THE BASTARD BOY

The Bastard Boy

JAMES WILSON

faber and faber

First published in 2004
by Faber and Faber Limited
3 Queen Square London WC1N 3AU
Published in the United States by Faber and Faber Inc.
an affiliate of Farrar, Straus and Giroux LLC, New York

Typeset by Faber and Faber Limited
Printed in England by Mackays of Chatham, plc

A CIP record for this book
is available from the British Library

ISBN 0–571–21514–9

2 4 6 8 10 9 7 5 3 1

For PJW
and for ANRW, TOCW and KW
with love as always

I

I write.
I know my name.
Ned Gudgeon.

I had supposed myself beaten – robbed – and thrown into a ditch.
But this is not a ditch.
My watch is in my pocket yet, tho' it wants winding.
My head throbs fit to burst, but nothing is broke.

II

Second day . . .
. . . not of my confinement – I cannot with certainty say when that
began – but of my writing.
I recall . . .
I recall my name:
Ned Gudgeon.

III

Third day
Tho' I still wake with an aching head, and have no conception how I
come to be here, yet little by little the fog about me lifts, and I begin
to recover my scattered wits – which is as well, for G–d knows, they
have pressing enough business here.
   What is this place?
   A room four paces by three – a bed – a table – a chair – pen, paper
and ink – a privy closet, emptying into a stream below (whose gush
and gurgle gave flesh to the phantom ditch). A small square window,
thro' which I hear birds – tho' it is set too high and deep for me to see
them. The upper part of the door is a hatch, which gives not on to the
outside, but rather on to a kind of box or cage, where food and drink

are left for me – though how, or by whom, I have not the smallest notion, for the first I ever hear of it is the outer grating closing again.

In short, indubitably a prison – but unlike any jail I ever saw or conceived of.

And *if* a jail, why do I not hear the cries and groans of my wretched fellows?

'Tis depressing to the spirits, and giddying to the brain, to write *third*, *fourth*, *fifth* day &c., with no notion where it may end. I have therefore resolved to christen today *Thursday*, for no better reason, than that *third* chimes with *thur* – but 'tis only seven to one I am wrong. However long the journey, 'twill be easier to bear in lots of seven – for then, every turn of the wheel that takes me farther from home will, in a fashion, bring me back again.

IV

Friday
My new system works, by initials at least: *Friday* and *fourth* both begin with "f"; a small sleight of hand will make the "f" of *fifth* into a long "s" for *Saturday*; and *sixth* returns me to my path, with an "s" for *Sunday*.

Last night, racked 'twixt sleep and waking, an image came to me, which I knew to be neither dream nor fancy, but recollection:

I was standing in moonlight before a half-familiar house. Only one window was lit. I approached it – peered in – and saw . . .

Saw what?

I cannot now recall – but something that must surely be pertinent to my case; for I know that as my nose touched the cold glass, my heart suddenly began to beat so loud I could hear it.

'Tis a small enough hare, but may put up others.

V

Saturday
My first thought when I woke this morning, was: *My head hurts abominably.*

My second (as soon as I had opened my eyes): *I have been a great fool.*

For there, on the table, was a most material piece of evidence, which has been constantly before me – which I have used daily, as I do at this instant – and yet whose significance, until now, I had entirely missed.

It is simply this: there is no book here, no game, no instrument – not the least trinket or bauble that might occupy a man for ten seconds together – save only, *pen*, *paper*, and *ink*.

From which I must conclude: *I am put here to write.*

But write what?

I must take care to consider, before I answer that question.

VI

Sunday

This morning, half-asleep, I started up another hare.

It was night. I was looking in upon a stable-yard, where a great black coach was being got ready, as if for a funeral.

A footman glanced up – saw me – and cried out.

Then I was running from him – stumbling – the earth beneath my feet a great blanket, which might at any moment be snatched away.

Perhaps he supposed I was mad; or guilty of some offence.

I am neither, yʳ honours – whatever may appear to the contrary. Of that, at least, I am certain.

This evening I shall try an experiment: take a sheet of paper, and lay it before the door.

If I mistake not, it will give me notice of my supper.

VII

Monday

My memory returns – like a tide that first fills four or five pools, and then connects all together.

Besides which – it is now beyond doubt – I am not mad. The paper stirred; and not half a minute later I heard the outer grating open, and my tray slid in.

So it is delivered not by some wraith or vapour, but (even tho’ I cannot hear his footfall) by a human creature who must enter from outside – admitting with him, whether he will or no, a draught of air.

Looking at it anew, this is no more like a madhouse than a jail. What it most resembles is (as I imagine it) a hermit's cell.

Indeed – a man who had given over all ambition, and resolved to end his life in philosophy and reflection, might be quite content here – if he but knew himself secure, and had use of a garden.

VIII

Tuesday

The more I reflect, the more I am persuaded that I am fixed here to set down an account of my actions, and so vindicate myself (if I can) from some charge.

But of *what* charge, and of who my accuser might be, I still have no idea – or rather, I have a *surfeit* of ideas, for there are so many worthy candidates for both offices that it is impossible to choose among them, and say which is fittest for the work.

What is a man to do, that fears an attack but knows not which way his enemy will come?

He must fortify his position on every side.

Tomorrow, therefore, I shall begin a full narrative of my adventures.

When I am done, I am certain, there is not an unpartial man living would convict me of anything worse than ill luck, and prodigious folly.

IX

Wednesday

And so to work:

I must begin with a letter from my brother Daniel – for the most tangled and riotous ivy proceeds from a single point, and this is the root of mine. The year was '74 – the month, I think, September – the import, that he was very ill, and greatly desirous of seeing me, as he had something particular to say.

I ordered my horse saddled at once – bade adieu to my sulky wife (for we were engaged that afternoon at Sʳ Will. Sutton's), set off in a fine rain – and was with him by evening. His man Poist, a fat, fidgety fellow, flapt from the house in a great taking and grasped my hand with tears in his eyes. "Thank God you're come, Sir!" – "What! He is not dead?" – "No, but sadly altered, I fear."

And so he was. I found him not (as I had supposed) in bed, but sat before the fire in his study – but so shrunk and sorry I scarce knew him. He was a picture changed from paint to pencil – the meat all eaten from his bones, and nothing left but holes and shadows. His dog Frisk was at his feet, and on his knee an unopened book – as if to say, *I am come here by my own choice to read, and not because I am driven to it.* It was this feeble deceit, more than all else, that undid me. For death (I perceived it the instant he turned to greet me) was not to be cheated by so paltry a trick – it had set its mark upon him, and served him notice to quit, and would hear no appeal.

"Nay, Ned," said he. "What's the matter?"

"Nothing – but that it pains me to see you so."

"'Tis not so heavy. Hadley says I shall have another year, if I come through this." (But his hands trembled, and were cold enough to numb me, when I caught them in mine.) "Pray – come and sit by me. I have a kindness to beg."

"Anything you like, that's within my power." (And I pause to ask y^r honours now, before we come to the pith of the business: which one of you, under like circumstances, would not have said the same?)

"'Tis within your power," said he, with something like a smile; "but I fear 'twill not be greatly to your liking. Or to your lady's."

The exertion of speaking made him cough, which he tried to conceal by affecting to laugh.

"If you know some canting parson", he gasped, "that wants matter for a sermon, here's the very tale for him. Tell him 'tis his for a guinea."

"A sermon on what subject?"

"Ah – the heedlessness of youth." He coughed again; and as he took the handkerchief from his mouth, I could not but see upon it a constellation of blood-spots. And the wretchedness of age. He seized my wrist. "'Tis a hard measure, Ned, for a man to see his wife and child die before him. And to know his last hope of ending his journey in peace is to find something he carelessly cast aside years before, when it had scarce begun."

"What thing is that?"

And this, y^r honours, as well as I can remember it (and leaving out frequent sputterings, and snatchings at breath) is how he answered me:

"How old were you, Ned, when I was ordered to America? Fifteen? Sixteen? A boy, still, at least – so my letters to you were full of battles and fortifications and savages, and not of those tenderer adventures I might have confided to an older brother. Then, when I at length came home, I had little enough inclination to talk of what I had seen and done and suffered – especially after I was married, for then I knew that every particular of my story could only pain poor Sophie. So if you wonder at my never mentioning this before, I can only say – I did not mean to deceive you, but a fit occasion never arose to speak of it.

"I dare say, tho', you will not be greatly astonished by my little drama – or, at least, by Act One of it – for I was but four-and-twenty, and it is not to be imagined that a hot young fellow, in the full vigour of manhood, will not seek out the friendship of women, when occasion presents itself. And occasion presented itself almost as soon as I had stepped ashore in Virginia.

"We still awaited two regiments from Ireland – General Braddock was much occupied with quartering, enlistment of provincials, &c., &c. and, when I asked leave to visit relatives in Carolina, was good enough to give it. From the warmth of my reception at Fiskefield, you would have supposed I was a returning hero, who had already fought the French unassisted, and driven them from the Ohio country, rather than a conceited young fellow whose courage was yet to be tested; for it was near the end of Uncle Fiske's two years in America, and he was glad to make a show of me before his friends and neighbours there. Among whom was Mr. Catchpole, a small merchant from Wilmington, and his daughter – an eager, hot-tempered, impetuous girl of sixteen.

"We met at a ball, my third or fourth night there; she danced well enough – *ooh'd* at my conversation, laughed at my jests – and fixed me throughout with a stare that burned me halfway across the room, and drew my eyes to hers whether I would or no. At length she flushed – said the wine and company had made her giddy, asked if I would go outside with her, and take the air.

"It was a cool night – I put my coat about her, felt her tremble, and knew 'twas not entirely the cold. 'Shall we go by the stables?' she said. 'I dream sometimes I am a horse.' So we did.

"The rest of the story may be easily guessed, Ned – tho' not, I fear, so easily excused. But consider: I had passed two months penned in a ship, with none but men (most of them little better than hogs) for company; in two months more I should be in battle, where a chance shot might kill me, or make me old in an instant – can you wonder, then, when life was so hard and uncertain, that I plucked her sweeter fruits when I could? After that first night we contrived to meet four times more, on one pretext or another – and then a summons from General Braddock put a sudden end to our sport.

"She plied me with letters – misspelt, girlish things, full of sighs and tears and clumsy avowals – but (to my shame) I never answered 'em. In truth, I had little enough time – my days were spent preparing my men for the trial to come, my nights wondering privately how well I might meet it myself – and in the few moments I had leisure to think of Miss Catchpole at all, I contrived to persuade myself that silence was the kindest course – for (or so I supposed) 'twas the surest way to smother the flames of her attachment to me, which even the merest note must serve to keep alive.

"Then we were dispatched to the back-country, and suffered the cruel rout at Monongahela – which for a few weeks drove everything from my mind, save the howls of the savages and the cries of my dying men. By the time we limped back to Virginia in August, and I was again given leave to go to Carolina, I confess I had half-forgotten Miss Catchpole, and had no expectation of even seeing her again – for in the interim Mr. Coleman had taken Uncle Fiske's place, and at once set out to inspect the plantations in the Indies, leaving only his poor wife at Fiskefield, who knew no-one, and saw no company. So we led a quiet life – which fitted my mood pretty well, after all that I had seen.

"But one evening, as I returned from a walk in the park, I heard a sound from a rhododendron close by. I at once grasped my sword and lunged forward (for my fancy was so disordered that I still imagined an Indian behind every bush, until reason told me he could not be there), but was stopped by a gasp, and a frightened 'Wait!' Whereupon Miss Catchpole stepped out, much altered – her clothes stuck with snags and prickles – her face wan – her manner grave and earnest. 'Good G–d!' I said. 'Whatever is the matter?' To which her hand replied before her tongue, by going to her belly. 'What, you are with child?' She nodded. Without thinking (for I was still too astonished to think) I cried out: 'And believe it's mine?'

"Ill-considered, I know – tho' a natural enough question, surely, if a man could but find the right way to it; but from her response you would have thought I had accused her outright of being a whore, and a liar too. She flung herself upon me – grabbed my sword – tried to prise it from me, and (when I would not loose my grip) bit my hand, more savagely than any dog. Look – here – you can still see the scars. I at last got my arms about her, so she could hurt me no more – and at once she melted against my chest, sobbing, and saying *I was a heartless brute, no better than an Indian, &c. &c.; but that she had never loved another, and never could; and tho' I might be deaf to her appeals, surely I could not ignore those of my own child – who cried out, even now from her womb, that I must marry her, and save 'em both from dishonour.*

"Marry her! – a provincial hoyden who could scarcely read – who thought of nothing but dancing and horses – whose dowry would be a hogshead of tobacco and a barrel of salted pork? 'Twas unthinkable – unless I forsook home and station, and removed wholesale to America or the Indies, where her deficiencies would appear less remarkable, and invite less reproach. And what then of poor Sophie? Had I not, on the very eve of my departure, called on her father and told him how matters stood 'twixt her and me, and said it was my firm intention, if I should return, to ask his permission to marry her; which he had heartily approved? To break my word, and her poor gentle heart, was more than I felt I could do.

"But Sophie was not before me; and Miss Catchpole was in my arms, saying *she would sooner die than live without me; and if I would not make her my wife she would take a gun, and blow her brains out.* I was a fox caught in a hole, Ned, that's the truth of it; and after an hour I had almost surrendered – conceding every article save one: that I must have more time to consider, before giving her my final answer. At which she howled, 'You are a d–d coward, who has not the courage to say no to my face, and so resolves to put me off, that he may say it in a letter, and thus avoid seeing its effect upon me!'

"'Tis hard to be called *coward* – especially when your bravery has lately been so sorely put to the test, and will shortly be so again. For which reason, perhaps, I was unreasonably enraged – felt the Arctick enter my heart, and turn my words to ice.

"'Very well, then,' I said. 'I say it to your face: no.'

"At which she dropped down in a faint; and I was obliged to call the house-servants – one of whom, a capable young negro woman, seemed to apprehend our situation at a glance, and at once undertook to care for Miss Catchpole until she was well enough to be taken home.

"I gave orders that the lady was not to be admitted again; and, for want of a more worldy confidante, told Sally Coleman of my dilemma. She was too generous to censure me, but (being as friendless there as I was) quite unable to help me practically – save by asking, *Was there not a trustworthy American among my fellow-officers, to whom I could turn for advice?* This was good counsel; and the next day I wrote to a young Virginian with whom I had served, setting all before him – and was not disappointed; for he at once undertook, in the most liberal manner, to act as my agent, engaging an attorney, who was known to have served other gentlemen in like cases, and who agreed (for a fat fee) to negotiate terms with Miss Catchpole and make provision for the bringing-up of her child. I gave my friend a sum I supposed sufficient to the purpose and left to join my regiment at New York, where I had a miniature painted, and dispatched to Carolina as a keepsake for my bastard. Shortly after, we were ordered north – where, as you know (*grâce à M. le Marquis de Montcalm, et à ses sauvages*) I soon lost my liberty another way.

"For more than a dozen years, after I came home and was married, I heard nothing more – and had so far forgotten the whole business that even after Sam died I did not think of it, but supposed I must resign myself to dying childless. But then, a little more than a year ago, I received a letter from Miss Catchpole, saying *that my son by her, Jeffrey, was approaching manhood; and that a chance had arisen to buy him a fine property at a very reasonable price – which (since she was penniless) she hoped I might furnish, so as to set him up in life as a gentleman.*

"I could not but feel that – coming at such a time – this was an act of Providence. For was not this Jeffrey, no less than Sam, my own son? – and might he not supply Sam's place – if not in my affections, at least in filial duty, and the eyes of the law? 'Twas the touch of sun at midwinter – the first I had felt in many a cold month. She asked I should direct my reply, under cover, to my Virginian friend (for the mails could not be relied upon in the place where she lived); and I at once did so, saying *that the boy had no need of an estate in America; for, if she would send him to me, he should live with me, and complete his education at my charge, and inherit my property here.*

"But there was no answer. I wrote again: still nothing – a third time: the same. And now – now I begin . . ."

But what he began he could not tell me; for his words had undammed a mill-race, and he was tumbled away by emotion, choking and weeping and wiping his eyes with his blood-stained handkerchief.

"Perhaps", I said, "he has removed to some other part of the country. 'Twould be little enough surprise, after so many years."

Daniel shook his head; and, when he had breath again, said: "Why then does she not write to tell me so?"

I could not answer this objection, so held my tongue, and waited for him to go on. At length he cast down his eyes, like a man ashamed, and said: "You know I set no store by dreams, Ned; yet I was visited by one a few nights ago, that has troubled me every hour since – and was, indeed (I cannot deny it), the final prick that drove me to summon you here. I thought I was in America again – not (as I usually dream) in that accursed forest, but at New York, and about to take ship for England. But before I could embark, my young friend Lieutenant Litton hurried up to me, in a great sweat – 'Sir, you are wanted for duty!' – 'But I am ordered home!' – 'First, Sir, there is a final service you must perform.'

"He turned and led me to a great square, thronged with a silent press of sullen-faced people. In the centre, surrounded by soldiers, was a scaffold, brightly painted and decked in flags, so I knew not if it was a place of execution or merely a stage.

"'Come,' said Litton, conducting me up the steps.

"'What!' I said, laughing. 'Am I then to hang?'

"He said gravely: 'The hangman has deserted. You are to play his part.'

"The prisoner was then dragged on to the platform – a lank, desperate young fellow, twisting and trying to throw himself down, at sight of which the crowd set up a groaning roar. The guards held him with his back to me, but as they placed the noose about his neck, he turned. And in that instant I knew (though I know not how) he was my bastard.

"'What has he done?' I said.

"'He is a traitor. You must dispatch him.'

"I stepped forward; but whispering as I did so, 'This is but a play, is it not?'

"'No!' screamed Litton. 'He must hang!' – 'He is my son!' – 'Do your duty!' – 'I cannot.'

"But at that the boy sprang free of his guards and grasped my throat (tho', in the way of dreams, he had been bound but a moment before). He trembled with fear, but anger was a stronger master.

"'Nay, old man,' he said, 'I want not *your* mercy.' And with a look I shall not easily forget (for the hatred tortured him like a knife, screwing his face with pain) he spat at me.

"At which I woke."

When he was done, Daniel was silent for perhaps half a minute, and then began to weep softly.

"You should not be troubled by that," I said. "I dreamed once I was a great fish, with a hook in its mouth."

But he shook his head: "I fear 'tis true – she took my money, and laid it out on a traitor's education for my son."

"But why?" I said. "There are some rascally hotheads in Massachusetts, I know, that have fired some of their fellows, and made them suppose, like spoilt brats, they shall have what they want if they but squall enough; but most Americans are surely as loyal as my neighbour Grimley – and heartily sick, I make no doubt, of all these cowardly and dangerous anticks."

"She hates me," he said, "and has turned him against me – and against his country – for my sake."

He stirred in his chair like a shot bird, that tries to move its wing and finds it broke.

"'Tis a hard thing, I know," he said, "to ask a man to leave home and seek the heir to a fortune he might otherwise hope to receive himself. But I beg of you, Ned – go and find him if you can, and bring him to me."

I hesitated, and attempted to think; but in truth there was no thinking to be done.

"I will try," I said.

Had I not done so, y' honours, I should not be here now, and writing these words.

"What, then!" said my wife. "Are you no more than a dog, that must go when it's whistled for?"

"He is my brother."

"And I am your wife. And Sarah is Cully's wife, and like to be brought to bed of their first child in a month or two. So you will break up two families, to mend one."

"I'll leave Cully behind, then, and find another servant on the way."

"And what of me? Do you think I shall want nothing while you are gone?"

What she would want most, I knew, might easily be supplied by visiting the pillory from time to time, armed with a basket of rotting fruit; but experience had taught me better than to say so.

"And if you are murdered by savages, what then?"

"Well . . ."

"I shall be penniless!"

"Nay – you will have the estate."

"Not if I marry again."

"Why, then, your new husband will provide for you."

"What man will have me, if I've no property of my own to bring him? You have used up all else I ever had" – here making a mighty effort at tears, which ended in no more than a puking gulp, and a red face – "my youth . . . my beauty . . ."

I had been set upon in this manner so many times before, I knew there was but one course I could take to restore peace. So I sighed, and said: "Very well, then; I will change my will, if that will satisfy you."

"Satisfy!" she cried – tho' in a steadier voice. "How may I be satisfied, when you have abandoned me?"

"I fancy you'll jog along well enough without me," I said.

Perhaps y^r honours (depending upon *which* honours they may be) are in haste and anxious to get to America at once; in which case I must disappoint you, by lingering a while longer in England – tho' no more than I disappointed myself, for tho' I felt no relish for my commission, yet, once I had accepted it, I saw there was nothing to be gained by delay, and was impatient to be gone. But there was business to be done – a wretched harvest to finish getting in, and rents and leases to be settled, and cases to be heard; so that it was not before the end of September that I at length wrote to my Uncle Fiske in Bristol to ask his assistance in getting to Carolina. A week later I received a reply, saying *that he and cousin Coleman would be happy to place their brig the* Sweet Jenny *at my disposal, when she had returned from her present voyage; but that as no-one could say when that would be, I should set out at once, and lodge with him, so as to be ready when she arrived; for the captain would not wait.* This puzzled me for an instant – for if the ship was at my disposal, surely it was the captain's *duty* to wait; but then, reflecting that he must accommodate himself not only to my whims but also to those of tide and weather, I dismissed it from my mind.

That same afternoon, therefore, I took leave of my tenants and then rode into the village, to drink a last glass with my neighbour Grimley. I was surprised to find him deep in conference with Sr Will. Sutton (for they were not well acquainted, and I should have supposed that Sr Will. would have considered it beneath his dignity to set foot in Mr. Grimley's house); but when Sr Will. rose to greet me, my confusion was at once dispelled; for his manner was that peculiar compound of attentiveness and abstraction a man usually sees but once every seven years.

"What," I said, "is there to be an election?"

"Indeed, Sir, indeed; the King has dissolved parliament; and the writs are issued. I did myself the honour of calling upon you earlier, but you were abroad about your business – very commendable, very commendable, I'm sure – so" (with a sly look at my neighbour) "I came directly to Mr. Grimley's, to . . . to . . . But this happy chance permits me to ask if you . . . if I may hope . . .?"

"I fear I shall not be here," I replied. "Indeed, my express purpose in coming was to say, I leave at first light tomorrow."

"Why, where are you going?" asked Mr. Grimley.

"To America."

"America!" he cried, evidently astonished.

"You must be careful, then," said Sr William (with that forced jocularity with which he might have kissed a baby), "not to take any tea with you, or you may be set upon by Mohawks and lose your scalp for your trouble."

I contrived to laugh, and thought it but a small price to pay for being excused the poll (for tho' I liked Sr Will. well enough then, yet I considered him a weak and supine member, that would have voted to transport his children and declare war on his mother, had the ministry but told him the King's good government required it). But if I thought so easily to escape the burdensome business of the election, I was greatly mistaken – as you shall shortly see.

Here again, I fear, my ignorance trips me into a quandary; for – having no idea who y^r honours may be – I cannot guess how intimately acquainted you are with Bristol. If of the blues (as I conceive one party), I dare swear you know it better than I do; but if of the buffs, or the red-white-and-blues (which is equally probable), 'tis more than likely you have never even set eyes on the place, and could not fix it on a map to save your lives. If I strive to please both, I shall indubitably end by satisfying neither; so if you are of the blue persuasion, I can but counsel you to take the next paragraph at a gallop, and o'erleap it at a bound.

Fancy yourself, then, jostling with me in the Wells coach that dull October day – straining northward across the Somersetshire hills, buffeted by wind – and then at length, far into the afternoon, beginning to descend through woods and pleasant sloping meadows into a broad valley. Suddenly, sprawled before us is a great filthy city. No notice given – no suburbs, coyly hinting at what is to come – everything unbuttoned, and open to the eye, as much as to say, *We're plain folk here, and you must take us farts and belches and all, or go elsewhere; for we'll put on airs for nobody.* A single glance takes in towers and spires; chimneys and workshops and wharves, and huddles of mean houses crammed between them, wherever they can find space; thickets of masts and spars in the pools below, and here and there a merchant's mansion on the beetle-browed crags above. The very river seems to be taking its ease here – for it lies slack, and leaden, and full of noxious waste – until, a mile or two to the west, it suddenly remembers its modesty and, gathering up its skirts, hurries into a deep gorge to conceal its blushes. And over everything lies a thick, poisonous smoke – from mines, and iron foundries, and china works, and glass houses rearing up like diabolical cones – that chokes the lungs, and clothes the walls and windows in black – which a fanciful man might suppose an apt outward expression of inner darkness, as if the city could not trouble itself even to hide its own greedy and illiberal soul, but must make a display of that, too, for all the world to see.

I was set down at length at the Three Kings in Thomas Street and, engaging a porter to take my trunks, set off at once for my uncle's house. I had entertained some hopes that Bristol might have improved since my last visit (for, save for once or twice when I had been compelled to pass through it in my way to London, it was a full five years since I had entered the place); but, if anything, it seemed worse than I remembered. The buildings were in their usual state of disrepair (for the Bristolian will always count himself a shrewd fellow, that spends fifty pounds a year patching a decrepit old tenement rather than three hundred building a new one that will last him out); so that if you looked up to see a shop-sign swinging in the wind, you were like to be hit in the eye by a slate or a clout of plaster. The crowds in the streets appeared noisier and more offensive than ever –

ear-ringed sailors with brown teeth and black tattoos; drunken soldiers looking for a woman or a fight; foul-breathed shopkeepers bellowing for custom; draymen demanding way for their laden sledges (which are used in place of waggons, for fear the weight of wheels will break through the pavement and open up the sewers – tho' it could scarce smell viler if they did). Just as I came to the Back, where I thought I should be tolerably safe, a great torrent of people suddenly burst from King Street, all jigging and jumping and crying, "Cruger! Cruger!" (tho' who or what "Cruger" might be I had no idea), and swept past me, tossing me as if I were no more than a fallen leaf. It is my custom (or was then) always to carry a stout stick, cut from a tree in my own park; and had I not employed it in my own defence, I should indubitably have been knocked down.

It was with some relief to my spirits, therefore, that I came out at last into Queen Square, where many of the principal merchants have their houses – Quakerish, village-green affairs in red-brick, which, if not the height of fashion, are yet regular and elegant enough, and arranged around a neat central garden planted with trees. I paused there a moment to gulp the air – and then knocked on my uncle's door.

It was answered by Joseph, his negro man, who smiled when he saw me; for we had known each other since boyhood.

"What, still here, Joseph?" I said. "Not claimed your liberty yet?" (For it was two years since Lord Chief Justice Mansfield had ruled that a slave became free when he set foot in England.)

But before the fellow could reply, my uncle himself appeared at the dining-room door, clutching a pipe and followed by a great billow of tobacco smoke. He peered into the hall, let out a cry – then hobbled towards me, his mouth set in a strange alloy of pleasure and disappointment, as tho' he was both glad to see me and wished I was somebody else. He must have heard my question, for he clapped his hands over Joseph's ears and, laughing, said: "Hush, have we not trouble enough with the colonists; and will you now turn our blacks against us, too?" At which poor Joseph could do nothing but shuffle from one foot to the other, and grin foolishly.

Uncle Fiske had always been something of an original – believing, as he told me when I was thirteen or fourteen, that *a man must make a figure, or he'll be overlooked*; but, as so often happens, what began as affectation had become habit; and now he appeared (as they say) a kind of

15

caricature of himself, for not only was he swathed in a morning-gown of scarlet silk and wearing a small turkey hat in place of a wig, but even his sharp nose and thin wide lips seemed more pronounced than ever. He clamped my shoulders, and leaned back to examine me.

"Ned, Ned, Ned!" he said – his eyes big and weeping with wine. "This is a fine trick – a fine trick, indeed – and you could play it a deal oftener and hear no complaints from me or your aunt. Come in, boy" – tho' I was then nearer forty than thirty – "come in." And taking my elbow he led me to the dining-room, stopping to glance at me several times as he did so, as if he feared I were an apparition and might vanish again if he failed to keep me in his sight.

The air was hot and hazy, the table strewn with the flotsam of dinner. At one end, in the half-light of a failing candle, sat an elderly woman, flirting her fan to whisk the smoke away. I thought at first she was a stranger to me; but then she rose and came towards me, and I saw it was my aunt, tho' so changed I hardly recognized her; for if the last five years had merely made my uncle more like himself (or, rather, more like a satirist might have drawn him), they had carried her from the middle into old age, bending her to a permanent stoop, and riddling her face with lines and broken veins, so that now she might as well have been his mother as his wife.

"Ned," she said. And then, craning her poor stiff neck to kiss me, "'Tis the arthritis."

"And the brandy," said my uncle. "Those French devils always know where to strike us. Tell me, Ned" – squeezing my arm, and half-whispering – "where is a man's fortune?"

"In his head?"

"Nay, in his feet; for without 'em he can't be active, and attend to his affairs, and see his servants don't abuse him. So, naturally, I needs must have the gout. And where is a woman's?"

"In her disposition?"

"Nay, in her face!" cackled my aunt. "And 'tis well I no longer have to trust to mine, else I should be on the parish."

"Sit down," said my uncle, drawing out a chair for me. "We knew not when you would come, so we did not wait dinner. What will you eat?" He waved at the table.

I saw a greasy charger of meat smothered in sauce; half a pie; a dish of tiff-taff-taffety-cream – and felt my stomach turn.

"Nay, I am well enough."

"D–n it! A man can't sit here with his belly full of pig and prunes, and see his nephew go hungry!"

"No, truly."

"Let me see," said my aunt, "if I can't make a magick spell and find something you'll like better." Which pricked my eyes, for those were the same words she'd used to tempt me with some tit-bit or sweetmeat when I was a child (to the despair of my father, who said, *If he won't have beef and bread, let him starve*), and delivered with the ruin of the same smile.

When she had gone, my uncle slid closer to me – gave me a glass of wine – twisted a scrap of scorched paper – placed it in a candle-flame, and lighted his pipe from it; then, turning to ensure that my aunt was out of hearing, said: "She's not returned yet."

"Who?"

"The *Jenny*."

"Do you fear she may be lost?"

He sighed, then said: "Nay, nay; 'tis a rough season – I've known ships later, and no harm done" (puffing a curtain of smoke, and watching me through it). "Now tell me: what takes you to America?"

"Some business of Dan's."

"Business! What! – does he buy land there?"

"Private business."

"Ah! – ah! – he wants his bastard, does he?"

I knew not what to say, but my eyes must have spoken for me.

"Don't look so shocked, boy. Did you suppose I didn't know? Has he written for the child?"

"Yes – but heard nothing."

"Ah, well" (shaking his head). "We may as well send you; for the Americans will buy nothing else of us. The whole world's run mad. Barker now, before he was selling 'em three thousand pieces of stuff a year. This twelvemonth past, he's sold not two hundred. Parrinder, the pipe-maker, has sent 'em not a single case. And 'tis the same with all the other trades" (shaking his head again, and spitting into the fire). "All we export now is men. I tell you, boy" (eyes twinkling suddenly in the haze), "if matters don't mend soon, your aunt and I shall be obliged to sell everything we have, and come and live with you and be a charge on our nephew."

"And would be heartily welcome," I said, "if you could but bring my wife to it."

17

"Oh, what – she still rides you hard, does she?"

I feared the wine had loosened my tongue, making me say too much of my own affairs; so I said: "They should be forced to buy."

"How?"

"Ten thousand men should answer well enough. A rabble of ungrateful colonists ought not to be allowed to bring us to our knees."

"But" (shrugging) "there may be another way: to slip in through the back door, while they guard the front."

"What – we must slink into our own colonies now, must we, like criminals!"

He did not answer directly, but lighted his pipe again, and pinched the hot wax of a candle till it bore the mark of his fingertips. At length he said: "Too much pride, and too much heat. We have built a tremendous house, that has made us great and rich and is big enough for all of us; and now we are running through it like two packs of children, howling abuse and waving torches at each other – a spark from any one of which could burn it down about our ears and leave us all cold in the ashes."

"Do you think then we should knuckle under, and not compel them to obey our laws and pay something towards their own defence?"

"That is what Mr. Cruger thinks."

"I don't know who Mr. Cruger may be," I said, "but I met a mob of his followers on my way here; and if he is as unruly as they are, he's little better than an American himself."

"He is an American – a native of New York – tho' he has lived here some years."

"Well, then, 'tis no great wonder. But why do you credit his opinion, when it must inevitably be so partial?"

"The Whigs, I hear, have chose him to be a candidate in the election. And some of 'em want Burke for the other."

"Burke?" I said. "He's half a traitor himself. 'Twas he lit the torch, by getting the Stamp Act repealed."

"Well, well. Two of my neighbours think he is the man for the hour and have solicited my interest for him. I've told 'em they must bring him to see me when he gets to Bristol and I'll judge for myself. Ah! – I hear your aunt – we must talk of something else, for she takes it very hard. But" (dropping his voice to a whisper) "I know they've sent for him to London, and promised him here within the week; so it's ten to one you'll meet him and can hold him to account, if you will."

*

So, indeed, it fell out; but not before another notable character had strayed on to the stage, who, tho' he entered unlooked for and unannounced, yet soon came to figure so largely in the drama that I must pause briefly to introduce him.

But not tonight. I have already been three days a-scribbling, and my hand is cramped with so much unaccustomed use; so I shall here set a period to my first chapter (as I may call it); and present him in the next – tomorrow.

X

Saturday
This morning for breakfast there was a peach and a glass of some pressed juice, of a fruit I did not know but which marvellously restored my stomach and my head – a marked improvement on my usual fare here.

I also received a clean set of under-garments; accompanied by a short note, which read:

> Sir: Be so good as to place your soiled linen in the door, together with your used dishes; and fresh will be provided.

It strikes me that perhaps yʳ honours are *rewarding* me for writing.

But, if so – how do you know what I am doing? You cannot have read my words yet, since they are still all here before me; and if I cannot see yʳ honours (or the servants you have set to guard me), how may you – or they – see me? I have examined every inch of the room, but can find nothing that might serve as a spy-hole. All I can conceive is that by some contrivance or other – a lens or a mirror? – you are able to observe me through the window and, having seen that I spent most of yesterday seated at this table, naturally concluded that I was about the business I was put here for.

There must be an experiment to test this hypothesis; but, having not time enough at present to seek it out, I must rather wait for it to fly into my mind – and meanwhile return to my story, where the actor I mentioned to yʳ honours yesterday stands all a-fidget in the side-scenes, impatient to make his entrance.

The occasion for this arose from the condition of my uncle, which worsened visibly in the days following my arrival. The old man tried to maintain a semblance of good spirits before my aunt and me;

but, little by little, his efforts became more threadbare: he grimaced rather than laughed – toyed with his food like a love-sick girl – drank two or three bottles in an evening, tho' he knew it could but inflame his gout – and sat long hours together in a sort of stupor, from which nothing but a knock at the door would rouse him, and then only long enough for him to limp into the hall and see that it brought no news of his ship. My aunt and I caught each other sometimes in anxious looks and exchanged sad, knowing smiles – but we were powerless to comfort him; for even to name the spectre that haunted him would have been to give it greater substance and so increase his disquiet.

On my fourth or fifth night in Bristol (I cannot now remember which) I was waked by the sound of somebody entering my chamber. In the darkness, I could see nothing; but the foot-fall sounded like that of a woman, and in my half-sleeping confusion I supposed it must be my wife and that something was greatly amiss – for it was many years since she had come to me when I was a-bed.

"What's the matter?" I said.

"Hush."

But still I did not know who it was, for a voice reduced to a whisper loses the stamp of its character.

"Who are you?"

"What" (fumbling for my shoulder with a cold hand), "are you dreaming, Ned? 'Tis your aunt."

"What's happened?"

"I am fearful for your uncle. He tries to keep it from me, but I know he has not slept a wink for worrying about the *Jenny* – I could not sleep myself, and heard him tossing and sighing and muttering all night. And now he has sent Joseph to rouse some chairmen, to carry him to Durdham Down, so that when the dawn comes he may look down-river and see if she lies off Portishead."

"'Tis madness. He'll catch cold, for certain."

"Or worse. Reddish, the theatre manager, was robbed there of nine guineas – but when I remind your uncle of it, he says only he won't be fool enough to carry so much."

"The chairmen will protect him."

"What, those cronies? They'd drop him and scuttle home if they heard a cock crowing."

"What of Joseph?"

"He's but a poor black, and cannot fire a gun. Will you go with him, Ned?"

And so we set out, in the last raw hour of the night, up Park Street, and along the Clifton road – my uncle wrapped in a blanket, shivering in his chair and wiping his breath every few minutes from the window, I walking beside him, with my stick in my hand and a pistol in my pocket. There was a cold silk mist, which almost blinded us, and only began to lift when we reached the higher ground and felt a breeze from the gorge ruffling the air; but by frowning through the glass and noting a milestone here and the grave of a suicide there (each time nodding grimly and raising his finger like a farmer counting sheep), my uncle contrived to plot our course. At length, just as the first cracks of dawn broke the sky behind us, he rapped on the glass and demanded to be set down next to a thick bramble bush bent hunchback by the wind.

At almost the same moment (so near, indeed, that I cannot now disentangle it from the clatter of the chair or say with any certainty which came first) we heard, no more than two hundred yards away, the sound of two shots and a cry of shock and pain.

The chairmen gaped at each other wide-eyed for a moment, and then bolted (so exactly as my aunt had predicted, that, had she witnessed it, she must have felt, mixed with a natural concern for her husband, a certain gratification at her own acuity). Having no thought in their heads but to get as far as possible from the noise, the silly fellows galloped off in the opposite direction, which took them in a few moments to the edge of the cliff; so that when I drew out my pistol and shouted, *Come back, you rogues, or I'll fire!*, they had no resort but to obey – sidling towards me with sheepish grins, and muttering jests to each other in an undertone, in a pitiful effort to preserve the last tatters of their dignity. I then told them *that so long as they remembered their duty, they might count on my protection; but that if they forgot it again, I'd shoot them like dogs*. I could not do either, however, without first loading the pistol, which I had been carrying empty; so (to avoid their seeing it), I added, "Wait here, and I'll find out what's amiss."

I marched fifty paces or so in the direction of the shots and – when I was certain I could no longer clearly be seen – concealed myself behind a tree, where I might charge my piece at leisure. No sooner had I settled to work, however, than I distinctly heard, from a little

21

way ahead, the most piteous groans and whimpers, such as a man only makes when he is terribly wounded; and I knew at once that I must go to his aid. When the pistol was loaded, therefore, I raised it before me and advanced prudently into the fog.

But had not gone ten feet when there was a sudden eruption of sound before me – cries and oaths, huffs and grunts; the gasp of a horse, as it suddenly felt the spur in its flank; a startled whinny, and the muffled drum-roll of hooves.

"Hold!" I shouted.

More curses (I made out *D–n!* and *hang* and *devil*), a smokey swirl of figures, a black carriage, insubstantial as a ghost, looming from the mist and as quickly vanishing again – then nothing but three or four pairs of running feet, which in little more than half a minute had dwindled into silence.

Thinking I might still find the hurt man (tho' I could no longer hear him), I edged forward, peering cautiously about me; but all I discovered, after five minutes' search, was a patch of crushed grass stained with a great quantity of blood. Satisfied that I had done all I could, I turned and went back.

The two chairmen must have heard the commotion and concluded that I had saved their lives by putting a gang of murderers to flight, for they greeted me with the sly manner (compounded equally of deference and resentment) of unwilling debtors and watched me closely thereafter, as if they dreaded nothing so much as my leaving them again. My uncle, on the other hand, seemed to have remarked nothing – or, if he had, to have accepted it with Stoick philosophy – for he was leaning on the roof of the chair with his back towards me, his eye pressed to his telescope.

"Do you see her?" I said.

He did not answer, but at length looked away and shook his head sorrowfully, and crept back into the chair like a whipped cur (tho' how he could be certain that his own ship was not amongst that distant tangle of masts and sails and pennants in the haze, I still do not know).

And now, y^r honours, we come to the meat of it. We had gone perhaps half a mile of our way home – the rising sun had melted the mist and turned the ground to a firmament of frost and cobwebs, and my two doughty fellows were beginning to relax their guard a little (even singing and chattering as they laboured) – when all at once, as we were passing an overgrown bush, a young man stepped out from behind it and blocked our path. He wore an elegant coat and breeches; but his wig was askew – his shirt torn and bloodied – and he carried both a pistol and a sword, which gave him a fearful appearance. The chairmen instantly froze again; but they knew better than to run this time, and looked cravenly to me for direction.

"Nay," I said, taking out my own gun and levelling it at the stranger. "Pray walk on." Which they did.

The young man smiled; made a small bow; stood aside; and, as I came to him, fell in step beside me, saying, "I perceive, Sir, you are a gentleman."

I nodded.

He glanced quickly over his shoulder, and then said: "I am in a slight difficulty, Sir; and it would infinitely oblige me if you would permit me to go with you and claim me, if we are challenged, as one of your own party."

I stared at him.

He was pale, and quaking with cold and shock; but he mastered his fear with the utmost grace, holding my gaze, and continuing: "My name is O'Donnell, but 'twould perhaps be as well for you to fix on another, and give me that instead."

"Cully," I said, half to myself, for that was the first thought that entered my head. But I was still unresolved whether I should help him or no; seeing which he did not – to his considerable credit – as another man might, presume on my answer by taking it for acquiescence and so try to sneak into my protection by the back door (as it were) – but rather looked me straight in the eye and said: "I give you my word, Sir, it is entirely a matter of honour."

I hesitated but a moment more; then I took the cloak from my shoulders and put it about his. "Very well," I said.

Whether it was the wisest or the most foolish thing I did in my life I shall leave you to judge hereafter.

Having brought Mr. O'Donnell to y^r honours' notice, I must now banish him again to the side-scenes, saying only that we reached Bristol without further adventure and that, after giving back my cloak and professing undying thanks, he made a bow that set him wincing with pain and disappeared into the crowd. There, I fear, we must leave him for the present, to return to my uncle and the election – for tho' I have two pots to boil, yet there is but a single fire to warm 'em, so they must cook by turns; but when both are done, I promise you, they will sit as happy together as beef and pudding.

I need not trouble you with the events of the next few days, save to observe (for it bears a little on what follows) that my constitution, accustomed to the life and diet of Somersetshire, took those of Bristol very ill. The sedentary habits of my uncle's house, the *largesse* of its table, the foul air enclosing it and the noisy crowds surging past its door in pursuit of one candidate or another soon provoked my bowels to outright rebellion – which had me in such torments that I despaired almost of suppressing it, and fancied I might be obliged to capitulate and live out my life under a commonwealth of bread and water. I therefore (in hope of bringing the enemy to terms before he pressed me to this dreadful extremity) launched upon a vigorous plan of reform, moderating my drinking – scrupulously refusing all products of the cow – and taking a brisk walk to Clifton or King's Down every afternoon, to promote my circulation and fill my lungs with something other than smoke.

Returning from which, one day about a week after our encounter with Mr. O'Donnell, I was met by my uncle in the hall. He was wearing a green velvet coat, piped in gold, that would have looked extravagant on a prince, and seemed more animated than usual, rubbing his hands anxiously and jigging on his goutless leg.

"Will you come in to dinner," he said, "for we expect company after and must make haste?"

So, having speedily changed my clothes, I entered the dining-room, where I found him seated not (as I had expected) with my aunt, but with a young gentleman I could not recall having seen before – a dapper youth of seventeen or eighteen, whose man's shape and dress were belied by his face, which still had the high-coloured softness of a child's.

"Ned," said my uncle, "this is your young cousin, Matthew Coleman."

Which took me, I confess, quite by surprise; for tho' the boy's mother had been our favourite playmate when we were children, her marriage to Mr. Coleman had led to an estrangement between us – and I had met Matthew only once: at her funeral.

So I was the more confounded when Uncle Fiske went on: "And I hope you and he will be friends; for he is going to America with you."

24

"Ay," replied Coleman with a smile as he rose and bowed, "if the *Jenny* is not broke up upon a rock."

I was naturally astonished by this remark (which seemed to show at best a puppyish lack of judgement and at worst a total lack of feeling); and even more so that my uncle did not reprimand him for it, but rather affected not to hear – tho' the sudden flush of his cheeks showed it had hit home. Feeling that on such slight acquaintance I could not upbraid the boy myself, I said coldly: "And what do you do in the colonies, Sir?"

"I am transported for seven years, for winking at the mayor's lady."

"Nay," laughed my uncle. "Had you forgot our house is Fiske and Coleman? This is my partner, now – as well as my great-nephew."

"Or something nearer than that, Sir," said the boy, "if wagging tongues are to be believed."

"Don't let my wife hear you say so," said Uncle Fiske, with a clownish roll of the eyes.

My uncle had not made such an effort at merriment for days, and I could not conceive why he was doing so now, merely in order to indulge an ill-mannered whelp who showed him neither consideration or respect.

"And where is your wife, Sir?" I asked – thinking a woman's presence might tame the young fellow's impertinence.

"She dines in her chamber. We have business to discuss – which is tedious to her, or something worse. Matt" (clapping Coleman on the shoulder) "will be a year in Carolina, to improve our estate there and learn up the trade – as I did when I was young, and his father, too. He promises very well, and will doubtless end by buying me out. But there's still a thing or two I can teach him – eh, Matt?"

"Indeed, Sir – a whole lesson book; but whether 'tis wise to open it before cousin Ned I rather doubt."

"And why is that?" I said (for his meaning could only be either that there was something discreditable about my uncle's precepts or that I was not to be trusted with them).

"Why that I think I must leave to your imagination," said Coleman; and both he and my uncle laughed – and were laughing still when Joseph entered with a greasy goose.

I can remember now few particulars of that meal; for it is in our nature to forget most what we understand least, and all the talk was of markets and cargoes and the declension of prices at Leghorn and

American flour going off at 18 shillings a hundredweight Firsts, and 16/6d a hundredweight Seconds, &c. &c. But if the *matter* of the conversation is long gone from me, its *manner* remains stamped on my memory and still has power to bring the heat to my face – for Coleman continued throughout in the same insufferable vein (indeed, as my uncle's claret took its effect, it emboldened him to yet greater brazenness), piling insult on innuendo and raising them into a giddy tower of impudence. My natural impulse was to ride to my uncle's defence and whip the puppy back to his manners; but I was constrained by my uncle himself, who appeared to see nothing amiss in Coleman's behaviour – and how may we protect a man that does not feel his injury? In short, I was a tethered bull, goaded by a terrier; and in my exasperation, having freedom to do nothing else, took refuge in eating and drinking, which I ended by doing to excess – with the result that, when at length the meal was done, and we heard a knock at the front door, both my temper and my belly were in flames.

Joseph was at once dispatched, to admit the company and conduct it up to the parlour, from which I took the private hope that it might include ladies, who could be expected to check the poison of Coleman's tongue; but when we went up ourselves I was disappointed to find that it consisted only of two more gentlemen – both strangers to me, and both pacing up and down, as if they were impatient to do what they had come for and be gone again. My uncle introduced the first – a neat, well-dressed man, with a reflective cast to his eyes – as his neighbour, Mr. Champion; that done, Mr. Champion presented his companion as Mr. Edmund Burke.

Consider this: I was half-drunk – a-boil with confusion, indigestion and anger – and suddenly found myself confronted with a politician, against whom I had long nursed a rooted grievance – and who turned out, now that I actually saw him, to bear a striking resemblance to my brother's fellow Poist, with a pale face like a fat girl's, and heavy jowls, and fleshy lips. This last accident added – unreasonably, I dare say – a strong spice to my prejudice; for whenever Mr. Burke expressed a view (which he always did with sickening eloquence), not only did I generally disagree with it, but I could not put it from my mind that it was being advanced by a presumptuous servant, who had no business offering an opinion on the subject at all, so that I could cheerfully have cudgelled him every time he opened his mouth. The only satisfaction I could hope for was that Coleman might be drawn into some ill-judged incivility and slapped down for his pains; but I was cheated even of that, for the wily lad had wit enough to hold his tongue, and sat bolt upright, his hands on his knees, with the fixed smile and jolted expression of a boy who suddenly finds himself among men.

For ten minutes, as Burke warbled about the glories of our constitution and the importance of the suffrage (on which points, in truth, it would have been difficult to take issue with him), I contrived somehow to follow Coleman's example and keep my horse on a tight rein; but when he turned to America, I felt it break free of my grasp and knew that, sooner or later, whether I would or no, it would have its head.

"I know, Sir," began Burke, addressing my uncle, "that this great city has been sorely hit by the present troubles."

"We are driven to the last pinch," said my uncle.

"And now, I fear, not only Bristol, but the whole country, sways on the edge of a precipice. I am not come here to squeeze your hand, and solicit your vote with idle promises – that is not, nor has ever been, my way. I am far from certain that even the wisest heads can now deliver us from the crisis we are approaching. But this I will lay before you: if I should have the honour of becoming one of the objects of your (I mean Bristol's) choice, I shall spare no exertion to resolve our unhappy contest with the colonies, to the satisfaction and advantage of both parties."

"Ah, now we come to it," said my uncle. "How do you mean to do that?"

"If it can be done at all, it must be by conciliation."

At which I could contain myself no longer; but burst out: "What! – and I suppose we must conciliate highwaymen too, and robbers, and every other man that chooses to break the law!"

"If the empire cannot be maintained by kinship, and common liberties, and the free tribute of trust and affection," he replied, with an unruffled good humour that maddened me the more, "it will not be held together by chains, however stout you make 'em, and however tight they're bound."

"The Americans are but boys," I said, "and need to feel the rod. But since the Stamp Act was repealed, they think they may do as they please, and now they are in a fair way to becoming ungovernable."

"Boys grow up, Sir, God willing," he said, with an iciness that told me I had found a nerve. "It is their destiny to be men."

"And men pay taxes," I retorted. "Do you know what mine are?"
Burke shook his head, and sighed, and raised his eyebrows.

"Four pounds a year. How much does an American pay? Sixpence!"

"Indeed, Sir. But there is a principle here that will not be reduced to shillings and pence."

"Principle! Are we then to be given lessons in liberty by a gang of slave-drivers, who see nothing amiss in buying and selling men and women, and cropping their ears, and branding them like cattle?"

"No man could find slavery more repugnant than I do, Mr. Gudgeon. But that is no reason to deny the colonists their just rights."

"And what of our rights," I roared, "that must run and protect 'em every time they are set upon by the French, or the Spanish, or the Indians, and bawl out for help!" (Here my uncle began to laugh.) "What of my brother, that was wounded, and tortured by savages, during the late war?"

"I am sure he did his country great service," said Burke.

"He did indeed; but it appears now that is to be clean forgot."

At this my uncle broke out again, in a great explosion of mirth – of which the cause, I could not now fail to see, was not (as I had supposed) my wit, but rather my intemperance – which put me in such a rage that I at once turned to him, and said: "May I ask, Sir, what you find so immoderately droll?"

"He goes – he goes –" (scarce able to speak, and pointing at me) "there himself."

"What?" said Champion. "To America?"

Uncle Fiske nodded. Coleman smirked; but neither Champion nor Burke, I noticed, permitted himself even a smile.

"In that case," said Champion gravely, "I should counsel you to set aside your opinions, or at least to keep them to yourself."

"Why?" I said. "You think they will get me tarred and feathered?"

"They will bring you few friends."

"A man who will stand silently by, while his king is traduced and his country dishonoured, is a scoundrel; and I shall happily wear a feather or two, if that be the price for defending them."

"That is well said," said Burke; "and yet I urge you to heed Mr. Champion's advice, and take it in the friendly spirit in which it was meant."

There was something so ineffably condescending in his manner that I dared not trust myself with him any further; so, getting up and bowing, I said: "You will, I hope, excuse me; but I feel the need of some air."

"No, no!" said Burke, forestalling me and moving towards the door. "It is we who should leave – we have imposed on you enough."

"I hope, Mr. Fiske," said Champion hastily, as he followed him, "that we may count on your interest and –"

"Nay," said Burke – as sanctimonious as a bishop – "I'll have none of that, Sir; he has heard what I have to say, and must vote as his conscience directs."

To which my uncle smiled and nodded – removed his turkey hat – and bowed with a comical flourish that made them laugh.

When he had taken leave of them, he came back into the parlour, and said: "It must be wearisome, Ned, for you to be locked up here, with none but old people and politicians for company. You need society, and diversion."

I saw Coleman smile, but could think of no reason for it. "Truly," I said, "I have no cause for complaint."

"Nay, nay – tomorrow I'll send Joseph, to take a side-box at the theatre for you."

"'Tis quite unnecessary."

"I insist."

The other pot begins to boil again.

XI

Tuesday

A fine breakfast again this morning – juice of the same strange fruit I had on Saturday, and hot bread wrapped in a cloth, and a dish of coffee. And no bill accompanying it (which is just as well, for I have no money here) – so offering me greater proof yet, if any were needed, that this is no ordinary prison. It seems, indeed, now I come to reflect upon it, almost as if *you* are paying *me* for my labour, for you seem to favour me with better fare whenever I complete a chapter.

But if this is so (and no mere accident), it only puzzles me the more how you can know what I am about.

On which score: last night I dreamed I was a painter, at work upon some great historick canvas; and when I woke I knew this at once for a clue, that would show me how I might test my hypothesis – which, after a minute's reflection, it did.

29

In truth, it is so simple I am surprised I did not hit on it before: if I sit in my accustomed position, so that all that may be viewed from the window is my back, and *appear* to write but in reality occupy myself another way, by drawing a picture or some such, yᵗ honours (if I am right) will be unable to discern a difference and reward me just the same. So – here is Mr. Burke:

And here: O'Donnell:

I own I am no artist (my Burke is the sixth of seven attempts, and O'Donnell the last of three); yet the girlish pout of the one, and the hungry-dog eyes of the other, are not so far from the mark – and I cannot deny a certain satisfaction in setting them down so true, with no drawing-master to help me but my own fancy. But the experiment has cost me, I fear, half the morning, and advanced my story not a jot – so now (save for waiting for tomorrow, and observing the upshot) I must leave it be, and return to Bristol – or else nightfall will cheat me again before I am done.

My uncle's house was a mere five minutes' walk from the Theatre Royal; and I knew that, if my limbs and digestion had no greater satisfaction before being confined for three hours in a frowzy, airless prison, they would indubitably take their revenge by harrying me mercilessly from farce to tragedy – for which reason I set out early, resolving to go by way of Brandon Hill and Cotham. It was a hard, grey afternoon – the wind steely and ill-tempered, the clouds all slashed to threads and put to flight across a bloody sunset – yet drubbed and buffeted as I was, I felt exhilarated; for to fight such a day, and triumph against it, was to be master of myself again.

I had almost completed my circuit, and was descending St. Michael's Hill, which – as y honours will know, if you are of the blue, or Tory, persuasion (as I find today I imagine) – is a tumbling higgledy-piggledy of gothick tenements, daubed here and there with a whore's face of fresh plaster and new windows – when I saw, some way off, three or four ruffians swaggering towards me. I tightened my grip on my stick, and quickened my pace; but after a moment they turned into a dilapidated building with a weather-beaten sign batting in the wind above the entrance, which I took to be a tavern, and I thought no more about them.

And would, doubtless, have never done so again, had I not, as I came to the same place, been stopped by a sound from within – a long, dreadful wail, like the shriek of an untuned fiddle, answered at once by an angry cry and the nauseous swell of mocking laughter. I set my shoulder to the ill-fitting door, and went in.

It was close and crowded within – the air full of smoke from a dozen pipes, and tallow candles, and a fire of cheap sea-coals. In the middle of the room stood an old woman, in a court dress of green brocade, surrounded by drunken, jeering men and beating the air before her, as if their taunts were flies and she might buzz them away. As I entered, one of her tormentors – a burly fellow with half an ear missing and a raw scabbed face – broke from the others and raised his hand against her, crying, "Why, you d–d b–!" His lips were lathered with rage, and he would undoubtedly have struck her, had not another man – a demi-giant, who towered above the others by six inches or more – restrained him.

"May I be of service to you, Madam?" I said.

At which she turned, and stared a moment; and then, pointing at me, cried: "Him! I'll have him!"

31

The half-giant laid a hand on her shoulder, and murmured in her ear: "Nay, nay, he's not for you. Will you not look at Mr. Grace" – here nodding towards her attacker, and touching him with a sausage finger. "It's a pretty young fellow, is it not? You shall take his arm, and make the girls sad to see him spoken for, and have a dozen of port after, to sup with your friends."

"He is naught" – shaking her head furiously, like a dog dispatching a rat – "naught but a common sailor. My father was a member of the Africa Company – the Africa Company, mark – and hired and discharged such as him without thinking of it. I'll have a gentleman, or a merchant, or I'll have nothing."

"Madam – madam," purred the half-giant in the emollient tone of a tailor trying to persuade a gentleman to take the suit he has made, tho' he protests it does not fit; "I pray you – recall – 'tis only a matter of business." He smiled, and squeezed her elbow; but his pig eyes (made piggier by drink, which had puffed his cheeks into great wallets of flesh) were cold and fearful, speaking of money wasted, and reputation lost.

"Nay – I'll not be insulted," she said; "I'm not fallen so low as that. Let me have him" – staggering suddenly towards me, and trying to reach me through the crowd – "and we'll say no more."

"Madam!" He kneaded his hands – caught my eye – and, hoisting his eyebrows in a signal of comick despair more mimed than spoken, said: "She does not understand, Sir."

"No more do I," I said.

"Ay, you understand well enough," hissed the ruffian Grace, showering me with spittle. Then he grasped my arm with one hand, and the old woman with the other, and – heedless of the throng of people separating us, who were obliged to make their escape as well as they could – thrust us towards each other, crying: "If she wants him, she shall have him!"

Our heads collided with such force that I was dazed, and I recollect nothing for the next few moments. When I recovered my senses I was once again outside, pinioned between two sturdy fellows, and followed by a jostling, laughing gang, which pressed us forward at a kind of trotting walk. In the vanguard was Grace, rolling and swaying and sharing a bottle with two of his companions, who burst into snatches of lewd song after every swig. The sun had gone – a blustering autumn night was in the making – and in the dark I feared I might be robbed or killed, and no-one the wiser.

"Where are you taking me?" I said.

But my captors only laughed – and none too kindly.

I turned, and saw the old woman a little behind me, and behind her a long straggle of people, and wondered if they supposed she was a witch and I her familiar, and we were to go the stake together. But if so, she seemed to have no apprehension of our fate, for despite a swelling bruise on her brow she looked contented enough, and gaily waggled her fingers at me and gave me what was plainly meant to be a winsome smile – revealing a mouth full of ruined teeth, whose stench reached me even at the distance of half a dozen paces. A little to her left (tho' separated from her by two or three fellows with kerchiefs, and ear-rings, and oxen shoulders) was the demi-giant, who appeared more dejected than ever, but contrived a watery simper when he met my glance, and flapped his hand, as if to counsel patience and assure me all would be well – tho' with so little conviction, it only made me the more uneasy. He looked anxiously about him, and then called out in a half-whisper: "Nay – tell me, Sir, are you a freeman or a freeholder of this city?"

"What is that to you?" I said.

He had hoped, I fancy, that none but I had heard his question; but in that he was disappointed, for it was not the demi-giant but Grace who (without turning his head) answered me: "Why, it means he may have your vote the cheaper."

"What vote?" I cried. "I have no vote in Bristol."

"That is soon mended," said Grace.

"Nay, nay!" called the demi-giant; "I pray you, Mr. Grace, be not so hasty: Mr. Brickdale is a good man, that remembers his friends" – here Grace let out a snort that might have had him sued for slander. "Allow me but a moment to talk to the lady; I'm certain this may all be amicably composed."

"Ay, 'twill be composed, sure enough," said Grace, "– in bed! If we're not to be paid, at least we'll see some sport."

His companions responded by prodding each other and giving a great guffaw; which, acting as a kind of fuse, soon ignited a general explosion and set the whole crowd hissing and crackling with laughter. A moment later we rounded the corner at the bottom of the hill; and Grace, turning to address me for the first time, pointed to the tower of St. Michael's and said: "What is that?"

"You know very well – 'tis a church," I replied.

"And what business goes on there?"

33

Being unwilling to indulge his insolence further, I said nothing; and at length – having cast about in his fuddled brain and found some means to suggest that it was my foolishness rather than his weakness that obliged him to furnish his own answer – he went on: "Why, you're a dull fellow. Know you not where a man gets wed?"

"Indeed," I said, "but I have a wife already."

"Don't tell the parson, then, or you'll be taken for bigamy," saying which, he entered in the churchyard gate.

It was at this instant that I became aware of a change in the crowd behind me; for it was no longer pushing us forward, but had stopped and fallen silent (save for some fevered whispering), leaving me and my guards suddenly becalmed, like three boats after a gale. Grace, however, was too far ahead to remark it and, without turning his head, strode deliberately on into the churchyard, in plain expectation that the rest would follow – instead of which they all stayed in the street, coughing and shuffling like a gang of schoolboys apprehended in some mischief by their master. I turned, saw the crowd all frozen like a coop of frightened hens – but not (for a moment) the fox; and then, as my eyes adjusted to the gloom, I spied a figure I had not remarked before, in conversation with the half-giant. There was something familiar in the way he stood – cockily, legs astraddle, one hand on his hip; and when he saw me he at once beckoned to me to join him. I hesitated – looked at my guards – but they pointedly refused to return my gaze and made no effort to restrain me as I began towards him. I heard Grace calling from the church door, "Come, boys, the parson's waiting!" But the only answer he got was a new epidemick of coughing, and a few whistled bars of "Lillibullero" from a man ambling away with his hands in his pockets and his gaze fixed firmly on the ground.

"Your servant, Sir," said the newcomer as I approached. He wore a heavy coat and his face was shadowed by the brim of his hat, but I knew him at once by his voice.

"Why, Mr. O'–"

"Cully," he said softly. Behind him were two or three men with hang-dog looks and downcast eyes, who used the diversion of my arrival to break from the crowd and skulk off into the darkness. O'Donnell paid them no heed, but jerked his head perfunctorily towards the half-giant (who cringed as if he had been struck) and said: "I have been attempting to explain to this unfortunate gentleman – what is your name, sir?"

"I am Parkes – Samuel Parkes, y'r honour."

"I have been attempting to explain to Mr. Parkes the seriousness of his error – which would, I am sure you agree, be almost comical, were its consequences for him not so fatal." Here he looked at me – not winking, or smiling surreptitiously, as another man would have done, but as solemn as if were taking his oath in court. "What say you, Sir? Can you not find it in yourself to feel sorry for him?"

There was something actorish in his manner, as if he were giving me a cue, to which he expected me to respond in a character other than my own; but as I had no idea what he was talking about, I could only gape at him in astonishment.

"Is it possible," he said – his eyes fluttering with exasperation at my slowness – "that even a man of your experience does not know what the rascal is doing?"

I was obliged to shake my head.

"This – this fat scoundrel is an agent, charged with getting votes for the Tory interest; and having used up his share of the electors, and found it insufficient to a majority, has been ordered to manufacture more."

"Manufacture!"

"Indeed – 'tis easily done: the franchise here (as y'r honour must know) is confined to freeholders and freemen of the city, and you may become a freeman by marrying another freeman's daughter, or his widow. So – what to do? Why, scour the workhouses, and the alms-houses – where she" (here nodding towards the old woman) "was discovered – for freemen's relicts, and then find husbands for 'em, who may be counted upon to sell their votes to Mr. Brickdale for seven-and-six apiece."

The riot of corruption in late years had produced such strange growths, I could not conceive there was yet one so exotick that it retained the power to shock me; but this, I confess, froze my tongue.

"Most of these unions," said O'Donnell, "end at the church door; but a ceremony is provided for 'conscientious couples', who stand either side of a grave and repeat 'Death us do part' – which they suppose acquits them of all obligations to each other and allows them to regain their liberty. But your intended bride is plainly too addle-witted to understand such niceties. She evidently supposed she was marrying in earnest and, having rejected the man selected for her, determined to have you instead – little knowing that in doing so she was sealing Mr. Parkes' death warrant." He turned and, throwing his head back, looked the wretched fellow straight in the eye. "You have, sir, I think, a just grievance against Fate. There must be five thousand men in Bristol would serve your shabby turn, and yet she needs must direct you to his honour here – the very officer sent by parliament to supervise the election and ensure the probity of the suffrage."

I at last caught his drift and – resolved not to disappoint him again – did my best to assume the part he had presented me with:

"Indeed" – shaking my head with what I hoped was an appearance of stern wonderment – "'tis cruel – 'tis very cruel. I was on my way to the theatre when he set upon me; but this is a greater tragedy than I could have seen played."

"I nev – I never meant you to marry the lady, Sir," stammered Parkes; "but Mr. Grace there–"

"What, you even admit it, do you, before his face?" groaned O'Donnell. "This" – appealing to me again – "goes from bad to worse."

"Ay," I said, "'tis a hanging matter."

"I naturally yield to your greater knowledge, Sir," said O'Donnell; "but I should have supposed drawing and quartering as well – for surely 'tis tantamount to treason to frustrate the purposes of the King in parliament?"

"A nice question, which the lawyers shall doubtless make much of."

"But every candidate does the same! And there's at least a score of other fellows as bad as I am," gobbled Parkes frantically.

"Oh! oh! oh!" cried O'Donnell, striking his head as if he were in pain. "Is there no end to your folly? For now we must have those twenty names of you; and if you won't give them gladly, the hangman must pluck them from you with screws and pincers" – which set the miserable ninny quaking so much he could no longer stand, but fell to his knees, so bringing his face about to a level with ours.

"Why, he's a fine 'un," said the old woman (who had been deserted by her companions and was now staring admiringly at O'Donnell), "and speaks like a gentleman poet. Let me wed him."

"Hold your tongue, you mad hag!" roared the half-giant, which so amazed her that she could not at first reply, but merely looked at him, and then viciously kicked him in the haunch – so hard she must have hurt her foot, for she hobbled as she set off up the road, muttering something about her father, and shaking her head at the sorry state of the world. But Parkes was too occupied with the agonies to come to concern himself with those he had just received, and – without so much as a wince – turned to us, and sobbed:

"I beg you, gentlemen – I am but a poor man – I was a serge-maker; but that's all gone now – I have a wife, and three children yet living; what is to become of them?"

"You should have considered that before you abused this gentleman," said O'Donnell. "The law says they must be seized, and hang with you; for the infection of rebellion may spread like the pox, from man to wife, and from mother to infant" – at which the wretch seemed to give up hope altogether, and – collapsing like a great mountain of meat, from which the bones have been suddenly removed – beat his head on the muddy road as if he would knock his brains out. I glanced at O'Donnell, who showed no sign of relenting, but rather shook his head sorrowfully, murmuring: "I'll not deny 'tis sad; but it cannot be helped – 'tis the price we pay for our liberties." And he prodded Parkes curiously with his foot, provoking a most dreadful groan of despair.

Hearing this, I resolved to intervene, for O'Donnell, having masterfully suggested that we held a strong hand, had now all but thrown his advantage away, by recklessly staking a fortune on it we did not possess; and I feared that when the half-giant discovered our pockets were empty and that he had been humiliated by threats we had neither the means nor the authority to carry out, he would take a terrible revenge. So I said: "Perhaps, after all, some other way may be found."

"Truly?" said O'Donnell. "I cannot think of one."

"The law may be merciful as well as just. How many children did you say you have?"

But Parkes was past answering, which spurred O'Donnell to prod him again, and pull him up by his collar, saying: "Speak, dog, when his honour addresses you" – from which I knew he would not obstruct me, but would rather go along with me as readily as I had with him.

"Three, I think you said," I continued; "and I would not see them suffer for your great wickedness – nor your wife, neither, if she be an honest woman."

"Oh, she is, your honour, she is!"

"Very well, then. For their sakes we shall on this occasion overlook your offence, and let you go."

"Oh, I thank your honour!" – clasping my legs, and burying his head in my boots – "I thank you!"

"But if you ever do the like again . . ."

"I shan't, your honour, I swear it!"

"Be sure you keep your word," I said, disengaging myself.

The remnants of the crowd were edging away in a cowish huddle, and we would, I think, have made good our escape, had not Grace at last wearied of waiting and set off back towards us, to discover what invisible enemy had scattered his army. Arriving at the church gate just as we were passing it, he stopped abruptly, stared open-mouthed into O'Donnell's face for a moment, and then cried out: "That's him! That's the murderer!"

"Oh, damnable!" said O'Donnell, and began to run.

And I – having no other recourse – ran with him.

I recall little of the next few minutes – save that they showed me, for the first time in my life (tho' not, as yʳ honours shall see, the last), what it is to be hunted. Within a moment, the alarm had spread – and as if by some natural law, the sudden change of fortune seemed to exert a magnetick tug on the crowd, which at once reversed its own dissolution and recoalesced into a baying mob. We jumped, we twisted and puffed and ached through streets I had known since boyhood, and yet which now seemed as unreal to me as places glimpsed in a dream; for *my* world was shrunk to breath and blood.

By Stripes Street, and Jonny Ball Lane, and Lewins Mead, and a dozen little alleys between Needle Street and Broad Street we dodged and darted; until at length we emerged into the squalid bustle of Wine Street, where (the crowd being so dense) I thought we should be safe. But in this I was mistaken; for, as we came to the end, I heard a cry and, looking up, saw two of the fellows hoisting Grace aloft – who was pointing at us, like the figure of Fate in a painting and bellowing: "There! There! 'Tis them!"

"D–n!" muttered O'Donnell; and then, turning to me with a bow: "Your servant, Sir."

"What are you going to do?"

"Why" – turning, for he had quickened his pace and was already some way from me – "draw them off a little."

"Nay," I said, "let us draw them off together."

"They are here on my account–"

"But would not be here at all, had you not come to my assistance. Come – I know a place."

"Where?"

"Here." And, pointing towards the bridge, I began to run.

Which will doubtless surprise yr honours (if you be the honours I take you for); for the bridge, as you know, leads to Redcliff – a notorious stew of vice and corruption, where no gentleman of yr eminence ever ventures, save to ease his itch (thereby, almost certainly, acquiring another), or on the King's business. But it was as familiar to me as Uncle Fiske's garden – I knew every lane in it, every fold and corner and hole – and was able to lead our panting huntsmen as pretty a dance as you could have seen that day in Bristol. I drew them into a blind alley, from which we contrived to escape by a plasterer's ladder; I bribed a boy to say we had gone one way, and then went the other; I led them on to Redcliff Parade, hard by the harbour – from which (as I had intended) they concluded we meant to take a ferry and wasted a minute scouring the river for our boat, while we turned back again, and melted into the evil-smelling shadows between the houses. When at length we emerged in Guiney Street, our pursuers were so far behind we could not even hear them.

"Ah, an inn," said O'Donnell, seeing the distant lights of the Ostrich. "'Twas well thought of. I should be honoured, Sir, if you would permit me to entertain you."

"Nay," I said, "they will not give up so soon. They know we must get back by the bridge or the harbour or not at all and, having posted guards by the river, will search every ale-house and bawdy-house in Redcliff. And if they don't find us, our fellow-drinkers, as like as not, will cut our throats for sixpence, or sell us to a slave-ship captain. We must hide yet awhile."

"Where?"

I pointed to Mr. French's yard.

"Is there a gate?" asked O'Donnell, bending his neck back to see the top of the wall.

"'Twill be locked, I hope."

"Then how may we enter?"

"There is a hole," I said, guiding him into the lane.

"Are you certain? I see nothing."

"Unless Mr. French has undergone a reformation, and become more concerned for his property."

Finding my way by touch, and by the map of memory, rather than by sight (for there was no light, save a glimmer from the harbour), I came at last to the hole – which, far from having been repaired, had grown even larger, with a pile of rubble at its foot that might have been dropped there on purpose to make a step for us. The opening was barred by a rotting plank, smeared with plaster; but two blows from my boot soon removed it, and we climbed through, and set it back again behind us.

"This is most excellent," said O'Donnell, looking about him (tho' he could make out nothing of the weeds and broken stones and rusting chains that I saw so vividly in recollection).

"Nay," I said; "we are not done yet. If they know this place, they will not scruple to look for us here. We must go one step more."

So saying, I led him into the darkness of the cave.

On which subject – 'tis grown dark here, too, and I am tired and (having no candle) cannot see to write more; so shall here set down my pen, and pick it up again tomorrow.

XII

Friday
This morning a mystery.

A simple breakfast, quite lacking yesterday's festoons and flounces. And with it a note:

Pray, Sir, no more pictures.

How came my pictures to be discovered? and: is this merely the jest of an insolent turnkey, or some manner of *instruction* from yʳ honours?

I must ponder these questions – but first, profit from the daylight, to return to my tale.

I see, looking back, that I abandoned yʳ honours at the mouth of the cave in Mr. French's yard, and left you standing there all night – a discourtesy for which I would ask your pardon, were it not that it neatly serves my turn; for by now you must be so cold, and stiff, and bewildered, that I am spared the necessity of describing those feelings in myself, and need only refer you to their pale counterparts in your own minds – to assist which: the cave was very chill, and very damp; silent but for the drip of water, and distant groans and gurglings from the river (from which it is easy to understand the superstitious belief that such places are inhabited by monsters); and so black I could not see

40

my own hand, let alone my companion, which gave me the strange illusion of being entirely alone; so that it was something of a jolt when O'Donnell said, from no more than two feet away: "You have a double advantage of me, Sir – for while Fate has furnished you with a brace of names for me, she has given me not a single one for you."

"Gudgeon."

"Your servant, Mr. Gudgeon. This place is gloomy enough. How long do you propose we stay here?"

"Until we have satisfied ourselves they are gone."

"And how may we do that?"

"We shall hear them pass. They may brush us close, but will not dare to enter here, I fancy – for the common people generally think it a resort of ghosts."

To which – to my great surprise – he said: "The common people may well be in the right," and stamped, and shivered his lips, like a nervous horse that feels the cold; and then fell silent – so giving me leisure, for the first time since I had heard the old woman's shriek, to reflect rationally on my situation, and muster my thoughts – which, as y^r honours may suppose, were none of the most cheerful, being compounded of one part discomfort, one part uncertainty, and three parts the most abject confusion. All Bristol seemed a bedlam – half the population driven mad by the election and the order of society quite turned on its head, with a mob of drunken thieves and cut-throats pursuing a gentleman in the name of the law – which brought me to another question, that I liked still less: I could not conceive a man of O'Donnell's character fleeing like a common criminal, unless he knew himself to be guilty – or at least believed there was evidence for supposing him so. I did not, of course, imagine I stood in any danger from him myself; but 'tis undeniably unpleasant to hide in the dark next to a man who may be a murderer, and to reflect that, if he is, and you are taken together, as like as not you will hang as an accessory to his escape.

And his mind, I think, must have been running in the same course – for after a minute or two he said: "Life deals strangely with us, does it not? Will you hear a story?"

"Gladly." (For there was a deliberate quietness in his manner, that told me I should get more from it than mere diversion.) "Tho' we must take care to speak soft, that others may not hear it too."

"Why, then . . . Last year when I was at Bath I met a young lady

41

from Bristol – Miss P. – for whom I soon conceived the warmest passion – which she reciprocated, with all the fervour of an ardent heart. Our love, tho', was denied the open road; for her father – a rich dealer in other men's misery – intended her for the son of a fellow merchant; so we could only advance it by skulks and sneaks – chance encounters, snatched meetings in back streets and starry gardens."

"I should not suppose that would be an easy course for you," I said.

"No, but 'twas all the hotter for it; and within a month I could conceive no thought of happiness without her, and she (so she said) none of life itself without me. And knowing her father would never consent to our marriage, we resolved to elope."

"How old was she?"

"Nineteen. I might have frozen my heart, and waited till she reached twenty-one; but she said she could not – that it would burn her up entirely and leave me nothing but ashes for a wife. So we laid our plans – made our escape – but had got no further than Salisbury when we were overtaken by her brother, and four stout fellows."

"How . . .?"

"Her maid – who had been party to our secret, and handsomely paid for it – could not resist the opportunity to make a penny more, and betrayed us. Mr. P. set me on the road, saying I might go where I pleased, and to hell, for all he cared; but that if I tried to see his sister again, he would have me whipped. At which I threw myself on him, and struck him, demanding satisfaction (my poor love all the while sobbing and screaming, and pleading with me to stop, for her sake); but his men pulled me away and rolled me in the dust, and before I could recover myself they had ridden off. After which Miss P. and I wrote to each other every day, contriving a shadow post office to get our letters delivered; but I made no attempt to break the embargo on her, tho' it chafed me raw – for she swore it would kill her if I was discovered. Instead, I shut myself up in the country, and composed a play, *The Bristol Merchant*–"

"Why," I cried, "I'm sure that is the very comedy I was to see tonight!"

"Ay," he said, "it has enjoyed some small success. But it did not please Miss P.'s brother, who protested that the character of Mr. Pennyproud was an unflattering picture of his father, and young Mr. Pennyproud of himself, and Kate Pennyproud of his sister, &c., &c. – and demanded I should withdraw it at once. I naturally refused, at

42

which he sent two of his louts to bastinado me. But I easily outwitted them and, leaving them locked in the cellar of my lodgings, went straightway to his house, and called him out. Some angry words passed between us, but at length we appointed for next morning on the downs – where in the due course of things we met, and each hit the other; but he was the more grievously hurt, and died a short time after. Which would have been all, save that by an accursed chance I was observed by some contemptible rogue, who was debauching a house-maid in the brambles, and at once threatened to go to the justices if I did not give him my purse–"

"Grace!" I cried.

"The fellow at the church?"

"Yes."

"Truly" (laughing), "fortune favours you marvellously with names. I had no notion of it. So, to continue: my wounded shoulder prevented me from dealing with him as I should have wished, and I was forced to flee – which was when I had the great good luck to happen upon you."

He was silent then, and seemed to be waiting (anxiously, as I thought; for his breathing was more than usually rapid) for me to respond; which at length I did:

"I am obliged to you, Sir, for your candour."

"I am glad," he said, with a cheerfulness that suggested I had relieved him of a heavy burden. "I then, of course, had the great ill luck to meet him again, this evening."

"Why were you there?"

"Like you, Sir, I was on my way to the theatre; but when I saw what they were about, and that you were its butt, I resolved to intervene. For, as you will readily appreciate – having been frustrated in my own marriage, it would have been insupportable for me to see you wed, and enjoying the bliss I had been denied."

He paused; and I was once again dumbfounded, for there had been no discernible change in his tone, so that for a moment the matter and the manner of what he had said were at war in my head, and I could not decide between 'em. A second's reflection, however, told me he must have meant it for a joke, and I began to laugh; but still he made no response, so that at length I wondered if I had been mistook. And then, quite suddenly, he laughed himself – a high, boyish, unconstrained *huh-huh-huh-huh-huh*, as quick and regular as the whirr of a pigeon's wings.

"Hush!" I said, for at that instant I thought I heard a sound outside. He stopped at once, and we both listened.

For a moment there was silence; and then, from beyond the wall, a man's voice muttered: "'Twas a laugh."

To which his companion replied, more quietly: "Unlike any I ever heard."

"Nay," said the first, "I'll swear 'tis them. Let's bring 'em out."

And then, two blows – a splintering – another blow – a tired sigh as the board fell again on the grass – and a figure crawling through the hole, clutching a lantern. He stumbled to his feet, patting the mud from his breeches, and stood peering into the darkness about him, his light held high, showing us his pale face and blinking eyes – as if he had just been born into our world and was making himself familiar with it. Seeing nothing but stone chippings, and the broken capital from a demolished arch, and the rotting skeleton of an old boat, he at last seemed to give up and turned back towards the opening in the wall – but as he did so, he remarked the mouth of the cave. He stared at it for some time, licking his lips and swallowing so hard we could see his throat working.

At length he called out: "There's a cavern here."

"I know," replied his companion. "And I tell you, 'tis haunted!"

"Bah!" said the first, putting all his bravado into his voice and leaving none for his face, which remained the very picture of fear. "Do you come in and help me!"

"Nay! Two of us won't be enough for them. I'll fetch Billy and the crew!" And leaving no time for a reply, he was gone – at (to judge from the slap of his footsteps on the road) a headlong gallop.

His companion – who had some shreds of courage in him – hesitated a moment, and then, very slowly, advanced towards us, stopping and squinting into the gloom with every step.

"Let us rush him," I whispered; but all the answer I got was a hand on my arm, bidding me be still.

At the time, I supposed O'Donnell must have been overcome by some sudden, unaccountable fit of timidity; but afterwards I was obliged to acknowledge he was right – for the sound of a fight would indubitably have brought the others running and led to our capture; instead of which, he waited until the fellow was almost upon us, and then – without warning – began to laugh again.

The sound was so strange and unexpected that it frightened even me; and the effect was ten times greater on our poor pursuer, who stopped – let out a gasp – rolled his eyes up – and fell down in a faint, clattering his lantern on the ground, where the glass shattered and the candle spluttered out in a pool of water.

"Come!" said O'Donnell; and twenty seconds later we were once again in the lane. At the end he hesitated – then set off back the way we had come; but I caught his coat – whispered, "Nay, 'tis better by the harbour," and hurried him 'twixt the floating dock and the Ostrich (skirting the puddles of light from the windows, where we might be seen) to the river. There we soon found a ferry-man, and engaged with him to take us to the other side; and he had almost done so, when we heard a wild cry behind us, at which he idled his oars, and (steadying them with one hand, and scooping the other behind his ear) bellowed: "What?"

The response was an eruption of noise – five or six excited voices, all competing to be heard above the rest – from which I could make out only a few words; but they were enough to convince me that we were discovered: *Come back!* and *murderer* and *guineas*.

"Pray continue," murmured O'Donnell, "and converse with your friends when you are done."

The fellow closed one eye and looked from one to the other of us, like a huntsman appraising hounds; then, saying nothing, he slipped his oars into the water. But instead of continuing, he turned the boat with a couple of strokes, and began to take us back.

"Turn again," said O'Donnell, "or I will kill you," and drew out his sword with his left hand (from which, tho' I had seen no evidence of it before, I knew his right must still be injured), and held it at the man's throat.

The boatman did not hesitate, but obeyed at once (tho' with a sigh and a snarl); and in two minutes had landed us at the jetty. As I helped O'Donnell up the ladder we heard another rash of angry shouts, and then the furious thrash of oars in water; and, looking back, saw Grace kneeling in the bow of a ferry thronged with men, and flailing the air with his arms, as if he thought to speed their progress. But all (to him) to no avail; for even a tired man may outrun the fastest rowing-boat; and by the time we heard the commotion of their arrival (all scraping wood, and oaths, and cuffs aimed at the wretched boatman who had cheated them of their prize), we were already safe in Queen Square.

Where I shall leave y^r honours, before my uncle's door, while I essay another experiment:

IIIIIIIIIIIIIIIIIIIIIIIIIIIIIIIIIIIIIIIIIIIIIIIIIIIIIIIIIIIIIIIIIIIIIIIIIIIIIIIIIIIII
IIIIIIIIIIIIIIIIIIIIIIIIIIIIIIIIIIIIIIIIIIIIIIIIIIIIIIIIIIIIIIIIIIIIIIIIIIIIIIIIIIIII
IIIIIIIIIIIIIIIIIIIIIIIIIIIIIIIIIIIIIIIIIIIIIIIIIIIIIIIIIIIIIIIIIIIIIIIIIIIIIIIIIIIII
IIIIIIIIIIIIIIIIIIIIIIIIIIIIIIIIIIIIIIIIIIIIIIIIIIIIIIIIIIIIIIIIIIIIIIIIIIIIIIIIIIIII
IIIIIIIIIIIIIIIIIIIIIIIIIIIIIIIIIIIIIIIIIIIIIIIIIIIIIIIIIIIIIIIIIIIIIIIIIIIIIIIIIIIII
IIIIIIIIIIIIIIIIIIIIIIIIIIIIIIIIIIIIIIIIIIIIIIIIIIIIIIIIIIIIIIIIIIIIIIIIIIIIIIIIIIIII
IIIIIIIIIIIIIIIIIIIIIIIIIIIIIIIIIIIIIIIIIIIIIIIIIIIIIIIIIIIIIIIIIIIIIIIIIIIIIIIIIIIII
IIIIIIIIIIIIIIIIIIIIIIIIIIIIIIIIIIIIIIIIIIIIIIIIIIIIIIIIIIIIIIIIIIIIIIIIIIIIIIIIIIIII
IIIIIIIIIIIIIIIIIIIIIIIIIIIIIIIIIIIIIIIIIIIIIIIIIIIIIIIIIIIIIIIIIIIIIIIIIIIIIIIIIIIII
IIIIIIIIIIIIIIIIIIIIIIIIIIIIIIIIIIIIIIIIIIIIIIIIIIIIIIIIIIIIIIIIIIIIIIIIIIIIIIIIIIIII
IIIIIIIIIIIIIIIIIIIIIIIIIIIIIIIIIIIIIIIIIIIIIIIIIIIIIIIIIIIIIIIIIIIIIIIIIIIIIIIIIIIII
IIIIIIIIIIIIIIIIIIIIIIIIIIIIIIIIIIIIIIIIIIIIIIIIIIIIIIIIIIIIIIIIIIIIIIIIIIIIIIIIIIIII
IIIIIIIIIIIIIIIIIIIIIIIIIIIIIIIIIIIIIIIIIIIIIIIIIIIIIIIIIIIIIIIIIIIIIIIIIIIIIIIIIIIII
IIIIIIIIIIIIIIIIIIIIIIIIIIIIIIIIIIIIIIIIIIIIIIIIIIIIIIIIIIIIIIIIIIIIIIIIIIIIIIIIIIIII
IIIIIIIIIIIIIIIIIIIIIIIIIIIIIIIIIIIIIIIIIIIIIIIIIIIIIIIIIIIIIIIIIIIIIIIIIIIIIIIIIIIII
IIIIIIIIIIIIIIIIIIIIIIIIIIIIIIIIIIIIIIIIIIIIIIIIIIIIIIIIIIIIIIIIIIIIIIIIIIIIIIIIIIIII
IIIIIIIIIIIIIIIIIIIIIIIIIIIIIIIIIIIIIIIIIIIIIIIIIIIIIIIIIIIIIIIIIIIIIIIIIIIIIIIIIIIII
IIIIIIIIIIIIIIIIIIIIIIIIIIIIIIIIIIIIIIIIIIIIIIIIIIIIIIIIIIIIIIIIIIIIIIIIIIIIIIIIIIIII
IIIIIIIIIIIIIIIIIIIIIIIIIIIIIIIIIIIIIIIIIIIIIIIIIIIIIIIIIIIIIIIIIIIIIIIIIIIIIIIIIIIII
IIIIIIIIIIIIIIIIIIIIIIIIIIIIIIIIIIIIIIIIIIIIIIIIIIIIIIIIIIIIIIIIIIIIIIIIIIIIIIIIIIIII
IIIIIIIIIIIIIIIIIIIIIIIIIIIIIIIIIIIIIIIIIIIIIIIIIIIIIIIIIIIIIIIIIIIIIIIIIIIIIIIIIIIII
IIIIIIIIIIIIIIIIIIIIIIIIIIIIIIIIIIIIIIIIIIIIIIIIIIIIIIIIIIIIIIIIIIIIIIIIIIIIIIIIIIIII
IIIIIIIIIIIIIIIIIIIIIIIIIIIIIIIIIIIIIIIIIIIIIIIIIIIIIIIIIIIIIIIIIIIIIIIIIIIIIIIIIIIII
IIIIIIIIIIIIIIIIIIIIIIIIIIIIIIIIIIIIIIIIIIIIIIIIIIIIIIIIIIIIIIIIIIIIIIIIIIIIIIIIIIIII
IIIIIIIIIIIIIIIIIIIIIIIIIIIIIIIIIIIIIIIIIIIIIIIIIIIIIIIIIIIIIIIIIIIIIIIIIIIIIIIIIIIII
IIIIIIIIIIIIIIIIIIIIIIIIIIIIIIIIIIIIIIIIIIIIIIIIIIIIIIIIIIIIIIIIIIIIIIIIIIIIIIIIIIIII
IIIIIIIIIIIIIIIIIIIIIIIIIIIIIIIIIIIIIIIIIIIIIIIIIIIIIIIIIIIIIIIIIIIIIIIIIIIIIIIIIIIII
IIIIIIIIIIIIIIIIIIIIIIIIIIIIIIIIIIIIIIIIIIIIIIIIIIIIIIIIIIIIIIIIIIIIIIIIIIIIIIIIIIIII
IIIIIIIIIIIIIIIIIIIIIIIIIIIIIIIIIIIIIIIIIIIIIIIIIIIIIIIIIIIIIIIIIIIIIIIIIIIIIIIIIIIII
IIIIIIIIIIIIIIIIIIIIIIIIIIIIIIIIIIIIIIIIIIIIIIIIIIIIIIIIIIIIIIIIIIIIIIIIIIIIIIIIIIIII
IIIIIIIIIIIIIIIIIIIIIIIIIIIIIIIIIIIIIIIIIIIIIIIIIIIIIIIIIIIIIIIIIIIIIIIIIIIIIIIIIIIII
IIIIIIIIIIIIIIIIIIIIIIIIIIIIIIIIIIIIIIIIIIIIIIIIIIIIIIIIIIIIIIIIIIIIIIIIIIIIIIIIIIIII
IIIIIIIIIIIIIIIIIIIIIIIIIIIIIIIIIIIIIIIIIIIIIIIIIIIIIIIIIIIIIIIIIIIIIIIIIIIIIIIIIIIII
IIIIIIIIIIIIIIIIIIIIIIIIIIIIIIIIIIIIIIIIIIIIIIIIIIIIIIIIIIIIIIIIIIIIII

XIII

Monday

Very well, y^r honours.

I am persuaded.

I am at a loss to know how, but I perceive that you (or y^r agents, at least) read my words.

This morning's breakfast: very plain – only the note more fanciful than yesterday's. The effort of covering paper, evidently, left none for finding jam:

> *Sir: A page of 'l's does you no service. Be so good as to continue with your story. First, tho', answer this: how came you to know Redcliff so well, and Mr. French's cave, if they were such discreditable places as you describe, and you a gentleman?*

To which, y^r honours, I reply:

First – as to the page of 'l's: I thought it possible you had observed I was drawing pictures, not from seeing the things themselves, but from the action of my arm as I worked. To test which, I wrote the same letter over and over, knowing that only if you saw the page itself could you have told what I was about. It was, I concede, a wrong hypothesis; but you find a hypothesis wrong only by putting it to the trial, do you not? – for which reason I think any reasonable man would judge it just and rational.

Second, I think I catch y^r drift: you try to close the circle about me by saying, *Redcliff &c. is the haunt of criminals; on his own admission he is well acquainted with it; therefore he is a criminal.* But that, you will permit me to observe, is false logick, akin to saying, *All the murderers were crippled; therefore, all cripples are murderers.* I was three years at school in Bristol as a boy, during which time I lived with Uncle and Aunt Fiske, and know Redcliff and Mr. French's cave only because they were favourite haunts of me and my playfellows – which I might, under different circumstances, have found witnesses to attest to, but must now (for sundry reasons that are already apparent, and others that will become so) ask y^r honours to accept on my word alone.

Since I am still here, at least, and you ask me to go on, I deduce nothing I have writ so far has merited a hanging – unless, of course, you leave me merely to twine the noose thicker for my own neck.

*

Whatever the case: we had reached (you will recall) Queen Square; where Joseph answered our fevered knocking.

"Were you not at the theatre, Sir?" he said, admitting us.

"This gentleman and I were waylaid, and have been fleeing for our lives," I said (which had him peering past us, his eyes white with apprehension). "Quick – shut the door." And then, when he had done so: "Where is my uncle?"

"In the aerie, Sir" (for so Uncle Fiske called his private apartment).

"Why, then we'll roust him out," I said, leaping on to the stairs.

But Joseph skipped nimbly past me, and turned, blocking my way. "He has giv'n orders he's not to be disturbed."

"We'll not disturb him," I said, beckoning O'Donnell to follow me; but still Joseph did not move.

"I am sorry, Sir; but he was extremely hot on the matter – saying that if the King himself called, he was not to be admitted."

"Doubtless because he would not wish His Majesty to see so many goods on which he has not received his due. But we shan't peach. Come, boy, let us go up."

"I cannot."

My temper was frayed so thin by all that had passed that it was now little more than a thread – and for some reason (which I still cannot fully account for, for of all the men I might have blamed for my adventure that day, Joseph was the least deserving of it) this continued obstinacy was the final chafe that snapped it. I felt the blood mustering in my cheeks, and heard myself roar, "Out of my way, Joseph, or by G–d I'll box your ears!"

But tho' he trembled, and braced himself by clutching the banister rail, yet still he did not move; and I sprang forward, raising my hand to strike him.

"Nay, nay," said O'Donnell, grabbing my sleeve and pulling me back, like a dog that has slipped its leash. "The fellow is only doing what he is bid – and I wish I had a servant I could trust to do the same. If you must have ears, and nothing else will do, then box mine – for they are far guiltier than his." And he interposed himself between us, and bowed his pale head towards me – in so ridiculously solemn a manner that, in spite of all, Joseph began to laugh.

But I was not to be pacified – knocked them both aside, and was already on the second flight before they had sufficiently recovered themselves to give chase – which they did with a will, gaining on me with every step; so that at length our advantages exactly cancelled one another, and we all arrived together, and tumbled through the door like a pack of noisy children . . . to discover my uncle seated at the table with a man I had barely thought of since leaving home, and the last I might have expected to encounter there: Sr Will. Sutton; who looked equally startled to see me, and – quickly reviewing his stock of emollient phrases and finding for once he had none equal to the occasion – held the back of his hand to his mouth and gave a cough so unbelievable it would have had an actor jeered off the stage.

But my uncle was not so easily ruffled and, smiling, said, "What, Ned, did the play not please you?" – though I noted that while his eyes met mine, one hand was busy gathering up some papers scattered 'twixt Sr Will. and himself, and arranging them so I might not see what they were.

"I tried to stop them, Sir," said poor Joseph, before I had time to reply.

"Nay, Joseph," said Uncle Fiske, "you cannot suppose I meant my nephew."

"No, indeed," said Sr Will., finding his tongue at last, and setting it to work on its customary greasy business. "And I must intrude upon you no longer, Sir; for politicks should never keep a man from his family. I trust, tho'" – rising, and collecting his papers – "that I may mention our understanding to the gentleman we spoke of, and tell him he may count on your interest?"

To which Uncle Fiske raised his turkey hat, and grimaced, and bowed comically – exactly as he had to Burke, and with exactly the same effect.

"Very well, very well, Mr. Fiske," said chuckling Sr Will. "No – no – please – I would not trouble you for the world – the gout, I know, can be very irksome, and your man here will perfectly suffice. My compliments on your excellent news"– and bowed himself from the room, and waited for Joseph to light him downstairs.

"What news is that?" I said, as the door closed.

"Why, the *Jenny* is returned, and no harm done; and when she is unloaded will set about making ready to take you to the colonies, Ned."

"Excellent, indeed," I said – for, as you may imagine, I was, by this time, heartily sick of Bristol and anxious to be gone. "And who is the gentleman you were speaking of?" (tho' I knew that, since Sr Will. was a Tory, it could only be Mr. Brickdale) – which brought a rare blush to my uncle's cheek, and a sheepish smirk to his lips.

49

"Nay, Ned," he said, laughing and laying a hand on my arm. "If there are two favoured runners in a race, the man's a fool that bets on only one of 'em." And then, catching sight of O'Donnell, who had retreated, and waited outside the door: "Who is this gentleman?"

"Mr. O'Donnell," I said (tho' from the spasm that twitched his cheek, I divined O'Donnell would have preferred me to use some other name); "to whom I am indebted for my honour."

"And I to you, Sir – twice over," said O'Donnell, with a bow, "for my life."

"Indeed?" said Uncle Fiske. "That sounds a tale worth the hearing."

"I fear you are mistaken, Sir – 'tis very tedious," said O'Donnell, staring past him, and into the shadows beyond.

"Nay, an old dog sees no sport, and must hear what the frisky young fellows are about, or else die of dullness." He hobbled to the door, flung it open and shouted, "Joseph! When you are done, bring us another bottle!" then turned, flourishing his hand: "Sit down, gentlemen, I pray you, and be easy."

Which we did; and it was only as I took my chair that I remarked –

Nay, there's something I must tell you first: this aerie was a long, low-ceilinged room, which from boyhood had always seemed mysterious to me, and spiced with a kind of danger; for it was stuffed with objects from every corner of the earth – savage masks; feathers and snake skins; silks and pots from China; the tusk of an elephant; twisted little figures of gold from Africa; a great jug in the form of a negro's head – all of which made strange shapes and shadows that (to a child's eye) seemed possessed of some malignant power. And more especially so in the dark, so that it had been my custom, from the age of three or four, whenever I went there at night, to stay in the circle of light about the table and to avoid peering too closely into the surrounding gloom, for fear of seeing something that frightened me – a peculiarity that must have stayed with me, thro' force of habit; for it was only as I sat down that I observed what O'Donnell must have been staring at behind my uncle: a figure, sitting stone-still in the corner.

"Why, cousin Coleman!" I said.

"Oh, ay, ay!" said Uncle Fiske; "you've been so quiet, Matt, I'd almost forgot you was there! Here" – catching Coleman's arm, and dragging him forward – "Mr. O'Donnell, allow me to introduce Mr. Coleman."

Coleman and O'Donnell bowed, stiff and haughty as a pair of curs, each trying to sniff the other's purpose.

"Now, Sir," said Uncle Fiske, sitting down, "your story – and we'll have as much blood and cursing as you please."

"No, truly, Sir," replied O'Donnell.

"Come, man, don't be shy – you can trust me – mayn't he, Ned? – you tell him . . ."

"I do not doubt it, Sir," said O'Donnell, looking steadily at Coleman.

"Oh!" said my uncle, "that's the way of it, is it? Nay, you may depend on Matt, Sir, my word upon it: he looks like a boy, I know, but he's wise as Solomon – and as sparing with other men's secrets as if they were guineas. Ned and I – we're blabberers beside him. Now – what's the lady's name? – for I suppose there is a lady?"

But O'Donnell was not to be moved, and shook his head. "I hope you will pardon me, Sir; I am a little tired, and must beg to be excused."

My uncle was unused to being denied a thing, when he had expended so much pleasantness to get it, and I saw the colour rise again to his face – which he tried to conceal by lighting his pipe, and making a screen of fumes. And had not recovered his temper when Joseph entered, and toppled a glass as he set the tray down, smashing it on the floor; which provoked my uncle to bat him with the back of his hand, and snap out: "How now, Master Clumsy, you'll be sent back to Jamaica, will you? – for you're plainly fitter for the fields than for a gentleman's house."

"That, friend, you should know, the law now forbids," said O'Donnell to Joseph; and then, turning to my uncle: "And if he is returned, you'll not find another man to replace him, that knows his duty so well."

"Nay, nay, Sir, I do but jest," said Uncle Fiske. "You know that, don't you, you monkey?"

But the poor fellow looked far from easy, and trembled as he withdrew.

"Let me tell you my tale," I said hurriedly. "'Tis at least the equal of his for drama, and its superior for comedy."

"That's true enough," said O'Donnell.

My uncle nodded and grunted; and I launched upon a detail of my adventure, puffing up the most ludicrous and grotesque particulars, so that they became (as it were) the principal personages of my history. And was gratified to remark that even Coleman cracked a smile; and Uncle Fiske positively rocked and laughed; so that after a minute or two I believed I had successfully diverted him from his purpose.

But in this I was mistaken; for when I had done, he turned again to O'Donnell, and said: "And now yours, Sir, if you please."

"I pray you, Sir, not to make such a test of my manners; for I cannot."

"Cannot!?" He narrowed his eyes – then turned to Coleman: "What say you, Matt, to a man will not sing for his supper?"

Coleman smirked, but said nothing.

"Rather must not," said O'Donnell. "For to do so would be to abuse your hospitality."

"How! – my hospitality?"

"By placing you at best in a quandary, and at worst in some danger."

"Hmph. So – what" – he was very busy with his pipe; then looked up suddenly – "you have killed a man, have you?" And, a moment later, when O'Donnell did not respond: "I think I heard young Godfrey died in a duel, tho' his father makes pretence 'twas an accident. Did you not hear that, Matt?"

"You forget, Sir," said Coleman; "I am as sparing with other men's secrets as if they were guineas."

"Ah!" My uncle acknowledged the hit by slumping in his chair, and prodding the air with his pipe-stem. "You have me there, young Solomon. Do you see, Mr. O'Donnell? The grave itself is not more discreet."

"Tho' perhaps a jot warmer," murmured O'Donnell; and at once bit his lip.

"What!" said Uncle Fiske, with a chuckle – like a man who divines that a jest was intended, but has not heard its substance. "I hope, Sir," he went on, "you will accept a bed of me tonight; and I'll keep company with my thoughts, and consider how we may be of further service to you tomorrow."

It was perfectly plain, from this abrupt change of manner, that my uncle had suddenly seen some advantage that might be gained from O'Donnell's predicament, which (tho' I could not guess what it was) yet left me a little uneasy; and O'Donnell, I think, was equally apprehensive, for he stared at Uncle Fiske, pale and unsmiling, for some seconds before replying. But at last (doubtless reflecting that it was a lesser evil to be in my uncle's clutches than risk falling into Grace's) he bowed and said: "I am very much obliged to you, Sir."

*

The wind rises – the tide turns – the *Sweet Jenny* tugs at her moorings, impatient to be away. Only a moment more, yʳ honours – and then, I swear, we shall be embarked for America.

The next morning, when we breakfasted, Uncle Fiske told us he had sent Joseph early to the Exchange coffee house; who had returned with the intelligence that three or four mobs were scouring the city for a man of O'Donnell's description (one, indeed, bursting in upon the place while he was there), in hope of receiving a reward for his capture – as a result of which my uncle counselled us to pass the day within, and keep from the windows; which we did.

The day after, my uncle summoned us to a conference in the aerie.
"You are looked for everywhere," he said to O'Donnell; "and not just by the rabble; for a press-gang from one of the ships lying at Kingroad, who were hired as bludgeon-men for the election, have joined the hunt – which is more dangerous yet, for they know their business, and make it almost certain you will be taken if you venture out. For which reason," he continued, "you must, I think, for your own security, go abroad for a while; which may best be accomplished by your accompanying my nephew to America, as his servant – and so enjoying the protection he may offer you against prying passengers and officious excisemen, whose suspicions are liable to be aroused by the sight of a man travelling alone. And if Ned is agreeable, I, for my part, will undertake to give you free passage."
I was, if truth be told, far from agreeable; but I could not abandon O'Donnell to be hanged, and was at a loss for a better plan to save him. So I grunted my assent.
"You are most generous, Sir," said O'Donnell. (I studied his face, for any sign he was not in earnest, or that he suspected my uncle's kindness might carry a price; but could see none.) "I wish there was something I could do to repay you."
"Ah – well – perhaps there is now, at that," said Uncle Fiske. "Since the troubles with the colonies began, it has been hard for us to communicate anything of moment to our American friends; for the excisemen seize our letters and read 'em – so we may write nothing of politicks, and little enough of business. And the government now keeps a register of emigrants – who are subjected pretty well to the same strictures – from which only gentlemen and their servants are exempted. So . . ."

"You wish us to deliver something?" said O'Donnell.

Uncle Fiske nodded. "To a gentleman with whom I have had dealings these many years, and whose confidence I should be very sorry to lose, for no other cause than a foolish quarrel between brothers. Tell me, Ned: whom does Dan propose you should see?"

I told him.

"That will fit very comfortable. You, Sir" (to O'Donnell) "seem a quick-witted young fellow, who'll easy enough out-fox His Majesty's clods." (Picking up a sealed letter that lay before him.) "What do you say?"

"I should be honoured, Sir," said O'Donnell, taking it.

"It bears his name, but not mine. This, on the other hand" – taking up another, that was closed but unwritten upon – "bears mine but not his, tho' it carries the same seal; so that if he opens them together he shall know they are both from me. So you will take this, Ned, if you please" – holding it towards me – "and deliver it at the same time."

I took the letter – tho' not without a faint misgiving, that it might bring me some unexpected mischief.

"But pray" – mumbling his voice and frowning at the door – "not a word of it to Matt. 'Tis none of his concern, and there's no reason to trouble him with it. Do you understand me?"

"Entirely, Sir," said O'Donnell – and suddenly smiled.

That afternoon, Joseph was dispatched to O'Donnell's lodgings to retrieve his possessions, and to take a handful of letters he had writ to the post office.

For three weeks thereafter we lived as prisoners in my uncle's house, keeping within doors by day, and taking such exercise as we might in the small garden at night – a regimen which taught me a trick that has proved of great utility since, and continues to serve me now, *viz.*, how to run, and jump, and walk a mile, in a space no more than a few yards long.

At last the night came, when we were conveyed by boat to the river-mouth, and slept for a few hours in a pilot's house before boarding the *Sweet Jenny* at dawn.

The question of what we might do in America had seemed scarcely real (and so not worth the considering), while we were yet in England and uncertain whether we should be able to escape the dangers we faced there; so it was not until we were safe within the cabin, and had a map of America opened before us, that I at last asked O'Donnell if I might see the letter my uncle had given him. After ensuring we were not observed, he slipped it from beneath his undergarments and gave it to me.

"That's well," I said, handing it back. "My brother tells me he's as gentleman-like a man as we may hope to meet in America; that he did him great service, and can be counted on to use his good offices in our behalf, and furnish us with such assistance as he is able."

And I give y^r honours my solemn word – that is all the name Washington signified to me then.

XIV

Thursday

Y^r honours have the whip hand of me, I'll not deny it; but I am not to be trained like a dog – tossed scraps from the table when I die for the King, and thrashed when I piss on a chair-leg. The reason I did not write yesterday was simply this: having worked fourteen days without cease, I resolved to devote the fifteenth as best I could to exercise and musick – for which, plainly, you think to punish me, by giving me a stale crust and water for my breakfast. But I shall not be starved into submission: I picked up my pen again this morning from choice, not hunger – and, indeed, find I return to my task with some relish; but if I am to tell my story, it must be at my own pace – which is a sharp trot, and not a gallop. If not – if this is nothing but a charade, and I am to hang at the conclusion of it, willy-nilly – then let us make an end of all these feints and manoeuvres, and be done with it now.

I have tried this past hour to make a sketch of the *Jenny* (for until I have plain evidence to the contrary, I shall presume y^r honours to be in earnest, and continue with my tale); but am chastened to find it no better than a child's drawing, with a hull like a log and three sticks for masts. So – pray – imagine: a fat, squat merchantman of three hundred tons, designed with no thought to comfort, but only to conveying the largest cargo, and getting the greatest profit, possible – even when (as in this instance, and I doubt not many others) the cargo included fifteen wretched emigrants, who were kennelled in the steerage with the hard loading, and allowed on deck but twice a day. In order that no opportunity might be lost to turn a penny more, the sailors were obliged to sleep in the straw next to the livestock, so that their meagre quarters might be crammed with barrels of oats and pease; and even the cabin was more than half a store-room, with butts and chests, trunks and chairs and a harpsichord (destined for the Carolina ladies) all lashed to the sides – so shrinking the floor that six men could barely stand there together.

The want of space immediately provoked a difficulty; for there was but one *stateroom*, in addition to the cap'ᵗˢ; and that being no more than a closet, five feet by six, with two narrow beds, constructed one each side of the cabin, the question naturally arose: *Where should we all sleep?* O'Donnell – who could not have played the servant more heartily if he had been at Drury Lane – suggested that Coleman and I should take the chamber, and he would make shift on the cabin floor; but Coleman – greatly to our surprise – would have none of it, saying *that he was a seasoned sailor, and might as easily sleep in a cot swung from the roof.* When I protested, he replied *that he would not impose upon two gentlemen, who must naturally expect to find themselves in sole possession of such accommodation as the ship could afford.* And was as good as his word; for not only did he retire *to* the cabin at night, but withdrew *from* it every morning, so that we should not be disturbed in its use during the day – with the result that we were as comfortable as two men might be under such conditions. When the weather permitted, indeed, we could almost escape our rolling, leaping little world altogether; for O'Donnell sat at the table lost in his scribbling, and I had an elbow-chair fixed close by the stove, where I might read a book and forget, for an hour or two, the cries of chicken above my head, and of children beneath my feet – the songs and jests of the sailors, half lost to the wind – and the endless thrashing and shivering of the captive sails. But these advantages were purchased at a price, which largely undid their benefits.

I should cut a less contemptible figure in my own eyes – and doubtless in yʳ honours' too – if I could pretend that it was the consciousness of my own good fortune that made me uneasy, when so many other miserable creatures were enduring the most pitiful privations all about me. But that, I fear, would be to elevate a small cause into a great one; for what principally concerned me was Coleman's conduct, which made such a powerful contrast to his previous manner towards us. The greatest dolt in existence could see he had no liking for O'Donnell and me (and in truth we had little enough for him); but neither of us could ever have supposed that his antipathy was so fierce as to make him prefer weeks of cold, sickness and confinement to a few hours every day in our company. This mystery occupied me for the first part of the voyage, and was then compounded by another, that made me more uneasy yet.

It arose some weeks after our setting out (of which I shall say nothing, for crossing the Atlantick is a tedious business; and rather than trying yʳ honours' patience with too particular an account of it – *21st day, a flat calm; 22nd, another; 23rd, a tremendous gale,* &c. &c. – I shall relate only those few episodes that bear directly on my story), when we had just passed the Azores. Around eleven o'clock in the morning, as I warmed myself before the stove, and O'Donnell (whose delicate sense of smell made the cabin more of a purgatory for him than it was for me) was taking the air on deck, I heard a sudden cry from without, and then a brisk tattoo of steps on the boards above me.

I sprang up, and was almost at the half-door, when it opened, and the master, Capᵗ Tallis, entered – hat blown half from his head, and pearls of water shimmering on his coat and boots. He barely acknowledged me, save to say in passing: "I fear, Sir, there's a storm in the making."

"I feel nothing," I said.

"Listen," said Tallis – a broad, oak-faced man, who wore no wig, and cropped his hair into a great silver brush. "Do you not mark the change?"

And – now he spoke of it – I did: the slap-slap of the sea had grown more insistent, as if it had lost patience with us, and was anxious for us to be gone.

"Fill your lungs now, if you have a mind to," said Tallis; "for in half an hour, if the wind don't mend, I must order the deadlights up, and close the hatches" – and at once sat down, and turned to his charts.

Which I took as my signal to leave, for he plainly could spare me no more thought, and I did not want to divert him from his work. To avoid cluttering the main deck (which I knew, by now, to be where most of the sailors' business was done) I climbed the companionway to the poop – and there found two or three hands attending to the mizzen mast, and Coleman and O'Donnell standing as far apart as they could without one or other of them falling into the sea. I came up by O'Donnell – who leaned against the rail as easy as if he were on dry land, snuffing the wind like a fastidious dog – and watched the bustle below. A second seaman had joined the helmsman at the wheel; a dozen more swarmed in the rigging, shortening sail; and the mate (an irritable American called Kirke, who resembled a shiny turtle in his leather coat) strode about like a pig-herd, *shooing* the emigrants back to the hold. Most of them went uncomplainingly; but one – a young woman – resisted, saying *she would sooner die here, under God's sky, than be smothered and crushed to death in the steerage.*

"Puke on her, if you have a mind to it," murmured a voice at my shoulder – at which I turned, and saw Coleman (to my great surprise; for it was many days since he had spoken an unnecessary word to us) smirking at me. "'Twill make her warier of standing on deck," he said; and then, pulling his hat about his ears and huddling into his coat, set off down the stairs towards her – doubtless to lend his authority to the mate's.

But had taken no more than three steps when all at once there was a tremendous jolt, and a giant hand seemed to pluck the little ship from the waves and set her down again at an angle of ninety degrees – as if she were no more than a boy's toy, and her master had tired of sailing her across the pond and resolved instead to send her against a flotilla of ducks. Coleman vanished; O'Donnell and I were flung to the deck; at the same moment there was a terrible crash from the steerage, which shook the boards beneath us, making me think the hull was holed. A second's awful silence . . . and then an eruption of groaning and wailing such as I had never heard – proceeding (it seemed), not from the several voices of fifty beings, but from the throat of a single wounded animal.

My first thought was of the seamen aloft, who must, I imagined, have been thrown overboard; but when I looked up I saw two or three of them still meshed in the mizzen-mast rigging, like flies in a web. Then another sound claimed my attention: the howls of an injured child, and the sobs (so I supposed) of its mother. O'Donnell heard it too, and – being surer on his feet (for the ship was now rocking from side to side so violently that I could not walk, but only crawl) – got to the stair-head before me. When I reached it myself, I looked down on a scene of pitiable disorder: broken spars; torn canvas; loose ropes whipping and twitching like hanged men; hands scrambling towards the wheel – all heedless of young Coleman, who lay pale and doubled with pain, clutching a hurt ankle and protecting himself as best he could from their kicks; and everywhere barrels, that had broken free of confinement and were rolling this way and that, crushing everything in their way (including two unfortunate chicken) before splitting up on the sides, and adding their own contents to the swelling tide of spilled oats and rain-water and feathers washing across the deck.

In the midst of this confusion stood O'Donnell, helping the young woman we had seen earlier to rise from the wet timbers, where she had evidently been thrown. She seemed quite distraught – attempting repeatedly to throw him off, but then losing her footing and having to cling to him again. He soon secured her, and began to stroke her hair (from which the bonnet had blown clean away), and to murmur, "Hush! Hush, now, what's the matter!"

She did not answer at once, only shaking her head furiously; but then, suddenly subsiding, said, "The child! The child!"

"What, is it yours?"

She nodded. "But I fear she is killed."

"Let us go there together, and see," said O'Donnell, leading her towards the hatchway.

Observing which, Coleman at once raised his hand, and called out: "No! No! You must not!"

"What!" said O'Donnell, turning.

"'Tis – 'Tis –" (grimacing, and struggling to order his thoughts). "'Tis too dangerous!"

"Why then do you carry infants there, and women?"

"Oh, D–n you!" groaned Coleman. "Do as you are told!"

But O'Donnell either did not hear him, or was too occupied with comforting his companion and helping her avoid the debris strewn in their path, to pay him any further heed; and was almost at the hatch when Coleman bellowed after him: "Stop, you murdering scoundrel! I forbid it!"

O'Donnell stopped – stiffened – braced himself against the mast, and said: "Some allowance, Sir, I know, must be made for your present circumstances; but if you ever repeat that insult, I swear I shall have satisfaction for it"; and went into the hold.

I set off down the poop ladder, intending to follow him and see if I might assist him; but that instant Coleman – doubtless wondering (as I was) where the cap' was in this emergency, and perhaps thinking he might be induced to use his power against O'Donnell – roar'd, "Captain Tallis!" and, as I reached the deck, the top of the half-door opened, and a fearful face peered out, the eyes dazed, and a great

59

gash on the forehead, from which two rivers of blood poured unchecked down his cheek and on to his neck.

"I am hurt," said Tallis, his voice slow and dull. "I was struck by a lantern."

"So am I, D–n you!" snarled Coleman. "You're wanted here."

Tallis blinked, and shook his head, to clear the mist from it – then stepped outside, looking about him, trying to estimate the damage to his ship.

When he saw me he said: "This is no place for you, Sir, I fear. You will oblige me by going below, and staying there, until this crisis is past."

"But may I not be of service to you?" I said. "At the least, I am able-bodied."

"If I have need of you, I shall send for you," said the cap*, and, taking my arm, pushed me towards the cabin.

Which was a sorrowful sight: the lights all extinguished – my chair overturned – the floor carpeted with biscuits and molasses from the master's Lazarus (as he called his private store), which had burst open like its ruder brethren on the deck. I crouched by the dying warmth of the stove, but knew better than to revive it; for any fire in such a savage storm might easily escape and set the whole ship ablaze. After a few minutes, the carpenter appeared and began hanging the deadlights – so snuffing out the last sullen gleams of day, and leaving me in utter darkness. At length – cold, blind and sick, and wanting any other occupation – I retired to my bed, and contrived somehow to doze – to be roused, some time later, by the sound of O'Donnell creeping into his place, on the other side of the stateroom.

The motion of the ship had changed: we were now pitching instead of rolling, in a manner I knew would have me puking in an instant if I got up; so I tugged my blanket about me, and tried to find my way back to sleep; but was prevented by O'Donnell, who – unaware, I suppose, that he had waked me – had no sooner lain down than he began to laugh softly to himself.

"What is so diverting?" I said at last.

He stopped abruptly, and was silent.

"Is it the child?"

"No, no."

"What, then?"

"The child was hit by a box, that is all."

60

"You must be in a strange humour, to find much mirth in that."

"I don't. But the child will mend. And . . ." He began again to laugh.

"And . . .?"

But he would not say more; and at length we both slept.

We kept pretty much to our beds for most of the next four days, as the storm completed its mischief – cracking the mast; breaching the cabin's defences (so, at a stroke, drenching every inch of our clothing, and depriving us of the means to dry it); and sweeping half of the poor emigrants' possessions into the sea, where we all feared we should shortly follow them. Since we were so much in each others' company and denied every other diversion but conversation, I thought it near certain that O'Donnell must sooner or later divulge the secret of the box in the hold. But, try as I might, I could not bring him to it: if I asked him outright – as I did a dozen times – he nimbly changed the subject, or made a jest of it; and if I lifted my siege, in hope he might relax his guard and return to the subject himself, he talked of every thing you can conceive (and some, I'll wager, you cannot) – save only holds and boxes.

This was irksome enough; but nothing compared to what followed, when at last the sea tired of buffeting us, and we were released from our captivity. We came out on to the poop to find ourselves aboard a useless hulk, bobbing impotently this way and that at the whim of the slopping waves – the mast broke, the rigging torn and tangled, sails ripped to threads and tatters. Coleman leaned on the rail, watching the little groups of sailors toiling to repair the damage. He turned as he heard us – scowled – and looked away again without a nod or a word. This exceeded even his customary rudeness, and deserved a reprimand, which I naturally supposed – when O'Donnell changed direction and walked deliberately towards him – he was about to receive.

Imagine, then, my amazement, when I heard instead: "Your servant, Mr. Coleman. I trust your foot is mended?"

Coleman twitched like a bullock struck by a pebble, and glowered furiously – doubtless fancying that O'Donnell was glorying in his misfortunes by affecting an exaggerated concern for them. Indeed I fancied so myself for a moment; for, tho' such gloating raillery would have been entirely out of O'Donnell's character, so too would have been the puppyish obsequiousness that seemed to offer the only other possible explanation. But the next instant put the matter beyond question; for as soon as he felt the force of Coleman's stare, O'Donnell sprang back, flushing – not the tormentor who has got his victim in a corner, but the humble well-wisher, that fears he has given offence.

"We shall talk of this later," he said, with a bow; and immediately returned to my side.

This strange alteration in O'Donnell's behaviour continued in the ensuing weeks – provoking an answering change in Coleman's, which grew more insolent almost by the day. Of the many instances I could give you, one will suffice:

One evening, as O'Donnell and I sat together over our wine, discussing how we should proceed when we got to America, Coleman swaggered into the cabin, seated himself in a chair, laid his injured foot on another and, taking up our bottle without the least ceremony, emptied it into his cup – which he then drained at a gulp.

Having thus warmed himself at our expense, he at once began to mock me, saying: "You put me in mind of Quixote, Cousin Ned. You persist in laying plans, and devising stratagems, as if 'twere the likeliest thing in the world you will find this boy – which, in truth, as any man of sense would tell you, is near impossible, for tho' there may be no want of candidates for the office, yet you have no means of knowing which of 'em, if any, is really Cousin Dan's son."

"Will not his mother tell me?"

"There may be as many contenders for her place as for his, one of whom will surely persuade you that her moon-calf or turkey-cock is the boy; and you will doubtless be as satisfied with him for a nephew as the mad Spaniard was with windmills for enemies. But Cousin Dan, I fancy, will not be so pleased; and you'll end by making both yourself and him a laughing-stock to the whole county – nay, the whole country."

"Why did you not say so sooner, if that is your opinion?" I said.

"I have my reasons," he said, with a smirk that made me want to bastinado him. At which, to my astonishment and dismay, O'Donnell began to laugh.

"Well," I said, "Daniel has more knowledge of the matter than you do, I suppose."

"Bah!" replied Coleman, looking me steadily in the eye. "He is a desperate old man, that will clutch at any wisp."

I rose, unable to contain myself, and thinking to cool my temper in the sea air.

As I reached the half-door, Coleman said, "At least Quixote had Sancho Panza to assist him, and not some Irish scribbler obliged to fly for his life."

I stopped – held my breath – turned. O'Donnell might (as it seemed) have lost all concern for my honour; but surely he could not ignore such an affront to his own? And indeed, he grew very pale – clenched his hands – and moved his jaw like a man chewing gristle, and wondering whether to swallow it or spit it out again.

But then, instead of leaping up as I had expected, he hunched forward over the table, fixed his eyes on a skittish candle, that could not choose whether to smoke or burn, and murmured: "I earnestly pray you, Sir, do not presume too far upon my patience."

Coleman appeared startled, and stared into O'Donnell's face for a moment. Then, after favouring us with a little laugh (which was meant to sound careless, but appeared only uneasy instead), he opened his coat – drew out a wine bottle – and re-filled his cup, all the while whistling softly to himself.

Unable to trust myself further, I stumbled out on to the deck, thinking, *Dear G–d! if I were a savage, I should suppose the young puppy had magick powers, that could make a man insensible of injury! – for has he not just done again the trick I saw him perform on Uncle Fiske? – and this time with a victim so jealous of his own dignity, that – had I not witnessed it with my own eyes – I should not have believed it?* This set me to wondering if there might be a kind of potion that had such an effect; which Coleman had discovered and secretly added to Uncle Fiske's and O'Donnell's wine, in order to disarm them against insolence. There were, I could not deny, some evident objections to this idea – *viz.*, what could possibly be his motive? and why, if it was so, had he not dosed me in the same manner? – but I resolved nonetheless to observe him closely over the next few days – and did so, but never saw him touch, or show the least interest in, any food or drink but his own; from which – since O'Donnell's strange transformation continued unchecked – I was obliged to conclude there must be some other explanation for it.

But what that might be I could not imagine; for when I spoke to O'Donnell about it, he merely laughed, and said: "You must remember, Sir, that Mr. Coleman is young; and the son of a merchant; and, not having received the same education as a gentleman, should not be judged by the same measure. He has, tho', many excellent qualities – to which, in time, I am certain, will be added good manners and decorum."

"This was not your opinion," I protested, "before you went into the hold."

To which he smiled, and shook his head, and said: "Come, Sir, this grows tedious – let us play at whist."

XV

Saturday
Another note this morning:

> *Sir: Pray be so good as to place each chapter in the door when you have finished it. You will thereby spare us both some inconvenience.*

Perhaps I might spare *yr honours* some inconvenience by this procedure (tho' having no notion of the means by which you have read my words until now, I cannot guess what); but I am not conscious of suffering any myself, that would be relieved by it in the least. But I am happy enough to follow it, if you wish – for it adds no great burden to me; and in serving y^r honours' purpose, I find by degrees I am also serving my own – discovering such a pleasure in writing as quite surprises me, and makes me suppose that, if ever I am freed from the necessity of scribbling for my life, I shall turn author, and scribble instead for my living.

It was my practice, when the weather allowed, to walk a mile upon the deck (a habit, I could not but notice, that provoked some furtive merriment among the crew – tho' why the sight of man taking twenty brisk paces along one side of the ship, five across to the other, and then twenty back again should have appeared so droll, I am at a loss to explain); and it was while I was thus engaged, on the third day of the ninth week of our voyage, that I heard a wild shout from the mast; and a moment later found my way barred by a human torrent that gushed from the hold – seamen, and women, and children, and a frail old man I had never seen before, who was almost trampled in the rush, all running and jostling to the sides of the ship and straining their eyes towards the horizon. From which I deduced, that America must at last be in sight.

And so it was, tho' at first no more than a purplish band, that you could scarce distinguish from the furthest shadowy reaches of the sea itself. Then came a pale rim, which grew at length into a waste of white sand, beneath a ragged fringe of melancholy pines. It was hard to conceive, and harder to bear, that so much British blood and British money had been spent to preserve so dreary a place – which, even now, looked fit only for wolves and savages; for (try as I might) I could see not the least evidence of habitation, or of the most rudimentary improvement. Observing which to the mate, Kirke, who stood at my shoulder, I unwittingly brought a great torrent of patriotick abuse on my head:

"Why, Sir, are the English all blind, as well as deaf? Look – there – can't you see – that's Berry's plantation!"

I followed the direction of his calloused finger, and saw a tiny notch cut from the forest, and something that might have been smoke.

"And there" – pointing at another spot, to the south of the first, and at least thirty miles from it – "that is Tack's! That's how thick settled we are!"

"Thick settled!" I said. "You might as well say the Atlantick is all land, because it has islands in it!"

He spat angrily into the sea, and turned his back on me.

By evening we could plainly see the mouth of a great river opening to receive us; a short time later, the cap' hung out his flag, and almost at once a small pilot-boat put out towards us. This encouraged me to suppose that we might get ashore that night – which the whole company heartily craved, not only for the general reason, that we had been penned up together more than two months, but also for a more particular one, *viz.*, it was the 24th December, and we all naturally hoped to pass Christmas on solid land. But in this we were disappointed; for the cap' said *'twas too late to reach Brunswick today; but he would order in some provisions, that he hoped would make our last night aboard more tolerable.* To which end, he quickly concluded terms with the pilot for the immediate surrender of a dozen of wine, and a turkey, and a joint of salt mutton.

I cannot tell with any certainty where we lay that night. It was already dark, save for a timid moon that peeped out behind surly clouds, and we were still some distance from the shore; and soon after we had anchored, the cap' sent the carpenter to fix the deadlights, so blinding the cabin altogether. I asked Tallis whether he expected bad weather (for it was then pretty quiet); he shook his head, and smiled, and said nothing; but soon answered my question another way, by ordering the cook (a fat fellow called Bird, whose face had been ravaged by the pox and looked like a sponge) to stir up the fire in the stove, and set about preparing our Christmas meal – which led me to conclude that he did not fear a storm, but had some other reason for sealing his ship up.

Tho' what that might be, I did not have long to consider; for the festivity soon began, with the cap[t] opening a bottle, and summoning us to pledge his health in it – which we did, in prodigious good spirits, knowing that our captivity was about to end, and that in an hour or two we should be tasting our first fresh food (save fish, and the two barrelled chicken) since leaving England.

The table was strewn with lighted candles – the wine (seized, no doubt, from a French privateer) so freely offered, and so markedly superior to the vile drench the cap[t] had brought with us, that it was impossible not to gulp it down greedily, and return for more. Even Coleman was unusually sociable and cheerful and, while saying nothing that suggested he had recanted his poor opinion, either of me or of my mission, yet contrived to avoid making us the butt of his facetious humour. In short, we ate and drank hoggishly, and were as merry and easy together as four such men could be.

With the result (which y[r] honours will soon guess at) that by the time the joint was boiled, and set before us, my belly was in torment at so much unaccustomed fare, and could no longer countenance it. The very sight of the meat, indeed – wet and grey, and ribbed with yellow fat – made me want to puke – an impulse I tried at first to master, by looking away while Tallis hacked the quivering flesh to pieces. But while nature allows us to avert our eyes, she does not make the same provision for our noses; and the hot rancid smell of it in my throat threatened such an uprising, if I did not immediately remove myself, that I was at length obliged to make my excuses and stagger to my bed; where I soon slept.

But my digestion was too aggrieved to let me rest, and an hour or two later roused me again, for the first of several journeys to the bucket; on the second or third of which, while I was yet about my business, I heard a thump, and felt a blow against the *Jenny*, that made her shudder. Imagining that we had perhaps drifted, and struck a rock, I felt my way through the cabin (dark now, and quiet), thinking to go out on deck, and ask one of the seamen on the night watch what was the matter. But when I reached the half-door, it was barred, and would not move even when I leaned upon it.

I turned back – knocked at the captain's stateroom, got no reply, and entered. It was empty, and the bed cold. I returned to the cabin, steeling myself to wake Coleman, but when I felt for his cot I discovered it had not been let down, but was still tied up against the roof. My wits were yet so fuddled with wine and sleep that for a moment I entertained the notion that they must have been waked by the sound that I had heard and gone to investigate its cause; but then I reflected, that in that case Tallis's blanket would have been rumpled, and Coleman's cot swinging where he had left it. From which I could but conclude they had not gone to bed at all.

With increasing apprehension, I climbed the ladder that led to the poop, only to discover that the hatch, too, was firmly shut. I began to pummel it, crying, "Ho! Ho, there!" but the next second there was another jolt against the side of the ship, which dislodged me from my perch and sent me tumbling back into the cabin. The shock of which gave me a bruised wrist and a grazed shin – but also, in the same instant, cleared my head, so that as I sat on the floor, cursing and rubbing my sore hand, I suddenly knew the noise I had heard for what it was; and understood why Coleman and Tallis were not a-bed, and what the business was that had brought them here, and why they had left me locked up while they pursued it – and I was hobbling back to the stateroom, to wake O'Donnell and tell him, when he spared me the necessity by that moment appearing himself, clutching a new-lit lantern.

"Are you hurt, Sir?" he said. "I heard you cry out."

"Bah! – a buffet and a scratch, that's all. What's hurt most is my opinion of my uncle, which I doubt can ever recover."

"Why?" (crouching down, and coolly examining my shin). "What has he done?"

"He has duped us, Sir – he and that rascal Coleman! Bringing us to America was but a pretext – a varnish, to cover up their true purpose."

"What, you mean the letters to Colonel Washington?"

"Washington be d–d! – I mean smuggling, Sir! Listen! . . ." (for even as I spoke there came a third blow to the hull) ". . . that is a little boat, slapping at our side. Into which, I doubt not, they are unloading their contraband, to escape detection!"

"You cannot be certain of that, Sir."

"No, I can only guess it! – for we are prisoned here, the door and hatch fastened to keep us from going out. Which seems evidence enough to me."

O'Donnell did not answer, but walked deliberately to the half-door – doubtless hoping to show that I had deluded myself, and my suspicions were groundless; but it yielded to his efforts no more than it had to mine. And – as if to add yet further weight to my case – no sooner had he finished than we heard from without the crack of a heavy chest dropped on the deck, and a flurry of muttered oaths and jests – which immediately put me in mind of his adventure during the storm.

"Come, Sir!" I said. "You were in the hold, and saw what was carried there, and puffed it into a great mystery, to prick my curiosity. Tell me – this box of yours: do you think the excise know of it?"

He said nothing, but looked as near confounded as I had ever seen him: pursed up his mouth – tapped a little minuet on the base of the lantern – and at length shook his head.

"Very well, then!" I cried, snatching up a stool. "Surely together we can break out, and expose this villainy?"

"And what then?" said O'Donnell. "You know, Sir, I hope, that I am not a man who will flinch from a fight, when any good may come of it, and it has the least chance of success; but we are two against twenty or more, and even if we contrived to overpower them, and escape in the boat, we should not know how to reach land, or what we might find when we got there. Better to keep our own counsel for the present, and see what tomorrow may bring."

It went hard enough down with me – for by now my temper was so roused, I could scarce curb it – but I was obliged to concede that he was in the right of it; and sorrowfully followed him back to the state-room – but could not sleep; for every bang and knock boiled my blood a little hotter, forcing me to clench my fists, and clamp my tongue to stop it crying out in protest at the abuse being practised upon me, and upon my poor unsuspecting country.

In the morning, I stayed a-bed until long past the usual hour, in hope that I should thus avoid Coleman (who, having come to his cot so late, would doubtless be equally late quitting it); for the fire still raged in my head, and I could not trust myself to speak to him until it had somewhat cooled. But, on entering the cabin, I found him seated at the table, writing a letter which, as soon as he saw me, he concealed by so placing his hands that I could not read to whom it was directed, or what it concerned.

"I trust you slept, Sir," he said, coolly – but was immediately betrayed by the colour rising to his cheeks, which he banished by biting his lips so fiercely that he winced.

"Well enough," I said, "but am now in want of air," and climbed at once to the poop – to find we were already under sail, and in the river: the *Jenny*, freed of her cargo, frisking after the pilot-boat like an unburdened pack-horse; the cap' leaning on the rail smoking a pipe, and squinting ahead, looking for something in the dense trees that enclosed us. After a minute or two he cried out and, turning abruptly, caught sight of me – which seemed for a moment to discomfit him as much as it had Coleman; for he started, and his mouth gaped silently like a fish's. Then he recovered himself – pointed with his pipe-stem – and said: "The fort, Sir. Fort Johnston," and without waiting for an answer, hurried down the stairs.

I thought at first he must be jesting; for the building, when at length (after much screwing up my eyes) I saw it, appeared little bigger than a parson's house, and was made of sand and crushed shells that looked as if they must be washed away with the first spattering of rain. Then I remarked the guns poking thro' the walls, and was persuaded of its purpose – tho' not of its efficacy, for it was hard to conceive an invader would long be deterred by a toy castle, that a regiment of village-boys armed with sticks and buckets might have levelled in an hour. Hard by it lay an old sloop, crusted in barnacles, which would have thrown as prodigious an obstacle in the way of an enemy's navy as the fort would have of his army.

We anchored a little way off, while Tallis went ashore in the ship's boat, carrying a satchel of papers – saying *that he was obliged to show his credentials, and pay certain fees due to the governor.* I remained alone, preferring the company of wind and drizzle to that of my fellow-passengers, one of whom was guilty of the most flagrant duplicity, and the other (I could not but feel, now I came to reflect upon it) of something little short of pusillanimity – which I thought I might justly reprove by keeping aloof from him for the present.

And it was well I did so; for otherwise I should have failed to observe a particular that might have ended our American journey before it had begun: that when the cap' set out again from the fort, an hour or so later, he came not alone, but accompanied by a second boat, in which I could plainly see six armed men and an officer. What the reason might be I could not immediately guess – but amongst the riot of possible explanations that tumbled through my brain, there was not one that was to my liking.

I hurried below again, to discover my cousin gone and his place taken by O'Donnell – who smiled as he scratched in his note-book, and regarded me (when he looked up) with the detached air of an author meditating a phrase.

"Where's Mr. Coleman?" I said.

O'Donnell waved his pen towards the cap''s stateroom, which I reached in three strides, and banged on the door – so provoking a peevish whine from within: "What?"

"I fear you have betrayed us, Sir."

"I have not betrayed you," he said – but in the unsteady voice of a boy that denies stealing apples, while his pockets bulge.

"Why, then, is Tallis bringing a pack of soldiers with him?"

To which he made no reply; so I tried to open the door, thinking to drag him out, and shake an answer from him. But it yielded only an inch or two before banging shut again – from which I deduced he must be leaning against it.

"D–n you!" I cried, pushing harder.

"Leave me be!"

I stepped back – then launched myself at the door, butting it so hard that it sprang open, hurling Coleman on to the bed and jerking something from his hand, which slapped on to the floor. He snatched it up again and smuggled it behind his back; but not before I had seen what it was: a prayer-book. Then he lay still, moaning, feeling a purple graze on his forehead, and sucking blood from his thumb, which seemed to have been pricked by a splinter.

"Come, Sir, 'tis a plain enough question," said O'Donnell, appearing in the entrance beside me. His tone was careless – but he had turned marble-white. "Why are they coming here?"

"I don't know!" said sulky Coleman.

"Well, then," said O'Donnell, "we must suppose that they are seeking either you or me . . ."

"Me!" cried Coleman. "Why me?"

"Why, Sir, on account of the cargo that you carried, and discharged last night."

"The cargo!" (his eyes bright – his cheeks a furnace – all at once more furious than fearful). "What do you know of that?"

"Enough to hang you, for a certainty. But you may count on my discretion – as I am sure I may on yours, if they have heard somehow of my embarrassment in Bristol, and mean to arrest me."

"But who told 'em, if they have heard?" I said – remembering what Coleman had been about when I had found him that morning, and wondering if he had given his letter to Tallis to take ashore.

Coleman said nothing – but his eyes confessed what his lips would not, for he could not meet my gaze, but stared fixedly at the floor. I should have pressed my advantage; but was prevented by O'Donnell, who laid a hand on my arm, and said: "Nay, Sir, this is not the time for that – we must resolve what we are going to do, without delay."

Once again, I had to acknowledge he was in the right; but seeing Coleman cowering – wig awry, hair dishevelled, eyes bright as a trapped stoat's – I could not entirely put from my mind the question: *Why did he bring this upon himself?* It was hard to believe even he would have done it from malice alone – and yet, if there was another reason, I was at a loss to imagine it; and was destined to remain so, for many weeks after.

"What say you, Sir?" went on O'Donnell, prodding Coleman's foot with his own.

"Why" – dully, his spirit quite snapped – "we should conceal you, I suppose"; and he lifted his head at last, and looked about him (in every direction but mine) for a hiding-place.

"Where?" I asked.

"Beneath one of the beds," said Coleman. "Or we could let down my cot, and raise it again with him laid within it."

"But that is to proclaim myself guilty, before I am accused," said O'Donnell. "If they search, and find me, my best defence is already gone, and I shall have no resort but the worst."

"And what is that, Sir?" said Coleman, reddening again.

"I am surprised you ask me, Sir. But, since you do – I mean, by turning King's evidence, and purchasing my life with yours."

For a moment Coleman was perfectly still – the contending forces within him so equally matched, as to paralyse him entirely. But then prudence triumphed over rage and hatred, and he nodded and said: "What then do you propose?"

"I propose—" began O'Donnell, but was interrupted by the sound of oars, and a sharp *ho, there!*, at which he said, "I think I must show rather than tell you," and leaped to the ladder, beckoning us to follow.

Which we did, emerging to find the cap' already on deck, and the party of soldiers swarming up after him, led by their officer – a thin, cattish fellow, who shivered in the cold, and plainly had no relish for his task, but wished only to be within doors again, curled up before the fire. He glanced this way and that – drummed his fingers on his sword – and scrupulously avoided engaging our attention until the last of his party had joined him, evidently fearing to declare his purpose before he had mustered the force to accomplish it.

Then, blinking up at us, he said: "I am Captain Sutcliffe. I am searching for Mr. O'Donnell."

"O'Donnell?" said O'Donnell.

"We are ordered to arrest him."

"O'Donnell." (Musing.) "O'Donnell." Then, to me: "I think he must mean that rough Irish fellow."

"Very probably," I said, seeing that I must go along with him once again, tho' I had no notion where he was leading me.

O'Donnell turned to Coleman – who nodded, grinding his teeth – and then back to Sutcliffe.

"You say his name is O'Donnell?"

"Yes, Sir."

"And what is his crime? Eloping off with a bag of potatoes?"

"He is an escaped murderer."

"Ah . . . Ah . . ." murmured O'Donnell, with such an appearance of sudden apprehension that I was almost deceived by it myself. "Then 'tis small enough wonder, I suppose."

"Why, Sir, what has he done?"

"Thrown himself off, and swum ashore, not an hour since. I imagined that being at sea for so long had made him mad, but now I see 'twas rational enough – for any man will prefer the risk of losing his life to the certainty of it."

"And what of the gentleman that was travelling with him?"

"He too – tho' being somewhat older, and of a cholerick temper, 'tis even less likely he will survive the shock."

I could not hear this, even then, without some indignation; to distract myself from which, I studied Sutcliffe's face, and made a mental inventory of the warring emotions I saw there, *viz., suspicion; uncer-*

tainty; *indolence*, and several species of *fear* – most prominent among them, that of being humiliated before his men and reprimanded by his superiors, which seemed equally likely whether he accepted O'Donnell's story, or challenged it.

"Are you Mr. Coleman?" he asked at length, narrowing his eyes and looking at O'Donnell sidelong, to show he was not to be duped.

"No, Sir, I have not that distinction" – and he pointed at Coleman, who nodded and bowed, as stiff and mechanical as if he had been a puppet and O'Donnell had just pulled his string. "You will excuse the gentleman if he does not speak much for himself – he tried to prevent the escape, and was badly beaten for his pains and suffered a bit hand. As you can see." At which Coleman obediently displayed his torn thumb, and lowered his head, so that the graze was visible from below.

Sutcliffe hesitated – stepped forward a few paces – stepped back again – then turned to Tallis (who stood at his side, looking utterly perplexed), and said: "Is that Mr. Coleman?"

Tallis nodded enthusiastically – here was a fact he could pluck from the confusion, and confidently attest to; and he embraced the opportunity gratefully.

Still Sutcliffe wavered, while behind him his men began to cough and shuffle – and one even went so far as to giggle, before his fellows nudged him into silence; which brought a flicker of panick into Sutcliffe's eyes – encouraging O'Donnell to press home his advantage.

"I presume, Sir, that your commission extends to the ship, and no further; in which case you must report the matter to the constables at once, and may then properly leave them to prosecute it – tho' I doubt they will need to exercise themselves greatly, for 'tis ten to one the cold and the wild beasts will do the hangman's business for him."

Sutcliffe's eyes brightened, for the first time since his arrival – a door had opened, through which he could see the tempting glow of his hearth; and, having considered a moment to be sure it was not a snare, he hastened through it.

"Thank you, gentlemen," he said – bowed – and retired.

An hour later, the *Jenny* was safe anchored in the port of Brunswick, and O'Donnell and I clambered from the ship's boat to take our first steps on the soil of America.

XVI

No more Tuesday, Wednesday, Thursday, &c. I shall set my clock now, not by days passed, but by chapters written.

Not only a good breakfast this morning, but a good dinner last night: rabbit stew, and a little wine, which 'twixt them soothed my belly and procured me a few hours' unbroken sleep. There must be many an author setting to work that wishes he was so well fed and rested – and not just in Grub Street, neither.

I see, looking back at what I have written, that what began as a rubble of words has grown by degrees into the foundation, or basement, of a considerable edifice; which – since (as I hope) my skill as an architect has grown with it, and our arrival in America seems to form a natural interval – I shall here lay off with a new course and, with y^r honours' indulgence, call the next story:

BOOK TWO

XVII

I know not whether the Atlantick or America is the greater area, but they exercise, in their vastness, a similar effect on the senses – for the one consists mostly of water and the other mostly of wood. The ocean, it is true, is always noisy; while the forest seems almost mute – but sound and silence alike appear equally devoid of meaning, so that a plain man might quickly die of tedium, and a more fanciful one suppose himself trapped in a great madhouse and end by going mad himself. For which reason, I shall proceed by the same principle I adopted before, and recount only those adventures that are pertinent to my story – for y^r honours no more need to be acquainted with every tree I met in America than with every wave I saw getting there.

By which rule, Brunswick may be dashed off in a paragraph or two – for, tho' the mate had assured me *it was the principal sea-port of the province,* it turned out to be nothing but a scattering of houses at the edge of the forest, with less regularity than an English village, and to have no more to offer by way of company than it did of architecture. We stayed that night with Mr. Quince, the greatest merchant in the place; who kept a generous table and a cheerful hearth, but whose conversation was remarkable only for introducing me to the *new system of politicks*, as he was pleased to term it. At dinner we were joined by several of his neighbours – including Mr. Dry, the collector of taxes, a more fanatick zealot yet; and to hear them inciting each other to rebellion, as carelessly as if they had been talking of the weather, you would have supposed the most admired accomplishment in America was not wit or learning, but treason. I observed to Mr. Dry *that to speak thus was to repay kindness with the basest ingratitude – for did he not owe his prosperity, his safety, and his occupation itself, to the gracious care of the very king he was defaming?* At which he sucked at the air, as if attempting to draw back some of the brickbats he and his companions had recently loosed there, in order to turn them against me. And he might have succeeded; for the next minute, instead of replying, or offering a new argument, he merely pelted me with the same tiresome phrases I had already heard: *What of liberty, Sir? – popery? – tyranny? – ministerial tools?* – like an enraged parrot trying to frighten a cat.

I looked at O'Donnell – one word from whom, I knew, could reduce the fool to silent confusion; but he only smiled, and refused to acknowledge my gaze. I could not easily pursue the subject further myself, without such a show of rudeness as would assuredly have had me put out of the house – and where should I have gone then, if every inhabitant of the place thought as Dry and Quince did? So I held my tongue until the toasts, when I proposed *The King and Queen*. Quince (to my surprise) raised his glass; but then replied, "And confusion to the King's false friends in the ministry; and success to his true friends in America, the Sons of Liberty, and members of the Congress – Mr. This, and Captain That, and" (here a knife-point seemed to touch the back of my neck) "Colonel Washington."

"Colonel Washington!" I said. "Of the Virginia Militia?"

"The same," oozed grinning Quince. "Will you drink to him?"

"As my brother's friend, if not the King's," I said; but soon after went up-stairs, pleading tiredness after our long voyage.

But – having grown so accustomed to being rocked and lullabied by the sea – could not sleep, and instead lay racked by fatigue and confusion and unquiet bowels, which conspired to paint my situation in the darkest colours imaginable. Here I was, in a strange country, abandoned by my companion, tricked by my cousin, and surrounded by enemies – among them, it appeared, the one man in America I had supposed I might turn to for help – which deprived me, at a stroke, not merely of friends and comfort, but also of the best hope I had of find-ing my nephew; for the only plan I had formed – *viz.*, to accompany Coleman to Fiskefield, where Uncle Fiske had promised we might be furnished with horses and a boy; and then go on to Virginia to solicit Colonel Washington's assistance in finding Miss Catchpole – depend-ed on two men I now knew were not to be trusted. But, try as I might, I could not devise a better; and at length reluctantly concluded that I must keep company with it until another way opened to me.

These thoughts were still torturing me when O'Donnell came to bed; and for a minute or two I considered laying them candidly before him, in hope the jolt might free the rusted mechanism of our friendship, and make all well between us again. But pride held me back – I hesitated – opened my mouth – shut it again without speak-ing; then heard his breath sink into the soft regularity of sleep, and knew the moment was past.

My cousin might have sent word ahead to the plantation and ordered horses to meet us; but that would have delayed us two days more in Brunswick, which he would by no means countenance – for now we were in America, he was eager as a young dog to get to his new home, and piss his mark on the wall, to show the other curs what a great fellow he was. In the morning, therefore, we dispatched a mes-senger to Fiskefield, to announce our imminent arrival; and a few hours later – having hired a waggon for our baggage, and Mr. Quince's phaeton for ourselves – set off after him.

The first part of the journey was pleasant enough – the road level, and bordered by wild fruit trees, so delicately tangled that with the low winter sun behind them, they formed a kind of wall of black lace, which made a delightfully picturesque effect. But what charms by day may oppress by night; and as it began to grow dark, the woods seemed to draw together and push menacingly towards us – so that it was impossible to banish entirely all thoughts of the fierce beasts (and, for all we knew, desperate men) that dwelt there. We asked the coachman, "How much further now?" to which he carelessly replied, with no more ceremony than if he were talking to a washer-woman, "Oh, many hours yet."

"Is there not an inn, where we might put up for the night?" I said.

But he only laughed – which, tho' it depressed my spirits, seemed to enliven Coleman's; for, after having sat in gloomy silence for the last ten miles, he suddenly found his tongue again – and with it his sarcastick humour.

"You fear, do you, cousin Ned, that you have cheated the fishes, only to fall prey to a savage or a bear or a wolf?"

"There are no savages here," I said (recalling Dan's story); "and the bears will still be sleeping. And I never heard yet of a wolf so hungry that it would attack a carriage."

"Ah, but the wolves of these parts, I hear, consider English flesh a particular delicacy – especially that of Somersetshire, which is known to be fat and sweet – and will venture any risk to get it. Tho' you, Sir" (turning to O'Donnell) "have no cause to be anxious; for they'll not resort to a skinny Irish carcase – no, not to save their lives."

I waited for O'Donnell to respond – wagering with myself, whether he would wink at this latest insult, as he had so often before; or (as I hoped) at last recover his pride and answer in kind, or demand an apology. But he made no reply at all – not a movement, or an intake of breath; so that I should have supposed him asleep, had I not seen the glint of his eye in the starlight. Which plainly surprised Coleman as much as it did me; for instead of laughing at his own waggery (as I had expected), he stirred in his seat, and said, in a parsonish voice that put me strangely in mind of Uncle Fiske:

"Nay, nay, gentlemen – you know I do but jest. And I hope when we are at Fiskefield you will not be in a hurry to leave again; for I swear, I shall make amends there for my raillery, by showing you some fine entertainment – if you will but linger long enough to enjoy it."

This sudden about-face (which came as near to an apology as I had ever heard Coleman utter) was as unconvincing as it was astonishing, and – as if by common consent – neither O'Donnell nor I indulged it with a response. And in that moment, I think, our poor bedraggled intimacy began to revive somewhat – tho' I did not know it at the time, and it was many weeks before I understood what had injured it.

I cannot tell how long we travelled that night, passing no habitation, and no other creature than bats and owls; but the stars were long gone from the sky before we finally turned off the road. For a moment, the trees seemed to press still more closely upon us; then, like a crowd whose curiosity has been sated, retreated again, admitting us to open fields, that shimmered dully with frost, with the dark bulk of a building rising beyond them. At first I could see little of it, for there was but one taper burning in an upper room; but as we drew nearer, lights began to appear first in one window, then in another – gradually revealing a sweetly proportioned facade that a baronet might not have been ashamed of owning. It would have been surprise enough, in such a wilderness, to find any house at all – save the witch's hovel in a childish story. To discover such a scene of enchantment as this seemed so strange that for a minute or two I wondered if I had fallen asleep upon the road, and come upon it only in my own dreams.

I had more or less mastered this fancy by the time we drew up at the door; but it at once broke free again, when three or four servants streamed out, holding up lanterns – just as I or y^r honours might have expected, save in one particular: they were all black. I had, of course, known my uncle's man Joseph and several other negroes in Bristol; but there they were exoticks, kept as much for adornment as for service, and quite outnumbered by their English fellows. To see suddenly a whole company of blacks in the characters of abigails and footmen was not unlike going to a familiar play at the theatre and finding the female roles taken by men, and the men's by girls. One of the women – about the middle age, with a grave manner and large watchful eyes – stepped forward and bobbed her head.

"You's welcome to Fiskefield, gen'lmen," she said. "I is Niobe."

"Oh, you is, is you?" smirked Coleman – with a hasty glance at O'Donnell and me, to see if we shared his great opinion of his own wit. "And do you know who I is?"

"Mrs. Coleman's boy, Sir."

Which quite nonplussed him; for he had plainly hoped for a more exalted title, and yet could hardly reproach her for impudence or ignorance – so drew himself up, and marched without a word into the house. And at once stopped again, so abruptly that I trod upon his heel. For a moment I could not see what had caught his attention, for there were but three or four candles lit, so that it was more like entering a cave than a hall. Then he pointed, and I spied in the shadows before us a great untidy pyramid of open-mouthed boxes – rudely stacked, with clothes and papers and knick-knacks spilling from them.

"What is that?"

"They's Mr. Wimsey's, Sir."

"And why are they here?"

"He say the mornin' soon enough to take 'em."

"Did he not receive our message?"

"Yes, Sir. But when you not here after supper-time, he say you prob'ly not come till tomorrow. He tell us to wait you, jus' in case; but as for him, he goin' to bed."

Coleman was enraged – a young prince, who comes to take possession of his kingdom, only to discover that the regent has not yet quitted the palace. He clenched and unclenched his fists, before trusting himself to speak:

"Be so good as to inform Mr. Wimsey that I have now arrived, and expect to see him here immediately."

Niobe shifted from one foot to the other, and glanced at the other servants – who seemed as uncomfortable as she was, and turned away. At length she said: "He say anyone go in there after he in bed get a whippin'."

"Does he, now?" – clenching his fists again – "Well, I say anyone that don't do as I tell 'em will get a worse."

The poor woman began to tremble; seeing which, one of the other servants – a slight mulatto boy of nine or ten – moved to her side and pressed himself against her. She stiffened, and shook her head – but too late to stop him blurting, "Please, Sir!–"

"D–n it!" – with a stamp of his foot that made the child skit back in terror. "I am master here now, and I will be obeyed!"

The woman did not protest or cry out, but shuddered, and dropped her eyes, as if preparing herself for the lash already. Then she nodded – took up her lantern – and began slowly to walk off.

I was half-insensible with fatigue and cold, and there was a good fire in the grate, and welcoming chairs before it – seeing which, it was easy enough to persuade myself I could do nothing to help her. Until, that is, she paused at the door, and turned to send the boy back again; for then I remarked the expression in her face: a kind of Stoick weariness, formed by years of unjust suffering, and the certainty that she could expect nothing else.

"Perhaps, Sir," I said, "I might go in her place, if she will direct me there."

"I too," said O'Donnell.

For a moment, Coleman was startled into silence, and did not recover his wits until we were halfway across the hall, when – plainly seeing he could not command us – he muttered, "As you please," with as great a show of carelessness as he could muster.

I confess I had expected she would thank us as soon as we stepped outside; but she said nothing – as if the bargain she had struck with Fate required her to be as indifferent to kindness as to cruelty. Going upon tip-toe, she led us across a frosty courtyard, bordered on two sides by low buildings which – even in the darkness – contrived to convey an air of neglect. There was a light showing in only one of them, which I naturally supposed to be our destination; but she hurried past it – tho' not before a small negro man (whom I took, by his appearance and his proximity to the horses, to be the ostler) came out and engaged her briefly in a whispered conversation. I could not hear what they were saying; but from the familiar manner in which he touched her arm, and her answering smile (the first, and almost the last, I ever saw her give), it was plain they were intimates, or something more. He bowed, laughing – flourished his arm towards his quarters – and then retired in-doors, leaving her to continue on her way.

She stopped at last before a snug cottage, conspicuously neater and straighter-roofed than its neighbours. Here she handed us the light, and then slipped into the shadows, before her part in the business might be detected.

We knocked loudly – I first, then O'Donnell, then both of us; but failed to stir up any response, so after a minute or so lifted the latch. But the door was bolted fast; and since it was plain we could only gain entry by setting fire to it or cudgelling it to splinters (which we thought something exceeded our commission), we at once gave up and began to return to the house. And had only taken a few steps when a casement opened on the upper floor and a suppressed, urgent voice called:

"What you wan'? The master sleepin'."

We looked up, and saw a black girl leaning out, clutching a blanket about her shoulders. In the yellow glow of the lantern she appeared no more than fourteen or fifteen.

I said: "Mr. Coleman is arrived, and would be glad to see Mr. Wimsey in the house immediately."

"Who you?"

O'Donnell held up the lantern so she might see our faces, and said: "This gentleman is Mr. Coleman's cousin, and I am his servant."

The girl glanced over her shoulder; then stretched further out, and whispered: "The master drunk. You hush a momen', you hear."

We listened. From behind her erupted a ragged snore, as rough and whistly as the snuffling of a hog.

"I wake him when he like that, he goin' to beat me bad."

"Then open the door," I said, "and we will wake him."

From her response, you would have thought I had torn my wig off and danced a jig on it. Her eyes grew round – she gaped in astonishment.

"You think that stop him?"

Before I could reply, O'Donnell said: "Very well, then. Good night."

"Good night, Sir."

"I pray, Sir," murmured O'Donnell, as we crossed the yard, "you will permit me to report what happened to Mr. Coleman."

"Gladly," I said, for in truth I could not think how to tell my young cousin without fuelling his anger and diverting it (since it was cheated of its proper object) on to the unfortunate slaves; and was thus not greatly encouraged, when we re-entered the hall, to find him pacing back and forth like an uneasy cat – plainly unable to devote himself to any other occupation, until he knew whether or not he was obeyed.

"Well?" he said sharply. "Where is the gentleman?"

O'Donnell strode leisurely to the hearth – took off his cloak – stretched his arms before the fire – and said (all the while studying some mark on his cuff): "I fear, Sir, Mr. Wimsey is unwell; but sends his compliments, and promises himself the pleasure of waiting upon you in the morning, if he is sufficiently recovered."

For a moment, all hung in the balance – Coleman flushed, and swallowed, and gnawed at his knuckle. Then, suddenly, the spring unwound – his shoulders dropped – he nodded, and scratched absently at the rim of his wig.

"Very well, very well. Now, gentlemen" – rubbing his hands, and even permitting himself a smile – "will you take some wine?" He turned to the remaining slaves, who had drawn together in a huddle, and plucked out the tallest of them with a jerk of the head. "You, sir – what's your name?"

"Dennis, Sir."

"Well then, Master Dennis, pray bring us a bottle – if Mr. Wimsey has been good enough to leave us one."

"Yes, Sir."

And when the fellow returned, with a grimy madeira, my cousin raised his glass and pledged: "Here's your health, cousin Ned. And yours, Mr. O'Donnell. Welcome to Liberty-Hall – where I hope you'll feel no constraint, but do just as you please!"

*

Yet it was wonderful, as it turned out, how *little* we were able to please ourselves – the reason given being always the same: *that Mr. Wimsey's negligence had made it impossible.* We could not set off on our journey, or even jaunt through the woods and fields; for Wimsey had allowed the number of serviceable horses to dwindle to only two – and they were required for Wimsey himself and Coleman to ride about the estate, surveying the consequences of his incompetence. The food was plain, the wine indifferent – and we could neither make nor accept visits, for there was no lady in the house to receive guests. For all of which, Coleman squarely laid the fault at Wimsey's door – much as a Methodist, every time he steps in a puddle or suffers a bruise, will blame Satan for it.

For the author of so much mischief, Wimsey himself (when at length we saw him) made a poor enough figure: being thin, stooped and trembly, with a sallow monkey face set in perpetual apology, and teeth so rotted they looked as if they must crumble at their first encounter with meat – which gave him the air of an old dog that could no longer even mumble a rabbit. Or such, at least, was the case when he was sober; when drunk (a state he had usually attained within two hours of rising), his manner was entirely different: the palsy left him; he moved with an unsteady swagger, and would raise his hand on the slightest pretext against any of the slaves who dis-pleased him – tho' generally they contrived to skip out of the way before he struck them and remain there until he had forgotten their offence, which was seldom more than half a minute. And tho' drink-ing added little to his conversation, beyond a rich seasoning of oaths and curses, it encouraged a whole catalogue of sounds and gestures – tongue-clickings and gurgles, eye-rollings and nose-rubbings – which suggested he knew a great deal about the matter we happened to be discussing, but was too shrewd to reveal it.

The want of occupation and pleasant company rendered our first few days at Fiskefield a tedious desert – which soon degenerated into something worse, as I observed O'Donnell grow paler and less vig-orous, almost by the hour. He began staying a-bed until after noon, and then usually kept to his room until dinner-time – when he would emerge to sit wordlessly at table and chew upon a piece of bread, before retiring again. This (as you may imagine) spurred Coleman to tremendous flights of wit, concerning the indolence of the Irish; but I could not help supposing that my companion must have been seized with some wasting sickness, that was in a fair way of killing him. But when I begged him to let me summon the doctor, he only shook his head, and said *it was the place oppressed him; and there was nothing the matter that would not be cured by leaving it.*

I did not press him further; but privately thought he was mistaken, and that his disorder must have a more material cause – which would eventually vindicate me, by expressing itself in some definite symptom. Waiting for which, put me in the unfortunate position of conniving at Coleman's endless excuses for detaining us; for tho' I was as eager as O'Donnell himself to be gone, yet I feared that the exertion of travelling might bring on a crisis in his disease, at the exact moment when I was least able to provide for its treatment. But no other symptom appeared; and at length the matter was determined for us by a violent course of events that neither I, nor O'Donnell, nor Coleman had intended, or would have imagined possible – tho' we all played an unwitting part in provoking it.

The seed was sown one day at dinner, when Coleman – having engaged to ride out with Wimsey the next morning, to see the sorry state to which he had reduced the rice mill – asked me, with every show of politeness, what O'Donnell and I intended to do to divert ourselves while they were gone. At which O'Donnell suddenly broke his habitual silence, by saying: "We hope to find some remedy for our horselessness, Sir; for we are impatient to be on our way at last."

"Why, as to that," smiled Coleman, "you know we have no horses to spare; and that you are in no condition to go far on one of 'em, even if we had. And by the time you are recovered, I hope we may have found some . . . diversion here, that will give you less reason to leave."

My own doubts concerning O'Donnell's health were as strong as ever; but if I failed to back him now, he would inevitably feel betrayed, and Coleman would suppose he had succeeded in weakening my resolve. So I said: "We must leave. Every day that goes by, 'tis less likely I shall find Miss Catchpole, and bring her boy to England, before my brother dies."

Coleman was about to answer me; but at that moment, Niobe entered the room, and he contented himself with a supercilious smile – from which you would have supposed that I was a fanciful child, that had just announced his intention to go to the moon, and be home again by supper. As if this were not aggravating enough, the next instant Wimsey favoured us with his own observations – consisting of an arch stare and a series of sounds like a boiling kettle, which provoked me beyond all restraint.

"What, then!" I said. "You know Miss Catchpole, do you, and my purpose in seeking her?"

He nodded – ogled – and tapped the tip of his nose.

"D–n you, Sir!" I began – but Coleman lifted his hand to stop me; saying:

"Let us talk of this another time"; and then, before I could resume, turned sharply to Niobe. "Yes, madam – what is it?"

"The other servants is askin', when you give the meat allowance?"

"What! How the d–l should I know?"

She flinched, but went on steadily: "The master – Mr. Wimsey – he give it Monday. But we don't get nothin' since you come – got to keep everythin', he say, for you gentlemen."

"Is this true?" – to Wimsey, who nodded wearily. "And how much should they receive?"

"A pound a week, when we have it. And a peck of flour."

Coleman frowned – nipped his lip – drummed his fingers on the table. At length he said: "Tell them they will get it the day after tomorrow."

If Niobe was surprised (as I was, for I had expected another torrent of sarcasm), she did not betray it, but bobbed her head, and said impassively, "Thank you, Sir."

When she had withdrawn, Coleman gazed thoughtfully out of the window, and muttered: "Plainly, there is more to be done here than I had supposed."

The sequel to this episode came the next day, and fell out thus: the morning was damp and misty, with little to tempt a man out of doors, and O'Donnell was occupied with scribbling; so after Coleman and Wimsey had departed, I went in search of the library, in hope of finding some diversion there – only to discover that it consisted of no more than a dozen beggarly books in Wimsey's office, at least half of which concerned the breeding and racing of horses, a subject that had evidently enjoyed first place in his affections before being toppled by the bottle.

I sat down, blew the dust from a volume of Addison, and opened it; but had read no more than a page when there came a knock at the door, and Niobe entered.

"If you are looking for Mr. Wimsey," I said, "I fear he is gone out today."

"I know that, Sir. I lookin' for you. I see you come in here, and wan' to tell you somethin'."

"Indeed?" I replied – a little coldly perhaps, for I could not conceive what she might have to say to me, unless it were a complaint against the treatment she received, which I had no authority to improve.

"I hear you talk 'bout Miss Catchpole, Sir. Why you wantin' her?"

"Miss Catchpole!" I said, and was about to ask what business it was of hers – but checked myself in time, and instead said, "Why, do you know her?"

"I 'member her, Sir. Why you wantin' her now?"

It was an impertinent enough question; but when I troubled to reflect, I could not see the harm in answering it – for she plainly had the power to help me, if I satisfied her of my intentions, but not to hinder me, if I failed. So I said: "She bore my brother a son, who may now inherit his property; and I am come to find the boy and take him home with me."

At which, to my astonishment, her eyes suddenly brimmed with tears; but she showed no other emotion, and went on steadily: "I 'member Captain Gudgeon, Sir. He tell me to take care of Miss Catchpole, when she drop down faint."

So Niobe was the "capable young negro woman" Dan had spoken of, who had attended Miss Catchpole after his last interview with her. My spirits at once stirred – for this was the first time another creature had confirmed the least particle of Dan's story; which – tho' it did not alter my material circumstances a jot – seemed to draw Miss Catchpole a little from the vapourish place she inhabited in my mind, and fix her in the concrete world, where I might hope to find her.

"And did you ever see her again?" I asked.

"Jus' one time, Sir, must be 'bout half a year after Captain Gudgeon go away. I goes to Wilmington along o' Mrs. Coleman, an' we see Miss Catchpole, comin' out a door by the Court House. I think then, she look like she big wi' chil'. Mrs. Coleman ask her where she been. She say, she been to see the attorney, who helpin' her get a house a long way from there."

"Ah!" I said – for was it not more than likely that this was the same attorney who had composed matters for Dan with Miss Catchpole; in which case – if he were still there – might he not be able to direct me to her now?

"She did not say where she was removing to?"

"No, Sir."

"And what of the attorney's name? Do you recall it?"

"I never know that, Sir. But I make a picture, show you the place."

I took a sheet of paper from Wimsey's desk – rested it on Addison – and gave it to her, with an inked pen. She quickly drew a small plan (which surprised me by its neatness), showing a cross-road with a square building in the middle of it.

"That the Court House," she said. "And there"– pointing to one of the adjacent corners – "that the attorney's."

"I'm obliged to you," I said, "and would like to give you something for your trouble. Tell me" (for I had little enough conception of how a slave lived), "is money of service to you?"

"Yes, Sir."

"Why, then" – taking a half-crown from my pocket, and handing it to her.

But she at once returned it, saying: "It not colony money, Sir."

"No, 'tis better than colony money – colony money is but a token of it, and there's not a shop or a tavern won't gladly take it."

"No, Sir" – shaking her head – "I give 'em that, they say I steal it."

I had not thought of this, and could not contradict it; so said: "Very well, then; I'll 'change it, and give you its equal."

And endeavoured to do so, with dreadful consequences; which – since it is grown almost dark, and my strength begins to flag – I shall describe in the next chapter.

XVIII

Peaceful sleep again the last two nights – and the clearest head I have had since coming here.

I begin to wonder if these blessings have been obtained, not by what you give me at supper, but rather by what you have *stopped* giving me? For perhaps (it suddenly strikes me) you contrived to read what I had wrote before by dosing me with some potion every night – removing the day's pages while I slept, and then returning them again before I woke. The aching skull and misty vision I suffered in consequence being the *inconvenience* I have now spared myself, by surrendering each chapter to you willingly.

Pray tell me, if you may, whether this hypothesis is correct.

Y^r honours, for your part, send *me* a note, asking: *What is my opinion of the institution of slavery?*

To which I reply, *I should have supposed that to be plain enough already; but, if it is not, I promise it will be presently.*

Coleman did not return till long after dinner, and then sailed in as if a gale bore him, puffed out with self-conceit, and trailing in his wake poor stumbling Wimsey, who bobbed and gybed there like a captive man-of-war. He called at once for supper; and then – unable to contain himself longer – launched without delay upon a recital of the day's successes:

"I think, gentlemen, you will soon see some improvement here. We dined today at our neighbour's, Mr. Vaughan; who was good enough to sell me some provisions, to supply our immediate wants; and to hire us his best overseer – a rare fellow, by all accounts – to ensure we can supply 'em ourselves for the future."

At this, I observed Dennis – who was waiting upon us – suddenly twitch, as if someone had pricked his hand; from which I could but deduce that he knew something of Mr. Vaughan's overseer, too – at least by reputation.

"Do you think that is necessary?" I asked.

"I do, Sir – entirely. A man that has a field, and leaves it to the weeds – or horses, and does not set them to the plough, or some other service – is a d–d fool. Nay, worse than a fool; for by neglecting his property, he defies the spirit of commerce that moves the empire, and makes us prosperous."

"Perhaps," I said. "But does he not also have a duty to the horses – and to the field, too, if you come to that – not to abuse 'em, merely to turn a penny more?"

"The two duties are the same, Sir – for it naturally follows, that if he abuses them, they will not serve him so well, and he will get less benefit by owning them."

I should have argued the point further with him, but was unwilling to do so before the servants – who could not fail to understand that they were the true subject of his allegory. So I said: "On the question of horses, Sir: could Mr. Vaughan furnish two or three for Mr. O'Donnell and myself, do you suppose?"

"Be patient, Sir, I pray you"; and then, not to be deflected: "I came to make this place profitable, and I mean to do it. I confess I was discouraged at first – to find buildings so disrepaired, servants so idle, crops planted so ill-advisedly, or no crops at all – 'twas almost enough to persuade me it could not be done. But having been to Mr. Vaughan's – which in point of natural advantage is not the equal of this – and seen what he has done there, I am convinced Fiskefield can be a fine estate, and very serviceable to the company – if 'tis but rationally managed."

Here he fixed Wimsey with a corrosive stare – a compound of scorn and triumph, that must have wounded the most insensible creature living. Which (to judge by his appearance) the wretched man might have been; for, lacking any other refuge from humiliation, he had turned for succour to the usual place, and was now so drunk the eyes fluttered up into his head and his stock of noises had dwindled to bubbling at the lips. I had small enough liking for Wimsey, but it was impossible to see him so reduced without a stirring of pity; so – hoping to relieve his disgrace a little, by asking him for something it was still in his power to give – I said: "Tomorrow, Sir, would you be able to oblige me with some Carolina money?"

He appeared not to hear me; but Coleman – as if he must snatch away even this thread of comfort, and leave his poor victim naked – at once burst in: "You've no need of Carolina money here."

"'Tis for Niobe," I said; and then, to Wimsey, "Will you help me, Sir?"

He tried to look at me, but could not command his head, which lolled suddenly. I thought for a moment he had fallen asleep; but then he muttered something I could not hear – clasped the edge of the table – pulled himself up (after two or three failed attempts) – took a few stately steps towards the door – and fell to the floor, with a crash that made the glasses rattle, and brought one of them tumbling after him.

Coleman scowled with school-masterish distaste; the servants gaped and shuffled and looked at each other, uncertain what to do; I immediately rose, to see if I might help the unfortunate fellow – but O'Donnell (who was nearest to him) reached him before I did, and at once dropped down and felt his pulse.

"Is he dead?" I said.

O'Donnell shook his head; and then, noticing there was blood on his fingers, wiped them on his handkerchief. At which, Coleman turned sharply away, and called out: "You, sir – Master Dennis . . ."

"Yes, Sir" – breaking from the others, impatient to be busy.

"Take Mr. Wimsey to his quarters; and, if you cannot rouse him with cold water, send for the doctor."

"Yes, Sir," said Dennis, grasping Wimsey beneath the arms and setting a boy to take his legs.

"I am ashamed to own you my cousin, Sir," said Coleman, when they had gone, and O'Donnell and I had returned to the table.

"Indeed!" I replied, feeling my temper rise – for if either of us was to blame for what had happened, it was surely he.

But then he leered at me roguishly, and said: "To buy a wizened peach, when you might have a fresh one."

"What the d–l do you mean by that, Sir?" – tho' even as I spoke, a pretty shrewd idea of the answer suddenly formed in my mind, which heated me the more.

"Nay, nay, don't be hasty, Sir," he said. "I mean Niobe."

"What of her?"

"Why, cousin – I told you, this is Liberty Hall; and nothing could be more gratifying to me than that you have found some diversion here to your taste. But I should have supposed you'd prefer something younger and riper – which you might have had, if you'd but consulted the full bill of fare before choosing your dish."

Enraged as I was, I could not help observing something curious as he said this: that he seemed as uneasy in the character he had assumed himself as I was in the one he had given me. Wimsey himself could not have winked and smirked more animatedly; and yet the very extravagance of his gestures betrayed their falseness – like the bluster of an indifferent actor, who, lacking true feeling, tries to counterfeit it by bellowing.

"I think, Sir," I said, "you mistake the nature of our relation."

"Ah, what, then – you attended her salon, did you, and discussed philosophy?"

I began to speak; but he was so tickled with this conceit he could not stop, but over-rode me:

"That were a fine thing indeed, I doubt not, to hear a congress of slaves debating reason, and the existence of the soul, and the reality of objects."

"She told me something that may help me to Miss Catchpole."

His eyes widened; his mouth opened; for a second, the pretence of being a man of the world deserted him entirely – or even of being a man at all, for he looked like nothing so much as a frightened boy surprised robbing the larder. Then he recovered himself, and – attempting a careless laugh – said: "You might have expected more than that, for half a crown."

"You forget, Sir, 'tis my purpose in coming here."

"Pish, Sir! When the weather improves – the roads are more passable – then will be time enough to pursue this shadow, if you must. You cannot think of it now, when I'm yet not settled here, and have only that dolt Wimsey for company."

"Let us not argue, Sir – I have told you, I must, and there's an end of it."

"What must we do, Sir" – turning to O'Donnell – "to make him give up his gypsy ways – at least for the present?"

But O'Donnell said nothing; and at length Coleman went on (with something near to panick in his voice, tho' he struggled to master it): "Tomorrow, gentlemen, let us make an excursion to the slave quarters – and there, I promise you, you shall both find something more deserving of your favours than Niobe."

I felt myself impelled in two contrary directions: to rebuke him (for tho', from the impassive faces of the servants, I could not judge whether they had understood his meaning; yet I longed to demonstrate beyond a doubt that I abhorred it); or to freeze him with silence – which I finally did, having twice seen the effect O'Donnell had worked with the same trick. And was vindicated; for Coleman fidgeted, and implored me with his eyes, to make some answer – any answer – that would release him from the prison he had created for himself.

But I held my tongue; and at length he turned away, and barely spoke again for the rest of the meal, by the end of which he was so sunk in his own thoughts that he hardly seemed to know we were there.

I was already in bed when O'Donnell knocked at my door. He was half-undressed, as if he had been on the point of retiring when some sudden impulse had seized him. The light of his candle made him look paler than ever, and so hollowed out his cheeks there appeared nothing between skin and skull.

"Pray forgive my disturbing you, Sir. I have been reflecting: I cannot stay here any longer."

"I know. But–"

"I cannot wait for horses. I shall walk, if I must."

I had never heard him speak with such urgency, and for the first time began to think that he might be in the right, after all; for there was still not a jot of proof that I was, even after two months, and his manner had a kind of desperate certainty to it that was impossible to dismiss.

"Let us talk of it tomorrow," I said – to buy myself sleep, and a few more hours to consider.

And we did – but under circumstances I could not have then guessed.

I slept late the next day; and rose to find a sudden improvement in the weather – which at once effected a similar change in my spirits. A few whiskers of mist still lingered outside my window, when I first peered from it; but within an hour the sun had cleared them, leaving the air clean and new-shaved – the sky a brilliant chalky blue, the lawns and paths veiled in frost. Even the forest hemming us on every side appeared less like a great ragged mob intent on doing us mischief, and more like an orderly army, with whom it might be possible to agree terms. Seeing which, and recalling what Niobe had told me, a kind of spring-tide seemed to rush in upon me, lifting my hopes (which twenty weeks with Coleman, and eight in America, had all but stranded) and setting them afloat again. My cousin might sneer all he pleased; but was not my judgement as sound as his, or sounder? And this morning, my judgement told me I might yet succeed in finding Miss Catchpole, and taking her son back to England before Dan died – provided only I delayed no more. All that remained to determine was whether I should accept O'Donnell's diagnosis of his complaint, and so take him with me; or my own, and leave him here, under the care of a doctor.

After breakfast, therefore (which I ate alone, for Coleman was up before me and O'Donnell still, as usual, a-bed), I went out, intending to ask Niobe's friend the ostler whether he knew a place close by where we might buy some horses – and at once spied a huddle of slaves before the stables, among them Dennis, and the little mulatto boy, and two or three gaunt field-hands I had not seen before, dressed in makeshift suits of sack-cloth that flapped about them like sails on a spar. I thought at first they were engaged in a game of some sort; for the boy was running this way and that between the others, who caught him every time and pushed him away, as if they were playing blind man's buff. But as I drew near, I observed his eyes were uncovered, and full of tears, and his face skewed by grief or anger – which suggested he was not a complaisant participant but rather an unwilling captive, hurling himself against the walls of his human gaol in hope of breaching them.

"What's the matter?" I called out, quickening my step.

They shuffled out of my way, saying nothing, as shy of catching my eye as a herd of oxen – tho' still careful, I observed, to keep the boy encircled. He, for his part, seemed to subside at sight of me – but the next moment erupted again, as a dreadful cry suddenly shook the door of the building, which made him leap and grimace and wail. Then he dashed at Dennis – bit his arm – and, small as he was, almost succeeded in breaking out, and was only restrained by the field-hand, who hastily grabbed him from behind, and held him like a roped beast.

"What is it?" I said again.

Since plainly it would have been useless to question them more, I flung open the door, to be greeted by another pitiful moan – shuddering, and without hope of relief, such as a mother might make when she is brought to bed of her child; and, for a moment, suspected that to be the cause, for I had no conception of where or how the slaves gave birth, and could see almost nothing in the darkness, which was diluted only by the light of a dirty window set high up in the wall. But there was a steamy fetor in the air, despite the chill – a foul stench of sweat and filth, that made me uneasy, for it seemed to have more of death than birth about it.

"What!" cried a voice – incredulous rather than angry; and the next moment a small man darted rat-like from the shadows, and stood in the mat of sunlight by the door, frowning and blinking at me. "Ah," he said at last, glancing past me; "you must excuse me, Sir – I supposed you was . . ."

"What – a slave?"

He nodded. "I told 'em, I'd a-hang any of 'em as come in here while I'm about my business. Seems like a hard measure, and wasteful, too, I know – but sometimes you have to make an example of one, to settle the others." He held a curry-comb, which he moved to his left hand, and extended the right. "I'm Oxley, the overseer."

I nodded.

"And you are?"

"Mr. Coleman's cousin. Mr. Gudgeon."

"Ah . . . ah . . . are you, now?" He took a broken pipe from his pocket – examined it, as if it was an oracle – then thrust it back again, muttering: "I think, Sir, you'd best go."

"Why?"

"There's some gentlemen enjoy the sport, but Mr. Coleman thought you–"

"What sport?" I said, stepping past him.

He ran after me, and caught my arm; but not before I had seen something that drove the wind from my lungs: two negroes, a man and a woman – both stripped naked – tied hand and foot to iron rings on the wall – and covered from neck to ankles in such fearful gouges you would have thought they had been mauled by a bear.

"What have they done?"

"Why, Sir" – his voice as thin and flat as sour beer – "that you should know as well as any man. At least in her case. Saying which, he seized her by the hair, and jerked her head towards me. Her eyes rolled – her brow was wet, and contorted with pain – but I knew at once it was Niobe.

"She has done nothing that I know of!" I cried. "What in G–d's name has my cousin been telling you?"

"That she's a blabberer, Sir, that must learn to keep her tongue from going a-wandering. And I reckon she will, when I'm all done. I never knew one yet that weren't the better for a good currying."

"Currying!"

"Yes, Sir." He flourished the comb, and fixed me with a steady gaze that challenged me to reproach him. "'Tis a trick I learned of Mr. Morgan, that oversees for Mr. Lee in Virginia. Give 'em a severe scraping – get a boy to rub 'em down good with hay for several minutes – then salt 'em, and unloose 'em. Nothing broken – not a day lost – but 'tis wonderful how it medicines their manners, and makes 'em attend to their business. Even sullen brutes like this one" – here grabbing the man's head, and twisting it as he had Niobe's.

It was the ostler, and tho' I have witnessed greater horrors since, I shall never be able to expunge from my memory his face as he looked at me. His lip was swollen with a thick scar, his teeth broken, his ears cropped – which moved me to rage and pity and admiration, all at once; for these, I knew, were the mutilations inflicted on those of his kind who rebelled against their fate – and so, in a manner, badges, that testified both to the largeness of their spirit, and to the wickedness of their owners'. My eyes pricked with tears. I reached, without thinking, a hand towards him; had he been blind, he must (I should have supposed) have known that I wished to help him; and yet he neither accepted, nor even rejected, my compassion, but merely stared at me, as if I were of no greater consequence to him than pen and paper would be to a drowning man.

"And what is his crime?" I asked the overseer – crossing my arms, and squeezing my hands against my chest, to keep them from assaulting him.

"I ordered him to help me, by a-scrubbing her with the hay, to get the dirt out of the bitch. But he refused . . ."

"That's all?"

He nodded. "So he got a lessoning, too. They been too long without a firm hand, Sir, that's what it is – and it's made 'em obstinate and idle. Let 'em feel the bit a little – learn who's master – and you'll scarce credit the reformation."

"Untie them," I said.

"I can't do that, Sir . . ."

"Why, then, I shall do it."

He tried to stop me, by snatching at my coat; but I threw him off (which was no great feat, for he was half my size), and had the satisfaction of hearing him stumble and fall; but had no sooner set to work than there was a whistle behind me and, turning, I saw two other men I had not observed before emerging from the shadows – one, a long-limbed fellow with a whip; the other, a fat, moon-faced boy holding an up-turned pitchfork.

"You'd best leave, Sir," said Oxley, brushing the dust from his breeches. "Afore we have to put you out."

"You'd be ill-advised to do that," I said.

"Would we, now?" He nodded, and whip and fork advanced upon me.

"If you so much as touch me, I'll see you thrashed for it."

The boy stopped, and looked uncertainly at Oxley – who set him in motion again with another nod, and then said: "You're a stranger, Sir, and an't yet learned how we go on here – that's the kindly way to view it, and I'm always kindly if I can be. But I'm warning you: you poke your finger in my pie again, you'll be sorry for it."

At which his creatures closed upon me. It would have done the poor negroes small enough service to have resisted, for a contest between one unarmed man and three ruffians could only have one issue; so I contented myself with calling, "I shall not let this rest, I swear it" – and left.

Dennis and his companions still lingered in the yard; and, conscious of their gaze and of the effect on their spirits if I should appear cowed, I walked rather than ran back to the house, and went directly to the study. The door was shut; but I could hear noises within, so (having knocked, and received no answer) I turned the handle – pushed it open – and only narrowly escaped hitting one of the servants, who had been attending to the lock and jumped back with a cry, clattering his tools on the floor. Behind him, at the desk, sat Coleman, with an open account book in his hands and a look of such alarm on his face you would have supposed I was the mob and had broken in expressly to murder him.

"Cousin Ned! . . ."

"Your overseer is abusing the slaves," I said. "Besides offering me the most insufferable insult."

"What!"

I began to tell him what I had seen; but when I mentioned the curry-comb, and the purpose Oxley put it to, he rammed his fingers in his ears, and bleated: "Enough – I pray you – no more. I am assured the man knows his trade – how he goes about it is his concern. As for his rudeness to you, Sir, I can but apologize, and beg you to remember: his is a hard, rough occupation, and doubtless ill-fits him for polite conversation."

"You confound cause and effect," I said. "'Tis his insolence makes him a tyrant – for, believing himself free of all restraint, he supposes he is at liberty to treat his charges as he will. You must go at once, and recall him to his duty – else he will quickly grow ungovernable."

"Nay, Sir, he is a slave-driver – that is his business; and he carries it on, I suppose, better than you or I should. I shall no more try to instruct him in it than I should a doctor come to attend a patient. Yes, sir?" – suddenly looking past me, with an irritable shake of the head – "What is it?"

"Please, Sir," said the servant, who was standing patiently at my shoulder, "I's done here."

Coleman nodded sharply; then, turning to me again, said: "Perhaps, cousin, sooner than condemn Mr. Oxley for punishing Niobe's viciousness, you should reflect on your own part in encouraging it."

"My part! What the d–l do you mean, Sir?"

"I mean, Sir – when she brought you a stolen article, you played the fence, and bought it."

"She brought me nothing! – only told me something . . ."

"Ay – and what did she tell you? She told you a secret that was not hers to tell. Thanks to Mr. Wimsey, the slaves here have come to imagine they may pilfer what they please, and they must learn it is not so. Why do you suppose I commanded a new lock for this door? 'Twas–" He stopped suddenly, glaring past me again. "Why are you still here, sir? Have you some observation on the subject you think it would profit us to hear?"

"No, Sir – you don't say I can go."

"Of course you can go, you booby" – at which the poor fellow leapt from the room, like a cat freed from a box. "I begin to wonder," went on Coleman, "whether they are capable of improvement, or we are vainly trying to make porcelain from mud; but you must under-stand, Sir – I do this not for my own sake, or upon some arbitrary whim. I am but the company's steward; and to discharge my obliga-tions, I must impress upon every slave that not only his own person, but all he sees and hears, belongs to the company. And that if he speaks of it to another person, he is guilty of theft."

This was so extraordinary a claim, I should (I see now) have kept my temper, and questioned Coleman more, in hope of finding out his motive for making it; but at the time it seemed no more than final proof of what he had already amply demonstrated, *viz.*, that he was beyond the reach of reason, and that I should gain nothing from debating with him further. And in that instant I resolved what I must do – tho' whether I was right or wrong, I still cannot say.

I bowed, and shambled out, with as much carelessness as I could muster; but after twenty paces or so – having first ensured I was not followed – I ran into the hall, and up the stairs. I had not forgotten O'Donnell's condition; but in the immediate crisis of our affairs, my anxiety about it had been thrust into a corner, and I at once rapped on his door, and went in without waiting for a reply.

I found him neither a-bed nor at his writing-table, but footing about the floor like a caged fox, as big-eyed and wan as he had looked the night before – until I told him my plan, which struck a spark of colour in his cheeks.

"Allow me five minutes, Sir, to put together a few necessaries, and prime my pistols; and I shall be at your service."

I returned to my room, to do the same office for myself; then took my knife and cut several strips from the bed-sheet. I was still thus occupied when O'Donnell entered – whereupon I held them up, like a sheaf of trophies, saying: "What do you say?"

"They will do very well, Sir – for the present."

We carried our bags downstairs – left them in the hall – and hurried into the study without a word or a knock. We were so quick, and Coleman was so startled, that he had not time enough to cry out, before O'Donnell had glided behind him and tied one of the strips about his mouth. Then we bound his wrists and ankles and slipped out again – securing the door by its new lock, and taking the key.

We rightly supposed we had nothing to fear from Wimsey, who must still be sleeping after the excesses of the previous evening; but I misjudged Oxley, who showed more spirit than I should have expected, dodging past us as we entered the stable, and shouting, "Help! Help me! – or I'll flay the skin off you!" But O'Donnell then gave him an earnest of our intent by firing one of his pistols and sending up a cloud of straw and dust a foot before the fellow's nose – after which he went meekly enough, to join the fat boy and the thin man in the corner where we had ordered them – and remained there, his face white and pinched with rage and every glance muttering revenge, while O'Donnell stood guard like a sheep-dog, carelessly weighing a pistol in each hand, and I untied his victims and used the same ropes to bind Oxley and his companions.

When I was done, O'Donnell stepped forward and addressed them as if he were giving the epilogue to a play: "You see who did this to you, and if I ever hear that another creature has been punished for it, I shall return and blow your brains out."

It was at this moment, just when I supposed the most difficult part of our undertaking was behind us, that we encountered our first obstacle. The experience of our first night at Fiskefield had taught me not to expect thanks from Niobe and the ostler; but I confess I expected to be rewarded with more than silence and sullen looks. They dressed themselves when I told them to – which must, indeed, have been painful; but from their scowls you would have supposed it was a worse torment than Oxley's, and I the crueller tormentor.

"We shall not leave you here," I said, thinking perhaps it was this that vexed them. "There are horses enough for all of us" (for, with the arrival of Oxley and his men, there were now five and in borrowing them we should at the same time be making good our escape and delaying our pursuers). "And, of course, you will travel under our protection. Are you" – to the ostler – "well enough to saddle 'em?"

Instead of replying, he drew Niobe aside, and entered into an agitated conversation with her – tho' it was so hushed, I could hear nothing of what they said. There seemed to be some disagreement between them, for she twice shook her head sharply; after which the ostler turned, with the sudden resolution of a gambler who has made his bet and surrendered his destiny to the cards; and said: "She go with you, Sir. She and her boy."

"Her boy?" I said – and at once answered myself, by remembering the little mulatto child and his evident attachment to her. "And what of you?"

"I take my chance, Sir. Come – we get the horses."

Which we did.

There – we are on our way again, yʳ honours.

I must to bed.

XIX

Yʳ honours will keep me at Fiskefield, whether I will or no.

You ask: *Did I not wonder, that the slaves should be so ungrateful?*

In truth, I had small enough time to wonder anything – save whether or not we should escape.

But now you prompt me to reflect upon it: I suppose the poor creatures, having been brought up from the cradle to expect nothing but the cruellest abuse, could not conceive such an article as a kind master, and so misgave my intentions in helping them – which, tho' a slight answer, is all the one I have; so – since I am not one of those literary upholsterers that plumps his words with horse-hair, to make 'em more commodious – I shall here (with yʳ honours' indulgence) close the matter up, and resume my adventure.

It seemed most expedient for us to go first to Wilmington, which lay at a distance of no more than fifteen miles, and offered us several advantages, *viz.*, bed and board for the night (for we could not, given the circumstances of our departure, throw ourselves upon the hospitality of any of Coleman's neighbours); the attentions of a doctor for Niobe, who plainly could not travel far without them, and if necessary for O'Donnell; and an opportunity to question the attorney concerning Miss Catchpole. We were some three hours upon the road – for, tho' Niobe bore her affliction with the utmost Stoicism, yet it caused her such pain that we had to stop every twenty minutes or so to keep her from fainting; but it was still light when we spied a church in a hollow before us, and then a scattering of other buildings, and at length came to the brow of a small rise. From which we looked down upon a tiny town, that was yet so neatly laid out, and contained so many good houses, that it seemed like a fraction of a great one – as if somebody had snipped a corner from a map of London, and pasted it on a patch of wilderness. Beyond it lay a broad river, speckled with ships and boats – which added force to the illusion, by putting me something in mind of the Thames at Southwark.

We had descended but a little way, past a cluster of fine villas, that I supposed belonged to the principal merchants of the place, when we were intercepted by a rabble of ten or a dozen men, who spilled across the road, crying, "Halt! Halt there!"

My first thought was that Coleman had somehow got word before us, and that they were soldiers, come to arrest us; but I then observed that, tho' some of them carried guns, they wore only shirts and breeches, and seemed under no authority, but milled here and there like drunken farmers at a fair. Which provoked a more alarming conjecture yet: that they were *banditti*, who meant to take everything we had, and then murder us.

"Do we know you?" said one – a boy of about twenty, with blue eyes and a Scotch-Irish voice blunted by drink. He stumbled towards me, seized my bridle (as much to steady himself as to hold my horse), and stared up at me, as if he might convince his pickled brain it knew me, if but he came close, and looked hard enough. His cheeks were hot; and when at length he said, "No – who are you?", I could smell the rum fumes on his breath.

"We are travellers," I said.

"Where from?"

"From–"

"From Brunswick," said O'Donnell, before I could say more. "Where we stayed with Mr. Quince."

"Mr. Quince?" muttered the Presbyterian.

"If you are not acquainted with him yourself, ask any of your fellows that is a friend to Liberty."

The boy retreated to his companions, who chittered among themselves like a congregation of chickens; and then turned back to us, with a face so blank it was impossible to tell whether he believed us or not.

"And what is your business?"

"These are uncertain times," replied O'Donnell – himself sounding more Irish with every word. "But if you have an officer that affects the same opinion as Mr. Quince, we shall be happy to satisfy him – and, in the meantime, to give the man a shilling that will conduct us to a respectable inn, where we may spend the night."

Our questioner seemed persuaded, and so did most of his fellows, who began to melt from our path; but one of them – a stocky, red-haired pup, with a round, white face teeming with freckles – opposed some objection, which required their congress to be reconvened. I could hear little of its business, for it was conducted in a hurried murmur, with frequent furtive glances in our direction; but after a minute or two, with the conclusive air of a lawyer delivering the fatal blow, the Presbyterian cried out, "Come, we are ordered to stop men leaving, not entering!" At which the others laughed, and at once began to drift away; and the Presbyterian beckoned us to follow him.

This we did – tho' not (in my case at least) with the easiest heart; for I could not but feel like a minnow swimming into a bottle, and feared we might not get out again, before Coleman had found us, and corked us up fast – and was not much reassured when, our way taking us past the gaol, the boy pointed to it and, laughing, said to O'Donnell: "You may thank Mr. Quince, that you do not lodge there tonight."

He led us down two or three unpaved streets, choked with little parties of men and miry with the tramp of feet; and stopped at length before a neat, square wooden house, so new-built it still smelled of resin and fresh pitch. Here he told us to wait – as off-handedly as if *we* were serving *him*, and not the other way about – while he went in; to return a few moments later, saying *he had spoken to Mrs. Ross, who had a bed we might take.* Then he held his hand out and, having received his shilling, left to rejoin his friends, with no more for farewell than a waggle of his fingers.

We committed the horses to the care of the stable-lad, and helped Niobe (who by now could hardly walk) into the inn – to find it furnished more like a gentleman's house than a tavern, with glazed copper-plate prints on the walls, and an elegant parlour, where three or four men sat at a fine mahogany table, lolling over a bottle. Which led me to suppose that America could not, after all, be wholly wanting in politeness, and that we might hope to meet with a more liberal welcome here than we had received since leaving England. And so we did (to begin with, at least); for we had scarce set foot in the place before we saw a handsome dark-eyed woman hurrying towards us, who smiled, and bobbed her head, and said, in a sweet singing voice like a bird's: "You are welcome, gentlemen. Shall I show you to your chamber?"

"Thank you," I said, "but first we must see our servant settled; for she has suffered an accident."

"Oh, the poor creature!"

"Have you an attick room–"

"Or any room," slipped in O'Donnell.

"–where we may put her?"

"No, Sir – the servants, when we have 'em, which an't very often, usually sleep in the stables. I'm certain we can make her comfortable there; she'll have straw, and a blanket . . ."

"Nay," I said, "the skin's all chafed from her; she needs a bed, and a fire."

"Perhaps she might have ours, then," murmured O'Donnell, "and we keep company with the horses" – an idea, I confess, that had not occurred to me, and did not greatly please me; and yet I could see the sense in it.

But the landlady blushed – looked quickly at the drinking gentlemen (who, however, were too much engrossed in their own affairs to pay any heed to ours) – laughed charmingly, and said: "Nay, nay – I have a better plan: there's a good fire in the brew-house, where we may set a truckle-bed for her, and another" – here smiling at the mulatto boy – "for the young master, if he will. The cat lives there; she has just had kittens, and may let you play with 'em, if you're good to her."

The boy gaped with astonishment, and turned to his mother – as if she might instruct him how to respond to such unaccountable kindness.

"And what of a doctor?" I said.

"There are two or three in the town, Sir . . ."

"Which is the best?"

"Why, Sir, the first folks mostly favour Dr. Cobham."

"Be so good, then, as to send to Dr. Cobham, and engage him to meet us here in an hour, if he is able."

Having arranged for our bags to be taken up-stairs, and Niobe and her son to their quarters, we asked the way, and at once set out for the Court House – for, being resolved to leave again early in the morning, we were conscious that we had little enough time to find the attorney and discover what he might tell us.

The sun had reddened and begun to sink towards the forest; the sky was streaked with cloud, the air heavy and unmoving above the town, as if it meant to squeeze the breath from it. The streets were still astir – little knots of people gathered at doors and windows, or crowded the balconies of the better houses; but they appeared quieter and soberer than before, as if they were waiting for a thunderous outburst, but uncertain when it would come, or from what direction. None of them took the least notice of us, much less offered us any mischief – and yet I found myself wishing I had brought my stick, or even my pistol; for they seemed so tightly wound I thought the first dash of rain might suddenly prick them into a riot or a rout.

If O'Donnell was troubled by the same thought, he gave no sign of it; but it put me in an anxious humour – which was not lessened by a small curious incident on the way. We had just turned a corner, and found ourselves before a busy shop, which immediately seized my attention; for through the window I glimpsed such a hotch-potch of goods as I should not have thought possible: hoes and Bibles, pans and prayer-books, saws and axes, and enough cloth to supply a tailor for a year – all jumbled up, as if they were the same kind of article, and might be wanted together.

"Look," I said to O'Donnell. "Did you ever see such a mongrel?"

He peered in languidly (for in truth he was totally indifferent to such matters); but the next moment suddenly gasped and drew back, as if he had been stung.

"What is it?" I said.

"I don't know about mongrel, Sir, but that's damnable."

I pressed my face against the glass – for a moment saw nothing that might explain his behaviour; then all at once made out two figures I knew, in earnest conversation with the shop-keeper. One was the freckled youth who, not an hour since, had argued against allowing us to enter the town; but the other I had not seen since our arrival at Brunswick: Kirke, the surly mate of the *Jenny*.

"Good G–d!" I said. "What have they to do with one another?"

"I cannot conceive, Sir; but I doubt it bodes good to us. Come – they must not see us." Saying which, he pulled me away abruptly, and continued on his way as carelessly as if nothing had happened – tho' it was some while before he spoke again.

It was impossible to miss the Court House, for it commanded the principal cross-road in the town, and was surrounded by a throng of loiterers, that eyed us suspiciously as we passed. The attorney's premises, moreover, still stood where Niobe had marked them – even displaying a painted board, that favoured us with his name: *Frederick Grylls*. But if we hoped we should now be spared further troubles, we were immediately disappointed; for there were four armed men standing at the door, who, as soon as we approached, coalesced into a wall, to bar our way.

"What is your business here?" said one – a country fop, that wore his own hair, and spiced his simple dress with a wide hat and an India handkerchief tied at the throat.

"We are come to see Mr. Grylls," I said. "What is yours?"

He laughed, pleasantly enough. "To keep Mr. Grylls shut up, till he signs the Test."

"What test?"

"Why – don't you know? The Committee of Safety says every housekeeper here must sign the Continental Association."

"What does it provide?"

"No importin', or exportin', or knucklin' down to tyranny." (Laughing again.) "You best sign it yourself, if you an't yet."

"And what is the penalty for refusing?"

"Nay – I'm only jokin'; I can tell you an't from here."

"What is the penalty?" I repeated – keeping my voice quiet, but feeling the heat flush my neck.

"To be exposed, and contempted as an enemy of the country."

By which, plainly, he could only mean, a friend to mine.

"And what happens to a man that is contempted?" I said.

"If he's a real bad 'un, that's got the d–l in him, he'll be tarred and feathered. But that won't be the way" – jerking his thumb at Gryll's door – "with your friend. He's sly as a 'gator. He's just makin' a show,

103

to please his English masters, an'll come round wonderful quick soon as he whiffs a pitch-barrel."

I could not strike the fellow; but it was impossible to hear such sentiments, without wishing to rebuke them. While I was pondering how it might be done, O'Donnell slipped in before me:

"Mr. Grylls is no friend of ours; and you may be quite easy that we shall not touch upon politicks with him – for we are engaged upon a purely private matter."

"What matter?"

"He has certain information, relative to this gentleman's family, which we hope to obtain from him."

"And that your only reason for coming here?"

"I swear it."

He wavered – stared – stepped uncertainly aside – then appeared to repent of his weakness, and sprang back again.

"Nay – I cannot: we are ordered to let no-one enter or leave, upon any pretext whatever."

"Perhaps we might send in a letter, then," said O'Donnell.

The fellow hesitated only a moment, before nodding, like a man relieved of some unpleasant obligation, and saying: "Ay, I suppose there'd be no harm in that."

I was – as you may readily conceive – utterly indignant that we were reduced to treating in this manner with a lawless rabble, and concluding such a shabby bargain with them; but recognizing that the only consequence of saying so would be to leave empty-handed, I held my tongue. One of the fop's companions was duly dispatched into the house for pen, paper and ink; O'Donnell gravely offered his back as a human writing-desk; and I scribbled a note, giving a brief sketch of my situation, and what I hoped for from him – and ending (I could not help myself) by wishing him a speedy release from his unjust captivity. Which done, the same fellow hurried it back into the house.

Not two minutes later, a pale, worn face, scored with heavy lines, and wide-eyed with anxiety, flitted into the window and peeped out. I knew beyond doubt that it must be the wretched Grylls, who – fearing this was but another ruse to make him betray himself – had thought to see if I really existed, before writing an answer. Having satisfied himself on this point (which took no more than an instant), he shrank away again; but not before some of the crowd about the Court House had spied him, and set up a jeer. The fop *shooed* at them with his hand, doubtless intending to soothe their tempers, and keep them at a distance, but succeeded only in producing the opposite effect; for two or three of them immediately detached themselves from the others, and stumbled towards us, demanding *who we were, and what treachery we were hatching?*

"Pah!" said the fop. "Don't talk of treachery. They have lawful business here; and I'm just helpin' 'em to it. Nothin' to get vexed over. He still an't leavin' his house afore he signs."

Which brought a truce, but not a victory; for tho' they fell silent, they still pressed about us; and when the door opened, and our makeshift courier reappeared, clutching Grylls' reply, they surged forwards, plainly meaning to seize it. But the fop forestalled them – plucking it up, and handing it to me; and I at once broke the seal, and read (as well as I can recall):

> Sir,
> I thank you for your kind wishes; and beg you will use your interest to consummate them, by securing my liberty; when I shall be honoured to do you any service that lies within the power of
> Y^r most humble and obliged sv^t
> Frederick Grylls

And had scarce finished, when one of the loiterers (a squat, red-faced rogue, with jowls as loose as a turkey's) snatched it from me and thrust it at one of his friends, crying, "Now! What does it say?" And then (when his accomplice had stuttered it out): "See! 'Wishes' – 'interest' – 'liberty'! They's ministry tools, come to help a traitor!"

I felt O'Donnell, who was squeezed against me, move his hand to his sword, and began to look about me, for an avenue of escape. But the fop, tho' he faltered a moment, did not (to his great credit) give ground:

"Nay!" he said. "You an't read many letters – which an't too surprisin', if you can't read. This gentleman just wrote the same any man would: 'by your leave', and 'humble respects', an' all such. And Grylls is tryin' to use it, to wriggle out of the hole he's in – same as he would, bein', as we all know, a reptile."

This set off a ripple of laughter, which spurred him to a further sally:

"Why don't you duck your head in a bucket; and maybe you'll think clearer?"

The ripple grew to a rolling wave; at which the fop took courage to turn to me and ask:

"Where are you gentlemen puttin' up?"

"At Ross's Tavern."

"I'll go there with you, to make sure you an't ruffled on the way"; and began to part the crowd, like a footman drawing aside curtains to make way for his mistress.

The turkey-faced scoundrel – who was not so drunk he could not see the tide had turned, and left him stranded – skulked back towards the Court House, angrily calling over his shoulder: "You're a fool; and I shall go straight to Mr. Howe, and tell him what you done." Which stopped the fop short for a second, and made him pale; but then he recovered himself, and with a brave attempt at a smile said: "Come, gentlemen – let us go."

We got back to the inn without further mishap – thanked our protector (who made us a gallant bow, and said *he wished us a safe journey, and a successful conclusion to it*) – and went directly to the brew-house, where we found Niobe lying on her belly on a little bed, and the boy squatting on the floor, teasing kittens with a twig. In one corner a copper bubbled over a fierce fire, making the air so hot and steamy it was difficult to breathe – which must, I supposed, have only added to the poor woman's torments, by sticking her clothes to her torn back.

"I am sorry for this," I said. "Shall I ask Mrs. Ross if she has another place, where we might remove you?"

But she only shook her head wearily, as if the question itself were yet one more unjust burden I had forced upon her.

"Well," I said, "at least the doctor will be here soon."

And he was – a tall, grave fellow, dressed as quiet as a parson, who bustled through the door not fifteen minutes later, clutching a weathered bag and followed by a shambling apprentice, reeking of cloves and balm.

"I am Cobham," said the doctor, holding out his hand and then, even before I had taken it, shifting his gaze to Niobe. "This is your patient?"

"Yes."

He began to undress her, without a word, and with as little ceremony or feeling as if he were examining a dog – until, that is, he removed her bodice and saw the gouges in her flesh, which had reddened and filled with pus, so you would have thought they were a nest of gleaming worms, that were eating her alive. At which he drew in his breath sharply, and frowned critically at me.

"Good G–d!" I said. "I hope you don't suppose I am responsible for–"

"I suppose nothing, Sir" (snapping his fingers at the apprentice). "Bring me a bowl of warm water, and a towel."

"But it was I that freed her . . ."

"I pray you, Sir, no more! 'Tis none of my affair, and the less I know of it the better."

"Why?"

"Why? Why, Sir? – Why . . ." (with a shake of the head, and a grim little smirk, that had not a farthing of jocularity in it). "Let me do what I am come for, and leave as soon as I may. That will be best."

"Are you then in trouble," I said, "like Mr. Grylls?"

"Nay, Sir," chided O'Donnell, laying a hand on my arm – but Cobham started, and his eyebrows flew up, showing I had struck the mark.

"I hope," he said – with the same unmerry smile – "my reputation is something higher than his, and will protect me from suffering the same fate – at least for the present. But yes – I am embargoed for refusing the Test."

"Why, in that case, Sir," I cried, "allow me shake your hand again!"

He did so, but not with any great warmth; and was plainly relieved when, a moment later, the prentice returned, with the articles he had asked for, and excused him from further conversation. He at once set to work, cleaning and drying and dressing the wounds, as quick and nimble-fingered as a seamstress, and with as little thought (or so it seemed to me) that the object of his attentions might have feelings – a delusion which, for all the response she made, you would have supposed Niobe was resolved to vindicate.

He had just finished, and was busy packing his bag while the prentice wrote out the bill, when there came a sound from the yard, like the sea sucking at a pebble beach, and then three or four excited cries. I thought, for a moment, that it was nothing but a party of high-spirited boys, running to play at some sport; but Cobham at once stiffened, and cocked his head. "I fear–" he began; but the next instant the door flew open, and a ruddy, stocky, bullish man burst in, one hand holding a pistol, the other resting on his sword.

"Mr. Howe!" said Cobham – trying to master the unease in his voice, and succeeding so well he appeared to be whispering.

"*Colonel* Howe," said the intruder. Behind him were twenty or so others, some of whom laughed. Among them, at his shoulder, was the turkey-faced rogue, who thrust a finger triumphantly at me.

"This is the gentleman, is it?" said Howe, approaching me, and standing so close his breath heated my cheek. "I am arresting you, Sir–"

"Arresting me? For what crime? And by whose authority?"

"There" – gesturing to his men – "is my authority. As for your offence – that has several parts, I suppose, but may be stated under one head: that you and your companion are agents of tyranny."

I began to protest; but he continued: "We have long suspected, that the ministry would attempt to undo our cause, by planting spies among us–"

"Spies!"

"Ay, Sir, spies!" he barked, his throat swelling and turning an ugly purple. "Whose object would be not only to report our doings to their masters, but to bring comfort to our enemies here, and" (with a curious glance at Niobe) "to incite our slaves to rebellion against us."

"That is the most ludicrous thing I ever heard," I said, "and a contemptible slander against both me and my country – and your country, too, for the matter of that; for 'tis your liberty as an Englishman, and the gracious protection of our sovereign, that allow you to indulge yourself in these dangerous anticks. Had the issue of the late war been otherwise, and you had found yourself a subject of the French king, then, Sir, I think you would have had reason enough to cry 'Tyranny!' – and soon discovered that you lacked the freedom to do it."

If this outburst surprised even myself (for I had not given it a second's consideration, and was startled to hear my own frankness), Howe seemed quite dumbfounded by it – staring, and gulping, and lolling his head, as if to ease some sudden hardening in the neck. I thought for a moment he was going to strike me; but at length he got the better of his passion, and contented himself with saying: "I confess I was not entirely persuaded of your guilt, when this gentleman" – nodding to the turkey-faced villain – "first came to me; but what I have seen and heard here has removed any last doubts I might have entertained. And I can only thank G–d that the ministry takes us for such fools as to imagine we might be deceived by so transparent a rascal as you, Sir. I shall post a guard at the door, and you shall stay here tonight, with your companion; and tomorrow the Committee will decide what is to be done with you. As for you, Sir" – turning to Cobham – "were I to consult my own opinion, I should hang you from that beam. But my orders do not extend so far – at least, not yet. So you may go. But let me warn you – for the last time: if you do not sign the Association, and conduct yourself according to its principles, you will suffer the consequences."

Cobham and his prentice skulked out, and Howe turned to follow him; but as he did so, O'Donnell stepped forward and muttered in his ear. I could not make out the words, but saw Howe's face change from impatience to anxiety to uncertainty. Then he nodded – and ushered O'Donnell into the yard before him.

Leaving me totally alone – save for Niobe, her boy, and the family of cats.

XX

I cannot deny it: y^r honours quite astound me.

I left you at the end of the last chapter at such a juncture as must (I supposed) have made you frantic, until you knew what happened next. Had our situations been reversed – you the authors, and I the reader – I swear I could not have slept, for thinking of it.

But you detain me yet again – throwing yesterday's words back in my face, and asking, *Why did I speak of myself, as the slaves' 'master'?*

I own that I could not at first remember having done so; but then read over what I had written, and found (in answer to your last question) the following – which I take to be the sentence you mean: "I suppose the poor creatures, having been brought up from the cradle to expect nothing but the cruellest abuse, could not conceive such an article as a kind master – and so misgave my intentions in helping them."

I can see that a company of wily lawyers (which, I begin to think, y^r honours may well be) might just contrive to tease and crimp this into an acknowledgement of guilt: for does it not imply that I consider *myself* the 'kind master' they could not conceive? – and is a slave not his master's possession? and am I not therefore confessing that I *stole* Niobe and her son from my cousin, and unlawfully made them mine?

To which I can only reply: it is as absurd and groundless a charge as Colonel Howe's – as I should have thought by now you would have known.

But since you are evidently blind to hints, and will credit nothing, unless it be set out like a covenant or a will, let me plainly state:

That I, Edward Charles Gudgeon, abhor, and have always abhorred, the institution of slavery;

That I believe, and have always believed, it is entirely foreign to a country, whose law and constitution are founded upon the liberty of the subject; and is therefore unlawful in Great Britain – an opinion with which several eminent judges have concurred;

That, by reason, it must therefore be equally unlawful, in any territory, where the authority of parliament extends;

That, consequently, tho' our American colonies practise it, they cannot do so legally;

That in escaping with Niobe and her son, therefore, I was not robbing Coleman of his rights, but assisting two of my fellow-creatures to regain theirs; and so finally –

That since I had no thought of profit – took nothing that could be properly considered property (save for the horses, of which I shall say something later) – and gained nothing by my actions, I may not be called a thief.

Which I shall vigorously maintain, before any court y^r honours please.

As to why I used the word *master*, I beg you to recall: I was *master* to half a dozen servants in Somersetshire, who freely gave me their duty, and enjoyed my protection – not because I *owned* them, but because in an ordered society each man has his peculiar station, and acts according to its obligations. Which, I think you will agree – considering Niobe's and my respective ranks in life – it was neither unreasonable nor unnatural to take as a pattern of the relations that might exist between us.

And now, with your leave, I will return to the brew-house.

My thoughts – as I am sure you will easily imagine, if you have any interest in my story save to see me trip – were none of the pleasantest; for, besides reflecting gloomily on my own lot, and reproaching myself for Niobe's (which, thanks to my meddling, must now be worse than the one from which I had rescued her), I was deeply disquieted by the behaviour of O'Donnell – which set up a kind of furious law-suit in my head, where the opposing counsels were played by different parts of my own mind. The defence maintained *that he was a man of unquestioned honour and courage, who would never desert a friend in an extremity; and that it was therefore certain he had only left because he had conceived another cunning stratagem to deliver us; and would return, as soon as this was accomplished.* To which the prosecution countered: *What, then, of his unaccountable conduct towards Coleman, aboard the* Jenny? *Did that not suggest an inconstant nature, that might suddenly fly off upon a new course, if it appeared in his interest? And if he meant to come back, why did he leave without so much as a glance, or a word of reassurance? Was it not more probable that – seeing this was a predicament from which even he could not extricate us all – he had resolved to save himself? Perhaps* (an idea that lathered me in sweat, and at once turned it to ice on my skin) *by agreeing to testify against me.*

At first I resisted this fearful notion; but as first one hour passed – then two – it grew, fattening on my unease – like the insinuations of Iago on Othello's weakness – until at length I had more than half-persuaded myself it was true.

So that it was with something like the sense of waking from a nightmare that I suddenly heard the door open, and saw O'Donnell enter.

"Come, Sir," he said. "'Tis supper-time, and then bed." Then – turning to Niobe: "I have ordered some food brought in to you, and we leave at dawn, as agreed. Till when – I wish you good night; and" (this to the boy, who was still playing with the kittens) "to you, sir, and your friends."

We supped in a neat dining-room, before a fire of fragrant cedar logs; but when I asked him *what spell he had used, to secure our release,* he only frowned, and flashed a glance at our fellow-guests, to warn me into silence. And when we had finally reached our room, and I thought it was safe to repeat the question, he yawned, and said: "It has been a long day, Sir, and will be a short night; let us talk of it again when we have more leisure."

But the next day, as we made our way northward, through New Exeter, and Hillsborough (and half a dozen other hamlets that bore the names of English towns, and showed so little regard for the relation of the originals you would have supposed someone had thrown every place in the country into a pot, and stirred it), he again evaded my inquiries – and was no more communicative that night, when we stopped at a mean tavern at a muddy crossroads, where, altho' we were obliged to share a room with two other travellers and a colony of fleas, yet he had opportunity enough to speak to me at dinner. So that I began to think he meant to keep it a secret, like the contents of the *Jenny*'s cargo; and rather than demean myself further, by pestering him with questions he plainly had no intention of answering, I resolved to hold my tongue.

And was thus not a little surprised when, at breakfast on the fourth day, after we had crossed into Virginia, and put up at another country inn (or 'ordinary', as the Americans call them – with some justice, for G–d knows they are ordinary enough), he said: "Perhaps, Sir, if it is not too tedious, you will permit me to relate what passed between Colonel Howe and myself?"

"Gladly," I said, "if you will."

"I think you should know it, before we reach Colonel Washington's – for 'twas he, in a manner, that secured our release."

"But how – surely, he did not even know we were captive?"

"No. But I told Mr. Howe that we had business with him, and that neither he nor the Congress would look kindly upon the committee that obstructed us."

"But why did he believe you?"

"I told him I could prove it, by showing him a message we were carrying."

"A message!" I began. "What mess–?" And then, all at once remembering: "Ah! Uncle Fiske's letters!"

He nodded. "I took him to our room – removed the one I was carrying from my bag, and gave it to him. He frowned and grumbled, but could not deny the name he saw there."

"But it might have been any thing – and from any one. Did he not demand to read it?"

"He did; but I told him, that tho' we were travelling in the characters of a gentleman and his servant, embarked upon a private quest, we were in truth commissioned by the English friends of liberty, to take an important communication to Colonel Washington, which we had solemnly sworn to give into no hands but his own."

"D–n it, Sir, you must be a finer actor than I supposed, if Howe was convinced by such a flimsy confection as that."

"I confess he wasn't – not entirely – but enough to make him hesitate, before calling me a liar, and tearing the letter open. Which – despite sighing, and harrumphing, and clicking his tongue, to show I had not duped him – he could not quite steel himself to do; so at length took me before a fellow-officer, Colonel Moor, in hope that he would resolve his uncertainty, about what best to do. Moor (unlike Howe) was not merely the husk of a gentleman, but the thing itself. But he was no more easily persuaded, and insisted they must see the letter – saying that, while he understood our predicament, we must also understand theirs."

"So – what? You opened it?"

"No, Sir – I refused, but said they might, if they pleased, go with us to Mount Vernon; and if, when he had read the letter, Colonel Washington did not confirm our account of it, I should cheerfully submit to any punishment they thought fit."

"Good G–d!"

"At which – after a second's delay more – they said that in the present crisis they could spare neither themselves nor any of their men to accompany us; but that I had sufficiently answered their doubts, and we might go."

"But you – both of us – could have been hanged!"

"Indeed, Sir – and 'twas doubtless seeing I was willing to run that risk that turned the scale, and made them believe me."

I should indeed be a great fool, had I failed to observe by now, that y^r honours do not so much read these pages, as rake 'em, to tease out any nit or grit that might be puffed into a speck of evidence against me – tho' I still have no fixed notion of who you may be, or of what charge you hope to prove me guilty. It is always cautionary, when committing a word to paper, to reflect it will be picked over in this way; and today it is doubly so: for I have now reached a place in the story where the very thing that would justify me in the eyes of one party must inevitably condemn me in the eyes of the other. This dilemma has kept me silent the most part of an hour, while I considered how best to extricate myself from it; but I have at last concluded that my best recourse is to continue as I began, by relating what happened, as accurately as I can – and trusting to the truth to vindicate me. So let me plainly state, before the curtain rises upon a character whose very name must move you either to loathing or adulation: that tho' my relations with Colonel Washington were wholly cordial, and he performed a service to me, for which I must consider myself for ever in his debt, yet nothing that occurred between us might be thought to have compromised, in the smallest measure, either his principles or mine.

I heard a rabid parson once, preaching upon the parable of the talents, who struck the pulpit, and roared: "To neglect what we are given by G–d is a damnable sin, that spawns a family of others: cruelty, ignorance, pride and ingratitude!" I dismissed it, at the time, as the ranting of a mad enthusiast; but now, seeing the manner of life in Virginia, I was obliged to acknowledge the truth of it: for the hoggish inhabitants of the place – blessed with an indulgent Nature and a generous King – seem equally insensible of both. They cut a field from the forest – only to abandon it again, after a few years, to fill with scrub and weeds, while they cut another; but if you tax them with this profligacy, saying *that with a little dung, and some proper care, the first might remain productive; and then they should have two fields, rather than one* – they only shrug, and reply, *Why? – we don't want for land, and we an't goin' a-hungry.* Much of the day, in consequence (lacking, or refusing, any better occupation), they spend in filthy inns, supping grog, wagering on cock-fights, and breathing drunken sedition. More than once, as we passed through the colony, some swaying, bellicose little tyrant told us that the wicked government meant to reduce them all to slaves – and then staggered home, where he might vent his rage on those unfortunate creatures forced to serve him, who knew well enough what true slavery was.

But from all these strictures of reproof I must exempt Colonel Washington. Favoured with a noble situation on the lofty banks of the Potomac, he has set about improving it by every means man can devise – and ended by making it (even on a smokey March day, when many of its charms were no more than shadowy suggestions in the mist) the finest small estate I think I ever saw. The farms are neat, well laid out, and so artfully placed, that they do not intrude upon the graceful parks and gardens – where the eye finds such delight, and is drawn so pleasingly to distant prospects, you might think you had strayed into Elysium. The house itself is not large, but elegant and sweet, with a fine portico that extends the full length of one side – giving it the air of a rustick temple set upon a hill. And when we stopped before it, and a cheerful mulatto came out to hold our horses (falling, as he did so, into easy conversation with Niobe and her son); and another opened the door, and politely asked us our business, I began to wonder whether, in such a place, and under such a master, even servitude itself might be tolerable.

"Is Colonel Washington at home?" I said.

"Yes, Sir. I believe he is just returned from his mornin' ride."

"Be so good as to tell him that the brother of his friend Colonel Gudgeon is here to see him."

"Yes, Sir. Why don' you gen'lmen wait right in here?" He ushered us into a low entrance hall – then turned, and disappeared through a door on the left. Which, less than a minute later, opened again; and a florid, well-fleshed, immensely tall gentleman strode out, still wearing his riding-boots. He glanced quickly from me to O'Donnell and back again – then smiled, and offered me a hand as big as a small ham.

"Mr. Gudgeon," he said. "I knew you at once, from your likeness to your brother. This is a most happy surprise."

"Thank you, Sir. But you must excuse me, that it is a surprise at all. I should, naturally, have written ahead, had I been able – but circumstances forbade it."

"'Tis no matter, Sir – we have a great many guests that arrive unannounced, and few so welcome as you." He smiled again – a slow, careful creasing of the face, accompanied by the discreetest hint of a twinkle in his eyes. "If any come now, we shall tell 'em the tavern is full."

"You're very kind, Sir. If you're sure we're not imposing upon you . . ."

"Not in the least. We are undergoing some improvements here, that constrain us a little at present; but my wife commands a whole company of post beds, that may be pressed into service in a crisis. You are how many?"

"Two," I said. "This is my companion, Mr. O'Donnell" – thinking it was neither politick nor necessary to continue the pretence that he was Cully.

"Your servant, Mr. O'Donnell. And" – glancing at the front door – "you have, I suppose . . .?"

"A black woman and her boy."

His eyebrows jumped – and I could not help wondering (for it was, undeniably, an eccentrick retinue for two gentlemen to travel with) whether he supposed Niobe to be my mistress, and her son my bastard. But all he said was: "Well, we have a servants' hall, where they may stay. Martin" – turning to the footman, who hovered behind him – "will take your bags, and I'll have your horses seen to. We dine at three, gentlemen – when I promise myself the pleasure of hearing news of your brother." He began towards the back-door; but stopped after a few steps, and said: "I should tell you, that in this house we keep most religiously to the five-minute rule." And then was gone.

"What is the five-minute rule?" I asked Martin.

"Why, Sir, every one must be at table five minutes after the bell is rung, or they go without."

If Colonel Washington's reception was singular enough (for he could not have accepted our visit more unquestioningly – shown less curiosity as to its purpose, or offered his hospitality more readily – had his house indeed been an inn, and he no more than its keeper), his conduct at dinner was more unexpected still. After our experiences of the last few weeks, and knowing Mr. Washington to be a principal actor in the quarrel with the government, I had prepared myself for a homily, at least, upon the villainy of the ministry. But as it turned out – tho' yᵣ honours may scarce credit it, if you are not yourselves acquainted with the gentleman – he did not speak of politicks at all. Save, that is (for I am sworn to be truthful), in one small particular, when he excused the want of any meat but pork and fowl by saying *the Continental Congress had forbid the killing of lamb and mutton;* and, when I asked the reason, replied, "Because, if we are to import no more animals, we must preserve those we have, to breed from."

For the rest, we roamed pleasantly enough through the weather, architecture and farming (he seemed especially curious about my experiments with cows and turnips, and told me of his with sheep and peaches) – until the table-cloth was wiped, and the pies and tarts appeared. At which point, he leaned towards me, and said: "Now, Sir, what of Colonel Gudgeon? He is well, I hope?"

"No," I said, "I fear he is not. He has an affection of the lungs, and is not expected to live the year."

"I am truly sorry to hear you say so." He leaned towards his wife – a small, handsome, round-faced woman, who (tho' saying little herself) had followed every word of our conversation as keenly as if she were watching a game of shuttlecock. "Colonel Gudgeon, my dear, served with me under General Braddock, and was a most valued friend."

"Indeed," she said – smiling, and rapping the air in mock-reproach – "you have no need to remind me of it." Then, turning to me: "My husband speaks of your brother often, Sir – and always warmly."

"And he, for his part," I said, "is deeply sensible of the service Colonel Washington did him."

"Service?" said Washington, frowning slightly, and fixing me with his blue eyes, as tho' he were truly puzzled.

"Why, yes, Sir – Miss Catchpole . . ."

"Oh. Oh . . . that . . ."

"Miss Catchpole?" asked his wife curiously – in a manner that plainly said, she had not heard the name before.

"Ay . . . ay – 'twas a small enough matter."

"Perhaps then," I said. "But not now. I must tell you, 'tis the occasion for our coming here."

"Indeed?" said Mrs. Washington.

"Yes – she bore him a son, and . . ."

"'Twas a youthful embarrassment," interposed Washington firmly, "in which I had the happiness of being able to help him. But the case is not uncommon in young gentlemen; and I would not see his reputation suffer for it. He was a gallant soldier – that is the material thing – who plainly perceived England's destiny in this country." Here his face creased again – a strange shifting of skin and muscles that puckered the mouth and stretched the area about the eyes, until it had come as close to an expression of merriment as it seemed capable of; and he went on: "The same could not, with any justice, have been said of most of his fellow-officers, who saw only savagery and wilderness here, and thought 'twas impossible it should ever be civilized."

"Of which this house, and your conversation, are sufficient refutation," said O'Donnell.

"Thank you, Sir," replied Washington – with a little smile, and a grave bow, that suggested he was of the same mind, tho' modesty forbade his saying so.

"Indeed," I said. "But as to Miss Catchpole, and her boy . . ."

"In a moment, Sir, with your permission," he said quietly, raising his huge hand to stop me. "Once, Mr. O'Donnell, when we were still in Virginia, Captain Gudgeon (as he was then) told me of a young

117

friend newly arrived from Ireland, Lieutenant Litton, who fixedly believed the air and climate of America were so unwholesome an Englishman could not thrive in it – with the result that, in a very few generations, we should all become pygmies. So 'twas arranged, that Litton should dine at a tavern one day; and then, when he had drunk a bottle or two, I should arrive with Captain Gudgeon, who would present me as an American pygmy – which, since I stand more than six feet, frightened the poor fellow half to death."

O'Donnell laughed politely, but in truth it was an indifferent enough jest; and – since Colonel Washington was plainly not the kind of man that would tell such a story to show his own importance – I could only conclude he had done so out of delicacy, so his wife should not hear the history of Dan and Miss Catchpole. And she, I fancy, thought so too; for the moment he was done, she smiled dutifully – then made her excuses, and left the room. Washington ordered the cloth removed and the dessert brought on – ensured our glasses were full – settled himself more comfortably in his chair – and at last turned to me.

"Now, Mr. Gudgeon: the lady you mentioned."

"Yes, Sir."

"What is your business with her?"

I briefly told him.

He listened attentively; and when I had finished, sighed, and said: "And how do you believe I may help you?"

"Why, Sir, I hoped you might tell us something of her subsequent life. And where she is now."

He shook his head. "I doubt I can tell you any more than you already know. About six months after your brother first wrote to me of his predicament, I received a letter from Mr. Grylls – you are acquainted with Mr. Grylls?"

"Only by name, unfortunately . . ."

"Well – 'twas he who had undertaken to compose matters between Miss Catchpole and your brother. Which (he said) he had done. But now, it seemed, she was being troublesome again – saying that she would be satisfied with nothing less than her own substantial property, where she might live comfortably with her child. But to buy such a thing, in the area about Wilmington, would have been excessively expensive – so, knowing that I had some interest in the development of the back-country, where land is cheaper, he turned to me for advice."

"And . . .?"

"I recommended a region in the western part of the colony, near Frigateville." He cracked a nut, of a kind I had not seen before, and meditatively pulled out the flesh, before continuing: "After which I heard nothing of her at all – until two years ago, when she wrote me, saying she wished to correspond with your family in England, and asking if she might have the replies directed under cover to me. To which I agreed."

"Where was she writing from?"

"From the Frigateville post office, as I recall. Or, at least, that is where my reply was to be sent."

"So Grylls did as you counselled?"

He shrugged his great shoulders. "'Tis a long time ago, Sir. There might be a hundred different explanations for her being there now."

"Are the mails to Frigateville not to be depended upon?"

He shrugged again.

"What other reason could there be, why she might want Dan to write to her here?"

He did not answer at once, but looked towards the window, where the last light of day was bleeding from the hazy sky. At length he said: "Perhaps she did not want to be found."

I confess this unpleasant thought had not struck me before; and my dismay must have found its way into my voice – for when I snapped *Why?*, it sounded (even to my ears) peevish and impatient.

"I could not say, Sir," he replied coldly. "I do not know the lady. Have you applied to Mr. Grylls?"

"We called upon him, but he could not speak to us."

"Indeed? Why?"

"Because he was being held prisoner. For" – here I had to check myself, and choose my words carefully; for we were approaching a powder-keg, and the least spark might ignite it – "for refusing to sign the Association."

"That does not surprise me, Sir. He was always" – his wintriest smile – "a man of unsound principles, that liked nothing so well as to play the lackey."

I exhaled slowly, to let out my temper; and said, as calmly as I was able: "Could you direct us to Frigateville, Sir? She must live near the place."

He paused, careful as a magistrate considering sentence – and at length said: "'Tis a pity you did not come a few days ago. I have just sent some of my people to seat my lands in the Ohio, and you might have travelled with them, for they go that way."

"But we may find it on our own, may we not?"

He nodded. "But be advised, Mr. Gudgeon: you may never succeed in finding Miss Catchpole – or your nephew. The back-country is plagued by troubles: these two years past we have been fighting the Shawnese, and she or her son may have been captured, or even killed."

"Good G–d! – I hope not!"

"Perhaps your brother must reconcile himself to being childless. From my own experience, 'tis not the worst calamity may befall a man. My stepson is an impetuous young fellow – but I am happy enough to see him inherit my property. Do you not have a son yourself, Sir, who might in time enjoy Colonel Gudgeon's fortune?"

"No – my wife and I have no children."

He was silent again – like a man who has come to a fork in the road, and cannot at once choose which direction to take. Then (as if he had suddenly reached a resolution, and was eager to be on his way again) he impetuously thrust a dish under my nose, saying: "Try the Mississippi nuts, Sir – I'll wager you've never tasted any thing like 'em, and they sit pretty well with the madeira. Tomorrow I'll show you my new cherry grafts, if you'd care to see 'em."

"I should, Sir," I said – grateful for the promise of a subject, that we might discuss without fear of a breach.

And it was as well I did – as it turned out.

XXI

Y^r honours put me in mind of nothing so much as a mad terrier-dog, that will worry an old shoe till all that's left of it is threads and tatters; and if (as you insist this morning) your motive is not to incriminate me before a court, I am quite at a loss to conceive what it might be. I shall, nonetheless, take the assurance in good faith, and answer it by acceding to your request, and trying to respond to your latest questions as temperately as I can.

You say: *I make much of my principles; but are they not injured by my relation with my Uncle Fiske? Surely every merchant in Bristol has dabbled in the Africa trade? Did I not even accept passage to America in a ship that might have transported slaves?*

Very well, y^r honours – but consider this: *We are not papists, that give their conscience into another man's keeping, but free-born Englishmen, that are guardians of our own; for which reason, I cannot be held accountable for Uncle Fiske's conduct, however abhorrent I may find it. As to the* Jenny *– if she* had *ever carried negroes (which I doubt), I cannot see how my going in her could have added one jot to their misfortunes.*

One point, tho', I will concede: that the knowledge of my uncle's business made me uneasy – and it was that, it strikes me (now I come to reflect on it) that kept me so much from Bristol, and put me in such a queasy temper when I was there.

And – here's the tender place, that it pains me to come near – I cannot deny that, as a boy, I loved Uncle and Aunt Fiske, more than any one in all the world, and was happier in Queen Square with them than at home in Somersetshire with my own parents. And *then* Bristol was a delight to me – a glass I had but to peer in to glimpse every country on earth; for there was sugar from the Indies, pelts from Canada, tobacco from Virginia, silk and porcelain from China, coffee from Arabia, peppercorns from India, ivory from Africa . . .

And slaves.

We seldom *saw* slaves, naturally (save for those few, like Joseph, that were kept as house-servants); but the whole city bore their mark – as the wretched creatures themselves bear their absent master's, scorched into a shoulder or a cheek. You might find it in the names of inns, and the black figures ornamenting the Exchange; in the bills inviting *wares for a voyage to Calabar,* or advertising *a ship of 280 tons burthen, well calculated for the Africa trade*; in the drunken songs of sailors, and the gangs infesting the vilest taverns, hoping to skim off the scum that had gathered there and force them into service aboard a snow bound for Guiney. And – for me – it was in the booty (for so I have since come to see it) filling my uncle's aerie; and in my aunt's bed-time stories of *Obbo, the poor little black boy, stolen by a wicked Portuguese.*

Once, when a Fiske and Coleman ship returned from some uncommonly profitable venture, my uncle gave me a small, rude, gold figure, saying *it had belonged to an African prince, and was now mine.* When I returned to my father's house, I took it with me; and for a long while after, soothed myself to sleep with it – clutching it in my hand, and imagining I was the prince myself, and the adventures I might have in his character.

For that is all the Africa trade means to a boy, yʳ honours: wonders, and marvels, and romance.

'Tis Sunday – by my reckoning, if not yours – and I mean to devote the rest of the day to bracing up my muscles with my customary exercise, and my spirits with some diversion other than authoring.

XXII

I had not supposed yʳ honours near enough to hear the noises issuing from my room. But 'tis, nonetheless, gratifying to find that I contrived to divert you as well as myself yesterday; and that, in consequence, I am confronted with only one question this morning: *What were you about last afternoon, Sir?*

What I was about, yʳ honours, was composing a glee – and, since it requires three voices and I possess but one, was obliged to sing the parts severally; which doubtless sounded ridiculous enough, but at least has spared me the labour of satisfying your curiosity on any more extensive point, and allowed me to return at once to my narrative.

The hours following our dinner at Mount Vernon were among the pleasantest I recall in America – or, indeed, anywhere else I have ever been. We passed the night in a quiet, well-furnished chamber – serenaded by a whole orchestra of sweet garden smells, that seemed to congregate beneath the window expressly to delight us – and rose to find the smoke clearing from the sky, and the sun already bright. At breakfast, our host chatted affably to me of hunting and horses – while his wife charmed O'Donnell by observing, "We an't been honoured with the presence of a dramatist before, Sir; but private theatricals is a favourite entertainment in these parts; and if you was to oblige us with a piece of your invention, you would never want for friends here, I promise you." And when we brought out the letters from Uncle Fiske, and laid them on the table, like a pair of new-caught fish, Washington so far unbent as to laugh out loud, saying: "By heavens! Why two of 'em? Would not one have sufficed to tell me what he has to say?"

"'Twas a precaution," said O'Donnell. "To protect him, in case we were intercepted. You will see your name and his do not appear together."

"Ah . . . nor they do. Is the matter of 'em so inflammatory, then?"

"He did not favour us, Sir, with a clue as to their contents."

"What! – that is a hard measure, is it not: to make a man carry something that, for all he knows, might have him hanged?"

"Perhaps, Sir," replied O'Donnell. "Tho' in justice to Mr. Fiske, I must say that while he may have risked our lives, he also very probably saved them." And he proceeded to recount our adventure in Wilmington; which I doubted the wisdom of, until he ended by saying, "And I hope, Sir, when you read the letters, you will find 'em equal to the heavy responsibility I was obliged to thrust upon 'em."

Washington's face creased, just enough to suggest a smile; and I at once understood, that by being candid with him, O'Donnell had not only given him an earnest of our honesty, but also inoculated him against hearing Howe's account of the incident – which it was almost certain he must do, at some point in the future, and could only make him think ill of us, had he not first heard ours. But – having no idea what Uncle Fiske had written, and recalling that he had already deceived us once – I could not entirely quell the anxiety, that something in it might seem to justify Howe's suspicions after all, and perhaps even move Washington to deliver us back to the Wilmington Committee of Safety. For which reason, I observed him closely as he read; but saw nothing that might suggest either anger or pleasure – or any response at all.

When he had done, therefore, and begun carefully re-folding the letters, I said (in hope of prising from him some hint of what they contained): "I did not know, Sir, that you and my uncle were acquainted."

"Many years ago," he replied stiffly, "at your brother's suggestion, I believe, Mr. Fiske joined me in investing in the Ohio Company, and has now been good enough to reaffirm his interest in the venture. I shall write and assure him that – despite our present quarrel with the ministry – nothing can lessen my warm regard for him." His mouth twitched again, into the semblance of a smile. "He is, indeed, a most singular gentleman. Tell me: does he still affect a turkey hat?"

Which told me, in an instant, my fears were groundless, and so buoyed my spirits, I almost shouted: "Yes!"

Washington nodded – gave a little growl of laughter – then rose from the table, saying: "Come – Mr. Gudgeon, Mr. O'Donnell – let us go and look at fruit-trees."

It was warm as a late-spring day in England – the soft, moist air full of scents and the musick of birds (whose voices were strange to me, but melodious enough); the sunlight flickering on the mighty river below us, and composing the garden into a charming pattern of brilliant colour and cool shadow, so forming as happy a union 'twixt the regular and the sublime as you could hope to see. Colonel Washington, gracious as a king, led us along neat paths and grassy walks, stopping every few paces to view *some peach kernels from Philadelphia*, or *the Black May Cherry I had of Colonel Mason, and grafted here but yesterday* – discoursing on all of them so engagingly, and with such good sense, I found myself wishing he was my neighbour in England – or I his in America – so that we might talk thus every week. All of which worked upon me to such an extent that after half an hour or so I was near to bursting out, *Come, Sir – let us be frank and open with each other – set aside our differences on politicks and slavery, and resolve to be friends; for G–d knows, there is more unites us than divides us.* And (tho' I am certain yʳ honours will think me a vainglorious coxcomb, or something worse, for saying it), I am half-persuaded that, had I done so, the dispute between our two countries might have taken another way.

But alas! it is in the nature of things, that such moments are short-lived and, once gone, cannot be recalled. I hesitated – opened my mouth – shut it again; and the next instant saw Washington's gaze stray past me towards the house, and his face assume a stern frown. I turned, and observed Martin, the footman, padding towards us.

"What is it?" said Washington, as the fellow came near.

"There a gen'lman to see you, Sir."

"Do I know him?"

"I don' think so, Sir. I an't never see him before. He say his name is Wimsey."

I drew in my breath sharply, and felt O'Donnell stiffen at my side like a pointing dog – but if Washington remarked it, he gave no sign of it.

"Did he say what he wanted?" he asked.

"No, Sir. He tol' me i's a private matter, jus' between you and him."

Washington shook his head, plainly perplexed, and sighed, like a man obliged to pick up an unwelcome burden. But before he could make his excuses to us, O'Donnell laid a hand on his arm, and said: "With your permission, Sir – this Wimsey" (addressing the footman) "– is he a watery-eyed, yellow-faced, rot-toothed fellow, that looks like a drunk monkey?"

Martin was so startled he could not contain a tiny shriek of laughter – which he then contrived somehow to recapture, and tame into a squeal of assent.

"Tho' I'd not", he added hastily (with an anxious look at Washington), "ha' use them words myself."

"In that case," said O'Donnell, "'tis a hundred to one we can tell you his business. But first" – glancing at the house – "do you suppose he can see us here?"

"I greatly doubt it," said Washington. "But we can make a certainty of it, if you wish"; and, without waiting for an answer, guided us behind a small octagonal garden house, where we were safe from view – calling over his shoulder, as he did so: "Tell Mr. Wimsey I shall be pleased to wait upon him presently."

Yʳ honours may think I was a slow pupil – and, indeed, I think so too; but by this juncture I had finally learned my lesson by heart, and knew that if the tongue existed that could talk us out of a difficulty – even with my brother's friend – it was O'Donnell's, and not mine. So I kept my peace, and listened – and, despite my apprehension, could not but marvel at how he told the tale: for, without ever being guilty of a lie, yet he tweaked some particulars, and trimmed others, to fit Washington's prejudices, as neatly as a tailor snipping and stitching a suit. Thus: Wimsey was a slovenly sot, who had not the least notion of good husbandry, or of how to manage an estate; Coleman was incompetent to keep slaves, not only because he lacked the education of a gentleman, but also because he was English – and hence unfamiliar with the right way to treat them; &c. &c.

When he was done, Washington cleared his throat – pinched his lower lip – stared at his boots – and at length said (in the sad, soft manner of a tender-hearted woman that likes her meat but regrets a lamb or a cow must die to furnish it): "I own, gentlemen, you put me in something of a quandary. G–d knows I have little enough love for slavery, and wish it might be done away with, and a better way found – and some day, no doubt, it will. But 'tis the system we have at present, and, without it, this" – stretching out his arm, and spreading his great hand, as if to grasp the landscape – "would still be wild forest, infested with wild people. I have lost three or four negroes myself, and should not look kindly on the man that helped or harboured them."

"Well, Sir," said O'Donnell, drawing himself up – as white and brittle as an icicle. "You must do as you think proper."

"So must we all," replied Washington. "But – I remember Mr. Coleman's parents, when they were living at Fiskefield. His mother was a sweet and sprightly lady; but I cannot say I loved his father. He was a true merchant – the very model of stony-faced usury, who would lend only to increase your dependency upon him. If (as you suggest) his son takes after him, I should not care to be his slave." He stretched out his hand – took a cherry bud – rolled it thoughtfully in his fingers, like a pawnbroker valuing a jewel – and then turned abruptly about, and asked: "What would you have me do?"

"Plainly," said O'Donnell, "you cannot please all parties. We will not surrender Niobe and the boy, without first fighting to keep 'em; and cannot in conscience buy them from Coleman, when we do not accept they are his to sell – so since (I suppose) he will demand nothing less, either he or we must in some measure be disappointed. But perhaps if we were to give you a generous – an exceedingly generous – sum for the horses, and you were to hand it to Wimsey, saying we had gone already but left him this, in payment of our debt – that might sufficiently satisfy everyone's honour, including your own."

I began to speak; but O'Donnell stopped me – moving his eyes so sharply across my face they seemed to graze my own, and prick me into silence.

Washington pondered a moment more; then suddenly flushed, and said: "Very well, I'll do it. How much do you suppose . . .?"

"That is the difficulty I was about to observe," I said (with a dark look at O'Donnell). "'Tis an excellent plan – save that I haven't the ready money to execute it. I could give you a bill, drawn on my brother's bank; but that would require me to go back to the house, where Wimsey would undoubtedly see me."

Washington hesitated no more than a second. "In that case," he said, "I shall pay him now, and you shall pay me after. 'Twere best, I think, for you to wait here until I return."

He was gone almost an hour; which made me fretful, for I could not conceive how the business could take so long, and feared that (improbable tho' it seemed) Wimsey might somehow have contrived to turn him against us, and was even now laying hands on the two slaves and removing them in chains. But O'Donnell assured me it was impossible – that once Washington had given his word, it was to be depended upon utterly; and, sure enough, when at length he reappeared, his ruddy face glowed, and his lips were pursed into a look of cattish complacency.

"'Tis done," he said.

"Thank you, Sir," I replied – surprised to feel the tears spring to my eyes, and wondering if Washington could see, in them, the gratitude my voice was suddenly unable to express.

"We are infinitely obliged to you, Sir," said O'Donnell, with a bow. "Was he very vexed?"

"A little, to begin with. But at least he won't return entirely empty-handed. He has the money, which seemed to please him."

"And will doubtless work the same effect on every tavern-keeper 'twixt here and Carolina," murmured O'Donnell, "who, I fancy, will be destined to get most of it."

The phantom of a smile flitted across Washington's face, and vanished.

"We ended by talking pleasantly enough of horse-racing," he said, "which seemed to soothe his feelings – and allowed us to part friends, I think, after a fashion. And now, Mr. Gudgeon – be so good as to favour me with your opinion of the white peach."

Having warned us of the difficulties that lay ahead, Washington plainly felt he had gone as far as friendship permitted in deterring us; and – since it was evident we meant to continue in spite of them – must now fulfil its obligation to assist us instead. When we left Mount Vernon the next morning, therefore, we carried with us not only the directions to Frigateville, but also two guns and an additional horse, called Hector (which he said we might return when we came that way again), that I at once took as my own – for its size and vigour made it more equal to the task of bearing me than was any of the others. He was also good enough to furnish us with a letter he had written, that (he explained) *clearly set out our purpose, in hope it might spare us further misunderstandings and unwelcome adventures.*

Had y^r honours seen us, carefully wrapping this precious document in oilskin and securing it within a little saddle-bag, you would have thought us no better than a pair of superstitious peasants, packing the supposed toe-bone of a saint, in hope it would ward off evil; and, looking back, I cannot deny our confidence in it seems almost childish. But consider: we had already observed, how Washington had turned back Wimsey, and how his very name had been enough to release us from Wilmington; so was it entirely unreasonable to hope that a letter from him might have the power to deliver us from any future crisis? We discovered, soon enough, how ill-founded was this belief; but I cannot altogether regret it, for (as is doubtless often the way with faith) the mere illusion of security buoyed up our spirits – making the next five days a pleasant holiday, rather than the torment of anxiety they would most certainly have been, if we had known the truth.

The weather was fine, the roads easy, the wooded country lush and charming, speckled with blossoming peach orchards and threaded by little streams fringed with judas trees, where we might rest and water the horses. One night we stayed at a vile ordinary (kept by a Mr. Johnson, the fattest man I ever saw, who also – to my astonishment – served as a justice, when he could sufficiently defy gravity to waddle to the adjacent court house); but for the rest we were obliged to put up at farms and plantations. And, in general, fared much better as a result; for tho' they grew smaller and more scattered, the further south and west we travelled, yet we always contrived to find one that would lodge us in a better room, and provide us with a better meal, than we might have found at any inn – and at less cost, too.

And, by the bye, while I am upon the subject of meals, I am obliged to record that for some reason or other the digestive torments I had suffered in England seemed gradually to diminish during this portion of our journey. Tho' (as will shortly appear) they still troubled me from time to time, they never recovered their former ferocity – as if, like a small tree overshadowed by a larger one, their vigour had been sapped by the greater difficulties that soon overtook me.

I wish, I confess, I might linger a little longer on this interlude – for it is, without doubt, the most agreeable part of our travels to recall, and introduced its own company of curious characters and amusing incidents. But – try as I may – I cannot persuade myself that any of them have the least bearing on the principal matter of this story; so I shall reluctantly close the curtain on them, and pass on – contenting myself with just two brief observations:

One: that on our way, we encountered two or three families of wandering poor, who begged the merest crust from us to keep them from starving – which led me to the surprising conclusion that such an abundance of land does not prevent some people suffering for want of it; and . . .

Two: that even in the remotest corners of the colony, every free man gets his substance by depriving another of his liberty; for there is not the least farmer that does not keep a negro or two, to labour next to him in the fields.

On the fifth morning, about an hour after we had set out, I heard a cry from Niobe's boy and, turning, discovered him pointing excitedly to the right. At first I could make out nothing through the clearing mist; but then – high above what I took to be the horizon – I saw a faint serrated line, shimmering silver-blue like a giant saw-blade.

"Look, Sir!" I cried to O'Donnell. "The mountains!"

But he had observed them too, and only nodded.

All through the day they grew bolder and darker, turning first to a rich, silky green, and then – as the sun began to descend behind them – a deeper and deeper black, till at length they resembled a great jagged wall, that it seemed inconceivable we should ever breach. And this idea must, I think, have lodged in my brain – for that night I was scarcely able to sleep (thanks to a surfeit of whiskey), and, when I did, dreamed that my nephew was held prisoner in a castle, and I could not get to him.

But, at breakfast, our landlord – a quiet, ruminative fellow, with watery blue eyes, and big freckled arms like a butcher's – said 'twas *impossible to miss the road, which we would reach in half a day, and which would then bring us, after only a few miles more, to Mr. Driscoll's, lately removed from Philadelphia, who had three handsome daughters, and would make us the best entertainment we should find within a hundred leagues.*

Whether the man was a villain, or we entirely mistook his meaning, 'tis now impossible to say; but the consequence was that we left an hour after our usual time, and by late afternoon found ourselves in a wild and desolate place, that bore not the least resemblance to anything he had described. Ahead of us, an ocean of trees surged up the sides of the mountains, clinging like spume to cliffs and tumbles of rock – and so closely pressed together, there scarce seemed room enough between them for a man to pass, let alone a horse. We could hear a stream falling a little way off, which gave us promise of water; but we were carrying almost no food with us and, tho' we remarked two or three large clumsy birds stirring the branches above our heads, knew we had little enough chance of killing any in the failing light. We had not passed a house for three hours – and that had been no more than a hut, where a surly, wall-eyed woman had sold us a little milk, all the while muttering *that the menfolk 'ud be back soon, an' we better be gone then, 'cus they didn' like her treatin' wid strangers.* This might have been an empty threat, meant merely to deter us from robbing or abusing her; but it suggested we were unlikely to be well received if we returned – and it was far from certain that we should even be able to find our way there in the dark.

We had just agreed that we should make shift where we were, and go back the next day, in hope of discovering where we had mistaken our route, when Niobe emerged from a rough tangle of bushes (which, doubtless, she had taken advantage of our pause to press into service as a privy), and hurried towards us, crying, "There a way through there!"

We followed her, and at once saw what had caught her notice: a little nick in the forest, opening on to a narrow track that rose sharply for a hundred yards or so and then wound out of view. I peered along it for a moment, before turning to O'Donnell and saying: "This cannot be the road he spoke of."

"Perhaps not," said O'Donnell, "but it is a road, and must lead somewhere; and, at the very least, takes us further in the direction we are going, rather than away from it."

"It might be no more than an animal path."

He sniffed the air – then shook his head, and said: "I smell horse dung. And" (prodding the earth gingerly with his boot) "you cannot see them plain, I know, but feel: the ground is pitted with hoof-marks. I propose we go on. If it is the road, we should soon come to Mr. Driscoll's house; if not, we may happen upon another. And, at the very worst, we can always find another place to camp, and stop there."

"'Twill be higher up, and colder."

"We have a tinder-box" (looking about him, and laughing softly), "and shall not want for fuel."

I confess I did not greatly like this plan, but could not deny the log-ick of it; so reluctantly agreed.

For the first half-mile or so the way was easy enough; but then it began to rise sharply, and to grow rougher and rockier – so we were at length forced to dismount again, to spare the horses (which were already tired), and lessen the risk of an accident to ourselves. And so continued – our faces lashed by twigs, and stones slipping and skittering beneath our feet – for nearly two hours; by which time it was quite dark, and a thick mizzling mist had formed, making it impossible to see ahead. After we had twice taken a wrong turn – finding ourselves on one occasion entering a gully, and, on the other, the gap made by a fallen tree, that almost tripped poor Hector – I waited until we came to a little brook, therefore, and ordered a halt.

"As you wish, Sir," said O'Donnell. "But I am certain we are not far from shelter now."

"What!" I said. "We could not be more lost, if we were in the mid-dle of Africa!"

"Pray, Sir – consult your nose."

I did so, but could make out nothing beyond the wet reek of the forest, and the steam of our own horses.

"Smoke!" said O'Donnell. "Do you not catch it? Someone has made a fire. And, if we continue, 'tis fifty to one we shall soon be sitting by it."

He was right: within five minutes I could smell it too; in ten more we heard the barking of dogs; and in another ten found ourselves walking beside a rude fence of split logs, which guided us the last hundred paces or so to an even ruder gate – so clumsily made, it could not have kept a child without, and only the most feeble-minded pig or chicken within. Beyond it lay a stinking yard, and then what we took to be a little house – tho' all we could see of it was an oblong slab of black cut from the grey of the night, with a faint yellow gleam from one tiny window.

We told Niobe and her boy to wait with the horses, and opened the gate – which so far forgot its duty as to fall over at the first push, as if it hoped immediate surrender would persuade us to spare its life. But the dogs had more mettle to them, and set up such a chorus of defi-ance as must have startled every bear and raccoon within a mile – with the result that, before we had reached the door, it had already opened, and a woman's head poked out, to see what was the matter.

"Madam!" I called, to reassure her. "Please don't be alarmed. We have lost our way, and wonder if you could oblige us with a bed for the night, and something to eat – for which, of course, we shall be happy to pay."

There was no reply – and for a moment I feared she might simply close the door again and bolt it shut. But she remained where she was, with one hand on the latch, and the other hidden from view – tho' whether with the intention of welcoming us, or rebuking us, or shooting us dead, it was impossible to say; for all we could make out in the darkness was the crimped edge of her cap. But when we were no more than ten yards away, she suddenly turned, and the dim light from the house caught one of the handsomest women I had met with in America – round-cheeked, bright-eyed, and with thick curls of golden hair clustering over a smooth brow. And yet there was something disturbing about her, too – and not just the shock of finding her in such a place as this: her plump lips were drawn into a wet, ingratiating grin, such as I had only ever before seen on an idiot.

"Can you help us?" I said slowly.

She shook her head; but with a smile, that made it a gesture of incomprehension rather than refusal. Yet her manner had such girlish grace and liveliness, that it was hard to believe her difficulty proceeded from a want of intelligence.

"Do you suppose she is deaf?" I asked O'Donnell.

"She heard the dogs well enough."

"Dumb, then?"

He shook his head. "I think she is German." And then, to the woman: "Deutsch, ja?"

"Ja! Ja! Deutsch!" she cried, laughing; and immediately unloosed such a torrent of jargon, you would suppose it had been penned up behind a dam, and O'Donnell had just plucked open the sluice.

"I hope you understand her, Sir," I said, "for G–d knows I don't."

"I once knew a young Hessian lady," he replied, "that looked something like her, and was good enough to teach me a few words – tho' I fear they are not equal to this."

He tried to answer her, but was so unaccustomed to lacking the means to express himself, the effort soon reduced him to blushing and stammering like a schoolboy. But at length – after a good deal of gesticulating, and laughing, and phlegmy, stuttering phrases that sounded like the death-rattle of a consumptive, he contrived to establish that:

i. The road to Frigateville lay ahead, and we should soon rejoin it in the morning.

ii. Her son, who lived with her, had been badly bitten by one of the dogs, and she would not put him from the bed to make way for us; but we might lay our blankets on the floor before the hearth, and sleep there.

iii. She had little enough food, for either us or our animals; but we might buy a few eggs and biscuits for our supper, and a chicken, which she would kill and cook for the morrow; and we could graze the horses in the little meadow at the back.

She seemed astonished, when Niobe and her son appeared – holding the door half-shut against them, and casting a questioning glance at O'Donnell, as if to make certain these were truly the attendants he had spoken of and not a pair of changelings substituted for them by mountain imps; but when he nodded, she made no further objection, and even went so far as to coax the shivering boy towards the fire, to let him know he was welcome.

It was the plainest dwelling I had seen yet, with scarce any furniture, and that as crude and unserviceable as the gate: a lumpish chair; stools lashed together with strips of leather; a table sliced from a tree-trunk, and still wearing the remains of its bark. The floor was earth, the ceiling mud, the candle-holders no more than two or three old bottles, worn dull with use and stained with dirty streaks of tallow; everything, in short, suggested want, and lack of refinement – save for one particular: above the fireplace ran a makeshift shelf, on which were arrayed fifteen or twenty brightly coloured little china figures.

O'Donnell seemed as struck by this strange company as I was; for he stopped dead the instant he laid eyes on them, and – as soon as the woman was busy with our meal – sauntered over to look at them more closely.

"There's a sad story here, I fear," I said, following him: "a respectable family, or something more, fallen into difficulties, and obliged to remove to the wilderness to fend for itself."

"Perhaps, Sir," he said indifferently – still examining the figures, and with a nod so cursory it was almost impudent.

"Had they been born to this condition," I persisted – proud, I must confess, of my own reasoning, and determined he should acknowledge it – "they would have known better how to provide for it." I touched my boot against a stool-leg, which wobbled perilously. "A peasant would have made a better seat than that."

"Very probably," he replied – tho' devoting so little energy to it, I could barely hear him.

"I own, Sir," I said, "that I am curious about such things; and should have imagined that, as a dramatist, you would be too. But since, evidently, you are not, and I cannot question her myself, I suppose I must content myself with ignorance."

He turned abruptly, and spiked me with his coldest stare.

"I fear, Sir, you flatter me, by presuming I am competent enough in her language to tease her history from her, without appearing insufferably impertinent."

This foolish disagreement was, without doubt, the pettiest we had ever known – which O'Donnell, I am sure, felt as keenly as I did. Yet, tired and irritable as we were, neither of us would take the first step towards ending it; with the result that we ate our supper under a frost, that froze all efforts at conversation to a standstill – and shortly afterwards retired to rest.

But no sooner had fatigue sent me to sleep than unease and discomfort woke me up again, and kept me shifting this way and that, and juggling a hundred thoughts in my head, until I was once more overcome by fatigue; and continued thus throughout the night – with waking and sleeping so intertwined, I could not with certainty say where the one began and the other ended. So that when, in the morning, I recalled seeing O'Donnell get up, and light a taper from the embers of the fire, and take a porcelain shepherdess from the shelf, and minutely scrutinize it, I supposed it was a dream.

And doubtless would still think so today, but for one small incident, an hour or so later, when I had gone out with Niobe and the boy, to see to the horses. It was another fine day; but the mountain air was sharper than I had expected, and after two or three minutes I came back again, to fetch my coat – to discover O'Donnell in conference with our hostess, holding the same figure before her, and urgently asking her a question concerning it. To which she replied with a word I could not hear; and O'Donnell said: "Transylvania?"

"Ja! Ja!" – laughing, and pointing through the window – "Transylvania man!"

XXIII

My breakfast this morning was well enough, but came unaccompanied by a note – from which I deduce *either*, that nothing I submitted to you yesterday appeared worthy of comment; *or*, I have at last sufficiently hooked yʳ honours' curiosity, to make you give over questioning, so as to delay not a second longer than necessary my resumption of the story and the moment when I reveal to you, the meaning of *Transylvania*. If the latter (as I naturally hope) – why, then, I promise you, you shall have part of your answer in this chapter, but must wait a little longer for the rest.

Having thanked our hostess (who seemed well pleased with the two guineas I gave her, and repeatedly called out *Danke, meine Herren! Danke!* as she reassembled the gate behind us), we set out; and within ten minutes had reached the road she had spoken of, where, with the sun to guide us, we took the way west. It was broader and flatter than yesterday's track – the ground churned in places by hooves and wheels, but easier going, for all that – and we rode at a steady pace, not wishing to tire either ourselves or the horses. We spoke little; but as the sun burned away the mist, it seemed to work the same effect on our ill-temper – so that by degrees our silence became companionable rather than angry, and now and then one or other of us would break it with a remark about the beauty of the scene, or the startling brilliance of a strange bird.

About two o'clock we met a man coming towards us, driving an old horse laden with sacks. He was as gaunt and ill-dressed as a scarecrow, but pleasant enough; and when we asked him, "How far we were from Frigateville?", replied: "I jus' bin thar, to git my corn ground; and b'ain't above four mile."

You might have supposed that, hearing our destination was so near, we would have been eager to press on to it at once; but travel-weary as I was, and having barely slept the night before, I was reluctant to enter the place, until I felt sufficiently restored to deal with the adventures it might bring – which, for all I knew, might begin with an immediate encounter with Miss Catchpole. And O'Donnell, I think, was of the same mind; for when I proposed that we should stop and rest, he immediately agreed.

We halted by a little brook – spread our blankets on the mossy earth – ate our meal of chicken and biscuits – then lay down, and let the musick of the water murmur us to sleep.

Which it did, only too well; for when we awoke, we found the warmth already fading from the air, and the light from the sky, and were obliged to hurry the rest of the way in deepening twilight. And came, at length, to the rim of a shallow valley – with a huddle of buildings clustered near a winding river below us, and beyond it the black sea of the forest swelling up to the horizon, where a great red sun was breaking, and bleeding away into strips of cloud.

As we descended, the gloom grew heavier by the minute, thickened by the onset of night and by languid curls of smoke from the chimneys. Here and there a few dim lights appeared; but – in the absence of any sound, save the clatter of our own horses upon the road – they made no more than a dismal dumbshow of conviviality, which only depressed our spirits further. But then we heard the regular beating of a hammer, and the thrashing of a mill-wheel; and soon found ourselves in a street of sorts, with rough houses on either side, and little parties of people hastening to and fro – who were plainly accustomed to travellers, for they spared us barely a glance; tho' when we stopped a young woman to ask her the way to the nearest inn, I observed her frown surreptitiously at Niobe and the boy, and fold the child she was carrying tightly against her shoulder, as if to keep it from seeing them.

The place she directed us to was Frigate's ordinary, a hotch-potch of wooden buildings – some one-storey, and some two; one with a parapet, and fine modern windows; another with gables, and mean little casements – all jostled together on a low rise close to the river-bank. The oldest of them (tho', in truth, it was only half the age of Queen Square, which Bristol still considers new; for to be the oldest house in a town as sudden as Frigateville means no more than to be oldest boy in a dame school) was a simple two-room tavern, to which the rest had attached themselves like barnacles to a rock. But the door was as thick as a castle gate, and heavily pocked and splintered; from which I drew the uneasy conclusion, it had been attacked by Indians – and not so long ago, neither.

The parlour was thronged with the most various collection of humanity I had seen in America: English men and women, of every station from the wretched to the prosperous; a lordly negro in a fine suit; two girls, prettily dressed in blue silk, but with hair so black and skins so dark I supposed they must be savages; and a whole company of children, squeezing between legs, and tugging at cuffs and hems. The air was foggy with pipe-fumes, and so hot from the press of bodies you might have roasted an ox in it, had you been able to squeeze it in – which is doubtful; for, in truth, we could not even find space enough to insert ourselves, and bobbed about in the entrance, like a couple of skiffs kept from harbour by the tide.

A large woman, that I took to be the landlady (for she made it her business to keep her eye upon the door), spied our predicament and began to nudge and push her way towards us; but when she came near, so loud was the clangour of conversation, and so strange our voices to each other's ears, we could not understand what she said, nor she us; and we were obliged to go out of doors again. Which was just as well; for she stank so evilly, you would have imagined she had been formed from rancid lard, and then glazed over to make her shine.

"Now, Sirs," she said, laughing, and dabbing the sweat from her brow with a filthy sleeve.

"We are just arrived in Frigateville," I said, "– like half the world, it seems; but hope you might yet be able to furnish us with a bed."

"Is it jus' the two o' you?"

"And our servants."

"Ah. An' where might they be?"

O'Donnell turned, and pointed into the shadows at the edge of the road, where Niobe and the boy waited silently with the horses.

"Well, now," said the woman, "that makes a difficulty. In the general way o' things, we don' see many servants here, from one month to the next; but happens tonight we got a house-full of 'em, what with that French fellow – you'd think he was the king himself, wouldn't you, the number he got travellin' with him? An' then there's the Scotchman, too, with his pack of Indians – and natural enough, folks don' like to share a bed with them, for fear they'll wake an' find their throats cut. You'd a pair o' men with you, we might ha' turned and turned about, and riddled you all in somewheres. But" (shaking her head), "– her bein' a wench . . ."

"Can you recommend us to another place?" said O'Donnell.

"Let me see – let me see . . ." She pinched her lip, and rolled it between her fingers, as if it might yield an idea, if she but worked it hard enough.

At length she said: "No – not one as won't most likely be stiffer packed 'n we are. But there's a room over the stable here, that an't took yet; an' we could find a blanket or two for you, and hang a curtain, to keep the negroes off, if that would answer."

"Very well," I said immediately – fearing that if we delayed, in hope of finding something better, we might end by having nothing at all.

"I'll jus' tell Frigate, then," she said, "case somebody else come."

"Hah!" breathed O'Donnell, as she turned. His eyes were round as an owl's, and the instant she had passed the door, he snatched a pencil and a corner of paper from his pocket and began scribbling.

"What?" I said (a trifle peevishly; for the sight of it put me in mind of his secretive behaviour the night before, and his conversation with our hostess that morning). "Some intelligence about the Transylvania man?"

It was a random shot, but enough to stop him – tho' not to jolt him into revealing more. He shook his head – resumed writing for a few seconds – then folded the paper up again, and murmured: "A small memorandum, Sir. Did you observe how she spoke as if we already knew every person she mentioned, and so required no explanation of who they might be? 'The Frenchman' – 'the Scotchman' – 'Frigate'. You would suppose the mere fact of her being acquainted with a man was sufficient to confer the same privilege on the entire world."

"Why should that be worthy of note?" I said – half-suspecting he was lying. "It shows nothing, save that the woman's a fool."

"Indeed – but would please an audience, I think, if I slipped her into a play. Mrs. Know-all. Mrs. Panacon."

"Humph – I cannot see the wit in that: setting a booby in the stocks, and exposing her to the ridicule of the crowd."

(And am still of the same opinion today – tho' must in justice testify that his judgement of the publick taste was vindicated, as any of y^r honours that have been at the theatre in London this year past will know.)

"The wit", he began, "lies in the–"

But I never discovered where the wit lay; for at that moment the foul-smelling woman reappeared, clutching a lantern, and bade us follow her – leaving O'Donnell time only to thrust his handkerchief to his nose and whisper, "Dear G–d! I hope she keeps her house cleaner than her person," before we were caught up in the bustle of bags, and ostlers, and servants.

She led us across the yard, up an outside stair, and into a spacious attick – that, for all it was in an outbuilding, seemed more like a house than half the houses we had stayed in. The roof was lofty and well beamed, with a pair of dormers on either side, a table and stools in the middle; and a small stove in one corner, which she at once set about preparing, saying *it could still get mighty cold o' nights, and she'd not have us shaking and shivering.* Before she had done, a fidgety girl and a lad in hessian breeches – who, from their blushes, were plainly lovers – arrived with candles and beds, and began setting them up, giggling and ogling at every slip and fumble, so adding a touch of hilarity to the business, which even had Niobe smiling. Then the reeking woman completed the transformation, by hanging the curtain to form two neat little chambers.

"There," she said. "I fancy you'll be snug enough now. Shall I have supper sent in for you?"

"We may as soon come to the supper, as the supper to us," I said.

"I's afeared, Sir" (shaking her head, and glancing at Niobe), "we can't make room for so many tonight. But it an't no trouble to find you somethin'. How's fresh-killed deer meat, and bread, and whiskey tickle you?"

"Admirably," I said. "We've tasted nothing but chicken and pig-flesh for a month."

"Ah – that's them meddlesome gentry in Congress. But they an't fixed to stop huntin' yet – and best not try, neither; leastways not here."

Our arrival in Frigateville had so depressed my spirits that I had resolved not to inquire after my nephew or his mother until the following day, in case I should receive a disappointment when I was least able to sustain it. But warmth, and merriment, and the promise of a meal – above all, the discovery of an American, who seemed friendly not only to me, but to my country – had worked such an effect upon me, that when she paused at the door and said *would we be wanting anything else?*, I found myself asking, before I had time to reflect: "Do you by chance know a Miss Catchpole?"

She frowned – squeezed her lip again – and at length said doubtfully: "No – I don't think so. An' I'd pretty much take my oath you won't find her here, 'less she's jus' passin' through, for I'm generally acquainted with all the folks in these parts."

At which O'Donnell smiled.

"She may not live in Frigateville," I said. "But her correspondence is directed to the post office here."

"Ah – well – that's another thing again. There's some fifty mile off get their letters that way – tho' I know most o' them, too, so I'm surprised I an't heard o' her. But my husband's sister keeps the post office, along o' the store, an' I'll show you to her in the mornin', if you wish. She'll be happy to help you, I'm sure, for she's the most obligin' woman you could hope to meet."

This connection was, I suppose, little enough wonder, in a town as small as Frigateville; and yet I could not help feeling there was something providential in it, which heartened me still further.

Whether this lightening of my mood effected a similar change in my companions', by some kind of sympathetick action, or whether they had reasons of their own for feeling cheerfuller, I cannot say; but it is certain that we were happier and more easy with each other that evening than we had ever been before – or were to be again. When the meal came, O'Donnell insisted we should sit down to eat together – and then himself affected the role of servant, waiting upon us with such footmanly gravity as to provoke a sound I had thought I should never hear: Niobe and her boy laughing. And when at last we retired, full of venison and drink, she muttered (for the first and last time in my hearing), "Thank you."

That night, I dreamed my wife came to me in my bed, and lay with me; and after, rested in my arms, and toyed with me, and called me all manner of sweet names I had not supposed she knew.

I woke late, my head aching fit to split, to find O'Donnell had risen before me, and gone out. He returned while I was yet dressing, to say *he had spoken to the landlady, who could still not accommodate us in the house, but would have our breakfast sent across, and afterwards wait upon us, to show us to the post office.* A short while later, the two giddy young light-heads appeared, swaying beneath great rough trays of ham and coffee and milk; but even their presence could not restore our gaiety, and we ate in silence, each gnawed by his own thoughts – which, in my case, were almost entirely occupied with the consequences of mixing game and whiskey. Then, when we were finished, we revived the fire in the stove, to provide some comfort for Niobe and the boy – for they were plainly tired, and there seemed little purpose in stirring them up to come with us, if they were to receive nothing but curious stares for their pains – and set out on our quest.

We found our guide in the tavern, which was already almost as thronged with people as it had been the previous evening – tho' so few of them seemed familiar, you would have thought that yesterday's entire company must have been snatched away at midnight and replaced wholesale with another. She was talking to a tall, stooped man, who wore a foreign-looking blue coat, and whose face was almost completely hidden by his wig, his upturned collar and a fine silk handkerchief pressed against his mouth – from which I guessed she smelled no pleasanter this morning than she had last night. But she was evidently waiting for us; for she already had on an out-door bonnet and, as soon as she saw us in the entrance, smiled, and advanced towards us. As she approached, she called to me: "You slept well, I hope, Sir? Not too chill a-bed?"

"Thank you – very well."

"There's a bite to the day, now, I know – but my sister-in-law keeps a fire, as'll have the frost off you in a minute."

"I'm sure we can find our own way to her, if you will but direct us," I said – as much (I confess) to spare myself as her; for the thought of the fumes rising from her in a hot, close place disturbed the uneasy peace of my belly.

"Nay, 'tis not so easily found – and besides, I'm always glad of a reason to see the good woman." And she at once strode out before us.

It was indeed a raw morning – the air sharp and smokey, and the tracks between the houses (for they could not be called streets) hard-ridged with cold, making us slide, and stumble, and fear a cracked ankle with every step. So I was not sorry to find that – despite the landlady's warning – the end of our journey was no more than two hundred yards from the beginning, and in reaching it we were obliged to turn but one corner.

The store (by which, I discovered, Americans invariably mean a *shop*) was a great squat building, that sat by the river-bank like a frog waiting for flies. On one side of it was a jetty and a pair of ferry-boats; on the other the mill we had remarked the day before, with a big crude wheel that groaned and clattered in the race so loudly you had to shout to make yourself heard above the noise – which created such an effect of bustle and activity that entering the place was much like going from a crowded street into the calm of a church. And, in truth, there was something of the popish chapel about the inside; for it was dark, and spiced with the scent of pitch and sacking, and full of strange objects crammed into corners and recesses: hanks of rope,

141

and almanacks, and pots stacked like so many reliquaries, and curved hoes, that would not have looked amiss in the hands of a bishop. I shall not try y^r honours' patience, by recklessly driving this simile to destruction, and describing the little knots of customers as worshippers – yet there *was* a kind of hushed solemnity about them, as they deliberated which spade or saw to buy, that I have never seen in England.

Mrs. Peckitt was not the paragon you would have imagined from her sister-in-law's eulogies on her – but an amiable enough woman for all that, with a round, soft face and delicate little ladylike hands that were forever fussing with her cuffs. She kissed the landlady fondly – and without apparent offence to her nose; then turned smiling to us, and curtsied, and bade us welcome. But when I tried to proceed to business (which I was naturally eager to do as soon as possible), she would not hear of it, saying *it 'ud not sit comfortable with her, to receive two friends of Mary in the store, as if they were strangers; and we must go with her into the house, and take our ease.* Plainly, it would have have been as impolitick to refuse, as impolite – tho' I could not but reflect that it was the first time in my life I had been taken for an inn-keeper's friend.

I am not such a cynick as to doubt that her hospitality was prompted by the most generous of motives; but they were alloyed, I think, with a tincture of pride: for, after ushering us from the back of the shop and down a broad unlit passage, she threw open the door at the end with a flourish, and held it wide, examining our faces as we entered, for evidence (I suppose) that we were agreeably surprised by what we saw – as, in truth, we were; for we found ourselves in a parlour as light and well proportioned as many I have seen in gentlemen's houses – and not much worse-furnished, with two or three good chairs, and a writing-table, and the portraits of a Puritan man and wife flanking the fireplace. O'Donnell and I both stopped, and looked about us, amazed; for the effect was so genteelly English, it was like moving from one continent to another in the space of a single step. Which evidently pleased her; for she blushed and smiled, and drew us to one of the windows, which commanded a fine view of the town and the mountains we had passed through the day before.

"When my brother came here," she said, "all that you might have seen from this place was forest, and rocks, and wild beasts."

"And when was that, Madam?" asked O'Donnell.

"Thirty years ago."

"And from England, I fancy," I said – for there was a stubborn flatness in her voice that had more of Yorkshire than America in it.

"Ay" – with a start, and a little simper – "we are originally from Wakefield. Tho' it half-pains me to own it, in the present difficulties. But today" (hurrying on) "there are four inns here, two doctors, a blacksmith, a Dutch church . . ."

"And a German," said her sister-in-law, nodding so heartily the sweat flew from her brow.

"A German, a Presbyterian, a still-house, a mill–"

Whether it was the sudden heat and the rank odour of the landlady, some lingering influence of the whiskey, or anxiety at what I might learn of my nephew, I cannot now say; but at that instant I felt suddenly faint, and was obliged to brace myself against the wall. Seeing which, Mrs. Peckitt abruptly stopped her catalogue of Progress, and said kindly: "Forgive me, Sir – I shouldn't run on so – you're tired with travelling. Please to sit down, and I'll tell the wench to bring coffee."

I did so; and was sufficiently recovered, by the time she returned, to say: "I hope, Madam, you will not think me uncivil, if I pass directly to the purpose of our visit here; for, to tell truth, I cannot rest easy, until I know your answer."

"Why, then," she replied, laughing pleasantly, and sitting beside me, "I hope I shall be able to satisfy you. What is the question?"

I told her; and was dismayed to see her frown and shake her head.

"Miss Catchpole?" she said. "No – I fear I cannot recall her."

"But surely – she would not have her mail sent here, if she did not live close by?"

"You are certain your friend was not mistaken?"

"Colonel Washington?" said O'Donnell quickly. "'Tis inconceivable."

I confess I was less confident on this score than he was; for tho' I doubted Washington would have wittingly misled us, it was not improbable that in the press of great affairs he could have mis-remembered so small a particular as Miss Catchpole's address. But to say so might have ended the conversation at once, by allowing Mrs. Peckitt to believe she had cleared the matter up, and need make no further effort on our behalf; so I held my tongue.

"Well, then, I am at a loss," she said, and gazed perplexedly off into the fire, muttering *Catchpole, Catchpole* to herself, and plucking so violently at her sleeves you would have thought she meant to have them off.

"Is it possible," said O'Donnell at last, "that she is employed as a servant in somebody's house; and her letters are to be collected with theirs?"

She started out of her reverie – looked first at him, and then at me.

"But did you not say she had a property of her own?"

"Yes – but that was many years ago, and her circumstances, I suppose, may have changed."

"Well – I can but see." And she rose, and went out into the passage.

Y^r honours may easily imagine the thoughts that swarmed through my poor brain while she was gone: *What if she finds nothing? Must we, after all we have endured, limp home empty-handed?* – which conspired with my thumping head and uncertain stomach to reduce me to a state of the most miserable apprehension. But thankfully, it was short-lived; for in less than five minutes Mrs. Peckitt flung open the door and hurried in, twirling a scrap of paper above her head like the colours of a defeated enemy.

"A very happy stroke, Sir!" she cried to O'Donnell – her eyes bright, and cheeks hot with triumph. "I have it! Her mail is directed under cover to Mrs. Craig, at Cicero."

"Who is Mrs. Craig?" I said, jumping up.

"A very spirited lady, who makes it her business to help less fortunate members of her own sex." (I could not help observing, as she said this, that her sister-in-law gave a complicit smirk; which at once had me wondering, whether by "helping less fortunate members of her sex" she meant "keeping a bawdy-house".) "So perhaps you were right, Sir, and Miss Catchpole suffered some misfortune, and found refuge with her."

"And where is Cicero?" asked O'Donnell.

"No more than thirty miles from here."

"Then let us set out at once!" I cried.

"You will not get there today," she said. "The road is very hard, and dangerous . . ."

"Harder than the road here?" I said.

She nodded – with the humorously indulgent look of a mother, whose child has asked, *Is the sea bigger than the duck-pond?* "There are *banditti* in the mountains, and only one or two houses on the road

144

where you may put up – and no certainty even they will be able to take you in. You had better buy stores for the journey, in case you are obliged to shift for yourselves upon the way; and then stay here tonight and leave at dawn. Think you not, Mary?"

"Ay – much better."

They both stood to gain, of course, by our accepting this advice – but after the kindness they had shown us, I could not believe they had any object in offering it but to help us, and ensure our safety; so I at once said: "Very well, then – we will."

The sun begins to set, and I am mindful I made a promise, when I began this chapter, that I have not yet kept; so I shall o'erleap the next few hours (when, in truth, nothing happened that was either very wonderful, or very pertinent to my story), and bring y^r honours to dinner that afternoon – where a great deal occurred that was both.

The landlady having told us *that a family of settlers had left that morning, and she might at last make a corner for O'Donnell and me (tho' not yet for the servants) in the dining-room,* we arrived there a little after three o'clock, to find two dozen or more people, seated at a pair of great tables. She placed us near the middle of the further one – opposite a little party, that seemed to consist of the stooped gentleman she had been talking to that morning (who still contrived to keep his face half-covered); the two well-dressed savages we had remarked the preceding night; and – between them – a high-cheeked, fine-featured man we had not seen before. Next to me was another stranger – a big, florid fellow, with a swelling belly that strained at the buttons of his well-cut coat and trespassed upon my arm every time he turned.

The food was plain – chicken, bread and coffee (which the Americans, it appears, drink as freely with their meals as we do beer); the conversation, for the first half-hour or so, plainer still. But then my fat neighbour observed that he had dribbled some hot grease on my knee; and, having breached the silence between us with his excuses, went on: "And where are you travelling to, Sir?"

"To Cicero."

"Cicero! I know the place well. What" – puckering his brow, so his eyes were lost in shadow – "what do you do there?"

I told him – and his face uncreased again.

"I am not acquainted with Miss Catchpole," he said. "But Mrs. Craig is a fine woman, and will, I am sure, help you all she can, if she

is at home. Tho'– I must caution you – you should not count on finding your nephew. Many children have been stolen from that part of
the country."

I felt as a man does when a cloud crosses the sun on a fine day and
the warmth shrinks from his skin – for did not this exactly echo
Washington's warning to us, barely a week ago? At the same
moment, I was aware that the other side of the table had suddenly
fallen quiet – that the men there had glanced quickly at each other,
and were now staring at us, like two cats watching a thrush; but I was
too preoccupied with my own unwelcome reflections, to attach any
significance to it.

"You mean by Indians?" I said.

"Ay, Sir, Indians . . ." he began; and was about to continue, when
the long-faced fellow said:

"Perhaps, Sir, a just man might think that fitting enough, if he but
stopped to consider what we have stolen from them."

His voice was quiet, with the breathy softness of a Scotch
Highlander; but you could no more mistake the anger in it than you
could a knife wrapped in a stocking. My neighbour was so plainly
astonished he was unable to reply for a moment, and merely stared
in return; but at length he rallied his wits sufficiently to say: "And
who might you be, Sir?"

"My name is McLeod, Sir."

"Well, Mr. McLeod – I can but say, that is the most singular opinion I have heard in my life. And I never met a man yet, just or not,
that would agree with it."

"Perhaps, then, you should extend your acquaintance."

O'Donnell coughed; and the fat man drew in his breath slowly,
fighting to master his temper; and said: "And what do you suppose
we have taken from them?"

"What is this place built on?"

"Their land, you mean? You cannot steal something from a man
that does not own it."

"The Indians own it, after their fashion."

"To own land" (shaking his head) "you must possess it, and live
upon it, and improve it – not merely roam over it, like wild beasts."

"That is not how the Indians live, Sir – as I can testify" (here gesturing towards the two savage wenches). "These are my daughters.
Do they look like wild beasts? Their mother is Cherokee, and I am

become more than half Cherokee myself, since settling among 'em."

"Then you should tell them, they may count themselves fortunate to receive any consideration for their pretended title."

McLeod's hand slipped to his side – reaching (I suppose) for a weapon, for the stooping fellow hastily shook his head, and put out his own hand to restrain him; and my neighbour barked a quick contemptuous laugh, and said: "You are become a savage indeed, I see."

"And what, pray, then, are you . . .?" said McLeod.

"I am David Hickling–" began the fat man; but McLeod pressed on without faltering:

" . . . an agent of the Transylvania Company?"

Which produced the same result in Hickling as my mention of Transylvania had in O'Donnell. He stopped dead – swallowed – flushed – and stuttered out: "What if I am?"

"Then you are a scoundrel, Sir – or at best the servant of scoundrels."

There was a breathless silence, which I expected any moment to erupt into a violent exchange; but then Hickling got up – bowed stiffly to me – and began to walk away, without a word.

"What is the Transylvania Company?" I asked – determined to trump O'Donnell for once, by discovering something on my own account.

"Why, Sir, a combination of hypocritical rogues, resolved to rob the Cherokee of their lands, under a pretence of law and commerce."

"How–?" I began; but was kept from saying more by a tremendous commotion breaking out that moment behind me. I turned, and saw Hickling at the door, clutching his wrist; and a woman, with whom he had evidently collided, kneeling on the floor where his great bulk had thrown her. As she got up, I saw it was Niobe – and plainly in some distress; for she looked wildly about her, and as soon as she spied O'Donnell and me, began hobbling frantically towards us, gasping with pain.

"What's the matter?" I said, rising to meet her.

"I see the master!" she sobbed.

"What – Mr. Wimsey?"

"No! Mr. Coleman – he out there!"

XXIV

Y^r honours must be made of stone. To be left at such a crisis! and to defer learning its resolution, merely in order to ask two foolish questions! – 'tis scarcely human.

I have already told you why I almost fainted at Mrs. Pickett's window – as you will easily see, if you trouble to re-read my account of our visit there.

As to why my first sight of Frigateville so depressed my spirits, I cannot say. But surely even such cloddish minds as yours must sometimes receive a powerful impression, either for good or ill, without being able to ascribe an exact cause to it.

And now – with your permission – I shall return to Frigate's ordinary.

My first thought was that Niobe was mistaken – for anxiety (I supposed) must have tuned her nerves to such a pitch that the glimpse of any fresh-faced young fellow in a crowd of strangers, with only the faintest likeness to Coleman, would be enough to set them jangling. I asked her, therefore, to go with me, and show me the man she meant; but she was so stricken with fear that she refused – so I seated her in my place, and set off on my own, to see if I might find him myself, and put her mind at ease.

But had got no further than the parlour door when I abruptly stopped again: for there, sitting at a table before an open bottle, and working his mouth meditatively about the stem of his pipe, was a familiar figure: Kirke, the mate of the *Jenny*, whom we had last seen in the shop in Wilmington. His companion had his back towards me – but I knew at once, from the sharp angle of his shoulder and the tilt of his head, that it was my cousin.

I turned slowly, and hurried back to the dining-room – where the entire company seemed to be anticipating my return, like an audience awaiting Mr. Garrick. I laid a hand on O'Donnell's arm – leaned close to his ear – and whispered, "She is right, I fear"; but for all the good it did I might have bellowed it out loud, for a drunken rascal at the other table at once called out: "Tell us! Tell us! Is it her master?"

Before I could check myself, I glanced towards him – and he must have seen the distraction in my face, for he immediately roared: "It is! It is! Look at him – it is!" For which his friends rewarded him with an ugly rip of laughter.

"Come," muttered O'Donnell, "this is not a matter for parliament."

"Indeed," I said; and we helped Niobe to get up, and made the most orderly retreat we could.

We found the boy hiding beneath one of the beds in our quarters, where his mother had dispatched him. Both of them were now shivering (almost the only time I ever saw Niobe exhibit any symptom of fear); so we bade them wrap themselves in their blankets, ordered them into the inner portion of the room where O'Donnell and I slept, prodded the sluggish stove into life, and told them to sit down before it. At first, Niobe was reluctant even to do this, saying, "We mus' go now, we mus' go now"; but when O'Donnell primed his pistol, and swore he would kill the man that tried to take her, she relented – tho' with a great sigh, that plainly told us she was still uneasy and conceding under duress. There was no lock upon the door; but we placed two stools against it, to impede any intruder, and give us warning of his approach; and then retired into the corner, to debate what we should do.

"You are, I suppose, quite certain?" began O'Donnell.

"Yes," I replied; and told him why.

He was quiet for a moment; then said, "'Tis the devil's work" – with such quiet gravity, I wondered whether he half-believed it, as he had half-believed in ghosts (or so it seemed) in the Redcliffe caves.

"Perhaps," I said; "but more likely Colonel Washington's."

He shook his head. "That is quite impossible."

"What – more impossible than the devil!"

"Washington is a gentleman."

"What of it? He would not be the first to betray a friend – especially if he saw some political advantage in it."

"What advantage?"

I reflected a moment; and then said: "Coleman is a proprietor in this country, as he is himself, and could doubtless do him some material service, if he chose – for which he might think disclosing our destination was a small enough price to pay."

"You quite mistake the man," said O'Donnell, angrily. "I tell you: 'tis inconceivable."

"So I must put aside my own opinion entirely, must I? and accept that of a young pup, that would sooner credit Satan with our misfortune than lay it at the door of an American rebel?"

He grew paler, and more hollow-cheeked, as if I had given him a stab of the tooth-ache – a sure sign that he was preparing to answer my thrust with one of his own. But our desperate circumstances must have dissuaded him; for at length all he said was: "Besides – 'twould have taken three days, at least, for a message to reach Fiskefield; and even if Wimsey had taken it, and Coleman had then set out at once, he could not have been here so soon."

Which was undeniable; so I said: "What other reason could he have for coming here?"

He shrugged. "But we may be certain that it does not concern us; and that he need not know we are within a hundred miles of Frigateville, if we but keep to our rooms tonight and leave at dawn as we intended."

I shook my head. "'Twill be common knowledge by bed-time," I said. And then, lowering my voice (for I did not wish to add to Niobe's anguish, by seeming to reproach her): "She could not have made it more publick if she had ordered bills printed and posted on every wall."

He was about to reply; but at that instant – as if Fate had contrived it expressly to prove my point – there came a sudden tapping at the door.

We glanced at each other.

"Perhaps it is only the servants," I whispered.

But he shook his head; and, indeed, I did not really think so myself – for we had heard no steps upon the stair, and the sound had a constrained urgency to it, like the scrabbling of a mouse that fears it may awake the cat.

Without a word, O'Donnell snatched up his pistol and concealed himself behind the curtain; and I began to tip-toe towards the entrance. As I drew near, there was a second knock – quicker and more muffled than the first. I seized one of the stools by the leg, as a makeshift cudgel; then pressed my back to the wall, and called out: "Who is it?"

"Friends," replied a man's voice; which – tho' it had spoken but one word, and that softly – I thought I knew.

"Mr. McLeod?" I said.

"Ay. Pray admit us, before we are observed."

I could not guess what business he might have with us, but it was hard to imagine it had any connection with Coleman; and if I refused, I should inevitably suggest we were trying to conceal something, and so plant a suspicion where perhaps none had existed before. So I set down my extempore tomahawk – kicked the other stool aside – and opened the door.

"Thank you," said McLeod, entering hurriedly with an anxious glance over his shoulder, and followed, at a statelier pace, by the stooping man – who made, now I saw him whole, and near at hand, a most singular figure, with his blue velvet collar pulled up about his ears, and his face shaded by a great hat. He walked with a limp, and carried a little cane, which gave him the curious air of a crippled fop who had strayed somehow from court and missed his way back.

McLeod looked about him, as if searching for something – and then, seeing O'Donnell emerge from his hiding-place, nodded, and said: "You know my name, gentlemen, but I don't know yours."

"Ned Gudgeon," I said. "And Mr. O'Donnell."

"Your servant, Sirs. This" – indicating his companion – "is Monsieur le marquis de Vieux Fumé."

We all bowed; and the stooping man lifted his hat – but then, instead of removing it, set it down again on his wig.

"I hope, gentlemen," he said (with scarcely a touch of foreign diction), "you will forgive this intrusion; but I could not help observing that . . . that unhappy creature . . . in the dining-room . . ."

"Our negro woman, do you mean?" I said.

He nodded – insofar as the architecture of coat and cravat about his neck allowed.

"She is, I presume, an escaped slave?"

"What if she is?"

"She is in great danger, I think?"

He paused, waiting for me to reply; but I did not give him that satisfaction, and at length he went on: "There were twenty-seven people in that room, Mr. Gudgeon – Mr. McLeod and I counted them, after you had gone. All of them heard her tell you that her master is here – and most of them will now tell somebody else – and within an hour or two, it is almost certain the story will have reached him, and he will seek her out."

"You will not, I trust, think me rude, Sir," I said (having no notion how a marquis should be addressed), "if I enquire, what is your interest in the matter."

"The interest of humanity," he replied. "I would spare her being recaptured, if I can."

Which I own, now I come to see it unadorned, seems unexception-
able; but it was spoken with such a rich sauce of jesuitical condescension as immediately had my bile rising.

"In that case, Sir," I said – loudly enough, I hoped, for Niobe to
hear – "you may rest easy; for we mean to ensure she is not."

"I am come to offer my service, in assisting you."

"Well, Sir – we are very much obliged to you; but please don't
trouble yourself further, for we are quite capable of protecting her
ourselves – and her boy."

"There is a boy?" – his eyebrows suddenly lifting.

I nodded – in such a peremptory manner, I thought it must end the
conversation at once. But they were not to be so easily deterred; for as
I was moving towards the door, intending to show them out, I heard
McLeod ask, "And what do you say, Sir?"

"Perhaps we might at least hear what the gentleman proposes?"
replied O'Donnell.

"Of course," said the Frenchman, inscribing a little circle in the air
with his stick, as if he were drawing in the sand. "What I propose is
that they should exchange rooms with two of my servants."

"And what would be the merit of that?" I asked.

"The merit, Sir" – with a sigh, as if it should have been perfectly
plain, and he was wearied by the necessity of explaining it – "is this:
if, when the master comes (which he is certain to do, as soon as he has
discovered from the landlady where you are lodged), he finds two
strangers here, in place of his slaves, he will be confounded. He cannot knock on every door and enter every chamber in the ordinary, in
the slight hope of happening upon their hiding-place; and will therefore be forced to wait until tomorrow and resume his search then. By
which time you – like we – will already be far away."

"Humph," I said doubtfully.

But O'Donnell must have mistaken my tone; for he turned to me
and said: "Indeed, Sir, most ingenious."

"Ingenious, perhaps," I said; "but quite unnecessary, when we are
prepared for him, and well-armed."

"Better, surely, it should not come to that, when the law is on his
side – and opposing him might make us murderers, as well as
thieves?"

Which put me in a quandary; for his argument was irrefutable –
and yet failed to answer my principal concern: that Niobe and the

boy were our dependants, and we should be failing in our duty to them if we entrusted their fate, at such a critical juncture in their affairs, to the first pair of strangers that rapped at our door – and not just ordinary strangers, neither; but a decayed French dandy, and a fellow who (by his own admission) was more than half a savage, neither of whom I should have allowed out of my house without first searching his pockets, to make sure he had not pilfered a snuff-box or a spoon.

Plainly, I could not state this objection directly; but it must have been writ upon my face; for as I was considering how best I might hint at it without causing offence, McLeod suddenly said: "Perhaps you should ask the woman herself, and let her decide the matter?"

"An excellent idea," said O'Donnell at once, gazing at McLeod with an open-eyed expression I had not seen before, tho' it looked very like frank admiration – and without leaving me time to offer an opinion, vanished behind the curtain.

I could not help thinking, while he was gone, that it was foolish and unfeeling to give a poor whipped creature such as Niobe the burden of determining her own destiny – when, as even the most incendiary democrat would have been forced to acknowledge, neither her education, nor her experience of the world fitted her to bear it. But I knew that to say so would only weaken my authority further, by casting me as a tyrant; so I held my tongue, and hoped she had sense enough to see it herself. And was gratified to observe, that the marquis seemed as unsettled as I was, as we waited for the conclusion of their muttered conference; for he walked up and down, whirring the air with his stick – like a great lame cat whisking its tail.

"Very well, gentlemen," said O'Donnell, when he at length reappeared. "She agrees to your plan – but only if I go with her."

Our visitors had plainly not expected this; for McLeod started as if a bee had stung him, and looked sharply at the marquis – who stopped in mid-step and stood quite still, staring at the tip of his cane. After a few seconds he drew himself up, and bobbed his head – tho' not with any great relish.

"I hope, Sir," said O'Donnell, turning to me and tapping the butt of his pistol, "that will remove your misgivings, too?"

I nodded – but was still not entirely easy.

I went with them, in case they should encounter Coleman on the way; but we crossed the yard without mishap, and I then waited in the shadow of a portal for the two servants that were to take Niobe's and the boy's places – who, it turned out (when they finally emerged), were the lordly negro we had seen in the tavern and a fluttering little fellow with a beak of a nose, about whom, despite a good deal of hand-flapping and my few words of school-room French, I discovered nothing, save that his name was François and he was a cook.

They seemed quite cheerful, and settled into their new quarters without complaint; but I could not quell my own anxieties, or stop myself straining to hear Coleman's approaching steps – and it was long after the jabber of conversation on the other side of the curtain had ceased that I at last slept.

I was waked by the sound of clinking harness, and stamping hooves, and hushed voices; and for a moment imagined myself back in England – for I had been dreaming I was at home, and Joseph had come from Bristol with a gang of rogues to steal my best nag, Merry. But then I observed that the window was of the wrong sort, and set in the wrong wall – and by degrees my memory unshuttered itself, and I recalled where I was, and what had passed the night before.

I got up, and hurried to the dormer – but the dawn was still too feeble to show me more than a few dim figures moving beneath the darkness like fish in a stream. I lit a candle – looked at my watch – and saw it was already long past four. Immediately I dressed myself, trying to suppress a queasy wash of fear that filled my mind with half-formed thoughts of theft and kidnap and murder – and then broke free altogether, when I pulled aside the curtain, and discovered the marquis's servants gone.

I went back for my pistol and stealthily descended the stairs – just in time to observe two or three horses laden with baggage ambling out into the road, and to hear the thump and clatter of several more, that must have gone before them, and already disappeared from view. At almost the same instant, a movement at the other end of the yard caught my attention; and, turning, I glimpsed a man hastening into the house. He was hugging his coat against the cold; his shoulders were hunched, and his face hidden – but there was something in his scuttling manner that put me powerfully in mind of Coleman. Seeing which, I cast away all caution, ran to the marquis's quarters and drubbed the door with my fist – so loudly, that a sleepy voice from above called out, "Quiet, there!"

154

There was no response, so I at once lifted the latch, and went in.

There was nothing to be seen, save for a faint patch of pewter-grey where (I supposed) the window was. But my nose told me what my eyes could not: that all was not well, for the air had the close, sour stink of a sick-room.

"Halloo!" I called softly; but there was not so much as a murmur in reply.

I moved forward gingerly, until something struck my shin – which, leaning down, I found to be an empty truckle bed. I edged round it, and found another, about three feet away, beneath a tangled blanket, that still bore a trace of warmth – which made it pretty plain that they must have slept here, and risen no more than half an hour ago; so I could but conclude, that they were among the party I had seen leaving, and that my only chance of rescuing them would be to take Hector and go after them at once. How I might succeed, when I was one man against so many, I could not imagine; but there would be time enough to consider that after I was on my way.

But I was forced to abandon this plan almost as soon as I had conceived it; for while I was fumbling my way back to the door, my attention was caught by something in the corner – a gleam of white, that, even in the gloom, I knew somehow to be skin. I stumbled towards it, dropped to my knees; and – with a jolt that seemed to knock my belly against my lungs – saw a pale cheek and a shadow in the shape of O'Donnell's mouth.

"Are you hurt, Sir?" I said.

He made no answer (I should, indeed, have been astonished if he had); so I put out my hand, and touched his skin. It was damp, but almost cold. I found his tinder-box in his pocket – groped about the floor, until I happened upon a candle – and lit it.

He was lying as if asleep, his coat pulled up about his neck, his shirt crumpled beneath his head to form a pillow. Next to him lay his pistol – which, so far as I could judge, had not been fired; for it was still primed. There was no evidence of a wound on him; but when I took his shoulder and shook it, he did not stir – tho' he was not yet stiff.

I placed my fingers at his throat and could not feel a pulse – so moved them beneath his jaw, and pressed harder – and the next instant received such a shock as might have killed me; for all of a sudden O'Donnell's eyes opened, and he grasped my wrist, and cried out,

"What! – strangle me, would you?" but in so quavery a voice, and with so foul an odour on his breath, that a superstitious man would have supposed he had died and a strange spirit seized his body.

"Dear heaven!" I shouted involuntarily, "– I thought you were dead!" I could feel my own heart thumping like a lunatick in bedlam, and a great spider of sweat starting out and crawling upon my back.

"And might just as well be," he groaned, in the same possessed voice, clutching his forehead – and then lay down again, wincing as his head touched his shirt.

"Whatever is the matter?"

But he only gave another groan; so I looked about, to see if I might discover the answer for myself. And soon discovered an overturned cup – empty, but with a lining of grey scum. I picked it up – sniffed it – and nearly puked; for it had the stink of cheap whiskey, mingled with another, over-ripe smell, that might have been staleness, but I feared was something else altogether.

"I think you have been poisoned, Sir," I said.

He began to shake his head; but the pain of it made him stop and cry out. He covered his eyes with his arm, and moaned: "No – whiskey – you . . . ."

By which I supposed he meant to remind me of my own head-ache the previous morning; so I said: "I was not struck down like this. And besides – 'tis natural, with my constitution, that I should sometimes be worsted by drink; but I have never seen it get the better of you." He said nothing; so I continued: "Who gave it to you?"

"What" (his voice a little more O'Donnell-like) "signifies that?"

"Why, Sir – I should have supposed it to be obvious."

"Well, then," he said wearily: "Niobe."

"Niobe! And how came she by it?"

"'Twas given her, I think, by the marquis."

"Then 'tis he must have adulterated it."

He tried to shake his head again, and repented of it as quickly as before. "Why?" he whimpered pitifully.

"Good G–d, Sir! has he quite pickled your wits? Do you not recall how unwilling he was, at first, to let you come here? And how he then considered, and appeared to change his mind? What was it, do you suppose, made him do that?"

He let out a sigh, that conveyed he did not know – and saw no reason to care, either.

"Unquestionably," I said, "'twas the recollection of this drug – which he doubtless carries to stupefy serving-girls, so he may debauch 'em, and which he suddenly saw he might employ upon you."

"To what purpose?"

My patience was worn almost to the bare threads; but I contrived to keep it from snapping – reflecting that there was no sense in flinging reproaches at him, until he had sufficiently recovered his reason to understand them.

"Why," I said, as calmly as I could, "to take our negroes from us."

Which seemed, at a stroke, to complete the business of waking him; for he sat up with a jolt, grimacing at the pain it caused him, and looked wildly about him, saying: "What! Are they gone?"

I lifted the candle, so he might see. He appeared dazed for a moment – struggled to get up – fell back – then rolled on to his knees, and slowly pushed and prised himself to his feet. He peered into every corner, as if to satisfy himself Niobe and the boy were not hiding; and at last said softly: "Damnable. He must have broken in."

I shook my head. "He did not need to break in, if you recall. He had but to take half a dozen steps from his own door, and lift the latch."

"I do not mean the marquis" (suddenly sharp, and three-fourths like himself again), "I mean Coleman!"

"They were in league. The Frenchman betrayed us, and sold them to Coleman again."

"He would not have done that, Sir, I am certain."

At this, my temper, which had been jerking at its chain like an enraged dog, finally broke free: "I would remind you, Sir, that 'twas you who insisted on bringing Niobe and the boy here – in defiance of my wishes, which you dismissed with your customary arrogance. I should have thought seeing this lamentable result" – kicking one of the deserted beds – "would have been enough to check even your over-grown self-opinion, and make you consider the possibility – for once – that I am right."

"I tell you, he would not deceive us . . ."

"But he has, Sir! Pray observe!"

"I do assure you–"

"By G–d, Sir, your impudence astounds me! First you seek to persuade me some slave-driving American rebel is beyond reproach . . ."

"What do you mean by that?"

"Why, Sir, Mr. Washington, of course! And now you try the same trick with a garlicky French mountebank. It seems a man only has to be an enemy of our country for you to think him the model of perfection."

For a moment he did not respond; then, sucking his breath slowly between his teeth, he turned towards me and said, so quietly I could barely hear him: "Your country, Sir, not mine."

I was quite dumbfounded: it was as if a knife had struck me in the back, and – tho' I knew at once the blow was grievous – I could not yet feel the pain of it, or judge its extent. For which reason I immediately left the room without a word, and latched the door behind me – fearing that if I answered him, before I had time to reflect, I might say or do something I should later regret.

It was some moments before a clear thought at last came to me, tho' (as the rain retreats first from the edge of the storm rather than its heart) it concerned only a marginal point. Debating whether O'Donnell and I could still continue together, or whether the breach between us was irreparable, and each must go his own way, I fell to thinking how we might divide the horses – and suddenly found myself wondering, if there were any left to divide; for would not Coleman have taken the opportunity to repossess them, along with his slaves?

Without pausing to consider further, I immediately ran to the stables – madly hoping I might yet be in time to intercept them, tho' reason told me it could not be so. A fat young ostler lay on a pile of sacks – doubtless thinking that, after being obliged to rise so early for the other party, he might now be allowed an hour or two's rest; but my appearance must have disabused him, for he instantly leapt up, crying: "Whatever is it?"

"Our horses," I panted.

"What of them?"

"Are they still here?"

"If they was here yesternight, they'll be here now," he said sulkily, as if I had no business troubling him with such a foolish question.

"Go and see," I said – and had to clutch my own wrist to keep from cuffing him.

"What's your name?"

"Gudgeon."

He looked at a chalked slate, to find the numbers of the stalls; and then sighed, and led me out, and slowly opened the half-doors, one at a time.

Even in the half-light, I remarked at once that Hector and the rest were all there.

"You see?" he said – with an air of priggish long-suffering that would have incensed a Stoick.

But such were my feelings, I could not rebuke him as he deserved; and instead said: "Here's half a crown. Have 'em saddled in ten minutes."

I set off back towards the marquis's rooms – but instead of going in directly, stopped at the entrance, to try to order my thoughts; for tho' this discovery had naturally relieved my anxiety somewhat, it had added, in about the same measure, to my confusion, and left me more unsure than ever what I should say to O'Donnell. We had, it was true, paid for the horses, through Washington's good offices; but I could not imagine a man as vindictive as Coleman allowing that to deter him from taking them back – particularly when, by doing so, he might materially injure us; for in the middle of the wilderness it would not have been easy to replace them. Which led me to another inconsistency, that I had not perceived before: if it was indeed Coleman I had seen in the yard earlier, and if – as I had hypothesized – Niobe and the boy were among the company that was departing at the same time, why had he not gone with them?

What, then, if I was mistaken? (Here I drew myself further into the shadows; for two figures had emerged from the tavern, and were crossing towards the stables; and I knew I must see danger in every quarter until I had sufficiently recovered myself, to get a bearing on where it really lay.) What if this was not Coleman's doing after all, and the Frenchman had seized the negroes on his own account? It was possible – save that I could think of no conceivable reason why he should have done so; for he was plainly rich and, if he had wanted slaves, could easily have bought himself a pair, without a fraction of the risk and trouble it must have cost to steal them.

I was still ruminating in this fashion, when I heard a noise above me and, before I could conceal myself further, saw O'Donnell on the stair. He clutched the rail, and descended a step at a time, as if the night had aged him fifty years; but he no longer seemed in pain, and his haggard face had taken on a tint of colour, like the first faint blush on a peach – which deepened, when he caught sight of me.

"I am happy to find you, Sir," he said, attempting a smile. "I have something I think will interest you – for it confounds us both."

"What?" I growled – for tho' his manner was conciliatory, I wanted him to know that I was not to be appeased so cheaply.

"This" – handing me a small piece of paper, so creased it must have been folded into a pellet. "'Twas in my boot."

"Your boot!"

He nodded. "A shrewd enough hiding-place, that ensures no-one else will discover it – and that I cannot fail to, as soon as I set my foot on it."

I looked down, and saw but three words: "wEE goE frEE".

"What is the meaning of that?" I said.

"The boy must have written it. He has a smattering of learning."

I shook my head, utterly perplexed.

"Plainly, they concluded 'twas too dangerous to remain with us, when we are so easily followed; and that they would fare better by themselves. And who knows but that they may be in the right?"

I was too amazed to speak; and he went on: "So there is nothing to detain us here; and we should make haste – else we shan't be at Cicero tonight."

Half an hour later, we were on our way.

I am now sufficiently well acquainted with y^r honours to know that what I have just written will provoke a question – so, to save you the trouble, I shall ask it myself: *Why, after all that had passed, did I so readily swallow O'Donnell's account of the negroes' disappearance, and agree to his proposal that we should go on together?*

To which my answer comes under two heads:

1. I had no better explanation of my own to offer, and a strong reason (tho' it shames me to say it) for accepting his: for if Coleman had taken them, I should have felt obliged to pursue him, and attempt to rescue them; whereas if the ungrateful creatures had willingly spurned my protection, without so much as a word of thanks, I should be acquitted of all responsibility for them.

2. Tho' I half-knew that the differences between O'Donnell and me had grown too great to be composed, and must eventually lead to a final parting; yet I hoped it might be deferred for some time yet – by which point (as I thought) I should have found my nephew, and begun my journey back to England, with him for a companion.

And – whatever you may think of my reasoning – it was as well I did.

160

XXV

I shall not try to anticipate y^r honours again.

You ask: *How, exactly, were Coleman and I related?* Which, I concede, at least has some sense to it; for it must seem strange indeed, that two cousins, who scarcely knew each other before, should have so quickly become enemies, when nature commanded them to be friends.

So: my mother, Aunt Fiske and Sally's mother were three sisters, the daughters of a notable Bristol merchant, Mr. Hicks; who – hoping that one of his children, at least, should make a good match, and become a gentlewoman – willed most of his property to my mother, and to any children she might have. This was intended as a sop to my father – who, tho' of good family, had little fortune of his own – and, to begin with, caused little enough ill-feeling. When I was a boy, Sally was as dear as a sister to me – we played and talked without restraint, insensible to any distinction of rank or wealth. But no sooner had she married Mr. Coleman than a chill set in, that by degrees turned summer into winter; and after they returned from America, I never saw her again.

The reason, I think (tho' neither he nor she ever said it directly) was that her husband believed Mr. Hicks's unequal settlement had cheated Sally of her just inheritance – in which, of course, he would have shared, and which their own son would eventually have succeeded to. I can only suppose that young Matthew was schooled in this resentment from the cradle – for, as I hope I have already sufficently shown, I should have been happy enough to jog along with him, at least when we first set out together; but he seems to have viewed me with the most implacable hatred from the beginning.

And that is all the intelligence on the matter I can give you.

The first two hours of our journey to Cicero were pleasant enough: the road easy, and dotted here and there with makeshift little cabins, that in other circumstances would have depressed the spirits, but that were given a look of bright-cheeked cheerfulness by the rising sun. At one of them, a small crowd of fair-haired children jostled from the door as we passed, and cheered us on with waves and halloos – imagining, I suppose, that we were settlers, bound for some still wilder place to the west; which set me wondering why we had never once been received in that manner before, for such parties must have been a familiar sight, on pretty near every road we had taken since Mount Vernon. It was a mile or so before I guessed the answer: that until now, we had been accompanied by Niobe and the boy, whose presence had made us seem like travellers of another sort, and plainly not to be trusted.

You may think me slow, not to have perceived it sooner – and so I was. But the truth is, that first morning I could not keep it in my own head that the negroes were no longer with us, with the result that I was forever looking back, to see they had not fallen behind – and, on discovering (or rather *re*-discovering) the truth, being struck by an odd compound of astonishment and anger and sadness and release, that rushed upon me like a breaking wave, and for a moment sent me reeling.

But their desertion did produce one immediate advantage, that became more evident as the ground began to rise again and the road – unable to scale the slope ahead by a direct assault – crept up on it by degrees: zigging this way, and zagging that, in great treacherous loops. With four riders, we should have been obliged to stop and rest every half-hour; but with only two, we were able to change horses instead, and so maintain a steady pace. Which would, I am convinced, have brought us to Cicero that night – had it not been for an unforeseen accident, that was to have the most momentous consequences.

We had begun to descend the other side, and were already congratulating ourselves on having passed the most taxing part of our journey, when – as I was rounding a bend – Hector abruptly halted. My first thought was to alert O'Donnell, who was close behind – and might have sent both of us rattling over the edge, if he had collided with me. Only then did I see what had frightened the brute: a horse like himself (of which only the rump and tail were visible) lying on the path before us. I dismounted, and continued on foot – observing, first, the rest of the poor creature, which was struggling to get up, and repeatedly falling back again, with piteous snorts of terror; then another nag, standing behind it; and finally an over-turned chariot, that sprawled across the road with one wheel in the air. Of its occupants, however, there was no sign at all – which led me to fear they had been flung on to the hillside below.

I hurried on, intending to see if I might find them, and offer them some assistance, if they were not already past receiving it; but had gone no more than five steps, when a voice called out: "You best stop there, or I'll kill you!"

I could not tell who it proceeded from, for there was still no-one to be seen; but from the sound of it, I guessed it was only a boy. But even a boy may fire a gun, so I obeyed, shouting, as I did so, "I am not alone, and we are armed!" – by which I hoped to intimidate him, and warn O'Donnell, at the same time.

But there was no response; so after a few seconds more I called: "We mean you no harm – only to help you, if we can; and to pass on our way, if we cannot."

"Who are you?" immediately came the reply.

"Gentlemen, engaged upon lawful private business."

I caught the stealthy pad of O'Donnell tip-toeing up behind me, and slipped my hand behind my back, and batted it at him, to keep him from coming further.

"You know there are *banditti* hereabouts?" said the voice at last.

"So we have heard. But you cannot take us for men of that sort!"

"Walk a little nearer."

I took five steps forward – which drew an audible gasp from O'Donnell at my folly – and stopped again.

"Nearer."

"No," I said. "Not until you show yourself."

After a moment, a figure began slowly to emerge from behind the vehicle, in several increments: first the tip of a crude fur hat – then the muzzle of a gun, which was pointed directly towards me – then a delicate, well-coloured face, that looked like no boy's I had ever seen – and finally a slight body, clad in a suit of animal skins that appeared too big for it, and that sagged about the shoulders, like the coat of a bloodhound. For a second or two I was quite confounded – for, try as I might, I could not sufficiently reconcile these conflicting elements to understand what I was looking at.

Then the stranger smiled, and said, "There!" – and at once I knew.

"Your servant, Madam," I said, stammering in my astonishment.

She bobbed her head quite prettily.

"Are you injured?"

"No. But my horses – as you can see – and my chariot . . ."

I called O'Donnell; then approached the vehicle – which, in truth, was hardly more than a sturdy little cart, tho' doubtless well enough suited for such a road as this, that would have shaken an English carriage to splinters in twenty minutes. It must have been thrown on its side with tremendous force; but the only damage I could see was to the wheel on the ground, which had fallen on a jagged rock, that poked between two shattered spokes. A little beyond was a clutter of bags and boxes, which had been heaped up to form a crude parapet – so giving the woman a particle of that protection to the rear that the chariot afforded her to the front.

"What of your husband?" I said.

"I was travelling alone. Save for my servant – who I have sent back to Dexter's."

"What is Dexter's?"

"The next house" – jerking her thumb behind her – "five miles or so that way."

"Is he on foot?"

"My servant? Yes."

O'Donnell at that moment arriving, I turned to him, and said: "To speed matters, one of us should take a horse, and find the fellow, and go with him to the house; while the other stays here with the lady."

"I will happily do either," said O'Donnell, bowing to the woman.

"You are very kind, Sir," she replied instantly. "You cannot miss the way. There is but one turning off the road."

If O'Donnell was as surprised as I was to meet a female that preferred my company to his, he did not show it, but at once set about helping me to make a gap, by shifting the chariot and moving a trunk or two. Then he coaxed two horses through, mounted one of them, and – promising to make all haste – was gone.

The woman watched him out of sight; before turning to me with a smile, and saying: "When I think of who might have happened upon me here, I count myself very fortunate 'twas you."

She was indubitably American; but her speech had a ladylike ease I had not heard for many a week. And its burden was more unfamiliar still; for I could not recall the last time I had been so prettily complimented by a woman – or, indeed, complimented by a woman at all, if I excepted the mad old hag in Bristol that had wanted to make a bigamist of me. For a second or two I was quite tongue-tied; from which condition I could in the end save myself only by imagining what O'Donnell would have said in my place.

"The fortune is ours, to be allowed to serve you."

"Oh! Such gallantry!" she cried, with a light clinking laugh, like a consort of wine glasses. "Will you please to be seated? You must be tired."

She waved me to a box, gracious as a hostess; and nudged another towards me with her foot, which she took for herself. Now I had a plainer view of her, I saw she was a handsome creature of my own age, or a little younger – round-faced, with dark eyes that sparked like a pair of flints when the light caught them, and a sweet curved mouth, petulant in repose, but charming in motion – who, in any other garb, would have been accounted something of a beauty. And perhaps she guessed what I was thinking; for, no sooner had the thought presented itself to me, than she blushed, and tugged at her sleeve, and said: "You must not suppose, Sir, that I would ordinarily appear like this before a gentleman. But a gentleman is the last thing I should have expected to meet on this road." She glanced at the ground; then smiled, as if at some sudden recollection, and looked enquiringly at me again. "Am I permitted to ask, what is the 'lawful private business' you spoke of, that brings you here?"

I told her; and then (so attentive was she) felt encouraged to say more; so that little by little – with nods, and questions, and a look of frank admiration that never left her face – she had pretty much our whole history from me. And I could not help feeling a certain gratification, when I was done, to see that she was moved almost to tears.

"Surely," I said – attempting a jocular tone, but conscious of a pricking in my own eyes, "'tis not so sad a tale as all that?"

She sniffed, and shook her head. "A heroick tale; and one that would make me very proud, if I were your brother. But" – sighing, and turning away – "But . . ."

"What?"

She shook her head again.

"Come – tell me."

She steeled herself to lift her face, and fix her gaze on mine. "I know Miss Catchpole," she said. "Indeed, she lives in my house . . ."

"What – are you then Mrs. Craig?"

"Yes" – her mouth pulled into a misshapen grimace, by the opposing forces of astonishment and dismay. "How did you guess that?"

"From what Mrs. Peckitt said."

"Ah, well . . ." She paused – then, like a horseman taking a hedge, blurted: "You will not find the boy, Sir. He was taken from her."

"What – by savages?"

"Yes – by savages."

This was grim news indeed – the grimmest I could have heard, save that he was dead; tho' I should have been a very great fool to be altogether surprised by it – for had not both Washington and Hickling warned us that it might be so? But there is all the difference in the world between a *possibility*, that leaves room for hope, and a *certainty*, that snatches it away; and I felt like a man approaching a wall of mist, that suddenly finds it is a wall of rock instead.

The shock of which was too great to be absorbed in a moment; so that it was a minute or more before I had gathered up my fugitive thoughts, and begun in earnest to consider the full import of what I had heard. Plainly, it was impossible my quest should now end in Cicero, as I had imagined; but where at length it would take me, and what I should do when I got there, I could not begin to conceive. And even if I succeeded in finding the boy and recovering him, what then? How would Dan (if he was still alive when I returned home, which was far from sure) accommodate himself to a half-Indian son, whose every gesture must recall to him the heartless brutes that had so cruelly used him during the late war?

Most women, I am certain (and most men, too, for the matter of that), would have been unable to resist the urge to say more – immediately plying me with particulars of time, place, and other circumstances, &c. &c.; but Mrs. Craig, with a refined sympathy that would have done credit to a duchess, held her peace – merely watching the effect she had worked upon me, with brimming eyes. But this delicacy allowed another sound – more distressing than any words – to break in upon my reflections: the huffs and scrabblings of the injured horse, which seemed to grow more desperate by the minute, mingling with and inflaming my own anguish; until it became quite intolerable, and – catching up my gun – I sprang to my feet.

"What are you doing?" cried Mrs. Craig.

"I am going to dispatch this poor animal."

"I pray you, Sir" – scrambling up herself – "don't!"

"There is no hope for him, Madam – he is dying, whether I help him to it or no – and you shall have one of ours to make good the loss, I promise you." Saying which, I set the gun to its head, and put the wretched brute out of its suffering.

"Oh . . . Oh . . .!" murmured Mrs. Craig behind me.

I turned, and found her pale, and shivering – as if by pulling the trigger I had blown ten degrees out of the air, and left her suddenly cold. "I am sorry," I said. "Were you very attached to him?"

She shook her head – clutching her elbows, and pulling them to her body. "'Tis the *banditti*," she said.

"What of them?"

"They lurk in the hills; and a shot will bring them looking for carrion. 'Tis for that reason I shouted my warning to you, rather than firing it."

"Well," I said – affecting an assurance I did not feel; for this possibility had never even occurred to me, and I could not but be alarmed by it; "O'Donnell will be back soon, and in the meantime you have me to protect you, if need be." And I loaded my musket again, and squinted along the barrel at an imagined outlaw.

But she only shook her head a second time, and said: "Let us hope there are none near enough to have heard it."

We resumed our seats, and sat for a minute in apprehensive silence; which she at length broke, by saying – with a curious, tentative smile: "You had best go back, Sir."

"What! You cannot suppose I would leave you at this crisis, before help arrives!"

"No, no; I mean after."

I shook my head. "I won't give the boy up now, having come this far and endured so many adventures. I shall go on to Cicero, and see Miss Catchpole, and learn all I can of his capture – and then do whatever I must to retrieve him."

"Miss Catchpole is not there, Sir . . ."

"What!"

"She is gone abroad, upon a matter of business."

"What business?"

"She – she did not say."

"Well – there must be others in the place, who could tell me something."

"No, no – 'tis impossible; the boy is lost, I swear it."

"What is lost may be found again."

"Please, Sir, I implore you: you have no conception of the risk you will be running – and all for nothing."

She gave a little sob, and bit her finger to stifle it; and the next instant the tears that had been slowly gathering in her eyes spilled over, and began to stream down her face. At this (as if they had only been waiting for that signal) my own feelings broke free of all restraint, so that in a moment I was weeping in concert with her; seeing which, she slipped from her box, and kneeled before me on the ground – and I slipped from mine, and kneeled before her – and in a moment (tho' I still do not know how it happened) we were embracing each other, and I felt the feathery touch of her breath on my neck, and heard her murmur, again and again: "Oh, Sir – oh, my poor Sir."

"Madam –" I began. "Dear madam" – but the words choked me.

"Hush," she whispered. "Hush." And slipped her fingers beneath my wig, and stroked my hair.

How many minutes we remained like that, and what the issue might have been, had we continued many more, I cannot tell; but at length there came a moment when I was master enough of my voice to say: "Perhaps, Madam, we might remove to some more . . .?"

To which she responded by clenching her hand to my head, and again whispering, "Hush!" – but this time with an urgency, that at once transformed it from a lullaby into a command.

"What is it?" I asked.

"Hush!" she said again – pulling away, and staring into the trees behind me, as still as a rabbit listening for a fox.

I turned, but could see nothing that might have caught her attention; so repeated my question – mouthing the words, and raising my eyebrows, to avoid speaking it aloud.

And she replied, by miming in her turn: "Do you not hear it?"

And then I did: a surreptitious rustling, close to the ground, perhaps twenty yards away.

"An animal?" I said in dumbshow. "A bear?"

She shook her head. I took up my gun, and began cautiously towards the edge of the forest – but had only gone a pace or two when I heard the sound again, louder and more insistent than before. It was followed, almost immediately, by a shrill whistle, a short distance to the right; and then another, about as far again to the left – which instantly told me, we had no chance of getting away by the road; for whichever direction we took, there would be men waiting to ambush us. And one glance down the steep slope below us was enough to persuade me that, if we attempted to escape that way, we would assuredly break our necks.

I turned back, and found Mrs. Craig frantically trying to fortify our position by piling the baggage at an angle to the chariot, so as to create a kind of simple ravelin, with its point towards the trees. Since it was better to be doing something than merely awaiting our fate like weasels in a trap, I set about helping her – tho' I knew that no precaution we could take would long protect us against an enemy we could not see, and who had the advantage both of greater numbers and higher ground. And I was plainly not alone in thinking so; for after a minute or two a thin, insolent voice called from the forest: "You might as easy spare yourselfs the trouble; for that won't do a piss worth o' nothin' 'gainst us."

I lifted my gun and loosed a shot into the trees; but succeeded only in rousing a bird, that rose screeching into the sky.

For a moment there was silence; then the voice said: "Try that one more time, an' I'll come down there direct and put the bitch's eyes out."

This was greeted by a chorus of sneering laughter from three or four other men, that put me unpleasantly in mind of the Bristol mob, and maddened me beyond bearing.

"I don't know who you are," I shouted; "but you're a d–d coward!" – and the next moment dodged behind the vehicle (where I supposed we should be safest), calling Mrs. Craig to follow me. Which she did; but as soon as I raised my musket again, and tried to find a target among the leaves, she laid her hand on my arm, and whispered: "For G–d's sake – 'tis the *banditti*! Set it down!"

And I reluctantly did so – reflecting that it was my impetuosity had brought this calamity upon her, by making me shoot the horse; and I must not now let it betray me into provoking a worse one. Which left me with but one feeble hope: that the rascals were waiting for the arrival of their leader, before they attacked us (for otherwise, why had they not done it already?); and that O'Donnell might get here before he did, and rescue us.

But this frail straw was snatched from me after only a couple of minutes, by the sound of hurried footsteps approaching from the forest – dunting the earth, and cracking twigs, and skittering stones, with no thought of concealment.

There was a great stirring of boughs; and then a second voice, deeper than the first, and more accustomed to command, cried: "Leave the weapons, and git to the edge!"

I hesitated; for to do so would be to throw away the last possibility of resistance, and leave ourselves utterly exposed. But when I looked for Mrs. Craig, she had already moved – and, with her, my reason for staying; for I could not defend myself, and not her. So I went after her, and stood at her side; and the next moment, the branches opposite to us parted, and a man stepped on to the road.

At first all I remarked was the brace of pistols he was carrying – which continued to occupy my attention until it became plain, from his sauntering manner and the loose way he held them, that he did not mean to discharge them immediately. This gave me leisure to observe that he was a well-made rascal, of about the middle height – with no wig, but a head of chestnut curls, and a pink complexion, that deceived me for a moment into thinking we had been made prisoner by a gang of youths. But then he stopped before us; and I saw a pattern of scars and lines upon his face that must have taken nature thirty or forty years to set there. And his mouth told the same story – for when he opened it to speak, it was entirely devoid of teeth.

"What passed here?" he said.

"One of the horses slipped, and took the other with it," said Mrs. Craig.

He nodded. "And the vehicle?"

"'Tis broke."

He stepped back, and looked appraisingly at the damaged wheel – glancing at us every second or two, to make sure we had not moved. At length he muttered, "'Tis not bad, not so bad" – and then yelled: "Ajax!"

A grey-haired negro – with a cropped ear, and a savage welt running from the corner of his mouth, as if some one had tried to extend it with a knife – limped from the forest, clutching a carpenter's bag, and at once set to work on the fractured spokes.

The captain turned to us again and said: "D'you know who I am?"

"I think so," said Mrs. Craig.

"Say the name."

"Lord Jack."

At this evidence of his fame, he could not resist a little smirk – which, since it showed nothing but gums, gave him the foolish look of a giant baby. But he soon quelled it; and went on: "And what d'you know of me?"

"That – that you will have it all," she said dully.

"Ay, ay," he said softly; and then, putting back his head to call to his hidden accomplices behind him: "D'you hear that? We will have it all!"

170

Which they saluted with a disorderly tattoo of cheers and whistles.

"And what else d'you know?" he said, inclining his head, and frowning intently into Mrs. Craig's face.

"You give but one warning."

"Ay. And if you heed not that?"

"You will blow our brains out."

"She has her lesson by heart," he said, nodding and turning to me. "I hope you have learned it as well." Then he swung up his arm, like a school-master setting boys to a race, and shouted: "Let us to work!"

At which signal, the rest of his company streamed from the trees – a spotty lad (that I supposed had spoken to us first); another negro; and – to my astonishment – a pair of bare-armed women in filthy breeches, with kerchiefs about their heads and muskets in their hands, and powder-horns swinging from their belts. Last of all came a quick, scampering little fellow, who seemed of a different order altogether – for he was somewhat older than the captain, and only three-fourths as tall; and had you seen him in any place but this you would have taken him for a tradesman, or clerk to an attorney. While the others began to pillage the bags, he presented himself before Lord Jack, like a terrier-dog eager to please its master – smiling up into his face, and wiggling his fingers, to show their readiness for whatever they might be commanded to do.

"Take up their guns," said Jack, staring at me all the while.

The little fellow at once set about it, squirming with pleasure – as if, having no tail, he must wag his whole body.

"Now," said Jack, cocking one his pistols, and waving it in my face; "where is it?"

I flinched, but said nothing.

He drew in an unsteady breath, and bulged his eyes.

"Come, Sir," muttered Mrs. Craig hastily, before he could speak again. She nudged me – thrust a purse under my nose – shook it, to make sure I had remarked it – and tossed it on the ground. Then she slipped her hand beneath her coat, and drew out a little jewel-box, which she threw after it.

The fellow's finger twitched on the trigger – and seeing there was no help for it, I reached for my own money; consoling myself, as I did so, by the recollection that there was more in my saddle-bags, that might yet be spared: for O'Donnell had secured our horses some way off, where the rogues had still not found them. Which led me to another thought, that stirred the last embers of hope, and brought them flickering back to life: was I not also carrying something else, that might prove an effective weapon against these desperadoes?

"Here is my pouch, Sir," I said, dangling it before him – and exerting my best talents to sound as O'Donnell had done in my hearing on so many like occasions. "But I counsel you to consider before taking it – for it will assuredly cost you your neck."

The effect was immediate – and far more gratifying than I could have conceived possible. The fellow shrank back – his vacant mouth dropped open – and for a moment he appeared overcome with confusion. Then he steadied himself, and said: "Say it again."

But having gained some small advantage, I was not easily going to relinquish it; so I replied: "You heard, well enough."

He stared at me a few seconds more, and then turned to the little man – who seemed as confounded as he was, and looked from him to me and back again with a wondering expression. "Why will it cost me my life?" asked Jack – in a voice from which all the bravado had drained away, leaving only a sour lee of anxiety.

"Because we travel under the protection of a gentleman, who will hang any man that robs or abuses us."

Jack glanced at the little fellow again – who at once nodded, as if I had confirmed something he already suspected.

"If you doubt it," I said, "I have a letter will soon settle the point."

He held out his hand.

"It is not here," I said. "I must fetch it."

He hesitated a second; then turned abruptly to the small fellow, and said, "Go with him. If you're not back in ten minutes" – here nodding at Mrs. Craig – "I shall kill her."

I set off, with the man-terrier trotting at my side. He still carried my gun, but paid it so little heed I could easily have grabbed it from him, as soon as we were out of sight. But what (tho' I did briefly consider it) should I have done then? I might have escaped myself – tho' even that was doubtful, when the *banditti* knew the mountains so much better than I did – but in doing so would have condemned poor Mrs. Craig to certain death.

"I am Tobias Tanner, Sir," he said. He waited for me to give my name in return; and then, when he saw I meant to remain silent, hurried on: "These are difficult times, I fear, Sir – difficult times. When 'tis hard always to know our enemies from our friends."

His speech had a Welsh edge to it, that led me to conjecture he was a transported thief, who (knowing no other life) had taken up the same occupation in this country, that had torn him from his own. And, as if to prove it, he pulled his head forward, to reveal a rash of raw pink skin about the neck, that looked as if it had been caused by a whipping.

"See!" he said. "See what my neighbours did to me!"

It occurred to me that a criminal should count himself fortunate to have received no worse punishment – but I was resolved not to humour him by saying more than I was obliged to; so held my tongue.

He made no attempt to interfere with me, or to pilfer anything on his own account, while I was removing the letter – tho' on the way back, he did importune me, like a child demanding a toy, saying: "Let me have it! Let me have it!"

"No," I replied. "'Tis for your captain"; and lifted it out of his reach, to make it plain I should not relent.

Seeing which, he wheedled sulkily: "He will only give it to me himself, for he don't read."

And so, indeed, it turned out – tho' Tanner himself was little better, and had to mumble the words aloud to construe them. And when he came to the end, it took him two or three runs at the signature before he had it: "Wa-shing-ton."

Which instantly wrought the most violent change I had ever seen in a man: his lips bubbled, making him dribble and spit; then he flung himself at me – kicking, scratching, cuffing, and heaping upon me such a deluge of insults as I had never heard – and cannot record for y^r honours now, since some of them I did not know, and most of the rest I had never seen writ down.

"Did you not see – did you not see?" I cried, parrying his blows as well as I could – for all I could conceive was that he had somehow mistook the name for another.

"Ay, we saw well enough," said the captain, approaching, and dragging the terrier off. "We are for the King and the governor, and your protector is a – scoundrel."

I could not have been more astonished if I had heard a pig preach a sermon; for I swear to y^r honours, Jack and his crew were the likeliest-looking set of rebels you ever laid eyes on.

"Take off your clothes," said the captain; and then, when I did not respond, struck my face with his pistol, and repeated with a roar: "Take off your clothes!"

I could think of but one reason why he should want us naked: so that our clothing should not be damaged when they murdered us, and might be added to their booty. But seeing Mrs. Craig begin to undress, I did the same; for all that was left to me now was to share her fate.

XXVI

My own feelings broke free of all restraint, and I began to weep in concert with her.

It is this you seize from what I gave you yesterday, to examine me upon. Why, for Heaven's sake? Surely even the most assiduous lawyer could not hope to turn my tears against me – especially when I have furnished him so much else that is more suited to his purpose? Or are y^r honours mere automata, with engines in place of hearts, whose only object in keeping me here is to learn what it is to be human?

A singular idea – but written only half in jest; for I cannot, at present, think of another hypothesis that better explains your questions.

But – in any event – to take up *this* question: *What feelings am I speaking of, and why did they overwhelm me?*

Surely it cannot be hard to guess the answer? Consider my situation: I had come half across the world, in pursuit of a boy that had just, once again, been snatched from my grasp; I had endured fatigue and hardship and danger on the way, and could now be certain of nothing, save that worse ordeals lay ahead; and in the midst of all, I had stumbled upon a woman, that had shown me such sympathy and tenderness as I had not known since I was a child. Is it so unaccountable that I should have been unmanned by these contradictory experiences, and the reflections they provoked? It is not strange to me, at least: for I have always found that it is only when they are alloyed with their opposites that sadness and sweetness, hope and regret, exert their most powerful effect on us.

And now – since y^r honours appear curious about such matters – I shall resume my story, by recording my emotions at the critical juncture where we left it. I have heard Dan speak of the minutes when he was wounded and made prisoner as being like a dream, and there

174

was something dream-like about this too; for I seemed to have been plucked from my own life, and at the same time to be observing it – as sometimes we may see ghosts or monsters while we sleep, and yet know they are but fancy, and we shall soon wake. But here there was this one difference: that the sleeping state seemed more real than the waking. Time had slowed, almost to one eternal tick of the clock; my fingers fumbled with buckles and buttons, that had been familiar enough in the humdrum world, but were grown strange and awkward in this one; and no more than two yards away, Mrs. Craig undressed before me – revealing such secrets as, even then, I could not look upon without a misplaced pang, that had me sorrowfully imagining a happier scene. And beyond her, our captors busied themselves: Tanner and the captain, a little apart, huddled together in private conference; the carpenter attended to the wounded spokes, as impervious to everything about him as a surgeon at a sick-bed; and the rest tugged hats and shoes and dresses from the baggage, and laughingly squabbled as to which should try them on – so that as quickly as Mrs. Craig removed one set of her clothes, they seemed to be bedecking themselves in another. And all happening in a kind of sluggish dumbshow, as if they were moving through water.

After I know not how long (it might have been five seconds or five hours), Tanner nodded abruptly, and hurried away to join the rest – who immediately left off their plundering and began to gather sticks and tinder, as if they meant to make a fire. Jack waited a moment, and then sidled towards us – shaking his head, and smiling, as a man does at the anticks of an idiot. He was evidently trying (incredible tho' it may seem) to tempt us into enquiring what had diverted him – as if, instead of his victims, we were no more than two idle acquaintances in an ale-house. When we failed to indulge him, he could contain himself no longer, and – with a glance towards the terrier-man – said: "He is for tarring and feathering you – as his fellows did him." And began to laugh.

"Tarring and feathering!" I cried – my voice swelling with the sudden hope, that this was the worst we might expect.

"Afore we hang you," he replied. "I said to him, 'How long d'you suppose we'd need to tarry here, to git down trees enough for the pitch, and birds for the feathers?'"

I was too amazed and horrified to reply; indeed, it was all I could do to keep from fainting clean away.

"What need the fire, if we are to hang?" said Mrs. Craig. I turned, and a little wedge of admiration forced its way into my fearful heart; for tho' she was trembling, her face and voice were still defiant.

"To put a brand upon you."

"A brand!" I repeated – scarce able to grasp the meaning of the word.

"Ay. A letter. I knows the shape of 'im, but not 'is name" – here inscribing a large 'R' in the air with his finger. "For 'rebel', see? I said 'twould be soon enough to do it after, but Tanner's got a snick o' learnin', an' he says a dead man's skin don't take it so good as a livin'. Nor a dead woman's, neither."

Which suddenly seemed to clear the confusion from my head; and I plainly saw what I must say:

"You may take Colonel Washington's letter as proof that I am guilty of some offence – tho' I strongly deny it; but this woman, I swear, is entirely innocent of any connection with either me or him. We are not travelling together – we do not know each other – we only met here, not an hour since."

"Why, then, you must skip pretty quick," he said, with a gummy leer – as pink and wet as a fresh wound.

"What do you mean?"

"Gus there" (jerking his thumb at the spotty boy, who was feeding the fire, and puffing it into a blaze) "says you was toyin' and pettin' when he see you."

"We – we –" I stammered; but could think of nothing more to say that would not merely expose us to further ridicule.

"If you're so sensible of her feelin's, we'll mark you first, and leave her till after," said Jack.

"For G–d's sake, why should we be branded at all?" asked Mrs. Craig spiritedly.

He lifted his eyebrows in surprise, as if he had supposed it too obvious to require explanation. "Why," he said, "to let 'em know you wasn't murdered, but killed accordin' to the law. Ajax there" – nodding towards the negro carpenter, who was now in earnest conversation with Tanner – "is a handy enough fellow; and he'll bend a fork or a spoon so neat it'll singe you clean as a lawyer's seal."

At which (as if he had been only waiting for this introduction before beginning) Ajax picked up his hammer, took a sliver of metal from his tool-bag, and – using a slab of rock as a makeshift anvil – began to beat it into shape.

I cannot say exactly why, but it was the sight of his thick forearm rising and falling, and the clanging death-march metre of his blows, that finally bore in upon me the reality of what was about to happen to us. And all at once I knew that I was not going to submit to being scorched like a bull-calf and then led to the gallows like a common pickpocket: I should (if I could) exact some price for my death, that would oblige them to shoot rather than hang me – and in doing so try to create enough confusion to give Mrs. Craig a chance of escape. But there was no time to reflect upon it further: if I failed to act now, the opportunity would be gone.

Perhaps y^r honours, in a like case, might have been able to devise another plan; but I could think of nothing better than to attempt to disarm him, and then – if possible – keep him hostage for long enough to deter his friends from following Mrs. Craig. So I stiffened abruptly – drew in my breath – and stared past his shoulder (muttering "Good G–d!" as I did so), in hope he should suppose I had observed something astonishing there, and would be unable to keep himself from looking to see what it was. And so it proved; whereupon I launched myself across the five yards separating us.

I reached him just as he was turning back – chopped one of the pistols from his hand – and contrived to knock him to the ground, and leap on top of him, crying to Mrs. Craig: "Run! Run!" But I had no leisure to see if she heeded me; for Jack was thrashing and jerking beneath me like an unbroken horse, and it was all I could do to keep my seat, and stop him grasping me by the throat, and squeezing the life from me. We struggled so for some seconds, grinding and bouncing in the gritty dirt – first one of us, and then the other, having the advantage; but always making so confused a target that his friends could not have shot me without the near-certainty that they would hit him, too. But then suddenly he began to scratch at my face, forcing me to screw up my eyes in defence, and in the same instant drew up his legs so violently that I was thrown a foot or more into the air. I was not quite toppled, even then; but as I came down again, my knee struck a sharp stone, which robbed me of breath, and paralysed me. Tho' the effect was only momentary, it was enough to allow him to scuttle from under me like a rat from beneath a log-pile, and scramble slithering to his feet.

I flung myself after him, but he skipped back, and I fell on a slab of raw rock, jarring my wrist and grating my cheek.

I tried to rise, but he delivered such a kick to my shoulder as drove all the force from my muscles and spun me on to my back.

I was powerless to move.

I saw him retrieve the fallen pistol, and poke it through his belt.

I saw him cock the other, and raise it towards me.

I saw his fellows press about him, with the hushed curious faces of a crowd at a publick execution.

I shut my eyes. I did not mean to, but I could not help myself.

I held my breath.

I heard a discharge, and felt a blow to my hand, that stung the skin but did not seem to enter it. From which I concluded that he had somehow missed, and the bullet had done no more than graze me on the rebound.

I held my breath again.

A second shot. But this one did not touch me at all – and was followed by a loud *ouf!* from the captain, and a sudden explosion of cries and curses from his companions, and the slap and clatter of running feet.

I opened my eyes.

Jack was lying on his face – his legs twitching – a forked trickle of winish blood spilling from his nose. Beyond him, the rest of the gang were buzzing like wasps in a bottle: knocking and tripping each other as they snatched up weapons, and casting about wildly (as we had, not an hour before) for some scrap of shelter that might protect them. But they were too late: three or four unseen guns fired from the forest above us, and the negro carpenter and one of the women fell to the ground. At which the rest immediately fled roaring along the road, or dropped frantically over the edge, in hope (I suppose) that they might save themselves by clinging to a root or a snag until the danger had passed.

There was a few seconds' pause – then a tall, big-shouldered young fellow carrying a musket pushed through the trees and sprang down before me. His face was weathered dark as a ripe apple; he wore no wig, but only a muddy nest of fair hair, bleached almost white in the sun, that looked as if it had been thatched on to his head by starlings; his breeches were torn and mud-stained, and his shirt grey with filth. Behind him came O'Donnell, and a small figure dressed in animal skins, that I took to be Mrs. Craig's servant; and then two more straw-haired youths – who, from their likeness to the first, must have been his brothers.

"You are not wounded, Sir?" said O'Donnell anxiously, hurrying towards me.

"No, thank G–d! You . . ." But I could not say more; and, naked as I was, put my arms about him, and wept on his neck.

He patted my back; and then gently pushed me away. "I know not how you come to be in this condition," he began, "but–" But then he suddenly broke off again, and – looking past me – murmured: "Ah, I see."

I turned, and saw Mrs. Craig emerging from behind a bush and advancing towards us. She had crooked one arm over her breasts, and dangled the other hand before her privates – but it was evidently modesty, not shame, that made her do so; for she walked beneath our admiring gaze as proudly as a queen entering a banqueting hall, and with as much consciousness that it was her due. And, indeed, I do not believe there is a man living that would not sooner have seen the jewels nature had bestowed on her than the most gorgeous diadem in the world.

"I compliment you, Sir," said O'Donnell – with something close to wonder in his voice.

"No," I replied. "'Tis not what you suppose . . ."

"Well" – very softly – "whatever the case . . . I think you should dress yourself. The Dexters are none too delicate. But that" – nodding at the little skin-clad servant, who was was trotting towards Mrs. Craig – "is another woman." And he caught my coat on the end of his gun-barrel – lifted it like a bedraggled standard – nudged it into my hands – and left abruptly to rejoin his companions.

I gathered up the rest of my clothes, and slunk behind the overturned vehicle to pull them on. But was only half done, when I heard a sudden commotion not twenty yards away: a cry – a meaty thump – a groan – and then O'Donnell shouting: "No!"

My first thought was that one of the brothers, his blood already heated with victory, might have been inflamed beyond endurance by the sight of a naked woman, and offered her some insult; so I hastened out again from my makeshift dressing-room, hauling at my breeches, and buckling my belt. But at once saw I was mistaken: for Mrs. Craig and her servant were nowhere to be seen, and the Dexters were all visibly still engaged upon bloodier business. The younger two were stripping the bodies of Jack and his female accomplice, with a slow, butcherly manner that suggested their victims were either dead, or past all possibility of resistance; while the oldest stood with O'Donnell beside the black carpenter – who was evidently still alive, and employing every desperate tactick he could devise to remain so. His eyes were white with terror; he writhed and kicked like a wounded rabbit, and clasped his calloused fingers in prayer – jerking them upwards, and muttering: "I's a good negro, I's a good negro . . . please . . ."

Dexter settled his grip on his gun, and pulled back the hammer.

"For God's sake!" said O'Donnell, laying a hand on his arm.

"He's no more 'n an animal," said Dexter, shaking it off again.

"This was not his doing," I said, approaching them. "He wasn't armed."

Dexter shook his head. "He's only a carpenter."

"He won't suffer so much this way, 'n if they take 'im agin . . . Runaway slave's goin' to be hanged, or cut up good, 'n' nailed to a tree."

"I's not a runaway!" said the wretched fellow. "Lor' Jack, he steal me!"

Dexter gave a foxy grin, that plainly said, *He's lying, and he'll not fool me* – then cleared his throat – spat on his boot – and aimed his gun.

"He can go with us–" I began. But before I could say more, Dexter had calmly crooked his finger about the trigger, and sent a bullet into poor Ajax's skull. Then, without a glance at either O'Donnell or me, he ambled off to join his brothers – carelessly blowing a country air between his lips, as if he could not be troubled to whistle it in earnest.

It was that that finally undid me. I waited for the sound of the shot to fade; but it gathered strength instead, echoing from the hillsides, and then entering into my own skull – bringing with it a great oily swell of darkness, that surged through my head, and churned my belly like sea-sickness. I retched and vomited – tho' I had eaten nothing for hours; and then, fearing my legs would no longer carry me, staggered to the vehicle again – set my back against it – and slid to the ground. O'Donnell was pacing up and down – his fingers thrumming on the hilt of his sword; his face so pale and hollow it might have been carved from chalk – plainly too occupied with his own thoughts to help me order mine. Which rampaged, in consequence, unchecked through my exhausted mind – a strange, jostling mix of thankfulness and anger and disgust – made the more confusing by all having the same object.

What liberated me at length from this dismal reverie was a surprise, as delightful as it was unexpected. I was staring numbly into the distance when, all at once, Mrs. Craig and her servant slipped out from beyond an untidy jumble of her boxes – where, I immediately guessed, she must have gone for the same purpose that had taken me behind the chariot. But while I had merely put on again the dusty travelling clothes that Jack had forced me to take off, she had got herself up entirely anew in a soft blue dress, and a broad hat decked with ribbons.

She looked about her anxiously, frowning and sucking her lips, until she saw me – when she suddenly laughed, and gave a frisky, coltish toss of the head, and picked her way towards me – tho' all the while looking at the ground, like a child that has glimpsed the sun, and turned away again, for fear of being dazzled.

"Now," she said, as she drew close, holding her hands towards me, and blushing. "Now, Sir, at last – I am fit company for you!"

I recall little of the next few hours – save in one particular, to which the rest is no more than the plain setting (as it were) that holds a precious gem, and shows it off to especial advantage. So: I cannot tell you how long it took us to get to Dexter's farm, but only that Mrs. Craig asked me to travel with her in her chariot, which had been patched back into a serviceable condition by the unfortunate Ajax; and that on the way she pressed herself against me, and laced her fingers through mine, and teased my bruised shoulder with her lips, murmuring *that she would soon make it better* – all beneath the eyes of her servant, and the brothers, and O'Donnell, which, altho' it occasioned me some surprise and embarrassment, yet I could not but find gratifying, for it must surely testify to the warmth of her feeling for me, that she was willing to make so publick a display of it.

I remember that the house, when at last we got there, was as rough as most of the others we had seen, tho' somewhat larger; that we were greeted by the Dexters' mother, and two or three sisters; and that the whole family showed Mrs. Craig particular attention, repeatedly telling her that she was welcome, and insisting that she should have a room of her own – which the girls furnished her by yielding up their own bed and withdrawing to share their mother's. I remember, too, sitting at supper in a cold parlour, badly lit by filthy tapers; but of the meal itself nothing save the constant sense of Mrs. Craig's gaze upon my cheek, as hot and bright as a lamp. And then seeing her rise, at the end, and make her excuses, saying, "It has been somewhat of a hard day," and begin towards the door – dropping, as she rustled past me, a pellet of paper, that fell at my feet, and that I supposed must be a note, tho' I had not remarked her writing it.

I remember leaning down, as discreetly as I could, and picking it up, and unfolding it, and reading: *You know where to find me. MC*

I know that, for propriety's sake, O'Donnell and I lingered a while longer, talking to Mrs. Dexter – but have so far forgotten the subject, or what any of us said, that you might show me a transcript of our conversation, and I should not recognize my own part in it; for all I was aware of was the dryness of my mouth, and the buzzing throb in my temple, and the thought of Mrs. Craig naked again, and in bed.

At last, after what he plainly thought a decent interval (his judgement in such matters was always admirable), O'Donnell got up; and – wishing the family good night – we went up-stairs ourselves, where he immediately lay down, and closed his eyes, and within a minute was breathing as gentle and regular as a child in a cradle. Whether he was really so soon asleep, or merely feigning it, out of delicacy, I could not say – and, in truth, I did not greatly care.

I thrust my head out – heard distant voices and a clatter of dishes, from which I knew the Dexters must still be below – crossed quickly to Mrs. Craig's room, and knocked lightly.

There was a murmur from within, so muffled by the thickness of the wood I could make out none of the words. But the tone was unmistakable; so I lifted the latch, and went in.

"Is that you, Sir?"

"Yes."

A long sigh – in which satisfaction and anticipation seemed to collide, and gradually shudder into silence. Then: "Shut the door, and come to bed."

There was but one small, unglazed window; and despite the chill she had left the shutter open, making a square of dim misty moonlight. But it was not, to begin with, enough to see by; so I found my way instead by smell – which was easy enough, for, masking the stench of smoke and farmyard filth, there was a marked scent of rose-water, that grew stronger with every step I took towards her. And then I heard the whisk of a sheet being thrown aside, and felt a pilot-hand reach out, to draw me in, and the heat of her body on mine; and then, at length, saw the pale glow and charcoal shadows of her bare skin. At which – tho' I had resolved to be quiet – I heard myself gasp, and cry out.

"What is the matter?" she whispered.

My throat was so clogged I could not reply, save with a kind of spluttering guffaw.

"I see," she said – and gave a little laugh herself, like the sound of leaves ruffled by a breeze. "Well, so long as it is nothing worse than that, I think I know the very thing for it."

Whereupon she found the breach in my shirt – slid her fingers through it – and drew them lingeringly down my chest, and on to my belly.

Only to discover . . .

But perhaps y^r honours may guess what she discovered – for I dare say your own experience of the world has taught you the lesson I learned at that moment: that a man is the most contrary creature in existence. For an hour or more, a brisk gale had been carrying me towards her – maintaining me at such a pitch of readiness as had obliged me to cross my legs and keep my coat hugged about me, so Mrs. Dexter and her girls might not see it. And now, just as I neared port, the wind had suddenly dropped – unstiffening my mainsail, and leaving it flapping uselessly before the harbour mouth.

"O, dear," she murmured. "What is this?"

"I – I . . ." But I could not say more.

"O – my poor gentleman! Let me see if I can help."

Which only added to my confusion; for the solicitude with which she said it put me strangely in mind of Aunt Fiske; with the result that, tho' she tried every art I could have imagined (and some I could not) to stir up the storm, and set me under way once more, my traitorous little bark remained stubbornly becalmed.

"Why are you not easy with me?"

Until that instant I could not have said – but the question itself seemed to furnish its own answer: for there was none of her former coquetry in it, but only a sadness and uncertainty that nearly broke my heart. And I knew then, it was *that* was troubling me: her frailty – our frailty; the naked vulnerability of this warm flesh, waiting patiently in the dark for mine, that might now – if O'Donnell had lost his way, or the Dexters had been from home, or a horse had stumbled, or any one of a million other small accidents had occurred – be cold and hard, and suffering the first touch of corruption.

"I almost killed you," I said.

"No!"

"I almost caused you to be killed, which is no better."

"But you" – placing her fingers on my cheek – "you were not to know."

I shook my head, but she did not remove her hand.

"You did nothing but from kindness," she said. "And I am sensible – very sensible, Sir – that you were ready to die for me, if you could."

"That is true. But – O my G–d! – it was near." And I began to weep.

"We are near death a hundred times a day," she said, raising her face to mine, so that her breath caressed my ear. "But look – we are still alive. We are alive! There! There! Come!" and slipped her fingers to my neck, and lay back, and drew me on to her.

And then, at last, the rigging strained, and the canvas filled.

XXVII

Y^r honours do not burden me this morning with so much as a word. I shall not presume to conjecture what the reason may be for your silence; but merely accept it gratefully, and return directly (as perhaps you are eager to do) to Mrs. Craig's bed.

I dreamed that night I was at home, and came upon an attick I had not known existed. I was fearful of opening the door, but willed myself to do it – to discover within a brood of curly-haired children, who as soon as they saw me set up a squalling chorus of *Papa! Papa!*, like so many hungry nestlings. I knew that I had somehow forgotten them, and that they would die if I did not ensure that they were fed at once; but – tho' I acknowledged them to be mine – I had not the least idea who their mother was, or where I might find her. And had just gone out again, to look for her, when I heard a leisurely, regular *chop-chop-chop*, that was at first part of the dream (where it proceeded from a great beast lumbering across the stable-yard), and then abruptly jolted me awake.

The room was dark, save for the first bleary glimmer of dawn at the window; Mrs. Craig slept peacefully at my side; the only sound in the rest of the house was the squeak and murmur of the timbers. The racket that had roused me came from without, and I could not immediately guess its cause – for some blows seemed no more than a whispering *shweek*, while others were a distinct *chink*. But considering the hour, and the place, and the dreadful events of the day before, it was impossible not to hear danger in it. What if the remnants of Jack's gang had re-assembled, resolved to take revenge – and were at this very moment constructing a fortification, from which to attack us? Or (more probably) demolishing an outbuilding, intending to use the wood as tinder to fire the house?

I got up from the bed, and squeezed my head through the casement. At first I could make out nothing but two or three dark smudges in the haze, which I took to be sheds and sties; but then, a little beyond the furthest of them, I saw a dark line and a small sliver of silvery-white with a round patch of grey at the end of it, that must be the source of the noise – for they moved up and down, up and down with every beat. I stared intently at them for some seconds, trying to arrange them into a familiar shape, before they suddenly resolved themselves, into an arm wielding a hoe, and a bare back, and a shaggy helmet of hair. From which I instantly knew, I was looking at the oldest Dexter boy.

My fear was gone; but for some reason the sight of him kept me at my peep-hole. My watch – which I could half-read by tilting it towards the east – told me it was not yet six o'clock; and yet here he was, already at work, chipping a little field from the rocky ground, where ten (or even five) years ago, there had been only raw forest. It seemed little less than astonishing to see such resolve – such pitiless disregard for his own comfort, or anything that might deflect him from his daily labour – in a youth that, not twenty hours before, had saved two lives, and taken three others. I could not, at that moment, have said whether I marvelled more at the hardiness of his spirit or the hardness of his heart; but this I plainly saw: that only a fool would choose to make an enemy of such a man, if he might hope to keep him for a friend instead.

As I watched, the rising sun thinned the mist to threads – spinning them into a yellow gauze, that spread slowly westward, until it reached Dexter, lighting the gold of his head, and the sparkling pearls of sweat on his skin. And then it moved on, gradually but inexorably, towards the black tangle of the wilderness, that had never yet known an axe or a plough – but (it suddenly struck me) was destined to fall before them, as surely as it was to feel the warmth of the coming day.

185

And perhaps I had still not entirely shaken off the grip of sleep; for I at once saw, in a kind of dream, how it would be then – the trees razed; a frame-work of walls and fences laid over the billowing hills; the angles and creases between them full of inns and churches and snug houses with smoking chimneys; and the rough roads scattered with crowds of playing children, who laughed, and jostled, and raced each other to the top of every rise, to set their gaze further to the west again. Among whom I glimpsed not only an entire regiment of little Dexters, but also (I thought) four or five infants like those in my dream – who, now I came to reflect, bore a strong resemblance to Mrs. Craig. Seeing which blurred my eyes, and made me giddy – so that I was obliged to withdraw abruptly, and turn back to the room.

Mrs. Craig was still asleep; but when I sat down beside her she stirred; opened her eyes; cast about uncomprehendingly for a moment; and then – evidently remembering where she was, and with whom – smiled, and laid a hand on my wrist.

"What is the time?" she asked.

I told her.

"Tch!" – clutching the sheet to her throat, and wriggling herself upright – "I must be up, then."

"Why so early?"

"I have lost a day – when I could ill afford it; for I was already late."

"Late for what?"

"An engagement," she said – then coloured, and added hurriedly: "A matter of business."

"Will you not tell me what it is?" – tho', in truth, I imagined I knew; for I could conceive but one answer that would bring a blush to *her* cheek.

She shook her head; but then – evidently guessing my thoughts: "But it is not what you suppose."

She had been so frank with me before, and spoke with such sincerity now, I could not but believe her – which naturally only made me all the more curious to find out the truth. But before I could interrogate her further, she smiled shyly, and lowered her eyes; and – letting the sheet drop – put out her arms towards me.

"Come here, Sir. There is something I must say to you."

It can have been no more than a few seconds before she continued; but that was time enough – so much nimbler are our minds than our tongues – for a whole pack of speculations to chase each other through my brain. Did she mean merely to relive the pleasures of last night before we parted; or had she grown so fond of me she could not bear to think of our being parted at all? Was it even possible she harboured some notion that our connection might be permanent? In which case . . .

"There are men and women live in the same house for thirty years," she murmured, "who do not see what we have seen together in a single day. Which makes us . . . more to each other, than many a married couple."

"Indeed—"

"Hush" (laying a finger on my lips). "So that I feel I may justly say, I have some claim upon your life."

"Yes. And I upon yours."

She sighed unsteadily, and then was silent – as if she could not continue until she had mastered her emotions; which unleashed my tumbling thoughts again. Was it true, then, that she really hoped to be my wife? And if so, must I inevitably disappoint her, by telling her I already possessed such an article; or could that difficulty somehow be overcome? Might I not simply stay in America – marry her here in the back-country, where no man knew me or my circumstances – share her property – strive to enlarge it – and breed a fine family to inherit it?

I had never before entertained such an idea – the audacity of it quite stopped my breath; but once it had taken root, it proved (to my amazement) strong enough to resist every argument I could fling against it. Yes – I should have to leave Mrs. Gudgeon; but what would be the harm in that, when our relation afforded her no pleasure, and she could better enjoy my estate without me? Yes – I was ignorant of almost every point about Mrs. Craig that society considers necessary for a man to know about his bride; but was not what I *had* learned at least as sure a foundation for a contented marriage as discovering the history of her parents and the size of her fortune?

"So when you hear what I have to ask," she continued at length, "I pray you will remember that . . ." But she still did not have command enough of herself to finish; and broke off again – swallowing so hard, I felt the working of her throat against my cheek.

The next instant, I was astounded to hear myself say: "You may find I agree more readily than you think."

She could not answer, but sniffed, and clung to me.

187

"I am no longer young," I went on; "and you . . . are not a girl. Fate gives us few chances of happiness; and –" (Here I faltered; for my voice seemed locked in my throat, and it was a moment before I could free it again.) "And if we do not seize this one, G–d knows if either of us will ever have another."

She shook, and squirmed her face into my neck, streaking it with warm tears.

"Madam!" I cried. "Dear madam! Come with me, and help me to look for my nephew; and after, let us pledge to keep company with one another all our lives –"

She thrust herself away from me – like a woman troubled by a festering thorn, who has resolved at last to pluck it out.

"I cannot," she sobbed.

"Why not? Have you a husband still living?"

She shook her head. "And you – you must not go on, Sir. That is my demand; and the last I shall make of you, I promise: give up your search for the boy. You have no prospect of finding him, and every prospect of – of – being – O!" And she renewed her weeping, more helpless than before.

I felt the prize slipping from my fingers – and, in my eagerness to lay hold of it again, blurted out, without pausing to reflect: "If you will not go with me, then let me go with you!"

She frowned, and bit her lip, and looked down at her clenched hands. Then she drew herself up; and – tugging the sheet about her again – said quietly: "This Fate of yours is a sarcastick fellow."

"Perhaps he is in earnest –"

"No" – tossing the idea aside, with a jerk of her chin – "if he had been in earnest, he would have contrived this encounter twenty years ago. We have been upon our own paths too long."

"But if I am willing to leave mine, and follow yours . . .?"

"It is not possible. You cannot cast off the history that made you what you are, and begin afresh." She sighed softly – as if I were no more than dandelion down, and an ill-considered puff might blow me clean away. "Go back to your brother, Sir, and tell him you did all you could to discover his son, and let him resign himself to dying without an heir."

It was the slap of cold water that returns a drunk man to sobriety. I sat in a sluggish daze, wondering at what, but a minute ago, I had come so near to sacrificing: my honour, my occupation, and the last hope of contentment for Dan. And all (I was forced to concede) for a chimera, that would almost certainly have vanished again as quickly as it had appeared.

"You are right," I said, rising. My skin was still tender from the impress of her body, and the sudden touch of the chill morning air made me shiver – telling me, in its own manner, what she had: that I was, and must remain, alone. And yet there was something salutary about it – a wintry satisfaction in having acknowledged the truth, and resumed the burden of duty.

"O! – I am glad to hear you say so!" she cried. "Will you go home directly, then?"

"No – I shall continue on my way."

"But–"

"I cannot forget my obligations, any more than I can my name."

"But you have fulfilled them already – more than fulfilled them! I can think of few men who would have done so much, and none that would have done more. If you persist, you will only end by depriving Colonel Gudgeon of a brother as well as a son. Your one obligation to him now is to help him bear his affliction with philosophy. His is not, after all, an uncommon case. Think how many men (and women, too) see their children cruelly snatched from them every day!"

"Enough, Madam – you shall not dissuade me."

"I implore you!"

"I am immovable," I said. And gathered up my clothes – stood in the corner – turned my back to her – and began to dress myself.

She did not speak again until I was buttoning my shirt – and then in a voice I scarce recognized as hers; for all the musick had gone from it, leaving just a dull husk of words:

"If you insist, Sir, then I shall give you a note to my daughter, who is at my house in Cicero, and will, I am certain, render you any assistance she can – tho' that will be little enough. But be sure you give it straight into her hand; for she is under orders never to admit a stranger; which perhaps you will better understand after our adventure yesterday."

"Indeed," I said. "Thank you." And bowed, and opened the door, and crept back to my own room, and the sleeping O'Donnell.

Having breakfasted, and paid our hosts for their hospitality (tho' not for coming to our aid against Jack's gang, for which they refused to accept so much as a penny), we left Niobe's horse for Mrs. Craig, to replace the one she had lost, and set out once more – clutching a letter directed to Miss Craig, at the Mount, Cicero, and guided by the youngest Dexter boy, Samuel, who said he would go with us, to keep us from becoming lost, and help us to protect ourselves in case we were troubled by *banditti* again.

As it turned out our journey was quite without incident – as if the god of adversity had unloosed his whole armoury against us the day before, and must now hold his fire until fresh supplies had reached him. The road wound ahead of us like a tattered ribbon of rock – sometimes reduced to no more than a single fibre by the encroaching forest, or severed by a fallen branch, but always plain enough in the smokey sunshine; and for six or seven hours we followed it this way and that about the hill-sides, up and down (but always more down than up), without mishap, and without encountering a single other soul upon the way. To drop, at length, into a great ocean of trees, that lapped about the base of the mountains, and rolled away to the west, gradually turning from green to blue, until it lost itself in the steamy sky.

"Not far now," muttered our guide (who had not spoken two words to us since leaving). "No more 'n four-five mile to Benjamin's."

"Benjamin's!" I said. "We are going to Mrs. Craig's!"

"I was thinkin' you'd want a bed tonight."

"Shall we not get one at her house?"

He shook his head.

"But she gave us a letter of recommendation."

"That won't help you. She won't have a man sleepin' there – cep' when the Indians is attackin'."

"Why not?"

He shrugged. "They might take what they an't paid for."

I could not guess what he meant by this – unless it was that she kept a bawdy-house and feared that, if she were not vigilant, the whores might deprive her of her livelihood by giving freely the favours it was her business to sell. But then it struck me, that even in such a wilderness as this (perhaps, indeed, more *especially* in a wilderness such as this) a brothel could not long endure that barred its patrons from passing the night within its walls. And I gratefully embraced the only other explanation I could readily think of: that a woman living alone here with her daughter must exercise the fiercest caution – for in the midst of such disorder as we had seen yesterday, and so far from the possibility of help, the least lapse might prove fatal.

After the perils of crossing the mountains, the last part of our way was easy enough – the air still and warm (tho' it was already late in the afternoon), and spicy with the smell of sap and fresh leaves; the path beneath our feet soft and muddy, crossed here and there with gushing brooks, and pocked with shallow puddles. And we had been travelling upon it not forty minutes, at an ambling pace, when we smelled wood-smoke, and heard the distant squeal of pigs; and shortly after came out in a rough clearing, still littered with the ruined stumps of trees half-clothed in moss. Between them stood four or five little huts, so crude you would have imagined they had been made by a company of boys to play at soldiers in: for they appeared to consist of no more than piles of logs, raised up on stone sills, and laid, one length-wise, the next cross-wise, the next length-wise, and so on – the ends all sticking out roughly, like a game of spillikins, and the gaps between stuffed with mud. Their doors were notches cut in the ends; a few unfilled cracks served as windows, and a hotch-potch of wooden slabs – crammed together like irregular teeth, and held down by makeshift frames – as roofs. So small were they, and so alike, that I at first supposed them to be a cluster of out-buildings; but when – after casting about in vain for a house – I looked again, I saw that two of them were distinguished by squat, tower-like chimneys, tacked to the walls furthest from the entrances, as if as an after-thought. From which I deduced that these must be the dwellings, and the others stores and workshops – tho' why, when land and materials were so plentiful, they had not been made bigger, and more convenient to their purpose, I could not understand.

As we approached, a gipsyish woman wearing breeches and clutching a gun appeared from the nearest house, and squinted anxiously towards us – until she recognized our guide, when her face relaxed into a smile, and she set her weapon down, and crossed her arms, and cocked her head, in a burlesque of chiding, and cried: "Is't you, Sam!"

He flushed, and gave an abashed grin.

"T'so long since we seed you, I thought you found yourself a new sweetheart, and forgot all about me."

"An't bin no call to come here," he mumbled, staring fixedly at his horse's neck. His confusion seemed so painful that I wondered for a moment if they had indeed been lovers; but then I remarked that her black hair was pencilled with grey, and there were lines about her eyes and mouth. From which I guessed that there must be a long-standing jest between them, such as a nurse-maid may sometimes make with a boy in her care – for surely it was inconceivable, even here, that a youth of sixteen or seventeen would woo a woman as old as his own mother?

"And now" – with an expression that quite belied her carping tone – "you'll be wantin' supper, I'll be bound?"

"I can't deny, I am mighty hungry. An' these fellows too, I s'pose."

"I'm makin' supper jus' now" – turning her smile upon O'Donnell and me – "an' I 'spec' I can tease it out, with a bit o' rabbit, and some biscuit."

"We needn't trouble you, Madam," I said. "If you can direct us to the tavern . . ."

She began to laugh. "This is Benjamin's place, as I told you of," muttered young Dexter – as if I had been guilty of some impropriety.

"You can stay here, an' gladly," said the woman, pointing to the next cabin. "There's space enough in there. Meantime, come and sit with Dadda, till the cookin's done. He's talkin' with another fellow; but they an't o' the same mind about the state o' the world, so I dare say you'll be sparin' 'em both."

She showed us where we might tether the horses; and then led us behind the hut, where we found two men sitting at a drunken table contrived from a plank and four whittled poles. Of the nearer, I could see nothing but his broad back and hunched shoulders, which for a moment seemed somehow oddly familiar – but I was immediately distracted from considering who or what they called to mind by the extraordinary appearance of the other. He was perhaps sixty – gaunt, and large-boned, with long white hair hacked off unevenly at the level of his jaw, so that it resembled an unruly wig. His face – when I first saw it – was raised gratefully towards the sun, like a basking cat's; but at the sound of our steps he jerked it quickly in our direction – then held it at a strange, broken-necked angle, as if he were merely listening to the noise, rather than searching for its cause. It was only when we had come within a few paces of him that I saw the reason: his eyes were as light-veined and lustreless as marble, and rolled uselessly up into his head.

"Here's Sam to see ye, Dadda," said the woman.

"Sam?" he repeated, gazing sightlessly at her – his lips hovering in a kind of tentative good-heartedness, that could not form itself into a greeting until he knew its object.

"Sam Dexter."

"Sam Dexter!" His dead eyes brimmed, and his whole counte-nance softened into a look of child-like delight, unalloyed by any taint of calculation. "This is a joy." He held out both his hands and, when Sam took them, pumped them up and down, as if they were dancing together at some country revel. "How do you, Sam?"

Sam stammered some awkward response; and then said: "I brung two friend o' Mrs. Craig along o' me."

"Indeed? Two . . .?"

"Menfolk – gentle . . ."

"I am pleased to know you, goodmen." His voice was unlike any I had ever heard – neither entirely English, nor quite Virginian; and so deep it buzzed in his throat like the bass string on a violoncello. "You are welcome to Cicero." He retrieved his hands from Sam, and extended them again – seeing which, O'Donnell and I, not knowing what else to do, seized one apiece. He gently stroked my fingers; and then (as if that were sufficient introduction) said: "What are you called, my dear?"

"Gudgeon."

"Nay – I mean, what did your parents call you?"

"Ned."

"Ned. Edward. That is a good name. And" – turning his attention to O'Donnell, and caressing him in the same manner – "you . . .?"

"Richard O'Donnell."

"Richard. O'Donnell. Yours, I fear" (his voice suddenly quiet and sad) "is something more of a burden. You carry the weight both of the conqueror and the conquered."

This seemed little better than the ramblings of a madman; and, supposing he would find it as whimsical and nonsensical as I did, I cast a humorous glance at O'Donnell – only to discover, to my aston-ishment, that he was biting his lip, and blinking tears from his owlish eyes.

"I am Benjamin," said the blind man, "and this is David." He nod-ded at his companion, who rose from his stool and turned towards us – and in that instant I knew where I had seen him before.

193

"Mr. Hickling!" I cried in amazement – unable, for a moment, to conceive how he came to be here before us. And then I reflected that, even if he had left Frigateville after we did, he might have overtaken us while we were at the Dexters'.

He made a little bow, but said nothing, and gave no sign of recognition.

"We sat together at dinner in Frigate's ordinary, not two days ago," I said. And then – laughing, and pointing to the grease-stain on my breeches: "This, indeed, was your doing. Do you not remember?"

He did not reply; but merely bowed again, and said, "You will excuse me, gentlemen; I have a survey to make."

And abruptly left – laying, as he did so, a book upon the table, that he had been holding in his hand. It was old and worn with use, and the back half flaked away; but on what remained I made out the words "Common Law of", and the letters "Eng".

Another man, I am certain, would have felt constrained to make some comment upon Hickling's ill-tempered departure, and perhaps try to explain it; but Benjamin seemed quite untroubled by it, and – after inviting us to sit down – resumed, as if nothing had happened:

"Martha is a wondrous friend to have, as I know, to my great happiness. But I am sorry to say, if you hope to find her at home, you will be disappointed."

"I know," I said (for my ear was now sufficiently attuned to his manner to understand that he must be speaking of Mrs. Craig). "We met her upon the road."

"Ah. Are you come here seeking wives, then?"

"Wives!"

"That is what brings most men to her house."

"No!"

He did not press me further, but sat with a sort of quiet readiness that invited me to say more if I wished it – without obliging me to do so, if I did not.

"We are looking for a boy," I said.

"A boy!" – as surprised as I had been, twenty seconds before.

"Yes – Miss Catchpole's son – my nephew."

And I again narrated my story. Which young Dexter plainly found tedious – for he left after a few minutes, saying, he would help Mary make the dinner; but Benjamin heard me out – uttering not a word, but nodding sympathetically from time to time, to show he was still following me.

When at length I was done, he said: "What is Miss Catchpole's Christian name?"

I was forced to admit I had never heard it.

"Then I cannot say whether I know her or not. But 'tis more than likely–"

"But surely – the boy . . .?"

"I have been here two years, and no child has been taken in that time. But perhaps before I came. Or before his mother went to the Mount. Most of the women there bring private griefs with them, that they do not choose to speak of."

"What are these women, then?" asked O'Donnell, suddenly – evidently struck by the same thought, that had occurred to me on the way here.

"The greater part of them are what the world calls ruined – poor creatures driven to desperation by want, or abused by some hard-hearted man – as Miss Catchpole was, Ned, by your brother."

"Oh, but remember!" I protested. "He was young, and in his country's service–"

"Yes – and fighting had murdered the pity in him" (grave, but more sad than censorious), "as it always will – so that he was able to cast her aside with as little thought as he would kill a Frenchman. So 'tis small wonder she came at length to the Mount. For Martha looks upon such women not with the cold eyes of men, but with the tender gaze of their Maker, that sees them in all their glory. And she takes them in, and clothes them, and waters their desert hearts with love, so new hope may grow there."

"And how do they live?" I asked.

"They work, as we are all enjoined to – tilling the soil, and rearing hogs and fowl, and hunting, and spinning, and sewing. Some will marry – for there is a want of wives in Eden, and the Mount makes a handy helpmeet for one of our new Adams."

"And–" I began; but got no further; for at this juncture Benjamin's daughter and young Dexter appeared with wooden plates and cups and jugs, and an old stewpot crusted with soot, which they set upon the table.

As if he felt my surprise (for I had naturally supposed we should be summoned into the cabin for dinner), the old man said: "It is our custom, when we may, to eat out of doors, where we are closest to the source of our being, and surrounded by His blessings." And as the woman and the boy sat down, squeezing their stools and insinuating their feet between ours, he bowed his head, and said a silent prayer over the food.

"And what of Mrs. Craig herself?" I said hurriedly when he was done – hoping to bring the conversation back to its course before it had escaped altogether. "Is she married?"

"She was, some years ago. To a poor blind brute – not blind as I am, but blind in the spirit – that used her cruelly: beating her, and spending her inheritance in drink and foolish investments, among them the supposed deeds to this land, which he bought from a trumped-up peddler claiming to be the governor's agent. But at last his own intemperance killed him, as it will; for those who live by the bottle must die by it. After which, she took what little remained to her, and built the Mount, as a haven for other women like herself; and resolved she would never wed again, unless the law was changed, that makes a wife her husband's chattel and forfeits her fortune to him."

He paused; but I said nothing; for the idea was so novel I could not even tell whether I approved or condemned it. And O'Donnell, for once, seemed to be dumbfounded, too – giving no more than a little snort of surprise, that whistled through his nose.

"And I salute her for it," Benjamin continued. "But for my part, I should go further, and make it impossible for any one, man or woman, to own another . . ."

"You speak of slavery," I said – grateful for the opportunity to agree with him. "Which I abhor, too, after all I have seen here."

"Not only what is called slavery," he said. "I mean, the power to command the service of a fellow human creature, or deprive him of the means to make a living. This" – stretching his arms wide, to encompass the forest all about us – "was given to our kind in common, and each of us has a natural right to what he needs – as our Saxon forebears knew. 'Tis a blasphemous corruption of God's purpose to vest all in the King – as William the Bastard did – and say we must have our title of him."

"But what of the Indians?" asked O'Donnell suddenly. "Were they not here first – as the Saxons were before the Normans? Or the Irish too, for the matter of that?"

"Do you see Indians?" said the old man, waving towards the trees. "That is but a pretext by the government, to deny us what is rightfully ours. There is enough land for all of us, if we are good husbands to it. Let an Indian set aside his savage ways, and come to Cicero, and fix upon the other bank of the creek for his farm, and I shall welcome him as my neighbour, and gladly."

I could not but conclude, at the end of this crazed philippic, that I had been right in supposing the fellow mad; and had I heard it in London, or Bristol, or even New York – where it might easily inflame the mob to some rash act – I should have felt obliged to remonstrate with him. But here, at the very extremity of the body politick, where they could infect only a few dispossessed whores and beggars, such views were doubtless harmless enough; and the only issue of disputing them, would have been to create ill-feeling, where none had existed before. So I contented myself with asking: "And what says Mrs. Craig to that?"

"Why" – with a sheepish smile, I should not have thought him capable of – "she says I am like an old monk, with his head full of angels and impossible beasts. She has no quarrel with property, if only women may have an equal share in it – for without it, she believes, the world will fall into disorder. And that is why she sent David to see me."

"What has he to do with it?"

"The Transylvania Company means to sell me my own home; and Martha says she will help me to it, if I will but sign the paper. But I have asked her, and David too: why should a man buy what is already his? God is my landlord here; and I hold his gift by the common law of England."

This provoked such opposite emotions in my breast, I did not at once reply – and Benjamin must have interpreted my silence as censure; for he at length said gently: "I perceive you are not of the same mind, Ned. But that is no cause for us to be enemies. Notwithstanding our differences, Martha and I love each other – and let us do the same."

For the rest of the meal, I – and he, too, I think – strove to obey this injunction, and avoid any subject that might cause the other offence. But it was a wearisome business; and I was so eager by the end to spare myself the labour of further conversation that – tho' I had previously intended not to call upon Miss Craig until the next day – I said: "How far are we from the Mount?"

"No more than two miles."

"I think we should go there now, and present ourselves to the lady, so that she knows to expect us tomorrow."

His face sagged with disappointment; for company was a scarce commodity in Cicero, and he had plainly hoped to enjoy ours for the whole evening. But it would have contradicted his philosophy, to try to detain us against our wishes; and all he said was: "'Tis easy enough to find. I can get there, even without benefit of eyes."

And so we went – riding through the darkening forest, with only the strangest, most vapourish notions of what this colony of Amazons might consist of, or how we might be received there.

XXVIII

Here's a strange thing.

Today – it being Sunday, and my hand weary with writing – I devoted to my customary diversions; and was rehearsing my new glee for the third or fourth time when – to my great astonishment – a fine contralto began to accompany me in the chorus, from without the walls.

It was the first human voice, besides my own, that I have heard since I was brought here.

And I wept at the sound of it.

And am now moved to recount the fact to y^r honours – even though 'tis next to certain you were the cause of it; for I can but suppose that the singer must either have been one of your number, or one of your servants.

So – you are not only my captors, it seems. You are become my confidants, too.

Tomorrow, I promise, I shall address your questions.

XXIX

I thank y^r honours. Yes – I was always accounted musical, even as a boy. Aunt Fiske used to call me her pretty skylark.

Why did I consider Benjamin's opinions mad? I should have thought it was plain: because (if acted upon) they would lead to anarchy and civil strife. An ordered society is as impossible without property as an upright tree without soil to hold its roots; and for this

198

reason: that only a man that has a stake in the preservation of society may be safely entrusted with its governance – as our constitution very properly acknowledges, by denying the vote to the poor. The farmer who owns the apples, can always be counted upon to drive the cart with care, as a matter of self-interest; but let a landless labourer have the reins, and he will beat the horses, and take every bend at a gallop; for he has nothing to lose if it overturns – and may even be able to snatch up a few pieces of fruit in the confusion, to smuggle home to his children.

I find it more accountable that you should ask me to enlarge upon the "opposite emotions" I felt when he had done speaking; for it is only now I reflect upon it that I wholly understand them myself. Consider: I had but that morning come from Mrs. Craig's bed; and the sound and smell and feel of her were still vivid in my memory, hovering about the edge of every thought and impression – and sometimes bursting in, and displacing them entirely. If it had appeared that she had been as great a lunatick as Benjamin, then I should have reproached myself for having been so near to marrying her – but rejoiced at my good fortune in escaping; if, on the other hand, she was a woman of sense, as I had supposed (and as, indeed, turned out to be the case), then it would exonerate my judgement from blame – but make me regret the loss of her more keenly yet.

Which I hope is a sufficient explanation; and will now resume my story.

Whether because he was blind, or merely because a man that imagines the best of everything will inevitably remember a road shorter and straighter than it is, I cannot say; but Benjamin was mistaken in telling us we were but two easy miles from the Mount. After the freshness of the mountains, the lowland air seemed heavy and damp; the muddy track was treacherous, ambushing us at every turn with hidden twigs and branches; and as the last streaks of day melted from the sky, I began to think we must have lost our way altogether, and should go back. And was about to say so, when O'Donnell suddenly cried out: "Ah!"

"What is it?"

"A light."

I peered ahead; but could not see it.

"No" – raising his hand – "there."

I followed his outstretched finger. A wavering yellow pin-head glimmered between the middle branches of a tree – so much higher than I had expected that if it had been brighter, I should have thought it was a star.

"'Tis likely enough, is it not," said O'Donnell, remarking my surprise, "you will find a place called the Mount, set upon a hill?"

The next moment – as if to prove him right – the path began to rise, and grow rockier; until, by degrees, our poor horses were climbing not so much a road as a flight of crude stone stairs, that threatened to send them tumbling, and obliged us to get down, and lead them. Until, quite suddenly, we came out at the base of a large mound – naked of trees, and surrounded by a low palisade.

Perhaps the memory of Mrs. Craig, and the knowledge that we were approaching her home, had made my senses susceptible of the idea – but I could not look upon it without being powerfully put in mind of a giant breast: for the ground seemed to swell deliciously, and at its peak was a circle of outbuildings – with a kind of small squat tower jutting from the centre, topped by the lit window that had served as our beacon.

"We might have slipped back six centuries," said O'Donnell – whose thoughts had plainly been running in a different course.

"Why?"

"Did you ever set eyes on a house that looked more like a castle? Observe: you have motte, bailey, keep, and" – here waving at a barred entrance, that extended two or three feet above the level of the wall – "barbican, too."

Which – as soon as he had drawn my attention to it – I saw was true. And in the same instant understood Sam Dexter's remark *that men might sleep there when the Indians were attacking*; for plainly this must be the best-defended place in the region, and the most natural refuge for its scattered inhabitants in times of danger.

We dismounted, and beat upon the gate; but the timbers were so massive, as to swallow the blows whole, leaving barely a whisper to rouse the inmates. So O'Donnell took up his musket, and rattled the end against the wood, bellowing the while, "Halloo! Halloo!" – in which I soon joined him; and in less than a minute, we were gratified to hear footsteps hurrying towards us, and a testy female voice calling, "Enough! Enough! I'm coming." And then, from no more than a foot away: "What do you want?"

"Mrs. Craig sent us," I said.

"On what business?"

"To speak with her daughter."

She made a noise, like the snort of a horse – as if she had heard the same threadbare story a hundred times before, from witless fellows trying to wheedle their way into the Mount, and wondered we had not taken the trouble to think of a better.

"We have a letter from her."

"Indeed? Let me see it, then."

"'Tis for Miss Craig . . ."

"I shall not open it."

I slipped it into the crack between two logs.

"'Tis Martha's hand, certainly," she said after a moment. "You may come in, and I will ask Sarah if she will see you. But you know you must leave again tonight?"

"Yes," I said. "We shall return to Benjamin's."

This appeared to satisfy her; for all we heard by way of reply was the decisive double *dunt* of a pair of bolts being shot, and the groan of a bar being raised. Then the gates crept open, and a small woman cocked her head out – dressed in the customary animal skins and holding a lantern before her to see us by – which, as its light danced on her face, afforded *us* the reciprocal opportunity to study *her*. She was perhaps forty, with close-set phlegmy eyes, and a big pinched nose that gave her the critical look of a sailor's parrot – and made me fear, for a moment, that what she saw was so little to her liking she was about to turn us away again after all. But then she nodded briskly, and said: "Come in."

She barred the entrance behind us (rejecting O'Donnell's offer of assistance with an irritable shrug); and then, without another word, hurried past us, and set off up the track towards the house.

"Perhaps," murmured O'Donnell, as we followed her, "Miss Craig is held a prisoner, and will let down her hair to admit us."

I knew, of course, it was meant in jest; and yet, as he said it, I could not help looking up at the highest window – and was startled to see it almost filled by the dark shape of a girl in an elegant dress. She lingered there for a few seconds – her head wistfully bowed, and one hand clutching something against her breast – before seeming to start, and then moving abruptly away, as if she had felt my gaze and must conceal herself from it.

"Wait here," said the woman, as we approached the house. And then, favouring us with not so much as a glance, she hurried in.

The onset of night is always melancholy, even when a man is close to home, and knows a cheerful hearth and a loving hand await him; but here, standing before a strange house, and surrounded by a gloomy wilderness that appeared blind to our very existence, the sense of solitude was so strong it seemed to assume physical form – breathing upon my skin, and gouging its fingers into my belly. And I think O'Donnell must have been touched by it, too; for he trembled, and hunched his shoulders, tho' there was still barely a hint of chill in the air. Seeing which, you might have supposed it the most natural thing in the world for me to have said something, so as to offer him (at least) the comfort of a friendly voice; or for him – observing that I was in a like condition – to have performed the same office for me. But for some reason or other, we both kept silence – leaving us (after we had hitched the horses to a misshapen post) with no occupation but to savour the sad odours of the dying day, and watch a thin rind of moon rising above the roof, and the bats flickering in its light, like dust in a ray of sunshine.

The gate-keeper was so long absent I began at last to think she must somehow have become distracted, and forgotten us entirely; but as I was about to knock, in order to enquire after her, she suddenly reappeared, saying *that Sarah was ready to receive us now.* And at once turned; and with as little ceremony as before led us through a dark, narrow hall – past the hot mouth of a great kitchen, where four or five females seated about a table gaped curiously at us as we went by; thence down a stale-smelling little passage, that was darker still – and finally into a small parlour, at the very back of the house.

The only light came from two smokey candles and the expiring embers of a wasted fire, by which I could make out nothing, but the shadowy bulk of two large chairs. But then, from the corner, I heard a little gasp, either of fear or exasperation; and, looking towards it, saw a young woman – who at once boggled and shrank back, as if we had taken her by surprise. By the way she held her head, and hugged something to her body, I would have sworn it was the same girl I had observed in the window; but if it was, she had changed her clothes in the interim – for in place of a dress she wore the suit of skins that seemed to be the soul of fashion in these parts.

I expected our parrot-faced guide to say something, by way of introduction; but she merely stood a little apart, arms folded and feet a-straddle, scowling – like a member of the royal body-guard, prepared to jump to her mistress's defence, if we should offer her the least insult. So at length I asked: "Are you Miss Craig?"

"I –" (so quiet I could barely hear her) "I am Sarah, yes."

"Naturally, I don't know what your mother wrote to you. But I suppose she said, at least, that we are looking for Miss Catchpole's son?"

"Yes."

"She told us that Miss Catchpole herself is gone from home. But we hoped perhaps you might be able to give us some intelligence concerning the boy?"

She did not reply, but glanced towards the other woman – with a curious quick movement of the head, that suddenly recalled her mother to me. In the act of looking away again, she stopped suddenly, and stared at something beyond my shoulder; and turning to see the cause, I discovered it was O'Donnell – who was gazing at her, as intently as she at him.

"In doing so," I continued, "you would be serving him, as well as us; for if we recover him, we mean to take him to England with us, and in time he will inherit my brother's property there."

"I fear – I fear I know nothing," she said – refusing to meet my eyes, and studying the floor instead. It was difficult to be certain in the dusky light, but I think she was blushing fiercely; for as I watched, the lustre of her cheeks seemed to deepen, from pearl to slate.

"You know he was stolen by Indians," said parrot-face – in the irritable tone of a tutor, whose charge has forgot his lesson.

"Yes – yes – that is true . . ."

"How long ago?"

"I –"

"Many years," snapped parrot-face.

"Yes," said Miss Craig – making a great effort to rouse her listless voice into some semblance of authority. "Before I knew her."

"Miss Catchpole, you mean?"

"Yes – Miss Catchpole."

"So you were not acquainted with him personally?"

"No."

"There are, I understand, several nations of Indians," I said. "Do you know which of them it was, that took him?"

She shook her head.

"What matters that?" burst in the other woman. "They are all devils, and will have used him in the same abominable way."

"But each, I suppose" – trying to master my growing anger – "has its own country? And if we are to have any hope of finding him, we must first know where to look."

"Believe me, you do not wish to find him. 'Tis near certain he is dead; and you will return home with nothing for your pains – save only a bone or two left by the dogs, if you are fortunate. And if by chance he is still alive, they will have turned him into a fiend like themselves. Do you think your brother wants a savage for an heir – that will burn his tenants' houses, and cut their throats, and steal their babes?"

She gave a snorting laugh, without an atom of merriment in it – like a lawyer sneering his adversary to silence. And I suddenly perceived that she was no common slut (as I had at first imagined, from Benjamin's description of the place), but a woman of some parts, who might have passed for the parson's wife, in a bye-country parish; and – in the same moment – that her conduct fitted her as well for the character of gaoler, as for that of protector.

"If that is the case," I replied, "we must see what education and a father's love may do for him. But" – turning to the girl – "I see, Madam, you are tired; and we have disturbed you, by coming here so late. Perhaps if we were to leave now, and return again tomorrow – so you had leisure to reflect a little, and make enquiry of the other ladies, to see if any of them remembers more . . .?"

"No!"

The word flew out so vehemently, you would have supposed it had been squeezed from her by a torturer; but the only visible sign of agitation was in her hands, which (as if they were too far from the seat of government to be reduced to obedience) were fluttering as wildly as a limed thrush – and revolving something between them that I guessed must be the object she had been clutching; tho' all I could see of it, was the glint of a shiny surface.

"You will forgive me, I hope, for observing it," I said; "but my question seems to have caused you far more distress than I should have thought possible, if you are truly as ignorant of it as you claim to be. Which leads me to wonder, if you are somehow prevented by some circumstance or other" (here glancing at parrot-face, in a manner I hoped made my meaning plain) "from telling us all you know?"

She did not answer at once, but continued working her fingers back and forth, back and forth – making me doubt, at last, whether she had heard me. But then she raised her eyes miserably towards O'Donnell, and said: "I wish – I wish I could give you something that would repay you for the trouble of coming here. But" – turning suddenly to me – "I cannot. Please – leave me."

"Madam–"

But she began to shake her head, and continued without pause – until it had ceased to be a gesture of denial or refusal, or a communication with us at all; but merely (it seemed) an expression of her own despair.

"Madam –" I said again.

But O'Donnell laid a hand on my arm, and muttered: "Come, Sir, let us go."

The parrot-faced woman turned us out of the house even more gracelessly than she had let us in to it – saying nothing, but huffing at our heels like an ill-tempered sheep-dog the whole way. Save only, that is, as we were approaching the kitchen, when she darted by us and shut the door, as if we were a contagion, that had already infected Miss Craig and would assuredly corrupt any other member of their company who had the misfortune to behold us for so much as a second. Such treatment would have been irksome at any time, and in any place; here, and after the grievous disappointment of our interview, it roiled me into a bubbling rage – and I was more than once upon the point of furiously remonstrating with her, by saying *that I supposed we had more to fear from her pox-ridden whores, than they did from us.* What stopped me was O'Donnell – who (tho' I knew he must be as sensible of the insult as I was) appeared to feel it not at all, but submitted to our humiliating rout as meekly and uncomplainingly as a child. From which I deduced that he had spied some danger, or been struck by some notion, that convinced him we must leave without a moment's delay; and I should have been a poor student indeed if I had not by now learned to trust his judgement in such matters, more than my own.

But if I had expected him to make me privy to his thoughts the instant the gate was shut behind us (as indubitably he would have done, at the outset of our adventure together), I was sorely mistaken. It was not until we were almost at the bottom of the rocky hill that he at length spoke – and then only to mutter, "Steady, sir – steady, now," to his horse, which had taken fright at the cry of an owl and skittered sideways, sending a shower of stones clattering into the bushes. To find I had dwindled so far in his estimation that he now considered me less worthy of conversation than a beast was yet another buffet to my bruised pride; but seeing I should learn nothing from him by any other means, I finally succumbed to my own curiosity, and asked: "What do you think Miss Craig was keeping from us?"

"I wish I knew, Sir," he replied – but so absent from his own voice, it was no more than a servant, dispatched to say the master was not at home.

Which suddenly recalled to mind his behaviour during the voyage – with such force, that I was goaded into snapping: "Anyone would suppose you had been in the hold of the *Jenny* again."

The effect was instantaneous, and far more gratifying than I could have conceived possible: he stopped – turned – stared at me in the watery moonlight, with wondering eyes – and at last breathed: "That is most remarkable."

"Indeed?"

"I was not certain you had seen it. And am still at a loss to imagine how you came to perceive its significance."

I had, of course, not the least idea what he was talking about; but could not resist giving vent to my feelings: "Perhaps I am not quite the fool you took me for," I said. And at once regretted it; for, by pretending to an understanding I did not possess, I saw I ran the risk of being exposed as a greater fool yet.

"Will you not tell me?" he said.

I attempted a foxy grin.

"Did your uncle mention it to you? Or did you contrive to guess it somehow, from the German woman?"

I was now in such a state of confusion, as I knew must become immediately apparent the moment I said anything; so I held my tongue – which I hoped he would construe as evidence merely that I was keeping my own counsel. But I think he divined the truth; for after a few seconds he nodded, and murmured, "Ah."

"What German woman?" I asked, as carelessly as I could.

"The one we stayed with, before we reached Frigateville. She had one of them, too – on the shelf above her fireplace."

"One of – one of –" I stumbled, painfully conscious that I was diminishing my small stock of credit with every word.

"One of the same china shepherdesses that Miss Craig was toying with, all the time we were with her."

I remembered the gleam between Miss Craig's fingers – and acknowledged that it might indeed have been caused by the glaze on a piece of porcelain, like the little figure (I now recalled) that had so captured O'Donnell's attention at the German woman's house. But what his interest in either of them might be, I could not begin to imagine.

I flung down the last farthings of my fortune: "What of it?"

"Why" – turning, so I could not see his smile of triumph, tho' I heard it well enough – "only that they came with us, on the ship from Bristol. There was a crate of 'em, split open, lying there when I went below to help the child. Half were thrown out, and smashed – but I could see well enough what they were."

I could not keep myself from laughing: "What! That is your great secret, then, is it! A box of broken knick-knacks!"

He did not reply.

I said: "There must be ten thousand such figures in America."

"And what are the odds that we should come upon two of them, in places that are so remote, and so bereft of all the other conveniences of life?"

"Well – perhaps you are right. But I fail to see that it matters a jot, whether they came with us, or not."

He did not speak at once; and when he did, it was in a tone so distracted, I could not tell whether he was answering me, or merely continuing the train of his own reflections: "The German woman said she had hers of the 'Transylvania man'. Hickling is employed by the Transylvania Company. We find Hickling here."

He was silent for a moment; then suddenly stopped his horse, and said: "I suppose, Sir, you can find your way back to Benjamin's alone?"

"What!"

"I mean to return to the Mount, and see if I can discover more."

"You will not be admitted."

"I shall admit myself. The wall is not so high."

"Let me come with you, then."

"No. I shall fare better by myself. I will be with you again by dawn, I promise." And turned about, and was gone.

For the next mile or so, my thoughts were entirely of O'Donnell: what his purpose was, and whether he would succeed, or was destined to be taken captive – and, if he was, whether I would hear the vengeful cries of the enraged harlots, and be obliged to go to his aid. But I heard nothing; and by degrees, became more occupied with the practical question, of how best to explain his absence to our hosts. If I told them the truth, their sympathies would inevitably be engaged in their neighbours' behalf – and perhaps move them to send a messenger, to warn the women of his intentions; if I said he had met with an accident, it was equally likely, they would dispatch a party to help him. And yet I could not think of another credible reason, that would keep a man from his bed in the middle of the wilderness.

As it turned out, I need not have concerned myself. Benjamin had already retired; and his weary daughter, blinking over a poor worn shirt she was mending by the glow of the fire, was barely awake enough even to greet me. She imagined, I think, that O'Donnell was without, attending to the horses, and that I had come in simply to fetch a lantern, to light us both to our cabin – on which point, I did not disabuse her.

And perhaps it was as well O'Donnell was not with me; for there were but three rough platforms in the hut, formed in the shape of a square 'U' – and one-and-a-half of them were already taken by young Dexter, who sprawled and shivered beneath his blanket like a giant crane. I had no wish to rouse him – so made myself as comfortable as I could in the space remaining; and soon fell asleep.

As – after a glass or two of the wine you have been good enough to send me – I shall now do here, in the more pleasant quarters furnished by yʳ honours.

XXX

Yʳ honours have no question for me this morning; which is curious – for (reading again my last chapter) I have found one for myself:

Why did O'Donnell and I not speak to one another, as we waited before Mrs. Craig's house? We had had no recent quarrel, that might have constrained us – indeed, he had treated me with unusual delicacy, after our adventure with the *banditti* and Mrs. Craig; while I would have been an unnatural brute indeed, if I had not still felt the warmest gratitude towards him for his part in our rescue. And yet there must, I suppose, have been *some* discoverable cause – unless a man's actions are entirely unaccountable, and he is no more than a feather, blown this way and that by forces he can neither control nor comprehend; which I do not believe – and (from your earlier interrogations) doubt you do, either. The only explanation I offer – *that it was for some reason or other* – appears, in this light, so idle and threadbare as to demand a better; which (tho' you do not press me to it) I give below:

O'Donnell and I were two boats, bound for different ports, that were tossed together by a great storm and swept briefly into the same way. When the wind dropped, each of us began to resume his proper path; but we were kept from parting by a certain mutual love and regard, which persuaded us – at every crisis in our relations – that the fatal moment might still be deferred a while yet. But day by day, our courses were diverging – until, by the time we reached Cicero, we had drifted beyond hailing distance, and could communicate only by means of signals, and a pair of telescopes. The final rupture was inevitable, and imminent – as was soon to be made plain; and yet, for a few hours more, neither of us could quite bring himself to admit it.

And now to the issue of it all:

I was waked by a hand upon my shoulder, and a voice, so near it warmed my ear, whispering: "Sir! Sir!"

I opened my eyes. It was still too dark to see. "Is that you, Sir?" I said.

"Yes. But – hush!"

"What is it?"

I felt his fingers tighten. "Get up quickly," he said, "and come out!" And without waiting for a reply, tip-toed to the door.

I shrugged on my coat – shuffled on my boots – and followed him, as quietly as I could. At first he seemed to have vanished; but then I caught a movement, about thirty paces away – and spied him standing there, close to the horses. Or rather, not standing so much as dancing – for he was shifting from one foot to the other, as fidgety as a boy.

"What's the matter?" I asked, as I approached him.

"We must go."

"What!" I mumbled, like an idiot – for I was still three-fourths asleep. "Go? Where?"

"Away, Sir. Back."

"Why?"

"Because we have been misled – and may soon be something worse, if we continue. The boy does not exist, I am convinced of it; and there are those who would sooner see us dead than in possession of the truth."

I felt myself begin to spin like a whipping-top, and should assuredly have fallen, had I not steadied myself against the remains of a tree.

"I am just come from the Mount," he said, "where I contrived to enter Miss Craig's apartment undetected, and spend an hour or two in conversation with her. She knows, I am certain, little enough of the plot –"

"Plot!" I groaned stupidly. And all at once, the strength flooded from my legs, and I collapsed on to the stump.

"But I remarked something that told me part, at least, of what she could not." He paused, as if he was suddenly uneasy; and then went on, more slowly: "You were right, Sir, in guessing that your uncle's ship was carrying more than us, and the wretched emigrants, and some china shepherdesses. There were also – there were also –"

In some dusty corner of my consciousness I knew I was about to learn the solution of a mystery that had occupied me for months; but the prospect, in my present agitated state, afforded me not the slightest gratification.

"Guns," he said. "I saw scores, if not hundreds, of guns."

"Guns?"

He nodded. "One of which Miss Craig now keeps, to protect herself. The identical pattern; the identical maker – Orrell, of Bristol. I asked her how long she had had it, and she said Mr. Hickling had brought it, a few weeks ago – at the same time as the little figure, and one or two other trinkets."

"But why" – for in truth, this was the only point, in all he had said, that I could easily apprehend – "why did you not tell me before?"

"Because I supposed they were destined for the Americans."

I was too confused to speak; perceiving which, he went on: "Seeing them, and recalling the trouble that Coleman had gone to to stop me finding them, I could only imagine that – despite his unamiable manner – he must be a friend of Liberty. And since I knew that you take a different view of the matter, I held my tongue."

I felt an explosion of anger, but – so remote was the cause from my immediate concerns – it seemed strangely distant, like a cannon-shot heard from five miles away.

"But now," said O'Donnell, "– now I see he must have had some other motive."

"What?"

"Why, Sir – gain. Profit."

"You mean, he is selling them to the rebels?"

"No, Sir – to the Indians."

"But the Indians – the Indians –" I stuttered, more puzzled than ever, "are surely – surely –?"

"What? The enemy? Indeed. But for this reason only: that they occupy the land. And you will recall that Mr. McLeod told us the Transylvania Company means to buy the land, or a great portion of it, from them?"

"Yes," I said doubtfully (for in truth I could remember little of what McLeod had said, but only that Hickling had taken offence at it). "But what has that to do with guns and shepherdesses and Miss Craig?"

"That is what I could not guess, and went back to the Mount to discover."

He drew in his breath to continue, but then seemed to choke on it – as if trying to suppress a sob or a laugh. I moved a step or two closer, and stared at him curiously. A few pale cracks were beginning to craze the eastern sky – affording me just enough light to observe that his eyes were bright, and his face more flushed with excitement than I had ever seen it. Which led me, dazed as I was, to wonder if perhaps he had enjoyed the same favour of the daughter that I had of the mother.

"Miss Craig would not answer me at first. But when I returned to the point a little later, she said, 'Well, I suppose there'd be no harm in it'; and told me that her mother is an investor in the Company – and was, indeed, on her way to Frigateville for some purpose related to it, when we met her."

"What purpose?" I said – recalling, with a flutter of unease, that Mrs. Craig would not tell me what her business there was.

"The girl did not know. But I think it was to meet Coleman."

I was like a peasant, who is shown a map for the first time and sees his village is not an island, but connected by a web of roads to Bath and York and London, and a hundred other places he has heard of, but supposed existed in a different world. I could not utter a sound; but felt my mouth working mutely, like a dying fish's.

O'Donnell went on: "The Cherokee will give up their title to twenty million acres – including the whole region about here; receiving, in return, a couple of cartloads of English goods. Plainly, the contents of the *Jenny* were Mrs. Craig's share of the purchase price – but had to be smuggled into America, because the Congress forbids imports from Britain."

I regained mastery of my tongue: "So what – she and Coleman are in league?"

"So 'twould appear, Sir. 'Tis a pretty enough conspiracy, is it not? Coleman buys cheap – because the manufacturers would rather take a penny for their goods than nothing – and exchanges them for a million or half a million or a fourth of a million acres."

"But how did he come to be acquainted with her?"

"From Miss Catchpole, I imagine." He paused, giving me time to reply; and, when I did not, continued: "She knew Miss Catchpole's history; and – when she first learned of the Transylvania Company scheme, two or three years ago – asked her to send to England, so the Mount might have a part in it. Perhaps she offered her her own stake in the venture, or perhaps some other inducement; whatever the case, Miss Catchpole did as she was bid – writing both to your brother, with her cock-and-bull story about his son, and to Coleman's mother – whom she supposed to be still alive."

"Coleman's mother!" I said, in an effort to rally my beleaguered forces – and shook my head, to suggest the idea was too fantastick to be entertained, even for a second.

"Why not? She had known her at Fiskefield; and doubtless remembered her as a kind lady, who had helped her then and might be expected to do so now." He waited again; and then – seeing I had no answer – resumed his relentless advance on my position: "Your brother responded by offering to take the boy, rather than give the money – which was so far from what she had hoped or expected that she never replied. The other letter was opened by Coleman – who at once saw the chance of becoming rich, and made his proposal."

There was such a weight upon me, I thought I should suffocate. I furiously summoned up every word spoken to me by Dan and Coleman and Uncle Fiske, by Washington and Mrs. Craig; but found nothing but cowards and traitors, that refused to contradict him. At length, all I could say was: "But you do not know any of this? 'Tis only conjecture?"

"Yes. But I would take my oath it's true. There is no other explanation will fit what we do know half so well. As, for instance, that Coleman was in Frigateville, when he could not have had time to follow us there; which is no great puzzle, if he was not following us at all, but had come to meet Mrs. Craig."

"What, then, of Miss Catchpole herself? And her son – for we know she had one?"

I thought for a moment I had found a flaw in his argument; for he was silent for some seconds. Then he shifted uncomfortably; and – holding my gaze with some difficulty – said: "You will take this very hard, Sir, I know – but I fear they are dead."

I began to retch, and only kept myself from vomiting by clutching my belly, and drawing in a great breath.

O'Donnell went on: "The boy, perhaps, died an infant; or was indeed stolen by Indians, many years ago. The mother – the mother –"

"What?"

"Mrs. Craig is a bold woman, Sir – bolder than any man I ever knew, save you. But boldness is bought sometimes at a fearful price. If she keeps her own daughter captive in the middle of a nest of harridans–"

"Oh, come!" I said. "Your imagination has got the better of your sense. You cannot say she is captive –"

"What word describes her condition better? She cannot leave the Mount – she is denied all society, save that of the sisterhood . . ."

"That is her account of it, perhaps . . ."

"Did we not see it with our own eyes?"

"She is mad, then, and–"

"She is no madder than you, Sir – tho' 'twould be small enough wonder if she were. She is a sweet, natural girl – locked away on her mother's orders, and obliged to smother every tender impulse of her heart, until the world is grown good enough to receive her."

"Good enough?"

"By granting her the same rights as a man. Which, of course, will be never – or not until she is long since dead." He hesitated, and seemed to consider carefully, before going on: "If Mrs. Craig will treat poor Sarah so, do you think she would show any more mercy to somebody not even of her own family, that stood in the way of her ambitions?"

"You do not – you do not believe she would have killed her?"

"Who would know it if she had, in such a place as this? By removing Miss Catchpole, and making herself Coleman's sole partner, she stands to gain two fortunes, instead of only one. Coleman would not care whether he was leagued with Miss Catchpole, or Mrs. Craig, or the devil himself; 'tis of no consequence to him what other pockets he helps to fill – provided he knows he is stuffing his own at the same time."

It was as if I had been slipping down a cliff, vainly snatching at roots and branches that would not support me; and all of a sudden something had arrested my fall. I remembered Mrs. Craig's tears of pity at the cruelty of my predicament; the tenderness of her touch on my bruised shoulder; the gentle sea of sighs and endearments that had carried her to the pinnacle of bliss; and the warm sweet smack of salt on my lips afterwards, as I kissed her weeping eyes – and I knew that, whatever else she was, she could not be a murderess. And if she was not, then Miss Catchpole must still be alive, and her son, too; for if they had died from any other cause, Mrs. Craig would surely have told me – since that would have been the most powerful reason imaginable why I should do as she asked me, and give up my quest, and return home; and it was inconceivable so intelligent a woman would have failed to avail herself of it, if it had lain readily to hand. So she was not a liar, either; in which case . . .

O'Donnell must have seen the drift of my thoughts; for he suddenly broke in: "'Tis possible I am mistaken on this score, Sir. I freely own, I do not yet know everything. But this I do: we are being led a dance, and should leave immediately."

"I mean to, Sir. I am going to the Indians, to seek my nephew."

He was, for once, quite dumbfounded. His eyes grew, until they seemed to occupy half his face; and it was some seconds before he had sufficiently recovered his wits to blurt: "I beg you to reconsider, Sir."

"D–n it, Sir. I am going!"

I was, I think, angrier than I had ever been in my life – tho' I am still at a loss to know exactly why. Part of the cause, undoubtedly, was O'Donnell's poor opinion of Mrs. Craig, and the certainty that nothing I could say would make him change it; but beneath that lay a deeper spring, that had long been penned underground, and had now found a fissure in the rock and begun to spurt out, whether I would or no. And O'Donnell was plainly in the same state; for all the colour had fled from his cheeks; and he had so far lost his customary composure as to quake visibly.

"Then you must go alone," he said at last.

"Very well – if you fear to go with me."

"I should have thought, Sir, I had shown beyond doubt that charge is groundless – and if any other man had made it, I should have called him out. But I will not play the dupe, not even for you – and if I cannot dissuade you from it, then you must act the part without me."

I could say no more; but turned, and walked off. But my eyes were so full I could not see my way; and stopped by the corner of Benjamin's hut, and waited there – more than half-expecting, every moment, the noise of approaching steps, and a hand upon my arm, and a rueful offer of peace. But the only sound was the steady beat of his boots as he gathered his possessions from the cabin – and then a soft neigh, and the slap of bags and saddle, and the huff and clink of tightening straps. And, at last, his voice, calling: "Adieu, Sir."

I stumbled towards him. Through the blinding haze he appeared as still as a churchyard monument; but as I drew close, I saw his head drop forward slightly, in a chilly little bow. I tried to return it; but was suddenly so overcome that I fell on him instead, grappling him to me.

"Thank you, Sir," I said, "for all your great service to me."

"And – you –" he began; but could go no further. He held my shoulders a moment; and then gently pushed them from him, and – without looking at me again – mounted his horse, and urged it towards the east.

I stood and watched, until the steamy maw of the forest had closed about him, and I could hear nothing, save the first cries of the birds greeting the rising sun.

The ordeals of that day were by no means the worst of my adventure; and yet I find myself strangely unwilling to recall them to my mind – of which the proof is, I was sat here twenty minutes this morning, pen in hand, before I contrived to write a single word. When I began my narrative – if I had remarked this reluctance in myself at all – I should not have thought it remarkable enough to merit a second's thought; but you have made me, by degrees, so curious to see into my own motives, that I cannot now continue, without first trying to discover the reason for it. And, after some reflection, have concluded, it is this: that that was the moment – tho' I did not know it at the time, and have never acknowledged it before – when I finally lost mastery of my own destiny. O'Donnell's boat was already beating towards the open sea, which (as I learned much later) would carry him in time to success and reputation; mine – tho' I continued to trim the sails, and turn the wheel this way and that – was being hurried along on a tide so powerful that whatever I did, or failed to do, the end must be the same. And perhaps it is not unnatural that man should shrink from the spectacle of his own impotence and blindness.

I had, to begin with, but one clear objective, after O'Donnell had gone: to avoid, at any price, encountering anybody else, before I had sufficiently unpicked my ravelled thoughts as to know how to proceed. I found a faint, half-overgrown track, therefore, and at once set off along it – taking care to stop every hundred paces or so, and look behind me, to see how I had come; for I knew that, in my confused and desperate state, it would have been the easiest thing in the world to miss the way back, if I let my attention wander for only a moment.

Often (as I think I have observed elsewhere) it is not until some time after we have received a blow that we begin to feel the full pain of it; and so it was on this occasion. With every step, the injury I had suffered appeared more grievous – until, by degrees, the extent of it seemed almost too great to bear. O'Donnell had been not only (as I suddenly saw) the most faithful friend and the truest gentleman I had ever known, but also the preserver of both my life and my liberty – without whose courage and quick understanding, I should assuredly before now have been hanged as a rebel, or imprisoned as a traitor. Recalling which, I could not but feel his loss as a virtual sentence of death; for was it not almost certain that worse dangers still lay ahead – and that one of them must indubitably prove fatal to me, when he was not at my side, to extricate me from it? There was but one small balm to my misery: the certainty that if I had chosen to go with him, it would have been blacker yet – for it is surely better to die clutching the tattered standard of honour, than to live comfortably in disgrace.

Woven through this gloomy threnody was a counterpoint of more practical concerns – most immediate of which was, once again, what to tell my hosts about O'Donnell. I had avoided the difficulty of explaining his absence last night, but could not count on being so fortunate today; and persuaded myself, in my over-wound state, that if I failed to contrive a convincing enough story to account for his disappearance, I should be suspected of having murdered him. And – even supposing I could get past that obstacle – what then? What course was still open to me, that might bring me an inch nearer to finding my nephew? I could think of but two possible answers – both of which had the thin stink of desperation about them: first, to seek out Hickling, who plainly knew something of Indian depredations, and might yet, if prompted, furnish some useful particular; or, second, to return to the Mount, in the slight hope of being better received, and meeting somebody there who could tell me more than Miss Craig had.

All of which bore so heavily upon me that I walked with my head bowed, and my eyes fixed no more than five yards ahead of my feet; with the result that it was not until a furious chorus of barking startled me into looking up that I saw I had come to the edge of another cluster of cabins. I say *another*, but for a moment I wondered if I had somehow made a circle, and returned to where I had set out from; for, at first sight, the two settlements seemed as like as a pair of pictures printed from the same plate. Then a man carrying an axe hurried from the nearest hut – which should have been Benjamin's, if this were really Cicero – to discover what had roused his dogs; and from his singular appearance, I knew for a certainty that I had never seen him before in my life. His face was grey and pitted as a piece of pumice – he wore no hat or wig – and where you would have expected to find hair, there was nothing but a cap of reddish skin, lined with gristly blue ridges, that descended to a point above his forehead.

I stopped – hoisting my eyebrows into a surprised look, that I hoped would convey I had mistaken my path, and would withdraw at once, without troubling him further. But already four or five others were following him, clutching guns or sticks, and with a frenzied sea of mongrels raging about their legs; and I knew that if I turned now, I should have the whole company snapping at my heels, and perhaps end by being beaten, or even shot, for my pains – for nothing excites a pack of curs so much as the whiff of fear. So I stood my ground; and, as they came near, raised my hand, and twirled it in a courtly greeting – which sufficiently astonished the hairless brute, as to slow him to an amble, and prise his mouth into a puzzled gape. The rest fell quickly into the same pace behind him; while the ocean of dogs, after surging ahead for a moment, suddenly observed that they had lost their masters, and retreated in a snarling wave, to howl and bristle at me.

Having achieved this temporary truce, I was at a loss what to say that might disarm the enemy altogether; but then I heard a half-familiar voice, that decided the point for me: "What do you here, Sir?"

I squinted into the crowd; and spied, amidst the strange faces, one I knew.

"Ah, Mr. Hickling," I replied – surprised, as I heard myself, both at the quickness of my wits, and the assurance of my tone. "This is fortunate, indeed! I am come to see you!"

"Me! Why?"

"That, Sir, I should prefer to tell you –" I said; and finished, with a significant nod towards the mob. Hickling at once understood the hint, and – with a shrug that served, at a stroke, to show his perplexity, and to shake off his companions – stepped out towards me.

"Yes – what is it?" he said, as he drew near.

His manner was peremptory; but he spoke quietly, and glanced over his shoulder, to see the others could not hear. It was, in truth, a small enough concession to delicacy; but, in my beleaguered situation, I could not but feel grateful for the least evidence of kindness – with the result that I suddenly found myself looking at him, almost as a friend.

"I will not deceive you, Sir," I said. "I am in something of a pickle; and hope you may be able to help me from it."

"Indeed?" (frowning mistrustfully). "How?"

"You recall I came to America, to find a boy?"

He nodded.

"My efforts have been confounded at every turn," I said, "leaving me in the sorriest predicament imaginable." And went on briefly to relate my history – omitting nothing, save the defection of O'Donnell.

He heard me out in silence – making no response, save to take a pipe from his pocket and rub his finger against the bowl, until it was shiny with grease. But when I was done, he did not hesitate an instant; but at once shook his head, saying: "No, Sir, I fear I can do nothing for you. Many hundreds of children have been stolen by the savages. And what has become of them – save only those few that have escaped, or been taken back again – it is impossible to say." And without waiting for a reply, he turned, and rejoined the crowd.

Fate pulls me inexorably on. Y^r honours will excuse me, I hope, if I pass quickly over the next few hours – for there is no pleasure to me in describing them, and nothing to be gained by deferring the inevitable end.

The discovery of Hickling at the strange settlement – where I suppose he had passed the night, finding the company there more congenial than at Benjamin's – had saved my neck, but closed, at the same time, one of the two remaining avenues I had hoped might yet lead me from the labyrinth. On my way back, therefore, I resolved to try the other way immediately – which would have the additional merit of sparing me the necessity of explaining O'Donnell's departure for a while longer, if I could but get to my horse without being observed.

On this latter point, I was disappointed; for, having slipped by the huts undetected, and concluded I was now pretty safe, I at last emerged – only to see young Dexter, busy saddling his own nag, not ten yards from Hector. I stopped, hoping to withdraw; but he had already heard me, and – looking up, with a suspicious scowl – called: "Ah, there you are. But where's the other fellow? Seems he jus' flitted, wi'out leavin' a penny for his vittles or his bed."

It was exactly as I had feared; but now the crisis was upon me, I again found the resource to meet it: "Did you not hear a noise, a little before dawn?"

He frowned with the effort of recollection; and then muttered: "Maybe I did."

"'Twas a messenger, come to call him away, on a private matter that would brook not even an hour's delay. He made me swear I would not say what it was – tho' 'twill not surprise you to learn that it concerns a lady. But I am still here, as you see; and shall be again tonight; and will pay for us both, I promise."

He considered a moment; and then grunted – with no very good grace, but with a little nod, that told me he was sufficiently satisfied; and after thanking him, and giving him a guinea for his trouble in bringing us there, I bade him farewell, saddled my horse and set off for the Mount.

I arrived in less than an hour – knocked upon the gate – and, short-ly after, heard the parrot-faced woman's voice asking me my busi-ness. But when I told her, she said *that Sarah had instructed, I should on no account be admitted again, under any pretext whatever.* I pleaded with her, but she would not relent – and at length lost patience altogether, crying, "Go now – or I will shoot you!" This was accompanied by the click of a musket hammer; which made it so persuasive that I at once left.

But had got no further than the bottom of the hill, before I felt such a great gust of fatigue as I knew would blow me clean out of the sad-dle – likely as not, cracking my head open on a rock – if I did not stop immediately. Which I did; and, after quenching my furious thirst in a little stream (for I had neither eaten nor drunk since the evening before), I lay down on the bank, and pulled my coat about me.

I must have slept some hours; for when I woke, the sun had already begun to sink in the sky, bloodying the tops of the trees behind me. I splashed water on my face, to rouse my sluggish brain; and then continued on my way.

After a mile or so, I heard hoof-beats coming approaching from the east. For one giddy instant I allowed myself to hope that O'Donnell had repented of his hastiness, and was coming back to find me; but then I turned a bend and saw a slighter figure than his, ambling towards me on a pony. At first, I supposed it to be a stranger; but as it drew near, I saw, with considerable surprise, it was Mrs. Craig's servant. We halted, and greeted each other; and – my pulse dunting in my temples – I asked *whether her mistress was with her?* To which she replied, *No; she had sent her back, to return the horse we had lent her.*

I felt, I confess, somewhat wounded; for we had naturally intend-ed it as a gift – which I had supposed Mrs. Craig to have understood, and accepted. But it would have been futile to remonstrate with the girl; so I contented myself with enquiring *whether she had met Mr. O'Donnell upon the way.* She answered in the affirmative, adding *that she had offered the beast to him; but he had said, my need of it was greater than his. So she had brought it to Cicero, and I should find it waiting for me there.*

Which I did. And also, to my astonishment, two other creatures, I had not expected to meet again: Hickling, and his hairless friend.

They were sitting by Benjamin's cabin; and rose, as soon as they saw me.

"I am glad you are returned, Sir," said Hickling. "I have some news you will be happy to hear, if I am not greatly mistaken."

He sat down again – gesturing to me, to do likewise. On the table before him was a folded letter, which he covered with his elbow – to prevent it, as I imagined, from blowing away, tho' there was scarcely a breeze.

"After you had left this morning, I mentioned your difficulty to Mr. Hody" – here indicating his companion – "tho' with little hope, I own, that he would be better able to assist you than I was. But by chance – or something more, perhaps – he can. He remembers your nephew well, and knows the place where he is held – and will, if you wish, take you there himself."

I looked at Hody.

He said nothing, but nodded vigorously, and sucked his lips into a tight grin.

"And I will come, too; and bring another handy young fellow or two with me – for if you are to go to the Indians, and come away again, you must be well protected. What do you say?"

It was the glow of a single candle, in a world of utter darkness. If I had lived in the age of superstition, I should have called it a miracle.

"Well?" he prompted me.

I had used up all my store of cunning. "Thank you," I said. "Yes."

XXXI

Pray continue, Sir, without delay; for we would not detain you longer than is necessary, at so painful a juncture in your story.

The delicacy of y^r honours' feeling does you credit – tho' I own I was startled to find it inscribed, not upon a separate sheet, but on the very page where I write myself. It is indeed strange, to discover another hand, where you expected to see only your own. I begin to imagine that y^r honours mean to turn author, and relate my adventure for me; for you speak as if you know it already.

Nay – I try to jest – but in truth I am troubled. How can y^r honours be so certain *that this is a painful juncture in my story*? Reason tells me, 'tis most likely you merely deduced it, from what I said yesterday; but I cannot entirely master the fear that you have somehow heard another account of what happened next – that could only have been furnished either by a murderous scoundrel, or by a double-dealing Tartuffe, neither of whom would have scrupled to slander me, in order to save himself.

This doubt lurks in my head like a cat in a dovecote – rousing my old speculations, and sending them into a fluttering whirr again.

Who are you?

Why are you holding me here?

What do you suspect me of?

Please y^r honours to make me easy, if you may.

Is it not remarkable, when you come to reflect upon it (as I never did before now), that while the human mind has succeeded in navigating the oceans, and mapping the skies, and unlocking the geometrick secrets of the world, it still knows almost nothing of itself. Of which I offer the following proof: for the past half-hour, conscious that my life may depend upon it, I have been dredging my memory for particulars of the following day's events, to set against the fraudulent testimony of my accusers – supposing, as I must, that such a thing exists. But for all the good it did me, I might as well not have troubled myself: for tho' the central image remains dreadfully vivid, the rest – save for a few incoherent flakes and patches – is worn away to the bare canvas, and nothing I can do is able to restore it. Whether this shows Nature's kindness, in sparing us useless anguish; or merely her thrift, in suppressing the recollection of small things, so that we may better recall great ones, I cannot say; but you are now, I hope, sufficiently acquainted with me to know that I shall not attempt to make good the deficiency, by inventing what I cannot remember. So I shall build my house with the bricks I have; and if there are gaps in the walls, that expose me to the insinuations of my enemies, leave it to y^r honours to decide which of us is more likely to be telling the truth.

Here, then, is what I recollect:

1. Hickling arrived about an hour after dawn. There were (I think) six men with him; but besides Hody, I can call to mind only one: a greasy, slouching, hang-dog fellow, who would not look me in the eye, and smirked at everything I said – as though I were either a great wit, or a great fool.

We left in a thin mist, that seemed to promise a fine day, once the sun had mustered strength enough to melt it. But the promise was evidently not fulfilled; for some hours later (it might have been two, or six, or any number between, for all I can say now), as I reached the top of a rise, I saw a churning sea of cloud rushing towards me from the west – and the next moment, felt a great buffet of wind, that flung a few stinging raindrops against my face. Why this should have stayed with me, when so much else has vanished, I cannot conceive; but I clearly remember thinking *that the weather in America was absurdly changeable, and we should all be very wet presently, if we did not take shelter beneath the trees.*

And perhaps we were, for all I can tell you to the contrary.

2. Tho' I had naturally expected that we should all travel together, my companions – without favouring me with so much as a word, or even a glance – set out at a feverish pace, which, try as I might, I could not keep up; for, besides not knowing the way, I was hampered by having to lead the two additional horses myself. As a consequence, my supposed guides were soon so far ahead that I often could not see them at all; but the road (tho' overgrown and swampy by turns) was plain enough – and reflecting that, since they had not troubled to consult my wishes, I was under no great obligation to consider theirs, I continued to stop, and rest the animals, whenever I felt the need. Provoking Hickling, on one occasion, to ride back, and ask me (none too pleasantly) *if I meant to dawdle the whole way?* To which I replied, "I am not dawdling, Sir"; and then asked: "Why are you in such a hurry?"

"Why, Sir – the men are anxious to be done with this affair as soon as possible; for they all have pressing business to attend to at home."

"Well – tell them they are engaged on my business now, and will be well paid for it; but that while they remain in my employment, they must match their step to mine."

This answer plainly did not please him, for he stared furiously at me, his cheeks flushed, and his throat working like an engine; but he said nothing, and after a moment turned abruptly about – stirred his poor brute with a kick – and set off towards his friends at an impatient trot.

We are nearing the fatal moment.

3. Some time later (again I cannot say how long) we forded a shallow stream; which so frightened my skittish pack-horse, I was obliged to leave it, and go over with the other two – and then dismount and return on foot, to coax it across. I remember the water seeping through my cracked boots, and the chilly touch of the wet

leather as I removed them, and – supporting myself against a tree – tried to shake them dry again.

I have forgotten what it was that made me start – perhaps a sound, or else just the mysterious knowledge we sometimes have that we are being observed.

I looked up. Hody stood perhaps a quarter of a mile ahead, at the crest of a low hill, gazing down at me.

I felt my shoulders clench, and my pulse break into a gallop – and could not at once imagine why; for surely there was nothing untoward in that? Hickling must merely have sent him back to find me, so that we did not become entirely separated – which should, if anything, have made me more easy, and not less.

Then my brain caught what my eye had already seen.

He was standing absolutely still, half-hidden by a jutting branch, and holding something before his face – which at first I thought might be a gun, but then, from its glassy glint, guessed was a little telescope. Not so much the manner of a shepherd seeking a stray lamb, as of a sentinel watching for the enemy.

I raised my hand, to signify I had spied him, but he did not acknowledge it; so I bent down, and slowly put my boots on – making a great lazy spectacle of it, so he should not think I was alarmed.

When I stood up again, he was gone.

My first thought was that I should set out for Benjamin's again without delay; but I soon saw the folly of this plan: for they were almost certain to overtake me before I could get there – and it is an invariable principle that, by showing a man you fear he means to harm you, you make it the more likely that he will do so. And what reason could they possibly have (now I came to ponder the matter more calmly), for wanting to harm me at all? I was able to think of but one answer, and that was: to rob me – and if that had been their intention, they might easily have saved themselves a deal of trouble by doing it before now; for – there being no constable or justice within a hundred miles of Cicero – they evidently had no more to fear from the law there than they did here. All of which led me, by degrees, to conclude that my stretched nerves must have betrayed me into seeing mere coldness and incivility as something worse; and that I should continue as before – tho' with greater vigilance, and having first stowed my remaining money in my boot, and ensured that my gun and pistol were both charged and ready to my hand.

It was that precaution that saved me.

4. I reached the top of the hill without mishap, and without seeing any further evidence of Hody or his companions; and found myself looking over a broad, stately, slate-coloured river, that wound itself in great serpentine loops through a shallow valley, before turning grace-fully from view. On the far side, a beetling, shaggy stone shelf crowd-ed right to the very edge – mocking the serenity of the water, like a mob of naughty schoolboys jeering and waving sticks; but on the nearer, directly below me, the land lay flat and submissive, almost as far as the eye could see. To my surprise (for I had grown accustomed to the wilderness, and did not expect to find it interrupted by any-thing larger than another miserable cluster of huts), a great swathe – extending perhaps two miles in each direction, and big enough to accommodate a pair of Frigatevilles – had evidently at some juncture been cleared of trees; but it must long since have been abandoned again; for the forest was now in a fair way of reclaiming it. The ground was already covered by a dense mat of brushwood, that rose here and there to knot itself about an old stump or a rock – and in a few places, little colonies of saplings had begun to establish themselves.

This discovery instantly rekindled my anxiety; for (reflecting that it must have taken at least a hundred men to make such a mark; and, being unable to conceive where they might have come from, or gone to, in the midst of an unpeopled desert), I began to wonder if Hickling was taking me not to the Indians, but back again towards the settled parts of America – where, perhaps, he hoped to earn some reward by delivering me to the rebels as a spy, or to the government as a traitor. But when I looked up, I saw the clouds to the left were tinged with silver; and knew that was where the sun was, and we must indeed be moving west.

While I was thus distracted, a sudden violent tug at my hand almost pulled me from the saddle; and, turning about, I discovered my flighty pack-horse had halted, and was shaking its head wildly from side to side, white-eyed with fear. I could not immediately guess what had alarmed it; but following the direction of its stare I saw a small dark cave beside the road – with a freshly fallen branch across the mouth, still covered in leaves, that twitched and whis-pered in the wind, like the lips of a sleeping beast.

I remember thinking: *If a man were attacked, that would be a snug hole to take refuge in, and defend himself.*

I dismounted again – held my hands before the poor brute's eyes – whispered in its ear – and led it by the imagined danger.

Would I had been so successful in protecting it from the true one.

We descended slowly – past abandoned fields, and little tangles of twisted plum and peach trees, that must once have been orchards – through the rotting remains of a palisade – and on to a wide straight track, that (tho' half-eaten by brambles), still had something of the air of a street. On either side was a series of overgrown lumps, which I had first supposed to be some natural peculiarity of the place – but now discovered were the ruins of little houses, caught in the grip of vines and bushes, that had choked them almost to death. Enough of the walls remained, however, for me to remark that they were quite unlike any of the other cabins I had seen – for they were larger, and made not of bare logs, but of wattle, plastered with a kind of reddish clay.

"Good G–d!" I muttered – forgetting, in my astonishment, that I had no companion to hear me – "this is an Indian town!" But I had no time to marvel further at it; for at that moment, the pack-horse abruptly stopped again, and snorted.

I remember glancing about, to see what had unsettled it now, and suddenly observing, as I did so, that the old huts offered such opportunities for concealment as would make it the easiest thing in the world to set an ambush here.

The next instant – from a building somewhat larger than the rest, standing in a kind of piazza about two hundred paces ahead – there came an answering neigh.

I at once dropped the leading-rope – turned – and set off back the way I had come, urging Hector into a run, and laying my cheek against his neck, so we might present a smaller target. Every second, I expected cries, or shots, or the clatter of pursuit behind me; but all I heard was the fading tattoo of my own spare animals' hoof-beats, as they trotted forlornly after us.

I began to think my fears must have been groundless; but then – just as I approached the top of the hill – there came a crackling of fire, and the fearful cries of a wounded beast.

I jumped down – led Hector into the shelter of the trees – tethered him behind a fat sycamore – snatched up my weapons – burrowed my way into the little cave – drew the branch after me, so that it formed a kind of natural parapet across the entrance – and peered down into the valley.

About fifty yards away, the wretched pack-horse lay twitching on the ground, as its terrified fellow thrashed and kicked beside it, furiously tossing its head in a vain effort to throw off the rope connecting them. Some way below, I could see two of Hickling's men approaching at a canter; while – in the distance – the rest were scuttling from their hiding-places, and running towards their horses. They were all still so far off, they looked as unhurried as crawling insects; but I knew this was an illusion, and that in reality I had no more than a few seconds to resolve what I must do: either to fire upon them, and trust to my own skill as a marksman and the impregnability of my position, to drive them off; or else to conceal myself as well as I could, in hope they had not seen where I had gone and would pass by without discovering me. What, in the end, decided the point, was not a rational calculation of the odds, but the thought that, if I took the second course, and it miscarried, I should be dragged out like a skulking schoolboy trying to escape a whipping, and subjected to who knew what indignities. Better, surely, to announce my defiance – and my readiness, if I must, to pay the price for it.

I lay down; discreetly levelled my musket at the nearer of the two horsemen; and – when he was close enough for me to see it was Hody – let fly. For the least fraction of a second I wondered if I had missed; then he suddenly stiffened in the saddle – let out a strange gargling cry, that frothed his lips with red – and tumbled headlong to the ground. It took me only a few moments to re-load my gun; but that was time enough for the other man to vanish into the forest – where, I guessed, he would await the arrival of his companions, and then join them in a combined foray against me.

I hastily looked about for anything I might use to fortify my defences; but could find nothing (aside from a few twigs and pebbles) but a jutting tooth of rock above my head – which resisted my every effort to dislodge it and remove it to a place where it would serve me better. After a short while, therefore, I gave up; and – having ensured that my musket was ready, and my pistol within reach – set myself to watch.

I remember wondering *why I was not more afraid*; and seeing, with a sort of sober amazement *that it was because I was alone*. In every other crisis, my anxiety had been inflamed, and my actions constrained, by the knowledge that not only my fate, but O'Donnell's, or Mrs. Craig's, or Niobe's, depended upon the upshot; now I knew that –

whatever the issue – the only life I should have upon my conscience would be my own.

I remember thinking *that having seen what happened to Hody, they would be fools indeed, to expose themselves in the same way; and would probably dispose themselves instead among the trees on the other side of the road, where I could not spy them, and where they might take best advantage of their greater strength, to harry me in concert.*

And so it turned out; for I heard and saw no more of them – until, after perhaps three minutes, there came a shocking double *crack* from the woods opposite to me. One bullet bedded itself in the fallen branch; the other chipped a flake of stone from the wall beside me.

I remember thinking *why were there only two?* – and reflecting that perhaps it was because, by some stroke of fortune, I had somehow contrived to wound the second rider, with the same discharge that had killed Hody. This thought provoked a little bubble of hope to leaven my depressed spirits; for if their numbers were really so reduced, I might yet have a chance of destroying them – provided I held my fire until they actually appeared, and then used both my weapons.

We are very near the end now.

Their next pair of shots shattered the wooden parapet. A second after, I was aware of an odd cold pressure on my left shin, and, looking down, saw a glistening rosy gash there. I thrust my finger into it, to discover if it was a wound of some consequence, or merely a scratch caused by a splinter – and touched a cruel little needle of broken bone.

I cried out – not in pain, for I felt none; but rather in horror.

In the same instant, there was a loud *dunt* from without, and everything – hands, leg, weapons – was engulfed in darkness.

I turned. A man's figure blocked the entrance. I could not see his face – for with the light behind him he was as shadowy as the monster in a nightmare; but in that last second of consciousness, I understood that he must have crept on to the roof, and dropped down suddenly upon me.

I saw he was holding a knife.

I tried to stand.

Something struck my neck; and the flood of darkness filled my brain.

*

228

I was stretched on my back, suspended between two torments, that had half my body apiece: a pumping throb in my leg; and a hot, stinging stiffness above my forehead – as if somebody had slit the skin, and inserted a red-hot wire there.

I felt movement – a regular swaying, that carried me up to the right, and down to the left again, like a boat tugging at its anchor.

But this was not a boat. I could smell horses – hear the soft whistle of their breath, and the trudge of their feet.

I opened my eyes; but the brilliance of the sun was another torture, and I at once closed them again.

I thought: *They suppose I am dead. As I shall be, soon enough.*

It was a voice roused me next: "Hush – he is stirring. Fetch some...!" But what was to be fetched, I could not tell. The words appeared to come from a hundred miles away, or from a different world altogether; for they had the balsamick tone of a fashionable doctor attending a duchess – giving me, for a moment, the wild notion that I was not in America at all, but at home in Somersetshire; and that my injuries had been caused not by Hickling and his gang, but by a fall from my horse that had knocked me into a coma, and my adventure no more than a fevered dream, cooked up by my jarred nerves as I lay insensible in bed.

But then I unscrewed my eyes – and found I was lying on the ground, wrapped in a blanket. The sky was pricked with stars, and eddies of flying sparks. The air smelled of crushed grass and wood-smoke – mingled with a cold, weedy dankness, that told me I was near a river. I could hear the spit and grumble of the fire, and feel its warmth; but when I tried to turn towards it, the back of my head seemed to wrench open – with such agonizing violence as to drive my other wounds, for a second or two, entirely from my mind.

"Pray, Sir – do not derange yourself."

He was nearer now – but directly behind me, so I still could not see him. But there was something familiar in his manner, that set me shuffling through my own recollections for the face that fitted it: Hickling, no; Hody, no; Sam Dexter, no. Benjamin I detained a moment longer, but then dismissed; for his strangeness, tho' equally marked, was of a different order. Perhaps I must go back further, to Coleman – or Washington . . .

No.

"You are very sick, Sir. You must – guard your strength."

Guard my strength? That, surely, was an odd enough phrase, that should direct me to the truth?

Lord Jack? No – he was dead. Tobias Tanner?

My reason began to slip. Perhaps it was the parrot-faced woman at the Mount. *She* was a guard.

Or the crowd of dogs at Hody's village.

A few more seconds, and I knew I should be unconscious again.

"Who are you?" I said.

He did not reply.

"I beg you–"

"Make yourself easy. I am a friend."

Friend. I clung to the word – as a boy hugs a toy, half-believing it will keep him safe from ghosts.

And so slept.

It was day when I once more came to my senses. I was lying still; and the sun pressed so fierce upon my eyelids I dared not raise them, to see where I was, for fear of being dazzled. But a chorus of sounds – the barking of a dog; the howling of an infant; the murmur of voices; the distant cries of playing children, and the pad and skitter of their feet – told me we were no longer upon the road, but had arrived in a town of some importance.

My first thought was *that I should be safer here, in the midst of so many people.*

My second, *that I must have been robbed; for the signet was gone from my finger.*

My third, *that perhaps I was beginning to mend*; for the pain in my injured leg had dulled to a sore throb. But when I tried to lift it, so I might probe the wound with my finger, it was as lumpish and unbiddable as a log.

I grimaced. The next instant I felt a shadow cross my face, and heard a muttered voice, not four feet away.

I opened my eyes, and saw a grotesque figure louring over me: tall – dark-skinned – unwigged – and with the hair all gone from his tawny scalp, save for a coarse black crest in the middle, that sprang up like the mane of a young horse. His ears were tipped with little tufts of white feathers – and so distended and deformed, they flapped about his cheeks like a hound's; his throat was cluttered with two or three medallions, engraved with superstitious signs, and

230

strung upon a black ribbon, and below them hung a great silver crescent – such (I imagined) as some devil of a Mexican priest might have put on, to tear the beating heart from his victim.

I tried to cry out. To my astonishment, all the noise I could make was a rattling gasp, like the croak of a dying pheasant. To which he replied by gingerly touching my brow, as if to convince himself that I was real – and then uttering a low, rumbling *hurrrr*, that put me in mind of nothing so much as the grunt of a hungry man when a piece of beef is set before him.

The next moment he turned, and shouted loudly, as if summoning others to the feast. Immediately the murmur of voices rose to an excited gabble, like the sound of a bee-hive roused to anger, and all at once a great jostling press of men and boys appeared, and closed about me in a tightening noose, until I began to fear I should be crushed. They were all as outlandish as the fellow I had seen first – and some even more so: daubed with vermillion, or pricked with hieroglyphick designs; or crowned with gaudy diadems sprouting plumes and quills. So strange and inhuman did they appear, it was impossible to guess their intention towards me; but from their wild gesticulations and noisy jabber, I could not but suspect it was unfriendly, or something worse; and I found myself praying (tho' to what or whom I did not know): *If I am to die, let it be quickly.*

Then the crowd suddenly fell almost silent; and two or three youths – after glancing quickly behind – sheepishly shuffled aside, to make a passage between them.

I thought: *Perhaps their king is come to save me.*

But it was not a king. It was a woman – dressed in a flapping petticoat, and a little beaded waistcoat – her hair coiled up, and aflame with brilliant ribbons.

She said something in a rough jargon, that seemed three-fourths composed of the letter "r"; and then leaned over me, and stared into my face.

My poor enfeebled heart fluttered with terror – for her hands were drenched in blood; and in one of them she clutched a butcher's knife.

I struggled to keep my wits, and think of some means to protect myself; but the grand combination of shock and weakness proved too powerful for me, and before I could even murmur a protest, I was tumbling back into unconsciousness.

Where I shall leave myself, until tomorrow.

XXXII

Be so good, Sir, as to give all the Indian words you recall, together with their meanings.

Thursday

Once more yʳ honours trouble me. Did I say these fearful creatures were Indians? Or, if they were (which I own to be a reasonable surmise), that I saw them again; or was long enough among them to learn anything of their language?

I said nothing of the sort; which seems to confirm my suspicion that you have already heard some account of my adventure – or, at the least, of this part of it.

But whose account it is – and to what purpose he might have given it to you – I cannot remotely guess. And since you have refused to answer my questions, or even acknowledge that I asked them, I can only suppose that you do not mean me to know.

So I find myself like a fish, that swims and swims – not knowing whether his exertions are carrying him to the freedom of the sea, or deeper within a bottle, from which there is no escape.

Which leaves me not only anxious, but also disappointed – for I had allowed myself to hope, we had begun (in some strange sort) to be friends.

But I see I was mistaken; and there is no help for it but to continue as before, trusting to the truth to protect me.

So – some Indian words:

Yoonwee – "a man"
Dickta – "an eye"
Ganega – "skin"
Hayoo – "Yes!"
Hunyahusker – "He will die"
Tsistoo – "a rabbit"
Gilli – "a dog"
Sagwalee – "a horse"
Sickwa – "a hog"
Nunda-igehee – "the sun"
Nunda-sunna-yehee – "the moon"
Kanunawoo – "a pipe"
Natsikoo – "I eat it"

Kanataluhee – "a *hominy* (stiff maize porridge) cooked with walnuts"
Anetsa – "a game or sport, to which they are much attached"
Tadeyastatackoowee – "We shall see each other"

And now – whatever the consequence – to my story again:

I woke shivering. My tongue was dry and swollen, and appeared glued to my palate. I heard a pitiful puppyish whimpering, which, when I opened my eyes, I found was coming from my own mouth – tho' even then I could not stop it.

I was lying wrapped in a sodden sheet. There was no light save for a single candle by the bed. As I watched, a figure emerged from the darkness and stood above me; and in the upward glow of the flame I saw an olive-coloured brow, surmounted by a wild bouquet of ribbons.

The woman with the bloody hands.

I was too sick to be frightened of her.

She bent over, and held a cup to my lips. I felt water trickle over my teeth. She took it away again, and put a spoon in its place.

I heard a voice sigh, "Feeeeeel better"; but whether it was hers, or the product of my own fancy, I could not say.

I tasted syrup. Soon the shaking eased, and I slept again.

For several weeks (I know now) I lay close to Death – and there were times I wished he would end my suffering by finally snapping the last tatter that attached me to life and taking me to himself. When I was conscious (if such a state may be called consciousness), my whole body seemed to have become a giant pounding heart – so noisy and violent as to squeeze everything else from my brain; when I slept, I was tormented by fantastick beings from the age of superstition – grinning succubi, and coiled, slimy demons, that laughingly pricked my eyes, and tortured my wounded leg and brow with red-hot forks. Once, when I woke, I thought I must have died indeed, and been d–ned for my pains: for there, at my bedside, was exactly such a creature as I had just been dreaming of – moaning, and rolling his eyes, and placing his slavering lips directly over my wound, as if he meant to bite it. Which astonished more than terrified me; for I had always believed that hell existed only in the mouths of priests, and in the minds of their credulous flocks.

But then I remarked the woman sitting by the bed; who – tho' I was still nine-tenths delirious – yet somehow contrived to make me understand that this apparition was an Indian conjurer, and meant me no harm.

When, or how, I began to mend, I cannot say; but I know that I suddenly came to my senses one day with a jolt. My chin and chest were cold and clammy, as if somebody had tried to rouse me with a wet sponge; but when I looked about me (which I was able to do only by shifting my eyes to right and left; for my neck was still immovably sore) I could see nothing but an empty chamber – about the size of the one in which I write these words. By the duskish light of the window I made out a neat little chest, and a chair, and a table close by my head, with a pitcher set upon it; and from another room heard the soft tinkling of a spinet – marred by hesitations and mistakes, but wonderfully soothing nonetheless: for surely there is no sound in the world that speaks more eloquently of home and peace and well-being?

I thought: *Where is this place? And how long must I have slept, to remember nothing of coming here?* – for I had not known such comfort since O'Donnell and I had stayed at Colonel Washington's.

Then I heard a step without; and the next instant the door opened gently, and the woman entered, carrying a basin and a white linen napkin. As she came near, and saw I was not only conscious, but staring at her, she suddenly stopped, and jumped back, with the startled squeak of a maidservant surprised by a mouse. Then she laughed, and said, "Oh! I think you sleeping!"

Her manner of speaking was the strangest I had ever heard: harsh and tender and musical all at once, as if she were simultaneously both angry and solicitous. "I help you drink," she said. "But the cup fall, and the water spill – and that, I suppose, wake you. So" – flourishing the cloth – "you know . . ." She smiled, and began dabbing vigorously at my breast.

I tried to speak; but all that emerged from my mouth was a pitiful whistle, like the sigh of a leaky bellows. But she remarked my effort, and at once paused in her work, and set her ear so close to my mouth that a wreath of her hair fell across my temple.

"What?"

"Where am I?" I whispered.

"Why – at Mr. McLeod's house," she replied. "I am his wife. He gone from home; but he tell me take care of you."

I knew I had heard the name McLeod before – and that not long

234

ago; but in my fuddled state could not immediately remember where or when.

"Your husband –?" I began.

But she spared me the necessity of saying more, by holding up her hand, and declaring: "You meet him at Frigateville, you remember?" And at once I knew him: the companion of the Frenchman, and Hickling's antagonist at dinner.

"But how did I come here?" I whispered.

She appeared to reflect a moment; then sat upon the bed – gazed into my eyes, as solemn as a doctor – and at length said: "Can you read a little?"

In truth, I doubted that I could; but my curiosity was so stirred, that I attempted a little nod, and silently mouthed, *I think so.*

She rose again – went to the chest – slipped something from a drawer – and brought it to me.

"Here."

It was a letter. I fumbled with it for a few seconds; but my hands were too weak to open it.

Seeing which, she took it back again, saying: "I do it for you?"

"Please –" I murmured.

She cracked the seal – unfolded the paper before my face – and held it where I might see it plainly.

This (as far as I can recollect it) is what it said:

Sir,

If (as I earnestly hope) you are ever sufficiently recovered to know where you are, and to wonder at it, here is your answer:

A few days since, while we were passing through the country west of Watagi, the Marquis de Vieux Fumé and I heard shots, not two miles distant; and hastening to discover the cause, found you, in the most desperate strait imaginable, close to the old town called *Tsiyahi*. You had evidently been set upon by a gang of lawless rogues, who had shot you in the leg; beaten you unconscious; and were in a fair way of removing your scalp – in the hope, no doubt, that the outrage would then be blamed upon the Indians. One of them (a hideous, mutilated fellow; who must at some time have suffered the same fate himself) was already dead – I suppose, by your hand; and we soon killed another of them, and drove the rest away. We removed the shot from your wound; and – tho' it necessitated a detour from our journey – determined to bring you to my house, where you could be assured of receiving the best attention possible.

I am sorry I cannot stay, to superintend your care myself; but I am engaged to go with the marquis, to assist him in his business. But I know (from my own experience) that you could have no more conscientious nurse than my dear wife; and if you rally enough to read these words, I am certain you will continue to mend, and I shall return to find you much improved.

Yours truly,

Ewan McLeod

"Thank you," I said.

At which she nodded, and smiled; and folded the letter again – so carefully and luxuriously, you would have thought it contained some part of its author, and she was showing her wifely devotion by the tenderness with which she caressed it.

"Sleep now," she said, when she had returned it to the drawer. And then, taking up the cloth and the basin again , tip-toed from the room.

I closed my eyes; and, for the first time in a week or more, drifted into unconsciousness of my own volition, rather than being flung there by force.

But this episode was but the first small victory in a long and costly war. Some days I made no progress at all against the enemy, or was compelled to retreat before him; others I would wake, half-drowned in sweat, and feeble as a blind kitten – but with a quiet pulse and a clear mind, that led me to hope my wits had finally returned to me, and would not desert me again. But then, after half an hour or so, I would feel a cold touch on my skin, and a tattoo in my ears, that grew steadily louder, like the drum-beat of an advancing army; and soon – however much I tried to resist – I would be plunged back into the terror of delirium.

Yet in spite of all these setbacks, little by little I inched forward – sipping a spoonful of tepid broth; mumbling a morsel of bread; and slowly increasing my periods of lucidity – until at length I had pretty much succeeded in expelling my nightmares from the day-time world altogether, and pressing them back within the borders of their own dark country, where I had no authority over them.

*

My time among the Indians sits so strangely with the rest of my adventure that I cannot treat of it in the same manner. In truth, to call it "time" at all is almost to deceive – for the hours and weeks did not pass there as they do elsewhere. There was, indeed, a clock in McLeod's house, which I could see when my door was open, and which his wife sometimes remembered to wind – but I soon gave up looking at it, for it measured the operations of another world, and told me nothing of consequence about the one I found myself in. I have had occasion before, when recounting the moment when I thought we were about to be shot by Lord Jack, to speak of the strange tricks our minds may play on us in an extremity. But while that was but an instant, that appeared to swell to an eternity, this was almost its diametrical opposite: a whole year (as I later discovered) boiled down to no more than a bubbling stew of thoughts and impressions – in which it is near impossible to tell in what order they occurred, or what passed between them. In consequence, tho' what went before is still clear and real enough, my Indian life, and its sequel, appear in recollection something like a long jumbled dream; and may be almost as quickly told.

Since y^r honours were evidently well acquainted with this portion of my story even before I began to write it, you perhaps already know how long I was confined to my bed in Mr. McLeod's house. But if you do not, I cannot help you to an answer; for (tho' reason tells me it must have been many weeks) all I can remember with any certainty is the endless cycle of day passing into night, and night back to day again. It usually began (if a cycle can be said to have a beginning) about dinner-time, or even before, when I was assailed by the noise of voices and footsteps without; and then, from some distant part of the town, the beginning of a frenzied commotion – stamping, and rattling, and howling, and roaring, as if the entire town worshipped Satan, and had gathered together to glorify their master and invoke his assistance for some terrible act. Of which I could not but fancy myself the intended victim – for this was the very unnatural racket that Dan had described, when relating his torture by the savages and the devilish dance that had accompanied it. It soon became evident, when I had heard it three or four times, and no-one had appeared to drag me to the stake, that it must have some other significance; and yet I could not wholly overcome my dread, and would try to delay falling asleep until it had ceased, and the house was filled again with the sweet stammering of ill-played Handel. But even if I failed, it would often invade my slumber – appearing to my confused senses as a sort of demon, that held me prisoner, until it was forced to set me free by the angelick voice of the spinet.

Sometimes I was waked early, by the imperious bray of a horn – which I at first imagined must be a signal, to warn of an attack; but later guessed was merely intended to rouse the Indians and send them to their labours. My breakfast arrived a little after, and generally consisted of tea (from which I deduced that the ban upon importing it did not extend to the savages), together with cakes of dense, bitter-tasting bread and honey. It was usually brought by Mrs. McLeod herself; but occasionally one of her two daughters, Flora and Nancy – who had been travelling with their father, but had plainly decided to stay when my misfortune carried them home again – did the office for her. They were charming girls: dark-skinned and black-haired like their mother, but more slightly made – and so graceful in their movements, they were as lovely to see as swans. You might have imagined they would have been easier with me than she was, since they spoke English more naturally, and had seen more of the world; but while they were always polite, they said little, and avoided my eye, and always left the room as soon as their business was done. But I soon came to perceive that – tho' the effect of this unwillingness was the same in both sisters – its cause was not: for whereas haughty Flora seemed merely to feel it was demeaning for her to be obliged to wait on me at all, poor gentle Nancy's difficulty lay in her excessive tender-heartedness and modesty – which made, respectively, the sight of my injuries, and the necessity of emptying my chamber-pot, an agony for her.

Mrs. McLeod, on the other hand, when she had finished washing me, and dressing my shin and scalp, would often linger some time longer, and try to engage me in conversation – asking me such particulars as how many children I had, where I lived, and whether I was a merchant, come to America to trade, &c. &c. She was as nervous and fidgety as her daughters – suddenly breaking off sometimes in the middle of a sentence, to puff my pillow, or smooth a wrinkle from my sheet, as if she had all at once remembered that was her true purpose in being there; but *her* anxiety, I think, arose not from the desire to escape, but rather from an apprehension of the great gulf that separated us, and how powerless she was to cross it.

238

Which plainly disappointed her – for she was a kind and intelligent woman, who saw I was troubled not only by physical injuries, but also by the want of company and intimacy, and was eager to relieve both conditions, if she could.

This leads me to observe (since yʳ honours have shown some curiosity concerning the Indian tongue) that language is a less trustworthy servant than you might suppose. I had always thought of it as a kind of currency, in which each token possessed a fixed value, and might easily be exchanged for its equivalent in another country – so that when travelling (for example) in France, you could as confidently use *cheval* for *horse*, as a louis for a pound. But my time among the Cherokee showed me the folly of this conceit. Mrs. McLeod knew many hundreds of English words, or perhaps even thousands – but what they signified in her head and in mine were often different things entirely. Consider, for instance, even so unambiguous a noun as *house*: for both of us it carried the notion of *abode* – but whereas to me, that was most powerfully represented by a Somersetshire manor, to her it could mean only a one-storey structure of wood and mud, such as the one in which we found ourselves. Or – more remarkably still – *rabbit*, which I wager conjures in yʳ honours' minds (as it does in mine) nothing more than the image of a long-eared pestilential little creature, that with a few of its fellows may afford a pleasant dinner. But the Cherokees (I learned, with some astonishment) see it not only as a source of food, but also as a potent god or spirit, that they call *Tsistoo* – who is the author of half the mischief in the world; and whose work, which is everywhere to be seen, makes him the subject of numberless droll tales. So, for the greater part of the time we were together, Mrs. McLeod and I were like two men that try to build a bridge from opposite sides of a river – but soon discover they are set on such different courses it is impossible they should ever meet.

It was, I suppose, the desire to find some other way across the chasm – even if only by a single rope – that prompted her, when I was strong enough to sit up a little, to appear one afternoon carrying a box of chess men and a board. She held them before her like a popish priest displaying a relic; raised her eyebrows into a question; and then – when I replied with a painful nod – smiled, and set them out upon the bedside table. After that, it became almost our daily custom to play two or three games – if *playing* it may be called; for tho' she knew the names of the pieces and the various ways in which they moved, she had not the least conception of how to form her own plan, or guess mine – with the result that I invariably routed her within three minutes. I tried sometimes to let her win, by exposing my queen, or failing to take hers, or the like; but – as if there were a fixed relation between us, that must ever remain the same – she always responded by making some even more foolish mistake herself, that forced victory upon me, whether I would or no. At which she would shake her head, and clap her hand over her mouth, and tremble with self-mocking giggles – like an awkward girl at her first ball who has dragged her partner the wrong way and wonders at her own ignorance.

So defective was my sense of time, I cannot even conjecture how many weeks or months it was, before I became aware that these contests had ceased to be a purely private affair, and turned into something like a publick spectacle. Ever since recovering my wits – and sufficient mastery of my head, to turn it where I pleased – I had been conscious that little bands of children would sometimes gather at the window, to peer curiously in upon me – and then run away again, as soon as their gaze met mine. But now we seemed to have attracted a permanent company of spectators, adults as well as youngsters, who stood their ground when we looked at them, and joined in Mrs. McLeod's sheepish mirth when she lost, with the complaisant cheerfulness of an audience at Drury Lane laughing at Tony Lumpkin.

One day, when the crowd was so unusually large that we barely had light enough to see the board, I said: "If we charged sixpence for admission, we should soon be rich." She plainly perceived from my manner that I intended it as a joke, and gave a little guffaw – but the rigidity of her lips and the uncertainty in her eyes told me she had not understood it; so – not wishing to confuse her further, and anxious to think of some other pleasantry she might better comprehend – I glanced out of the window again. And there remarked, among the wall of men standing at the back, the maned, tufted fellow, whose looming face had been the first sight to greet me on my arrival here. I could judge his sentiments no better now than I had then; but something had evidently caught his attention; for he stared unflinchingly at us, and his brow was ridged with thought.

I thrust a finger towards him – at which he appeared to wince, as if I had struck him with a stone – and said: "Who is that?"

"He is the son of a beloved man," said Mrs. McLeod – and then, for no reason I could imagine, fell into a furious fit of giggling.

It was (as far as I can judge) no more than a week later that, one afternoon, I heard Mrs. McLeod speaking to someone in the next room, and then the soft tread of her feet approaching my chamber. It was about the time in the afternoon we usually played together, and I naturally thought she was going to propose a game now; but instead she paused by the entrance, and called: "Are you awake?"

"Yes."

"A friend is come to see you."

And before I could reply, or speculate who it might be, the door opened, and – to my great astonishment – the same flap-eared man swaggered in, and stopped by the bed. Where he stood awhile, searching my face – with a kind of powerful watchful stillness, that brought the heat to my cheeks and gave me the unsettling impression he might stop my heart, if he chose, just by continuing to gaze at me. Then he clapped his hand to his chest, and extended it towards me.

Not knowing what else to do, I took it.

He nodded – jerked his thumb towards his own throat – and said: "Yanegwa."

I supposed this must be his name, and that I was expected to give mine in return; so I replied: "Ned Gudgeon."

"Negudge?"

"Ned Gudgeon."

"Negudga." Which small modification made it sound (to my ears, at least) so entirely Indian, I wondered if *negudga* was a word in his own tongue and, if so, what it signified.

He waved towards the chess board on the bedside table, and said: "Jess?"

"Chess."

"Tchess?"

"Chess."

"Chess."

I nodded.

He gave a little smile of satisfaction; then rapidly pointed from me to him and back again.

"You wish to play?" I said. But from the void expression of his eyes, I knew he had no idea what I meant; so (with some difficulty, for I was still pitifully weak) I picked up the box of pieces, and rattled it before him.

"Hayu!" he said – which it needed no interpreter to tell me denoted *Yes!*; for he smirked like a babe given a bauble, and his coppery skin gleamed with pleasure.

So I drew the board towards me, and took out the men. He made no attempt to help me arrange them, but merely perched on the chair watching me, as immobile as a kestrel – as if by observing attentively enough just once, he might stamp their disposition so indelibly on his mind as to be able to reproduce it himself whenever he wished. Then, when I was done, he held up his hand, to indicate I should not begin yet – and slowly rehearsed the moves permitted to every man. Considering that (as I later discovered) he had learned them only by seeing us through the window, his knowledge was little less than astonishing: for the only one of which he appeared unsure was the L-shaped hop of the knight.

As y^r honours may imagine, I won our first few games without difficulty; which he accepted with sufficient grace – tho' there always appeared a ripple of impatience and annoyance beneath his good humour; and, after one particularly galling defeat, he was so provoked by the laughter of the children at the window that he sprang up and angrily shooed them away. But – such was the astonishing rapidity of his progress – I was forced to purchase every victory at a higher price than the last; until at length, I found myself so pressed, I could only prevail against him by marching a pawn to the far side of the board and resurrecting my fallen queen. At which he flung up his hands, and cried out, his face liverish with anger – for since I had never been driven to this extremity by Mrs. McLeod, he could not have seen it done before, and plainly thought I was presuming on his ignorance, to cheat him of success. Whether he was threatening me with revenge, or merely protesting at my perfidy, I could not say – but his furious bellows were enough to bring Mrs. McLeod running into my room, and anxiously demanding *what was the matter?* When I explained, she nodded, and spoke to him in Cherokee – and must have convinced him that I had not acted improperly; for pretty soon he subsided again, like a dog that has been bristling at an approaching figure, and suddenly sees it is a friend. But from her flustered manner I suspect she was as unfamiliar with the rules as he was, and only took my part to preserve the peace.

After that, he came to play with me almost every day, entirely supplanting Mrs. McLeod as an adversary, and even depriving her of her office as umpire – for he soon became as much my superior as I was hers, and regularly thrashed me so roundly as to put the issue of our contests quite beyond dispute.

Why he continued with these engagements, when I presented so small a challenge to him, I could not then guess; but I have since concluded that – tho', once embarked, his pride drove him to excel at it – chess-playing was only a pretext for a larger purpose, *viz.*, to acquire some English, in hope thereby of gaining favour with Nancy McLeod – who was the only person I ever saw that could turn away his gaze and reduce him to blushes. At the end of three or four bouts, he would put away the pieces, and then linger beside the bed – suggesting an object by means of a sign or a small drawing, and telling me what it was called in his tongue, and demanding its English name in return. Which led, sometimes, to some very ludicrous misunderstandings – such as one day, when he stabbed the pencil first towards me, and then towards himself, and said: "Yoonwe."

To which, supposing he had confused "we" for "I", I replied: "No – you and I."

But he only shook his head vigorously, setting his long ears slapping against his jaw, and repeated: "Yoonwe!"

"You and I."

And so we went on – he scribbling childish drawings, from which all I could make out was they were supposed to be people, and I vainly trying to explain the difference between singular and plural – until Mrs. McLeod came in, and told me that yoonwe was Cherokee for "man".

By this means, I learned something of his language; and he (being by far the readier student) a good deal more of mine – so that at length we were able to converse a little, and discover something of each other's lives. He insistently questioned me concerning my home and family – not (like Mrs. McLeod) simply to make me easy, but to satisfy his curiosity, and form some conception of English manners and customs; while I responded by asking him about hunting, and what crops the Indians grew, and how they built their houses. And, once, whether he had a sweetheart – at which the tears rose to his eyes, and he said *he loved a maid, and hoped to wife her.* He did not mention Nancy's name, but later (as you will see) gave me such

243

proof that I had guessed right as I shall never forget.

And most heartily wish I might.

In this fashion (strange tho' it may seem), we changed by imperceptible degrees from acquaintance to companionship, and finally to becoming true and loving friends. We were like two trees, that have grown up so far apart, it seems impossible they should ever touch; but gradually plunge their roots deeper and wider, until at last they meet and tangle below the earth. It is impossible to compare my feelings for O'Donnell and Yanegwa; for (as I clearly see, now I reflect upon it) the Ned Gudgeon who travelled with the one was a different man from the Negudga who played chess with the other. There are shadows upon my memories of both, one blacker than the other – but I still cannot think of either of them, without a tug at my heart.

Little by little I grew stronger, until eventually I was able to rise from my bed unaided, and sit in the chair, wrapped in a blanket – where I stationed myself every afternoon, to receive my visitor. Yanegwa would enter a few minutes later, carrying a little stool from the next room – which so dwindled his height when he settled upon it as to give me the pleasant illusion we were on almost equal terms, and that with sufficient effort I could hope to beat him again. But try as I might, I never did.

One evening, I heard a more fearful racket than usual, that continued until dawn, and seemed to resume intermittently for several days and nights thereafter. During this whole period, I did not once see Yanegwa – which did not, at first, greatly surprise me; for I guessed the noise must betoken some especially important festival, that required his attendance – and tho' he had said nothing of it to me, I had long since learned it was his custom never to bid me adieu, or to appoint the time of his next visit, but instead to come and go at will, as heedless of the clock as a cat. Once, indeed, when I attempted – just as he was leaving – to engage him to play again the following afternoon, he seemed so affronted you would have thought I had proposed to set him in chains, and make him my slave.

But when the hubbub had finally abated, and a season of relative calm ensued, and still he had not reappeared, I began to grow more uneasy; and at length enquired of Mrs. McLeod, if she had any intelligence of him. To which she replied sharply, as if I had said something improper, *Why should I ask her? For what he did, or where he was, were nothing of her concern.* Which made me wonder, if perhaps some misfortune had befallen him, and she was reluctant to speak of it, for fear of distressing me.

And then, just when I had almost given him up, he returned again one afternoon – with no more ceremony or explanation than if he had walked out of the room but ten minutes before. But I could see at once that he had undergone some change: for – tho' he did not look sickly – his face was leaner that I remembered it; and there was a wild restlessness about him, such as you may remark in a generally quiet horse that has been driven into a lather and cannot settle again after.

We began to play as usual; but his eyes kept straying from the board, and after two or three games he suddenly pushed back his stool – jumped to his feet – and pointed towards the window. I followed his finger, and saw that it was pointing, not at our customary band of onlookers, but at the sky above – which was clear and blue, and tinged with a soothing honey-gold. I asked him, "What is it?" – and he began to reply, in the usual gallimaufry of Cherokee and English; but before he had said five words, I somehow or other guessed the meaning: that it was a beautiful day, and we should venture out for a minute or two, to relish it. Tho' it was a novel idea, it hit my fancy; and having wrapped my blanket about myself like a cloak, I leaned on Yanegwa's arm and limped with him to the door.

It was the first time since my arrival that I had clearly seen the town, or even any great portion of it – which may appear strange, for as soon as I was able to stand, nothing could have been easier than for me to poke my head through the window and discover what lay that side of the house, at least. Why I had failed to do so I cannot entirely explain, even to myself – but part of the reason, I think, is this: that within my room I was reduced to no more than a babe in the womb, who has no intimation that he must one day be expelled from Eden, and forced to take his place among his fellows, and assume the wearisome duties of manhood; but thinks (if he thinks at all) only of the present. If I looked out, on the other hand, I should see houses and horses and children, and men and women going about their business – which must inevitably connect me with the world again, and give me some measure by which to judge my own life, and my own fearful predicament. You may think this cowardly; but what, in all reason, was to be gained by reminding myself of a home and friends I should almost certainly never see again, and obligations I should almost certainly never fulfil? It could only have caused me needless pain, by ripping the scabs (as it were) from my mental wounds, when I lacked the power to bind them up again. But Yanegwa's invitation encouraged me to hope I was less helpless than I had imagined, and steeled me to make trial of my own strength.

So it was with some trepidation as well as pleasure that I now stepped through the door – and discovered a scene that quite took me by surprise. Below us, a clutter of perhaps three hundred mud-plastered houses (each attended by two or three smaller satellites, that might have been stores or privies) sprawled a quarter of a mile or so to the edge of a sprightly, bubbling river, and then continued their progress about the same distance up the other bank. Most of them were more modest than McLeod's, and wanted the refinements his possessed, of windows and a chimney; but they were sprucer and better kept than many an English cottage I have seen, and the little plots surrounding them – each one neatly framed by a thin ribbon of grass – seemed tolerably well tended.

Some way to the right was a kind of sunken square, with an obelisk in the middle, and two posts at one end (which I could not look upon without imagining a pair of wretched captives tied to them); and next to it a curious mound or hillock, that had plainly been constructed artificially – for it was too regular and abrupt to be a natural forma-tion. On its summit, dominating the entire place, was an immense earth-covered rotunda, perhaps twenty feet high, that must have been capable of accommodating several hundred people at once – and that, from its position and tremendous size, I guessed to be the temple or meeting-place where the revellers or worshippers I heard each night congregated to make their noise.

Further off, in every direction, stretched larger fields – covered in a spiky carpet of green, as if the harvest had been but lately gathered in, and scattered with peach and plum orchards. The whole spectacle put me so powerfully in mind of the abandoned town where I had been attacked that, if I had been a fanciful man, I might have imag-ined I had fallen asleep there, and somehow waked again thirty years earlier, when it was in its heyday. But there, I remembered, the old trees had twinkled with blossom; while here – tho' they still carried their leaves – the fruit was already gone from them, and they shiv-ered in the breeze like boats relieved of their cargoes. From which I deduced (with some amazement), that I had been a-bed for half the spring, and most of the summer.

But these reflections were at once put out of my head by three or four children playing before the house; who – as soon as I blinkingly appeared – stopped their tussling, and gaped at me, as if they were as astonished to see me out of doors as I was to be there. After a few seconds they suddenly turned and fled, jabbering like starlings – which led me to suppose, that my scarred face had frightened them, or even (for I knew Indians to be incorrigibly superstitious) that they imagined I had died, and was now a ghost. But a wonderfully short time later they returned again, with half a dozen eager friends – followed by a retinue of ancient men and women, and a pack of silly curs, that yapped and pranced to show they shared the general excitement, tho' they had no notion of its cause.

Yanegwa stopped, and bellowed a few gruff words, that were evidently intended as a warning – for the company immediately halted its advance, and for a second or two fell silent. But then one of the older boys (a smirking, insolent fellow of thirteen or so, who plainly fancied himself a great wag) broke from the others, and began limping this way and that – swaying, and stumbling, and jerking his arms, in what he imagined to be an imitation of my own halting gait. This witty jest earned him a little gust of admiring laughter from his friends – and, in the same instant, a furious reproach from Yanegwa, who cried out, and raised his hand, as if he meant to strike him. But having gained so much publick favour by his fearless satire, the boy was not going to lose it again, by too easily submitting to the censor; so darted to the other side of the throng, and then (having first glanced over his shoulder, to see he was securely out reach) resumed his performance there.

Yanegwa did not pursue him, but rather drew himself up – laid a hand on his heart – and began speaking in a sonorously rhetorical voice, like a minister addressing the House of Commons. Tho' (from what I have heard of that honourable body) to much greater effect: for within half a minute, the crowd was as quiet and tractable as the mourners at a funeral, and the lad had left off his jest and scampered away, for want of an audience. I had no notion what my friend had said, but could not but wonder at the force of his oratory, and imagine the heights to which it might have carried him, had he chanced to be born not in the wilderness, but in England. It was impossible not to conceive that (if he had the ambition for it) a man of such parts must have ended a Secretary of State; and died an earl, in a great columned house of his own making – the thought of which prompted me, when he was done, to ask: "Where do you live?"

He was evidently puzzled by the question; so I re-phrased it:

"Where – your – house?"

"There" – nodding abruptly to the right.

I turned, and saw the rotunda – and immediately thought that I must have mistaken its purpose, and that it was in truth a rude kind of palace, and he a rude kind of prince.

He must have seen the surprise and wonder in my face; for he shook his head as if I were mad, and thrust his finger towards a little cabin, much like all the others, close to the bottom of the mound.

"There?" I said.

"Yes." And then, as he looked upon it, his eyes suddenly brimmed with tears; and he slowly stretched out his arms, until they seemed to embrace not only his own house, but the rest of the town, and the fields, and the woods, and the mountains, and the sky itself.

He did not speak; but his expression sufficiently expressed his meaning: "This is mine; and I shall fight for it, and die for it, if I must."

And all at once, I thought: *He is of an age with my nephew. What if I find the boy, and he is grown such an Indian that he thinks and feels as Yanegwa does?*

For a moment I almost fainted clean away. Then I steadied myself, and slowly walked back to my room.

Thereafter, until I was prevented by the onset of winter, I went out often on pleasant days, either upon Yanegwa's arm, or else supporting myself with a stick; and stood there taking the air, or hobbled up and down before the door for a few minutes, or made a toddling circuit of the house. Tho' I never entirely ceased to be an object of curiosity, my appearance soon excited no more than a passing stare; and some of the old people, who seemed to have almost as little occupation as I did, and were for ever lingering about the place, at length knew me well enough to smile when they saw me, and come and shake my hand, and mutter a few words that I knew to be friendly, tho' I could not tell what they meant.

As with so much else in my Indian life, most of these expeditions are so blurred together in my recollection as to be indistinguishable from each other; but I must briefly relate one singular incident, that may be considered worthy of note:

On a bright autumn afternoon I was standing before the house as usual, when I was approached by a younger man – who plainly had some pretensions to fashion: for he was bedecked with jingling ornaments, and wore his horse-tail of coarse black hair drawn through a silver cylinder, and dressed with brilliantly coloured plumes. Something about the cast of his brow and nose seemed familiar – but only in the elusive way of something glimpsed in a dream, that flits into your head and is gone before you can grasp it; for I had no notion who he was – or even whether I had really seen him before, or had merely been struck by his resemblance to someone else. But he certainly appeared to know me, and laughed and chattered as if we were old friends – or, rather, as if he were a candidate, and I a voter: for his jocular manner, and his furtive glances to left and right, to see if we were observed, put me in mind of nothing so much as Sr Will. Sutton at election time. It was only when he had attracted a small crowd, and begun looking at my wounds, and rubbing them with his hot thick fingers, that I recognized him as the conjurer that had attended me in my delirium.

I could not, at the time, imagine why he had determined to examine me there, rather than coming to me in my chamber, like an English quack; but I now think he was making an advertisement of his supposed skills, in hope of getting more custom. For tho', undoubtedly, the real credit for my recovery belongs to Mrs. McLeod, and the resilience of my own constitution – yet it is equally certain that this distinguished fellow (who I later learned had intervened only reluctantly, when all other hope for me seemed to have gone) will have claimed it for himself, and sought to keep it in the publick view by every possible means. For when I told Yanegwa what had happened, he explained that the savages generally hold their spells to be effective only upon their own kind – with the result, I suppose, that the sorcerer that appears to have conjured a stranger back to health will be seen as a man of extraordinary powers, and can expect to find his services called upon by the best families of the place.

I thought I had done with this chapter; but when I read again what I have just written, I am struck by the question, how did I contrive to keep up my spirits during my strange interlude among the Indians, with none of the usual pleasures and consolations of life to assist me, and no prospect of ever enjoying them again? To which – thinking y^r honours may be curious upon the same point – I offer the following answer:

That a man without hope cannot be disappointed.

By which I do not mean, I was in despair; but rather that I accommodated myself to living as if happiness did not depend on attaining some future object, but only on relishing what I could in the present.

I had a bed, and food, and the use of McLeod's small library. I had Yanegwa and Mrs. McLeod for company. I had distant views, and the sound of rushing water, to please my senses.

Sometimes (strange tho' it may appear), when I saw the last remnants of the sun melting into the mist about the mountain-tops, and felt the chill of evening on my cheek, and heard the cheerfulness of the river, undaunted by the onset of night, I even seemed to have a surfeit.

If I stand on my chair, I can observe the same sun through my window now, and – despite knowing all I do – am touched for a moment by the same joy.

I had not seen it until this instant, y^r honours, but the lessons I learned among the Indians have served me well here.

XXXIII

Still no word from you this morning. But I thank y^r honours for the flowers that accompanied my breakfast. Besides delighting my nose and eye, they also cheered my heart; for it is not the custom for a man to give roses to his enemy. Which emboldens me to hope, that tho' you are constrained from saying so directly, you have come to think of me as something else.

During the winter months the greater part of the Indians shut up their mansion houses, and withdrew to smaller habitations close by, where the fire burned constantly, and they might live more snugly. But for some reason or other (perhaps because she thought I was still too weak to be moved) Mrs. McLeod determined to leave me where I was, and make me as comfortable as she could by plying me with blankets and inviting me sometimes to sit with her in the parlour – which, being blessed with a hearth and chimney, enjoyed an advantage denied to most of the Cherokee dwellings in the place. And, in truth, I was miserable enough – but I'll warrant there were thousands more miserable yet in England, while I was shaking and chattering in the wilderness of America.

It was, I should guess, one afternoon in February when I heard a sudden eruption of excited voices without; and the next moment Mrs. McLeod ran in, jabbering a confused mixture of Cherokee (at which she greatly overrated my competency) and English. I could scarce understand a word of it to begin with; but at length succeeded in grasping the material point: that someone had spied her husband approaching, and he would be home within the hour.

Having congratulated her on this excellent news, I asked if she could quickly find me a suit of clothes, so that I might dress myself, and venture out to greet him. At first she shook her head and tutted like a scolding nurse, saying, *I was still very sick; it was much too cold for me to consider going out of doors; and I should see him soon enough, if I would but stay where I was.* But I replied *that Mr. McLeod had saved my life, and I would be d–d before I welcomed him to his own house lying down, like a French despot at a levée;* and after some further argument she relented, and brought me my own coat, and a shirt and a pair of breeches that must have belonged to her husband – for the one was too short in the sleeve, and the other too long in the leg.

But I am obliged now to concede that she was right; for it was dusk when Mr. McLeod at length arrived – by which time my wasted frame was so frozen I was almost past shivering. And tho' he was, I think, truly glad to find me alive, and gratified that I had got up to greet him, yet, after so long an absence, he was naturally impatient to shut the door upon the world, and pass some hours of intimacy with his family. So I spoke with him only a minute or two, before pleading tiredness and returning to my chamber – where he promised to wait on me as soon as he had rested and attended to certain necessary business.

The next morning, as good as his word, he knocked on my door after breakfast, and briskly entered, looking much refreshed. When we had exchanged the usual courtesies, he settled himself in the chair – tugged at the knees of his breeches – and said: "We must take care, Sir, not to fatigue you unnecessarily; but we have a great many questions to ask each other. Which of us should begin, do you think?"

"I am so much in your debt," I replied, "'tis only right that your curiosity should be satisfied first."

251

He did not protest; but smiled, and said: "Very well. It made the marquis and me very uneasy to discover you at Tsiyahi by yourself, without Mr. O'Donnell. We could not conceive that he would have deserted you – so were forced to conclude" (here lowering his voice to a funereal tone) "that the scoundrels had murdered him first, and that his body was lying close by – where we should eventually find it, if we did but look long enough. But even a minute's delay would only have imperilled you further; so we reluctantly agreed that we must go on again directly, as soon as we had made the litter to carry you."

He paused, and gulped, and looked me sternly in the eye – as if he doubted I should tell him the truth, and thought to learn it from my expression. "But since then I have been haunted by the fear that he was not dead at all, only wounded – but, being too weak to cry out, could only listen helplessly as we rode away, leaving him to die alone."

"I can make you easy on that score, at least," I said – and related how O'Donnell and I had parted, concluding: "I am surprised you did not meet him, on the road from Frigateville."

"We came from another place," he said, "where we had business with a relation of my wife's." And then, after reflecting a moment, he shook his head, and continued: "I am happy to know Mr. O'Donnell is still living. But that is sad news, nonetheless."

His eyes were big with tears – that by some strange alchemy seemed to irrigate my own parched grief, and bring it into flower again; so that it was only with the greatest effort that I could keep from weeping myself.

"And why were you there at all?" he said at length. "There are no towns I know of, within two hundred miles of Tsiyahi, that have taken any prisoners for a dozen years or more."

"I was, I fear, roundly deceived. Hickling told me he and his friends could help me to my nephew, and I was desperate enough to believe him."

"That, perhaps" (raising a sardonick eyebrow), "is a misfortune from which Mr. O'Donnell could have preserved you."

This was not the sympathetick response I had expected; and I found myself stung into replying: "Indeed – if he had been a constant enough friend to continue with me."

"I do not know the cause of your quarrel with him," said McLeod quietly – sounding, for a moment, so like O'Donnell himself, as to make my neck tingle. "But I very much doubt whether you may justly accuse him of inconstancy." And then – before I had time to inflame our difference into something worse by an intemperate reply – he hastily changed the subject: "And what do you think was Hickling's motive for attacking you?"

"To rob me, I suppose."

"Why did he wait so long?"

So successfully had I contrived to keep the whole episode (together with everything else that did not immediately concern me) confined to some remote dungeon in my mind, I could not at once find the key to unlock it, and expose it to the light once more. But then I suddenly recalled the letter McLeod had left for me; and said: "Why – as you suggested – to try to deflect suspicion from themselves, by incriminating the Indians."

He nodded – sighed – frowned thoughtfully; and at length said: "You are acquainted, I think, with Mr. Coleman?"

"What!" I cried – thinking I must have misheard him.

"Mr. Coleman. He was the gentleman at Frigate's ordinary, was he not, who . . .?"

I waited for him to continue; but he seemed reluctant to finish the question, and left it dangling.

"Yes," I replied at last (tho' even this required me to rummage my brain for a second or two). "Why do you ask?"

"We did not, I fear, kill Hickling; but we did send him off without his horse. And when we searched his bags, found this . . ." He withdrew a slip of paper from his pocket, and handed it to me:

Sir, [I saw]

I send this by the hand of Mrs. Craig's servant, and trust it will come into no other but your own. 'Tis unnecessary to weary you with the reasons for it; but I wish never to see Mr. Gudgeon again; and the man that convinces me I shall not, will not be the poorer for it.

Yʳ &c. &c. &c.

M. Coleman

In my enfeebled state, I could not make nothing of it. My eyes fluttered back and forth over the lines; but I was unable to decipher their meaning, until McLeod finally said: "Why should he want you dead?"

Dead.

Dead.

Coleman wanted me dead.

And had paid Hickling to kill me.

"Well?" urged McLeod.

"I don't know." And indeed, I was quite at a loss to conceive Coleman's object – unless it were to be revenged on me, for taking his slaves. But tho' I did not doubt that he was vindictive enough to have me murdered, if he could do so without cost or danger to himself, yet it was hard to imagine that so grasping a fellow would have run the risk, and put himself to the expense, of hiring an assassin to dispatch me, unless he believed my death would bring him some material benefit. Which – since he had nothing to gain from my will, and no reason to suppose otherwise – was plainly not the case.

Even laying that question aside for a moment, there were several more I could not begin to answer. It took no great wit to guess that what I held in my hand was the letter I had spied on the table before Hickling, when I had found him and Hody waiting for me at Cicero. But how had Hickling and Coleman come to know each other in the first place? They had, of course, been together at Frigateville for a day or two, and might have met there; but Coleman would never have entrusted another man with so delicate a mission, if that had been the full extent of their acquaintance.

And then there was the matter of Mrs. Craig's servant. Was she merely an innocent cat's-foot in the affair; or did she know she was delivering my death sentence? More troubling still: did her mistress know?

No – it was impossible . . .

And then I remembered O'Donnell telling me that both Coleman and Mrs. Craig were implicated in the Transylvania Company. Of which Hickling was a servant.

And all at once I could not but wonder at my own folly, in believing I had been the victim merely of a series of accidents. For was it not dazzlingly clear, now I came to reflect upon it, that the connections between them were too numerous to be the result of pure chance? Far from being separate occurrences, they were all segments of the same net – that someone had artfully spread upon the ground, and then partially concealed with twigs and leaves to prevent my remarking the intervening links.

But not so artfully, that O'Donnell had been unable to see them.

Some reproachful quirk of my memory sent me back to my last

interview with him at Cicero. I heard the exact musick of his voice as he said, "We are being led a dance, and should leave immediately," and the sneering anger of my reply; I saw again his startled, wide-eyed stare – and suddenly knew, it expressed not (as I had supposed) wonderment at my resolve, but rather pain and bewilderment at the heat of my temper, and the roughness of my tongue.

A great tide of shame rushed in upon me, searing my cheeks, and stinging my eyes, and plugging up my throat.

"What is the matter, Sir?" said McLeod.

I could not speak, and shook my head.

McLeod pinched the letter. "I should not have shown this to you so soon. We will talk of it again" (here plucking it abruptly from my fingers), "when you are stronger. Now – no more of my questions for the present. What would you ask me?"

It took me a moment to recover my breath. Then I said: "Do you know Mr. Coleman?"

He shook his head. But his eyes had the too-fixed look of a liar, and he coloured slightly; and after a moment, knowing he had betrayed himself, he said awkwardly: "The marquis and I met him at the tavern, and spent a few minutes in his company there. But I should scarcely call that knowing."

"What did you talk of with him?"

"Why – why . . ." (suddenly quiet and mumbling) ". . . we talked of his slaves."

My heart beat uncomfortably fast – catching at my words, so they came out in sharp little bursts: "Do you mean – do you mean . . .?"

He nodded.

It was, I knew, to my great discredit that I had only now remembered Niobe and her son, and the part played by McLeod and the marquis in their disappearance; and – as is often the way – the apprehension of my own guiltiness made me readier to think the worst of others. So it was with almost a kind of hypocritical pleasure that I snapped: "So – what – your marquis turned Judas, did he, and delivered them back to Coleman for thirty pieces of silver?"

"No, on the contrary." He paused; and then continued very quietly: "He bought them from him."

I was too dumbfounded to speak immediately; and when at length I did, it was only to show my confusion, by stuttering: "What – why – you had no need of slaves, surely? – and if you had–"

He held up his hand to silence me: "The marquis had a very particular reason for wishing to acquire them."

"What reason? What has he done with them?"

"He has sent them to France."

"To France!" The idea of poor Niobe and the boy being imprisoned
for months in a ship, and then obliged to wait upon some puffed and
powdered lap-dog of a *marquise* so disgusted me that I could not say
more.

But my sentiments must have shown upon my face; for McLeod
murmured gently: "You have no reason to be anxious for them, Sir.
They will be well cared for, I promise." He paused; and then patted
my arm, and made to rise. "Now – I fear I've excited your nerves too
much, and quite worn you out. That is enough for one day –"

"No – one thing more!" I said, clutching at his sleeve. For a sudden
giddying thought had struck me: if the marquis was also acquainted
with Coleman, and if he had lied to me (as I now knew for a certainty that he had) concerning his intentions towards Niobe and her son,
then perhaps my encounter with him was no more accidental than
my meetings with Mrs. Craig and Hickling. In which case: was it
mere chance that he had been close enough to me, to hear the shots
when I was attacked? And, if not . . .

"What?" said McLeod – pulling his cuff free of my grasp, and edging towards the door.

"Why – why did the marquis not return to France with them, but
continue with you instead?"

"He was looking for someone else," said McLeod.

"Who?"

He did not answer at once; and when at length he did, his eyes (for
some reason I did not understand then, and still do not today) were
large with tears: "A white child brought up by Indians."

Which (as you may readily imagine) entirely robbed me of the
power of speech for some seconds. By the time I had recovered it, he
had bowed – said, "We will talk again tomorrow" – and left the
room.

After he had gone, I churned his words over and over in my mind,
until they were so trampled and muddy I scarce knew what they
meant. *A white child brought up by Indians.* Perhaps it signified nothing. The savages had, after all (it appeared), seized hundreds, or even

thousands, of captives; and there was no reason to suppose that we were both searching for the same one.

But had not this kind of reasoning been my downfall? When O'Donnell had remarked the resemblance between the china figures on the *Jenny* and the one in Miss Craig's hand, I had given him just such a reply. When he had discovered that Mrs. Craig was an investor in the company that employed Hickling, and shown convincing evidence that she might be connected to Coleman, I had dismissed the idea as fanciful – and almost paid for my folly with my life. Considering which – and the proof I now had, that the marquis was part of the same great net, and had deliberately set out to deceive me – I must surely be the greatest nincompoop in Christendom to doubt that his quest and mine were somehow related?

But why? What possible interest could he have in my nephew? How, indeed, could he have known I *had* a nephew, until I told him so at Frigateville – when he must already have been several weeks upon his journey?

I had to consider this question for some minutes before stumbling upon an answer – which immediately seemed so obvious, I was astonished I had not seen it at once: Coleman had told him.

And then a second point struck me: when I had mentioned my search for Dan's son, during dinner at the ordinary, the marquis had not responded with so much as a word. But surely – if his purpose had been entirely innocent, and he had not meant to cheat me of my prize – it would have been the most natural thing in the world for him to tell me he was engaged upon a similar quest, and perhaps even propose that we should travel together.

That seemed compelling enough; but, try as I might, I could go no further. I felt weak, and dreadfully cold; and my thoughts had suddenly become thick and sluggish, like honey poured from a jug.

As I tumbled into sleep, I could cling to only one of them: *When I am recovered, I shall pursue the marquis, and take my nephew from him.*

For some days thereafter I lay a-bed, sick of the chill I had taken. Sometimes McLeod would sit with me for an hour or two in the afternoon, reading a book in companionable silence, or – as I became stronger – engaging me in little bouts of conversation. But (as if by tacit common consent) we always confined ourselves to some uncontentious topick such as the weather, or a gewgaw of gossip he had picked up in the town – never once mentioning the marquis, or the child raised as an Indian, or any other large question that touched upon the future. His reason for this reticence (I suppose) was that he feared exciting me unnecessarily, and so perhaps provoking a relapse; and mine was much the same: for tho' I still intended to continue my search for the boy, there was little purpose in depleting my small stock of energy by trying to discover more, and form a plan, until I was in a condition to act upon it.

But after a while, these visits became shorter and less frequent – so that, in proportion as my appetite for company grew, the provision of it dwindled away. Which drove me at length to broach the matter with McLeod, saying *that I knew my care placed great demands him, when he was already fully occupied with his own affairs; and – in order to ease the burden both on his time and my conscience – might he ask Yanegwa to come and sit with me sometimes in his stead?*

But he only replied, very shortly, *that Yanegwa was gone away, on some private business; which hurt him as much as it did me – for he was a trader, and depended on the men to furnish him with skins, and could not long continue when (as had been the case this six months past) they were diverted from hunting by other concerns.* And then, before I could question him further, he hurried from the room.

It can have been no more than a week later that, one afternoon, I heard a number of horses arriving – and then the door opening, and the clack of half a dozen pairs of feet, and a hubbub of strange voices in the next room, that at length settled into what sounded like a momentous discussion. Which continued for upwards of two hours; before a sudden clatter of chairs signified it was at an end, and (after bidding his guests farewell) McLeod entered my chamber. He took his usual place beside me, but seemed very quiet and heavy; and after a few leaden sallies, gave up all attempts at conversation, and sat sighing, and staring silently at his feet – provoking me at length to ask *what was the matter?*

"Nothing," he replied.

"'Tis plainly something."

He gave another sigh, and said *he did not wish to trouble me, when I was still so weak.*

"You will trouble me a good deal more if you don't tell me," I said; "for then I shall wonder what it might be, and worry myself with a hundred groundless fears."

He hesitated; and then burst out: "The rebels have taken up arms against us in earnest; and 'tis very likely there will soon be a general war throughout the colonies. Which the government means to prosecute, by sending more troops to suppress the insurrection in the east; and encouraging the Indians to ally themselves with the loyal part of the population in the back-country, to fall upon the illegal settlers here."

"I do not believe it!" I cried.

"'Tis true. I swear it."

"No! – the King would never be so heartless as to loose savages against his own subjects –"

"Subjects, pah! They are the scum of the earth!"

"No!" I said. "I am certain, it is no more than a slanderous rumour, put about by the traitors, to stir up their countrymen!"

He shook his head, and said: "I had it just now, from Mr. Stuart himself, who is come to discuss how the Indians may best be supplied and armed."

I opened my mouth to speak, but was too shocked to find words; so he continued unopposed: "But I cannot deny I am dreadfully uneasy. Some of the young hotheads here have already left, and begun harrying the outlying farms, in punishment for the abuses they have suffered. Who knows what that may bring down upon our heads, before we are fully prepared? And if the war should go against us . . ."

He did not finish, but shook his head again, and rose stiffly to his feet – as if the minutes had swollen into years, and turned him to an old man before my eyes.

"I trust you will excuse me, Sir. There is to be a meeting of the council, and I must make myself ready for it."

That evening, the roars and screeches from the rotunda were louder and more fearsome than ever, and there was no tinkling spinet to save me from them. When at length I slept, the savage musick came with me into my dreams, and accompanied the wild gleeful dancing of the demons sent to torment me – that tonight, I saw, to my great horror and amazement, were not the usual scaly fiends, but Mr. Burke and Sʳ Will. Sutton and the King himself, who pranced and gibbered until their wigs broke free and slipped over their laughing faces.

XXXIV

Yet again, nothing from y^r honours this morning. You have not been silent so many days together since I began work in earnest. Which leads me to wonder if I have unwittingly written the fatal word, that will either hang me, or secure my release – tho', if that is the case, I am at a loss to guess why you should still confine me here.

Or is it perhaps merely that you are impatient to return to the story?

If so, you will not be disappointed; for, as you can see, I am myself so eager to hurry on today (for reasons that will soon become apparent, if you do not already know them), that I have chosen to forego my customary Sunday diversions, and picked up my pen again, to continue my narrative.

As the cold began its stubborn retreat, and spring raised her colours in the distant fields and forests, I at length found myself beginning to revive. It was as if I had been able to endure the ordeal of the last few months only by shutting up every unneeded room, and withdrawing to a little closet within myself, where every meagre resource might be applied to one simple object alone, *viz.*, remaining alive from one day to the next. Now, just as my Cherokee neighbours were leaving their winter huts, and re-entering their houses, so I, by degrees, found myself once more taking possession of my own unused limbs and faculties. I still limped when I walked – but my lungs strengthened, and my poor wasted muscles gradually thickened, till I was able to hobble two or three miles without difficulty. I continued to be disturbed by nightmares when I slept, but they were now so securely penned within their own domain, they could not pursue me when I woke again – thus freeing my mind from the exhausting torment of delirium, and allowing it to venture into regions unvisited for almost a year. So at last leading me – one day when I was sitting at coffee with McLeod – to essay a roundabout approach to the question we had both been at pains to avoid.

"You will observe, Sir," I said, "that I am now pretty much mended." I got up, and took half a dozen steps of a lame jig – which briefly thawed his grave expression into a smile.

"I am gratified to see it."

"I hope so," I said, "for it is entirely thanks to your kindness, and your wife's – and G–d knows you've had little enough else for your trouble."

He shook his head; but I persisted: "There is, I fear, nothing I can do to repay the debt I owe you. But perhaps I may at least reduce it a little, by removing myself from your house as soon as is practicable."

"There is no need to think of that –"

"Oh, come, Sir! – you are very good – but 'twere impossible I could have been other than a great burden to you, or that you shouldn't get on a great deal easier without me."

He was quiet for a moment; then (a little awkwardly) said: "But where will you go?"

"I must resume the search for my brother's heir."

Again, he did not reply at once; and when he did, his voice was slow and wary, like an advancing soldier fearing an ambush: "What – among the Indians?"

"If he is still with them."

McLeod sighed. "I must counsel you against it."

"Why?"

"It would be a dangerous undertaking. More than dangerous. Foolhardy."

"That did not deter the marquis."

"The marquis was not caught in the midst of a war. And, besides – he had a company of armed men, and me to guide him."

"And what became of him?"

"He found the child he sought –"

"A boy?"

He nodded, before quickly going on: "And returned with him to France."

We were both silent – he, doubtless, because he dreaded my next question; and I, because I hesitated to ask it. It would surely be but a poor return for all his great service to me, to press him on a point that must render him uneasy; and yet I knew that if I shrank from it, I should equally surely be failing in my duty.

So after a few seconds I steeled myself; and said: "Is it my nephew?"

He paled – swallowed – and then said swiftly: "I have no reason to think so" – adding, before I had to time to go on: "Death almost had you at Tsiyahi, Sir, and it was only with the greatest difficulty that we at length prised you from his grip. To go on now would be to deliver yourself to him again – with the assurance that he will not be cheated of you a second time." (Tho' his sibilant voice was as soft and musical as ever, it had dwindled by this point to little more than a whisper –

which I knew, from my recollection of his dispute with Hickling at Frigateville, was a sign of excessive anger.) "And so," he concluded, barely audibly, "cast away at a stroke all our efforts to keep you alive."

I did not at once answer him, but reflected for a moment on what he had said, and the manner in which he had said it. *I have no reason to think so* was not a direct admission that I was right concerning the identity of the boy; but perhaps it came as near to acknowledging it as McLeod felt he could, without betraying the trust of his late employer. And I could not help thinking that he intended some such construction; for if he believed I was mistaken, it would have been the easiest thing in the world for him to tell me so plainly. The genuine fervour with which he sought to dissuade me, moreover (for Garrick himself could not have counterfeited such emotion), suggested that he *knew* any further inquiries among the Indians would be useless.

"Very well," I said at last. "I shall return to England, and" – lowering my voice, and giving him what I hoped was a meaning glance – "pursue my search nearer to home."

He vigorously nodded his approval.

But before I could act upon the plan, my nocturnal horrors broke free of their confinement – spilled into the waking world – and became flesh.

The next day, McLeod took me to see his horses, and chose a fine, sturdy, broad-backed mare called Nunyu, that he said I might have for my journey. She was a gentle, imperturbable beast, and snuffing her steamy coat, and feeling the trembling warmth of her flank and the glove-like softness of her muzzle as I examined her seemed to refresh my senses, and stir the embers of a spirit of purpose and adventure I had supposed quite dead. McLeod smiled, and said *he could see he had judged right, and Nunyu and I should be friends; and tho' business prevented him from accompanying me himself, tomorrow he would find two or three other companions to go with me, and conduct me to the nearest British fort.*

As we walked back to the house, a sooty rag of cloud crossed the sun, and became fringed with fire – mottling the town with patches of shadow and slabs of dazzling, grained brilliance, that moved from one building to another, like a taper lighting candles; and in the same moment, the breeze strengthened, spattering raindrops against our

262

faces, and filling our mouths and noses with the mingled scents of smoke, and ordure, and wet earth waking to life again. And for the first time in many months, my eyes suddenly pricked with something akin to hope – tho' hope of *what*, precisely, I could not have said.

That night, I was blessed with the most peaceful sleep I had known since leaving home.

I woke from it suddenly, just before dawn – my pulse a-jigging, and my back dewed with sweat. I could not at first tell what had roused me; for there was nothing to be heard but a distant chorus of barking dogs – a sound so extremely common, I had developed the art of ignoring it.

Then, from some way off, came a noise that sent my heart skittering again: a shriek. Not of pain, or even of fear; but of utter anguish – as if it were announcing the end of the world.

I got up, and peered through the casement, but made out only the black contour of the McLeods' outbuildings, and the wall of forest rising beyond. I pulled my blanket about me, and hastened into the parlour.

There was a faint red glow in the room, that I supposed to be from the sunrise – tho' I was dimly conscious that it was not quite where I should have expected it. But I had no time to ponder this riddle further, for at that instant McLeod loomed out of the darkness towards me. As he did so, the shadowy form of one of his daughters emerged behind him, shrugging on her clothes.

"Ah, Mr. Gudgeon," he said. He was already dressed, and held a gun before him. "Are you well enough to use this?"

"Yes," I replied, taking it. "But–"

He grasped my elbow, and pushed me to the window. "See –"

I looked out. An angry blaze, as big as a beacon, burned on the opposite slope. It was too bright for me to judge immediately where it was; but there was something so shocking about its size and ferocity, I could tell at once it was not an accident, but a violent outrage.

"The palisade," said McLeod softly. "They will fire two or three other points, and then burst in, and set to work upon the houses."

"Who?"

"Rabble. Rabble." (So quiet I could scarce hear him.) "Scum." And then, more loudly: "I will take Flora, and see what may be done. If they cannot be held, we will return with the horses."

"Let me go too."

He shook his head. "Your shin –"

"I can walk."

"We may need to run. Besides – 'tis more than likely some of 'em will slip over to this side, and try to break in here. In which case, you will be able to protect my wife, and Nancy."

I nodded – for plainly this was not the time to argue. Without a further word, he took up another weapon from its place beside the door, lifted the latch, and beckoned Flora to follow him; which – having first armed herself in the same way – she at once did.

I watched them as they trotted down the hill – weaving between other scuttling figures, and sometimes stopping for a second or two to speak to one of them, or look in at the entrance of a hut, before hurrying on again. I could still hear the dreadful cry that had woken me; but now it had been taken up by other voices, that threaded it back and forth and back again – making a great net of despair, that seemed to snare the whole town in its meshes.

And then came the first shots.

I took a powder horn and a box of bullets from the chest where McLeod kept them – charged my own gun – and knocked at the door of the next room.

A faint female voice called something I took to be *Yes*.

I went in, and found Mrs. McLeod and Nancy bent over the bed, packing their bags by the light of a single candle. They did not even glance up at me.

"Are the windows shut fast?" I said.

"Yes," said Mrs. McLeod, with a sigh – like a long-suffering mother whose child has troubled her with a foolish question. Her face was taut with anxiety; but its expression was more one of weary resignation than of alarm – as if she had been obliged to flee in this manner many times before, and grown accustomed to it.

I returned to my own chamber, to close the casement there – then secured the front door as well as I could with the table and chairs (there being neither bolt nor lock) – and resumed my position by the parlour window. During my absence, the distant fire seemed to have reproduced itself – creating two or three little satellites which I knew must be burning houses. Between them I could see darting devils brandishing torches – who in a moment had another building alight, and then another, and then a third; so that as I looked, the blaze began to surge and leap towards me, like a hideous contagion I was powerless to arrest. So fast was it moving, I could only conclude the Indians were doing nothing to resist it – which baffled me (for I had always supposed that, whatever else they might be guilty of, the savages were not cowards), and made me itch to go down myself, and exact some price from the murderous rogues attacking us, for their barbarity. But I knew McLeod was right, in supposing my damaged leg would render me useless against so nimble an adversary – and, besides, was he not depending upon me, to defend his family?

Soon the flames had reached the river – turning it red, as if the water itself were on fire; and here, for a moment, I thought the Cherokees meant at last to take a stand: for the people below me seemed to throng to the bank. But then I remarked that the greater part of them were carrying bags and bundles, and that (far from stopping) they were all the time hastening towards the main entrance to the town – by which they evidently hoped to make their escape. A dozen or so brave souls did, indeed, form a line, to cover the retreat of their friends; but they were so exposed, and so greatly outnumbered by the enemy, that most of them were quickly struck down, and the rest forced to retire themselves. Whereupon twenty or thirty men on the further shore suddenly hopped from the darkness like rats from a nest, and – hesitating only to snatch up some burning timbers – dodged their way to the Indian boats, and propelled themselves across to the nearer side, to continue their business there.

No sooner had they arrived than there was a fearful tattoo of musket-fire from beyond the palisade, followed by the most pitiful wails and screams; and almost at once, a jostling torrent of terrified women and children began rushing back in through the gate. It was plain they must have found themselves caught in an ambush there, and preferred the risk (as they thought) of being burned to death within the town to the certainty of being shot without it – but now they faced both dangers at once: for the newcomers, remarking the savages' panick, set down their brands, and took up their muskets, and began killing the poor wretches, like so many rabbits trapped in a ditch. The smoke from the burning houses, rising ever thicker and rolling towards me in great black billows, kept me from seeing every particular of the scene – but it could not spare me the noise of it. To be forced to listen to such agony, when it is impossible to relieve it, is itself a kind of torture – and after struggling with my own weakness for a minute or two, I at length succumbed to it, and deafened myself with my fingers.

I wish to God I had not.

What roused me was a knock so hard that (tho' I could not hear it) I felt its tremor in the walls. I instantly unplugged my ears – stumbled to my feet – and glanced towards McLeod's bed-chamber.

Someone had slammed the door shut – with such tremendous force, that it was still quaking, like a newly beaten drum. From beyond it came the fractured, breathy sobs of a frightened woman, overlaid every few seconds by jabbering interjections from a man. I could not make out what he was saying, or even the language he was speaking – but the tone was unmistakable, and brought the sweat to my neck.

It would have been impossible to enter directly, without advertising my presence, and so losing the advantage of surprise; so I edged out, as quietly as I could, and – pressing my hand to my face, to keep from choking – hobbled to the back of the house.

The window of the room had been smashed open, and a log set below it, to form a kind of step – on which I gingerly raised myself up, to look in.

Mrs. McLeod was standing near the entrance, staring in horror towards the bed. I followed her gaze and saw Nancy stretched out among the bags – her arms pinioned by a big, broad-shouldered man whose face I could not see, and her legs by a smaller fellow in a felt hat, who was busy slashing the petticoat from them with a hunting-knife. She was throwing her head desperately from side to side, and crying *No! No!* – the words, in her terror, bubbling out in a white froth, and wetting the strands of hair flung across her lips.

"I pray – I beg –" said Mrs. McLeod, in a voice that was almost shockingly calm – as if she feared that by venting her true feelings she might ignite the fuse of some greater violence yet. And perhaps she would have done – for even this pathetick plea was enough to provoke the felt-hatted villain into laying the point of his blade on the girl's belly, and turning to her mother with a snarl, that plainly said: *One word more, and I drive it home.*

I got down, moved the log a few yards further from the house to a place where I knew I should not be seen, mounted it again – lifted my gun – and took aim. But then immediately encountered a difficulty – or rather a pair of difficulties: first, that the most skilled marksman in the world would have been hard put to it to hit the fellow with the knife, without also endangering his victim; and second, that even if I could accomplish that (which I greatly doubted), the girl would still not be safe from his companion – who might easily dispatch her – and her mother too, if he chose – before I had time to load again.

Had I had leisure to reflect, I might, perhaps, have been able to contrive a better plan, with fewer risks; but the next moment the large man shrugged impatiently, and muttered: "You best a-do what you come for."

And I at once knew his voice: Hickling.

"An't no call for hurryin'," replied felt-hat.

"We've business to attend to," said Hickling.

"We done three-fourths of it. An' a man's due some fun, after a hard day."

"There's fun enough in the other."

"Not" – here jerking his hips violently – "for the fightin' cock. 'Tis only natural, an't it, he wants his sport, too?"

"Be quick, then."

"You hear that, sweetheart? You ought to thank the man. He's tryin' to spare you" – flourishing the knife – "some o' this. Me, I'd sooner chew slow, an' savour each bite."

At which the poor girl began frantically to arch her back, and thrust and writhe – as if she thought that one last effort might yet free her from her tormentors.

"I said thank him!" roared the little man – suddenly leaning forward, and pummelling her face with his fist.

She gasped and whimpered with shock and pain.

"Thank him!"

She drew in a shuddering breath, and let it out again in the most pitiful moan: "Thank –"

"He did not hear you!" – striking her again, and spitting upon her cheek. "Louder!"

"No, no," said Hickling – as if this exceeded even his taste for cruelty.

Which seemed to embolden Mrs. McLeod to resume her own pleading; for she at once cried out: "Think of the good Lord! Think of Jesus!"

"What!" scoffed felt-hat, turning towards her with an incredulous grin. "Have we learned the savages so good, they're preachin' our religion to us now? You leave Jesus be, you d–d bitch, an' git prayin' to your own – devil – for it's goin' to be your turn next, once you seed this!"

"For G–d's sake," groaned Hickling.

"Very well." With a sudden violent tug, he ripped off the last shreds of Nancy's shift – and stood gazing at her nakedness for a moment, as if in wonderment – before (I scarce know how to write it, y^r honours, and yet it is what I saw) – before inserting the point of the blade in her privates.

All this time I had been looking along the barrel of my gun – waiting for him to move away a little, and so present me with a clearer target. But now, plainly, I could delay no longer.

My finger tightened on the trigger, and in the same instant Mrs. McLeod finally cast away all caution, and ran forward, evidently intending to snatch the weapon, if she could, so obliging me to hesitate again (for 'twas ten to one that if I had not, I should have killed her instead of him), and watch helpless as he repelled her attack with a blow to the shoulder that sent her tumbling to the floor; and then, almost in the same movement, and with a long grunting sigh, drove in his knife to the hilt.

I fired. He leapt back, clutching his neck – and for a second seemed caught in the air upon some invisible hook, before collapsing in a tangle of thrashing limbs. The next instant, I lost sight of him, as bulky Hickling appeared at the casement, and poked his gun towards me. He found me almost at once – and must, I think, have recognized me: for his eyes widened into a look of utter astonishment, as if he had seen a spectre. But he quickly recovered himself, and – calmly levelling his musket – pointed it directly at my heart, and cocked the hammer.

I knew I could not run; and thought it better to look upon my murderer than to be shot in the back vainly trying to flee him. Strange tho' it may seem, all I felt (so far as I can now recall) was a kind of melancholy regret that Hickling would have the satisfaction of dispatching me after all.

But then, of a sudden, he dropped the gun – which went off as it struck the ground, hitting the palisade behind me – and disappeared.

I re-charged my own weapon and limped to the window.

A coy author, or a lazy one, will sometimes justify passing over such and such an episode, by saying *that it defies description*; and I most fervently wish I could avail myself of the same excuse now – for indeed, the scene that confronted me in McLeod's bed-chamber is quite beyond my ability to depict it. Or, I will be bold to say, the ability of any man – for words are but flimsy dolls and puppets, that we twist this way and that to make one meaning rather than another; and while they may serve us well enough to suggest a tea-party, or a game at cards, or an insolent servant, yet they are powerless to represent the unsuspected giants and monsters that await us in the encircling darkness, when we stray from the little stage of our humdrum lives.

But – besides my duty to y^r honours – I am now sufficiently acquainted with myself to know that what I saw there will only haunt me the more, if I turn aside, and do not make the attempt to set it down. So:

Blood. A flood of blood. Spatters on the wall, as careless as drops of water flung from a pail. A great ugly well, darker than the rest, seeping over the bed, and dying skin and linen, wool and hair, the same wine-purple. Scarlet streams and rivulets, trickling on to the floor and settling there in spreading puddles – as if, irrespective of where they came from, they were destined to meet and mingle in a single red sea. And the sprawled bodies creating a similar illusion – the twitching hands and flailing legs seeming to have more kinship with one another than with the people they belonged to; so that for a moment it was impossible to tell who was where, and what was their condition.

Then Mrs. McLeod rose up, and separated herself from the confusion. She was as bloody as the others – tho' not, I deduced, from her own injuries; for she was able to stand unaided, and gave no sign of physical pain. But there was a look upon her face – the mouth a vacant cavity, the brow knotted in horror – that I had never seen the like of, and pray I never shall again. In one hand she held the knife. She had evidently plucked it from her daughter, and used it to stab Hickling, who lay at her feet. She must have struck him several times more after he had fallen, for there were gashes in his cheek and throat and belly. As I watched, his eyes fluttered – met mine for a second – and then rolled up into his head. He seemed to be trying to speak; but all I heard was a kind of long, rattling cough.

That sound suddenly made me aware of others. Perhaps the noise of the shots had stunned me, or else the evidence of my eyes had

been so overwhelming as to suppress my remaining senses; but –
whatever the reason – I had until that moment experienced everything in dumbshow. Now I caught the cries of the poor girl (here, in
truth, language fails me, for they were no more *cries* than a minnow
is a whale; and yet the lexicon contains no word for what they were:
not a plea for help, or a communication of any sort, but a pure, dis-
embodied distillation of agony). At the same time, I became conscious of another noise – a wild tattoo, accompanied by a babyish
babble – and, looking about, discovered her assailant, half-hidden by
the end of the bed, who seemed to be drumming his feet (tho' I could
not see them) upon the floor, as if he was trying to get up and could
not understand his inability to do so. His expression was one of perplexity rather than anguish: he held his hand out towards the empty
air, waiting in vain for someone to grasp it; all the while muttering,
again and again: *Mammy, Mammy, Mammy.*

I silenced him with a bullet through the skull.

As the echo of it faded, I felt Mrs. McLeod's gaze upon me. She
caught my eye, and then glanced away towards Nancy.

I forced myself to do the same. What I saw more resembled a
butcher's shop than a woman. No doctor in the world could have
mended her, or eased her suffering.

I looked at her mother again – wondering if she meant that I
should do for the girl what I had for her murderer. I do not remember
either of us speaking, but she nodded.

I re-loaded my musket.

When it was finished, I limped back to the other side of the house
– meaning, I suppose, to go in and offer what comfort I could, tho' I
do not recall thinking anything at all.

As I neared the door, I heard horses approaching through the fog,
and stopped to await them. Why I did not try to hide, I cannot say.
Perhaps, having failed to protect Nancy, I felt I should not now
attempt to save myself. Or else life itself, after all that had happened,
seemed not worth the cost of keeping it.

But it was not the enemy that emerged from the smoke, but
McLeod and Flora.

"We must go," he said shortly. "Where are . . .?"

"Your daughter," I said. "Nancy . . ."

He stared at me a moment – and then nodded, as if he had been
expecting it.

"I am sorry," I said.

He did not reply; but sagged, like a man carrying another on his shoulders, and went in.

I can write no more today.

Take courage, Sir. You are not so far now from the end of your journey.

XXXV

That is a strange, unsettling message to give a man.

What journey do you speak of? The journey I am recounting? My journey in this place?

Or do you mean the journey of life itself?

And for what do I require *courage*?

I beg y^r honours – whatever you intend towards me – let me first finish my story. If you are impatient, I swear I will make haste; but do not snatch me away before I am done.

That would be to inflict a double death.

To see the destruction of their town, and the dreadful murder of their child, would, I think, be such a mortal blow to most people as to make them give up the struggle altogether, and abandon themselves to sharing the same fate. What other losses the McLeods must have suffered, to harden them so to this one, I dread even to try to imagine; but after no more than five minutes I was amazed to see them reappear from the house, and – with stoick determination – begin to load the horses. The only delay was occasioned by Mrs. McLeod's insistence that we should not leave Nancy's body to the fire, but take it with us, so that it might be buried according to the custom of her people. She wrapped it in blankets, singing some strange, repetitious dirge as she did so; and I then helped McLeod carry it out, and tie it over the back of the girl's own mare.

They had brought Nunyu for me, and I was glad of it: for my shrivelled muscles could scarce exert enough force to keep my seat, and a more skittish animal would have taken fright at the noise and confusion, and almost certainly thrown me. Even as it was, I came close to falling half a dozen times, as the poor beast suddenly found itself in the midst of a gaggle of fleeing women, or stumbled over a charred corpse, or started at the crack of a great beam exploding in the conflagration. And when we at length came to a breach in the palisade, and found it almost closed by a wall of fire, she shied away so violently that I was able to stay on only by fastening my arms about her neck, and nearly throttling her. I finally succeeded in urging her through – aided by a volley of shots from below, but only at the cost of singeing her mane and tail, and making my clothes smoulder, and setting light to my hair – which (wanting a wig) I had allowed to grow long. It was this accident, by the bye, that caused the ugly purplish scorch you will have observed upon my face, if you have ever seen me; tho' so stupefied had I been by all that had happened, that – incredible as it may appear – I scarce seemed to feel it at the time.

I recall observing the others ahead of me, just as they were about to vanish into the haven of the trees, and prodding Nunyu, and muttering, "Come on, girl, come on!" to make her catch them.

I recall looking back, as I reached the margin of the forest – to see the dying town sinking beneath a churning ocean of smoke, and then, in its last moments, sending a final terrible signal of distress, as the rotunda suddenly erupted into red and yellow flames with a great despairing sigh, like a giant bonfire.

And then I recall nothing but an endless zig-zag through the wilderness – the colours of the world reduced to green and black and brown – no notion in my head of a destination, or of whether we were going east or west, or even up or down – and pausing only for a few moments now and then, to listen for the sounds of pursuit. Until at length, when the light was almost gone, McLeod said, "We will rest here"; and – having concealed our horses as well as we could in a thicket, and laid poor Nancy's body on a piece of open ground a little way off, and protected it with stones – we each of us took a blanket or a coat, and crept beneath a bush to sleep.

I was stiff with cold. A twig was burrowing into my shoulder.

And something was covering my mouth.

I opened my eyes. McLeod's head was no more than six inches from mine. He had crawled in beside me, and placed his hand over my face. When he saw I was awake, he removed it again, formed his lips into a silent, exaggerated *hush*; and then instantly withdrew – so noiselessly, that if you had been standing ten yards away, you would not have heard him.

I moved gingerly until I found a gap between the tangled sprays of my makeshift shelter. A thin grey light had begun to strain through the woods – by which I made out Flora and Mrs. McLeod, lying together as still as effigies. They had propped themselves upon their elbows, and were staring into the distance, frowning with the effort of listening; but listening to *what* I could not tell – unless it were the stirring of branches, and the first tentative snatches of song from early-rising birds.

I took my gun – wriggled into the open – and began to squirm towards them. But had barely gone halfway when my ears caught something that stopped me dead: the regular *sh-sh-sh* of trudging feet. Tho' so faint that they must yet be a great way off; so that – with the advantage of horses – we should easily be able to escape them, if we acted without delay. Or so I supposed. But just as I was about to say as much, I heard a low murmur of voices, not a hundred paces away.

I held in my breath. The women did the same. I was conscious of a shadow at the edge of my vision; and, turning slightly, saw McLeod creeping forward on his knees, his thumb so tense on the hammer of his musket that the knuckle shone white.

A pause. A curious grunt, and then the hollow rattle and grating of stones being picked up and set down.

For a moment I could not imagine what they were doing – and then I had it: they must have chanced upon poor Nancy, and begun to uncover her. Which was sufficiently alarming, for it kept them near us, when they might otherwise have moved on, but still – as long as we remained quiet, and the horses did not betray us – did not necessarily mean we should be discovered. For would they not conclude that the pile of stones was a hastily made tomb, and that the people who had placed her in it were probably long since gone?

For perhaps a minute we waited; and then, quite suddenly, the brittle silence was splintered by a most tremendous howling roar – that made me wonder, for an instant, if it was not a man, but a bear that had happened upon the body. But it soon dwindled into a series of distraught shouts, that were unmistakably human – at which the McLeods, after quickly glancing at one another for a second, all scrambled up, and began running towards it; calling out, as they went, a gabble of Cherokee words I could not catch. But since it was plain *they* were no longer afraid, there was no rational reason why *I* should be; so, after hesitating for a moment, to accommodate my nerves to this unexpected turn, I struggled to my feet and limped after them.

To find them with a dozen or so young Indian men gathered about the unwrapped corpse – all watching another, evidently of the same party, who was jumping and stamping, wailing and striking his chest, in a furious dance of sorrow. As he flung himself about, I remarked something familiar in the line of his brow and nose – in the bristly crest of his hair and the long dewlap ears, spiked with white feathers, that swung and slapped with every shake and leap.

It was Yanegwa.

His eyes brushed mine in passing, but did not linger or give any sign of knowing me. But as soon as he saw the McLeods, he stopped, and after a moment began to work his way towards them – still swaying from side to side as he went, and pounding the earth with his great feet to some urgent internal tempo. Not wishing to intrude, I kept my distance, and so did not hear what he said to them, or they to him (and probably would not have understood it, if I had); but pretty soon Flora was trembling and crying too, and then her mother, and then the little crowd of Indians huddled about them – as if they had all been unable to express their own grief until they had seen his. And at length even McLeod himself joined in – with a curious high-pitched lament, that seemed to have more of Scotland than America in it, and rose above the others', like a fiddle above a ragged consort of horns.

To witness such a display of unconstrained emotion, when I could not partake in it, and when my own feelings had been so wrung and trampled I scarce knew what they were any longer, seemed almost unbearable; so after a few minutes I moved away, and – spying a little path on the other side of the glade – began to wander along it. And had gone perhaps fifty paces, when I was startled to hear a female voice beside me calling, "Sir! Sir!"

Had I been inclined to believe in ghosts, I should have imagined it was poor Nancy's; for I had seen no-one, and the tone was very like hers. But as I looked about me, it spoke again, not far from my left shoulder: "Here, Sir! Here!"

I peered into the darkness of the forest; and, after searching for a moment, made out a flash of pale skin, no more than three or four trees away.

"We are bound, Sir. You mus' come to us."

Strange how our inconstant brains may tease us sometimes – delaying the recognition of an old friend when we meet him again, and yet allowing the merest inflection to conjure up some long-forgotten acquaintance with whom we have barely exchanged twenty words. And so it was now – so that even before I was near enough to see her clearly, I found myself bursting out: "You are Benjamin's daughter, are you not? From Cicero?"

"Yes!" (astonished, despite her weariness). "But how – who –?"

"I am Ned Gudgeon," I said – launching myself into the under-growth, and stumbling towards her through a sea of roots and bram-bles.

"Ned Gudgeon?" She was half-screened by leaves, so that all I could plainly make out was her head – which she tipped to one side as I approached, as if to study me better.

"I stayed at your house once –"

She said nothing, but continued to stare, her forehead wrinkled with perplexity.

But a moment later, another voice answered for her: "Ay, Mary, my dear – that is Edward. I know him by his speech."

"Your father too!" I said. And at that instant, saw them both – tied to adjacent sycamores, with their hands behind them, and their feet fixed to crude wooden trammels. Her face was recognizable – tho' dreadfully white, and marred by a bruise on the chin; but his seemed to have been smeared with soot or charcoal, giving it the appearance of a black mask. Behind them were four or five other women, and as many children – all secured in the same fashion, tho' none marked like Benjamin.

For a moment, Mary and I gaped at each other – and then she cried out: "Oh! What ha' they done to you?"

"To me?!" I said.

"Your head – your cheek –"

And all at once I recalled the scar on my scalp, and the burn I had received yesterday; which I was suddenly conscious (now my mind had been directed to it) had become exceedingly sore, and begun to throb.

"But what of you?" I said – deflecting her question with a shake of the head. "How come you to be here?"

"They fell upon us in Cicero. And all our neighbours, too. Killed I don't know how many, and burned the houses, and took the rest of us captive."

"I tried to talk to them, Edward," said Swinton, "– to explain, we are not enemies, and would help them till the soil, if they would, and live in peace with them like brothers. But I have not their language – and tho' their leader has a few words of English, I could not make myself understood."

It suddenly came upon me that the *leader* must be Yanegwa; and that his *few words of English* were those I had taught him during our games of chess; and the thought that he had put our lessons to such a use seemed so odd, I could not quite grasp it – so that it appeared in my mind like a circle that will not close, or four straight lines that refuse to be resolved into a square. And in almost the same instant, I understood something else: that Hickling's crew must have known Yanegwa and his friends were gone from home – so that by attacking the town when they did, they could be certain of finding it almost undefended.

"What of the Mount?" I asked. "And Mrs. Craig?"

"She and her daughter left the place," said Mary. "Not long after you came. But" – rolling her head, to indicate the wretches behind her – "some of the other women –"

I looked at them again, more carefully. All of them were sufficiently handsome, or at least sufficiently well made; but I did not remember having seen a single one of them before. The savages must have thought poor parrot-face not worth the trouble of taking, and dispatched her on the spot.

"Please," went on Mary urgently. "Please – let us go!"

I was suddenly paralysed. So many conflicting notions clamoured for my attention – so many different attachments for my loyalty – that I could not at once decide among them, or even plainly discern which was which. Would not to liberate the prisoners also be to betray Yanegwa – and through Yanegwa, Nancy, and Nancy's family, that had saved my life, and nursed me to health again? And yet not to do so would be to ignore the most basick promptings of humanity, and condemn these gentle innocents, who had made me welcome in their hut, and shared their meagre food with me, to who knew what horrors?

But Mary did not give me leisure to consider. As if guessing the tendency of my thoughts, she said: "You know what they mean to do with us! They'll take us for wives, and the children'll be torn from their mammies, and raised up savages, and learned to hate and kill their own people! And Dadda" – here jerking her chin towards him, and drawing my gaze back to his blackened face – "Dadda's marked for death!"

"But what – what will you do?" I stammered. "Where will you go? They will surely come after you – and even if they do not take you again, you will starve to death in the wilderness."

"That", said Benjamin, as solemn as a Methodist, "is as the Lord wills."

"'Tis better to starve," said Mary, "or git shot down as we run, than die as slaves."

Hearing which, even the most senseless clod must have relented; so – looking behind me, to see we were not observed – I at once set about trying to free her. But I had no blade – the knots were pulled tight – and some dissenting part of my own mind still assailed me as I worked, forcefully pointing out that I was condemning myself to fleeing with them, and to being hunted myself by my former friends. And this self-interested consideration, I fear, half-subverted my object – setting my hands a-tremble, and making my fingers clumsier than they would otherwise have been. With the result that I had only succeeded in untying Mary (who then immediately set about performing the same office for her companions), and was just beginning to fumble with the ropes binding her father, when he suddenly said: "Wait! They are coming!"

I stopped – listened – and heard running feet, and a chorus of raging voices, each seeming to try to outdo the rest in point of ferocity.

I began plucking and pulling frantically at Benjamin's bonds; but he whispered: "No – leave me – it is too late!"

And so it was.

Yanegwa appeared first – quivering, his copper skin burnished with sweat, and specks of white foam flecking his lips and the corners of his mouth. He appeared not to remark that Mary was gone, or that I was standing almost where she had been; but, looking only at her father, swaggered up to him – took a knife from his belt – and drove it into his eye.

I have spoken already of the inadequacy of words to convey the extremes of our experience – an inadequacy that becomes all the more apparent when they are worn threadbare by excessive use. So –

if you would know Benjamin's response, and your own imagination cannot furnish you with it, I can do no better than refer you to my account of poor Nancy's murder – for in truth, the agony of an old white man is not such a very different thing from that of a young Indian girl.

"For G–d's sake," I said. "Have pity!" – and, stepping forward, laid a hand on Yanegwa's arm. But he flung it off again so impatiently, it was plain he would not tolerate a second attempt; and I was reduced to pleading, "I beg you! I beg you! As we are – as we have been friends –!"

But without favouring me with so much as a glance, he withdrew his weapon; and – after first flourishing it at his companions, who were gathering behind him – lifted the second eyelid, and stabbed the pupil, as violently he had the first. Afterwards saying something, that from its taunting tone, and the laughter it elicited from the others, I deduce to have been a cruel jest concerning the uselessness of eyes to a blind man.

"It was not his doing! It was not his doing!" I cried. "I am more responsible for Nancy's death than he is –" and would have rushed forward again, to try to intercede; but that McLeod restrained me.

"You must not interfere," he said, leading me a little apart. "It is their way; and they will not be turned from it."

"I will pay them –"

He shook his head. "They brought him here with only one purpose. And consider what trouble it has cost them, to do it. There must have been a great want of male prisoners, else they would not have cumbered themselves with him at all, but dispatched him on the spot."

"But he is guiltless! I am certain he never hurt another creature –"

"And what creature had Nancy hurt?" he said. And then, seeing I was not able to reply: "He will die a terrible death; but the others will be spared, if they are not foolish enough to try to escape, or make themselves a burden. That is better, surely, than five hundred dying a terrible death – as – as . . .?" His voice grew thick, and his eyes bulged with tears.

"I cannot dispute it," I said. "And yet –"

He nodded towards the captives: "Look."

I turned, and saw Mary fling herself at Yanegwa's feet, to beg for her father's life. To which he responded by flipping her away with his toe, and gesturing to the other Indians to remove her; which two or three of them immediately did – not gently, but (I had to concede) not brutally, either. While they were tying her again to a tree, I became conscious of the smell of smoke, and a moment later saw four of their companions rush upon Benjamin with flaming brands, and begin burning the clothes from him, and scorching the flesh beneath – all the while laughing, and mocking his pitiful gasps and whimpers.

"Can I not at least do for him what I – what I did for Nancy?" I said, raising my gun.

He shook his head: "Then they would kill all of them – and you besides."

Benjamin began to mutter something that I think was part of the Lord's Prayer, before breaking off with a fearful shriek, as the remainder of the savages joined in his torment.

"I cannot bear this," I said.

"Then let us go. I have not much relish for it, either."

We returned to the glade, and waited by his daughter's body – unable to speak, or even to look at each other – listening to the dreadful sounds of Benjamin's end. Which at length seemed to fuse with those I had heard the night before, from Nancy, and from who knows how many more – so that they have become woven, in my memory, into a single hymn of human suffering and folly.

I am not mad, yᵣ honours. But if I were, that is the moment I should have become so.

I had intended to stop at this juncture and resume again tomorrow, but found I could not rest, for thinking of all that I had just described. If I tried to sleep, my vision was ambushed by the spectre of Benjamin's eyeless face, or the obscene viscous jumble of Nancy's body; if I resigned myself to staying awake, and attempted to follow another line of thought that would take me away from them, I was invariably driven from my course by the recollection of their noise – which seemed to form itself into a kind of hard, white icicle of pain, that bored through my brain from one ear to the other. My only defence against it was to sing – but there was something so uncomfortable in keeping such horrors at bay with airs from *The Beggars' Opera* and the like that I could not sustain it for more than a few minutes at a time; and at length I concluded that nothing would serve but to take up my pen once more, and write my way out of the wilderness.

But this remedy was denied me by a practical difficulty: it was by now almost dark, and I could hardly see the paper.

And then a curious thing: the hatch opened in my door, and three candles appeared upon a tray, accompanied by a tinder-box and some matches.

Whether this small charity was provoked by your hearing my snatches of "Over the Hills and Far Away" and "Polly, You Might Have Toyed and Kissed", and guessing the cause; or whether it is merely further evidence that you wish me to proceed quickly, I do not know – but whatever the reason, I thank you for it.

And shall now – by the light it affords me – get on with my story:

I can scarce say how I endured the next few days. I clung to my wits only by a thread – occupying myself by counting the hairs of Nunyu's mane, or plucking a leaf from a tree, and marking its shape, and the pattern of its veins, so minutely that I could have drawn it exactly from memory. I spoke only once, that I can recall; and that was to ask McLeod why, after killing Benjamin, Yanegwa and his companions had chosen to continue on their way, rather than coming with us – for I could not conceive why they should still wish to go home, when they knew that all they would find there was burned houses, and dead people. To which he replied *that they would first see if they might discover anyone still alive in the ruins, or hiding close by*; and were then resolved to go on to another town, called Chickamauga – the capital of the most irreconcilable chief of their nation – and cast in their lot with him. Which heightened one anxiety, while simultaneously relieving another; for tho' the additional men would undoubtedly have made us better able to protect ourselves, yet when I recalled what I had seen them do, I did not know how I might have borne their company.

For a week or more we travelled through the forest – stopping at nightfall – setting off again at first light – drinking from springs and streams – and eating nothing but bitter little biscuits made from our small stock of maize flour and baked upon the fire. One morning I thought to vary this diet a little, by shooting a plump partridge I spied on the path ahead; but when he observed me raising my gun, McLeod pushed it aside, saying *I should save my powder and shot; for we might have greater need of them hereafter*. And in truth, when I came to reflect on it, I found I was not sorry to be spared the sight of more blood, and the loss of another life, however trifling.

At length, on the seventh or eighth afternoon (as well as I can judge), we came to the top of a low rise; and, looking down, saw a wooden fort, standing black against the fishy gleam of a great river. From one of the corners flew the Union flag, which (tho' it surprised me then, and still does so now, as I write these words) seemed to stir some dim hope in me – as if it were a kind of seal, that gave a warranty of civilized conduct. And perhaps McLeod thought the same; for he turned to me with something almost like a smile, and said: "There – another mile, and we shall be safe."

The commandant was a Major Litton – a stout, short-breathed, red-faced man of the middle age, whose presence in such a place seemed quite inexplicable: for he looked as if he would have been fatigued by walking fifty paces to the coffee house, and found it utterly beyond his powers to board a ship, or cross half a continent. He listened to our story with some show of impatience – staring between us at a distant spot, tapping his finger-nail on the arm of his chair, and making little grunting noises in his throat, that might have been intended as sympathetic, but sounded merely uneasy – as if he had no notion how to respond to such a catalogue of woe, and thought it slightly ill-bred in us to burden him with it. And when McLeod ended, by saying *that having lost both his home and his livelihood, he hoped he would now be permitted to enlist in some company, where he might put his knowledge of the country and its people to the service of the king,* the wretched man appeared so discomfited, you would suppose he had sat upon a pin. He growled – puffed his cheeks – made a great performance of looking out of the window, which in reality was no more than a pretext for frowning at Flora and her mother, to confirm (I suppose) that his initial impression of them had been correct – and then got peremptorily to his feet, saying *we could talk of that again; but, meanwhile, he would order some tents put up, and a meal provided for us.* For which purpose, he at once summoned a corporal, and then turned away – picked up some papers from his table – and began reading through them distractedly, with weary sighs, and a few muttered *ahs* and *oh, dears.*

Naturally taking this as a general dismissal, we all trooped towards the door; but as I was following the others out, Litton suddenly looked up, and laid a hand on my shoulder, saying: "Wait – that burn of yours, now." And then, revolving me until my cheek caught the fading light, and squinting down his nose at it: "Yes –'tis as I thought – a d–d rascally singe, that'll play the very devil with you, if it don't get some attention." Without waiting for a reply, he immediately strode to the entrance and bellowed after the retreating corporal – in a louder voice than I should have supposed him capable of producing: "When you are done, my compliments to Mr. Gabbitas, and desire him to do me the favour of waiting upon me, as soon as he is able."

I could not help thinking that if he truly believed my case to be so desperate, he would have told the fellow to go to Mr. Gabbitas first – which led me to speculate that perhaps he had some other reason than my health for detaining me. And so it immediately turned out; for he took a bottle and two glasses from a cupboard, poured us each an inch or so of brandy, and – having invited me to sit down, and pulled his own chair towards mine – said: "Now, Sir, I hope you will be so good as to pledge me?"

I did so.

He took a great mouthful himself – rolled it about until his eyes smarted – swallowed it with a gulp – and went on: "I'll be plain with you, Sir – it isn't often you meet a gentleman in this damnable place. My captain, Lubbock, has read a book or two, and will get a thousand a year when his father dies, if the old man hasn't disinherited him – but he's a scoundrel, and two minutes of his company is enough to make me itch to take a whip to him. As for the rest" – shaking his head – "my dogs afford me more diversion – and better conversation, too. So you will easily conceive what a happiness it is to see you here."

He said this with a confiding air, that was clearly intended to gratify my feelings, and elicit an equally gracious answer from me; but I have never excelled at pretty speeches, and such small skill in them as I once possessed had all but rusted away over the past year, from lack of use. With the result that I could think of absolutely nothing to say; and he was eventually obliged to fill the silence himself.

"So tell me, Sir – I'm curious to know – how do you come to be in the middle of the American desert?"

I began to tell him my tale – tho' it sounded so strange to my ears as I related it, it might have been the history of another man altogether. But had got no further than my visit to Dan, when Litton's eyes widened, and – leaning forward excitedly – he said: "Forgive me, Sir, but I am conscious I have not the advantage of your name" – his eyes twinkled roguishly, and his mouth twitched into a simper –

"our Scotch chieftain, evidently, thinking it beneath his dignity to introduce us."

"Ned Gudgeon."

"Gudgeon! Good G–d!" (here setting down his glass so violently I thought it would shatter). "And your brother?"

"Daniel –"

"Colonel Gudgeon? That fought in the late war?"

I nodded – and all at once recalled what I had until then clean forgotten: that I had heard the name *Litton* before, both from Dan and from Washington.

"I thought – I hoped it might be – but –!" He gazed at the floor, shaking his head wonderingly, like a man rousing himself from a stupor; then quickly looked up again – his doughy face bright with pleasure and surprise – and burst out: "I served with him, Sir! I served with Colonel Gudgeon against the French – when I was but a young lieutenant, and he a captain! Is not this remarkable?"

"Indeed," I said – trying, without much success, to infuse some reciprocal warmth into my voice.

"You must stay here," he said, "and be my guest. I fear I cannot entertain you as I should wish; but at least you shall have a roof over your head, instead of canvas; and a bed to lie on, instead of a blanket; and the best fare my table can afford."

"That is very good of you, Sir. But what of Mr. McLeod and his family?"

He stared at me uncomprehendingly for a few seconds; then suddenly seemed to grasp my meaning, and said: "They will do better where they are. These Highlanders are proud, touchy fellows – little better than savages themselves, for the most part, in my opinion. And as for his wife –" He broke off, as if the impossiblity of eating with a Cherokee woman was so self-evident, I should see it myself after a moment or two, and break into spontaneous laughter at the absurdity of the idea, without his needing to point it out. But when I said nothing, and failed to acknowledge his sly smile with so much as a nod, he plainly concluded that I was not as quick as he had supposed, and went on: "I fear I do not know enough of spells and spirits and conjurations, to set her entirely at her ease."

"In that case, Sir" – feeling a sudden flush of heat at my neck and throat – "I must thank you for your invitation, and decline it."

He was so startled, he could not speak for a moment. Then he blurted: "Oh, come, Sir! I am obliged to furnish the Indians with arms – and own there was never a duty I liked less, when I see the use they put them to; but I am not ordered to treat them as my friends."

"I am indebted to the McLeods for my life," I began, "and cannot–"

"I am indebted to Sergeant Travers for mine!" he broke in, with the triumphant air of a man who knows he has an irrefutable argument, and cannot wait to dazzle his opponent with it. "But I do not ask him to dine with me – nor would he expect it."

The rage bubbled in me like hot bile, burning my throat; and – not daring to open my mouth, for fear of what might come out of it – I got up and left without a word, leaving him gaping with amazement.

Which may strike y^r honours as a quite disproportionate response to so small a provocation; and, indeed, I cannot entirely account for it myself. Perhaps the events of the past ten days had filled me with so much anger, and given me so little opportunity to vent it, that once I had reached the relative security of the fort, and found the external constraints upon me somewhat relaxed, I could no longer keep it in, but must loose it on the first object I discovered there. Whatever the reason, to find the world suddenly shrunk to the manners of a parsonage-house, and my friend and saviour, after all we had witnessed and endured together, banished (as it were) to the servants' quarters, seemed more than I could bear. I am glad Litton did not try to stop me; for if he had, I should indubitably have given myself still greater reason for regret, by knocking him down.

I found the tents at the edge of the central square, next to an untidy row of weatherboard huts that must have been the barracks. The McLeods had already taken possession of theirs; but their attempts to settle themselves were being obstructed by a slavering idiot of a soldier, who kept lifting the entrance flap and ogling Flora lewdly – while two or three of his companions stood by, urging him to *go on*, and *take the squaw*, and *give her a bit of good English meat*, and the like.

My mood must have been stamped upon my face; for the instant they caught sight of me, they all shuffled away.

I was not hungry, for some reason – only overwhelmingly tired.

I crawled into my own tent, and before I could even take my coat off, and pull it about my shoulders, was unconscious.

What signifies the word "property" to you, Sir?

XXXVI

Once I should have been astonished to see such a question in such a place – ay, and outraged, too. But now . . .

When I was a boy of eight or nine, Uncle Fiske took me to his friend Mr. Jennings's house, in St. Michael's Hill; and we sat drinking chocolate by the window of his bedchamber, to see a highwayman hanged. The poor wretch's name was Tompkinson – a handsome, swaggering fellow in a green velvet coat, with half a dozen women there to weep for him, and squabble over the favour of a last kiss. He caught my eye as he mounted the gallows, and smiled, and bowed to me; at which I said: "That is the finest gentleman I ever saw."

Uncle Fiske laughed, and ruffled my hair; but after he grew grave, and said: "Nay, Ned, nay – he has taken other men's property. Which makes him the enemy of society; for property is the cement that fixes it together."

And so I have always supposed since. Or *had* always supposed.

But I fancy *your* meaning is: it was property killed Benjamin, and Nancy, and all the rest. For without the hunger to seize from the Indians what they held in common, and possess it severally, and grow rich by it, the colonists would have had no occasion to murder them, or the savages to take revenge. And that hunger came from looking at men like me, and hearing us talk of *property*.

I cannot say if you are right, or not. I shall reflect upon it.

And meanwhile resume my journey.

Tho' Major Litton made no further attempt to seek out my society, yet his obligations to Dan were evidently still strong enough to prevent his simply abandoning me to the wilderness; and a few days after our arrival, I received from him a frigid little note, of which the sense – once it had been extracted from the husk of *honours* and *favours* and *your servants* – was this: *that Captain Lubbock and a small party of men would conduct me to Canada; where I should be able to take ship again for England.*

On a grey, unsettled morning, assailed by snarling gusts of wind, that spattered us with icy showers, and started the clouds into panick flight above us, the McLeods and I finally bade each other farewell. I tried to express my gratitude to them, and my fervent hope that the future would bring them peace, and a restitution of their fortunes, but – not for the first time in our relation – could not find words capacious and sturdy enough to carry what was in my heart. And they seemed to feel a similar frustration; for, after launching a few little sentences, that faltered and sank without reaching their destination, Mrs. McLeod shook her head, and seized me in her arms; in which she was soon followed, first by her daughter, and then by her husband. And so we stood, with the tears burning our eyes, and the rain pricking our skin, until I was summoned to embark.

Our party consisted of two nimble boats – one carrying Lubbock and myself, and the other six men and a sergeant. Whether it had been Litton's intention to punish my ingratitude, by appointing his adjutant to escort me; or whether there was merely no-one else at the fort to whom the office might have been entrusted, I cannot say; but I am certain it must have afforded him some satisfaction that – under the guise of doing me a service – he had contrived, at a stroke, to rid himself of Lubbock's company, and to inflict it on me. For the captain turned out to be even more insufferable (if such a thing were possible) than his commandant had suggested: a short, misshapen, opinionated fellow, with one eye bigger than the other, and pale scaly lips fixed permanently in a kind of sardonick quiver – as if the world had been created with the sole object of diverting him, and was constantly failing in its purpose. If I tried to be companionable, by offering an observation on the country, or the weather, or the slight resemblance I saw between one of his soldiers and the late Duke of Newcastle, he would reply with a murmured *Do you think so?* – that made it perfectly plain he considered me a silly fellow for remarking it, and could not trouble himself to set me right. This unremitting scorn soon paralysed my tongue; and since he seldom volunteered a comment of his own, we ended by travelling in almost unbroken silence – save for the whisper of the water, and the fidgeting of the canvas, or the sober slap of the oars. Which – while according pretty well with my depressed mood – deprived me of the possibility of being distracted out of it; so that I was left totally undefended against the pitiless assaults of memory and regret.

But it was not until the third day that I glimpsed the full extent of Lubbock's viciousness. We had just emerged into a great lake, that seemed as vast as the ocean – for it rolled towards us in frothy waves, and broadened majestically to a glittering horizon, on which there was not even the faintest shadow of a farther side. The sails were set;

and we were beginning to beat northwards at a merry pace, when I
suddenly spied – tucked into the corner between a headland and the
shore – a little farm, standing at the mouth of a stream. The house
was no more than a cabin; but the ground about it had been well
cleared and securely fenced with split logs; and behind it three or
four frolicking pigs were busy churning the yard to mud – giving the
place a truer air of settlement and agriculture than I had yet seen in
the wilderness, except among the Indians. But it seemed entirely on
its own, without neighbours in any direction, and (whether by
chance or design) was quite invisible, save when you were square
before it – being concealed, as you approached, by the promontory;
and as soon as you had passed, by the trees.

I supposed Lubbock had not seen it, for he was propped against
the side of the boat, with his eyes half-closed, and his hands folded
across his belly; and I did not trouble to point it out to him – knowing
that if I said, "Look, Sir; is it not surprising to find that here?", he
would only pout at me for disturbing him, and drawl, "Do you think
so?" But he must have been only feigning slumber, like a great lizard
watching for prey: for all at once he sat up; stared at it for a moment;
then turned, and called to the sergeant, "Put ashore, there, and fetch
us some dinner!" – as off-handedly as if he were dispatching a footman to his own larder, to bring back a pie – before immediately
resuming his former position; and preparing – to all appearances – to
doze off again.

"I hope you mean to pay for what we have," I said; for I had not
observed him give them any money; and doubted whether they
would carry enough themselves, in a place where they had so little
occasion to spend it.

But Lubbock only trembled slightly – in languid imitation of a man
shaking with laughter.

"Here –" I said, taking my purse from my coat, and holding it
towards him. "If you will call him back, he may use this."

Which provoked him into – for once – favouring me with a reply:
"Nay – you mistake the nature of the debt. The Americans should
pay us, for protecting them against the rebels."

"You will drive them to become rebels themselves, if you steal
from them."

"Do you think so?" he said, fluttering his mis-matched eyes con-
temptuously. And then, with a weary sigh – as if my foolish inter-

vention had robbed him of the hope of sleep – plucked a silver flask from his pocket, and clamped it to his mouth, like a suckling clutching his mother's breast.

"I shall call him myself, then," I said.

But had got no further than drawing the air into my lungs, when Lubbock quite knocked it out again, by roaring: "Be quiet, d–n you! While you are in my charge, you are subject to military discipline; and if you disobey an order, or interfere with me in the performance of my duty, I shall have you tied to the mast and returned to the fort to face a court martial."

Whether he had the authority to threaten me in this manner I greatly doubted – and, a year before, I would unquestionably have said so; but I knew that my rights in the matter were of little consequence, when I had no boat of my own, and when the men were bound to obey him rather than me – and experience had taught me, if not wisdom, then at least a degree of practical resignation before the inevitable. So I sat down, and barricaded my thoughts against despair, by directing them towards the boat – remarking the grain of the wood, and the graceful curve of the timbers, and the skill with which they had been shaped to their purpose, with the same minute care I had given to Nunyu's mane.

From which meditations I was roused, by a squeal from the shore; and, looking up, saw two soldiers holding one of the pigs across a log, while a third stood over it with a knife. The wretched creature was still kicking, when a woman ran from the house, shouting and waving her hands in protest; but the sergeant caught her, like a web entangling a fly – twirled her about – and hurried her back in again. Shortly after, one of his men followed, and then another; until at length only the slaughterman was left, butchering the carcase with the steady application of a man who knows his occupation, and finds satisfaction in it. I could not see what the others were about, but it was hard not to harbour a dreadful suspicion – which a sudden eruption of sound from the cabin soon told me was but too well-founded.

"They are raping that poor woman," I said.

Lubbock affected not to hear me, but ran his tongue about the nipple of his flask, as if trying to dislodge a last drop of liquor from the thread – with such lazy insolence, I could no longer keep my temper; and blurted: "You speak of duty, Sir! And yours is plainly to stop them!"

He turned quickly towards me, leading me to expect another hectoring reprimand – to which, this time, I was ready to reply. But instead he gazed at me, with a kind of astonished amusement, as if I had finally said something worthy of his attention – so that for a second I wondered whether after all he was no more than a common bully, that would leave off his blustering the instant you stood up to him.

But then he said: "Good G–d! – I do believe –" (shaking his head). "What is it, Sir? – the noise of it?"

"No!" I shouted – outraged that he could suppose my objection was merely to being disturbed. "'Tis what the noise signifies!"

He stared at me a moment more; and then said: "I own I should not have credited it; but any man could see that something's heated you. Shall I have you carried there, so you may take your pleasure with the rest of 'em?"

It was a second before I got his meaning – and then I found it so impossible to know if he was speaking in earnest, or merely smoking me, that I could not find an answer.

"For myself," he went on, "I have no taste for it. When I was sixteen, I debauched a maidservant in my father's house – which stamped such an indelible impression of disgust upon me, I could never bring myself to try the business again. But it wonderfully cheers the men, I know; and makes 'em less surly after – and if it were to work the same effect on you, Sir, no-one could be more delighted than I."

I was so appalled, I could not bear even to look at him, and was reduced to communicating my revulsion, by scowling sullenly at the water. Which caused me, by chance, to catch sight of my own distorted reflection – shivering and breaking and re-forming again with every movement of the surface: one moment folding my mouth in upon itself, or extending my purpled cheek, until it covered my whole face; the next, slicing off the top of my head and setting it back askew. And for some reason, this warped image appeared, just for an instant, a truer representation of my real self than I should have got from a mirror – as if, instead of being (as I had supposed) a well-regulated machine, ordered by some interior logick, I was no more than an arbitrary assemblage of limbs and organs and sensations, tossed first into one pattern, and then into another, by the endless motion of life, like seaweed on a beach. Which notion suddenly precipitated me into a dizzy descent; so that I seemed to be tumbling down a cliff, snatching at every passing tuft and root – only to find that none was strong enough to arrest my fall. I should find no refuge in my country – for *country*, I now saw, was nothing but an expensive harlot, that decked herself in finery, to dupe her infatuated slaves into thinking her better than the other whores; I could have no trust in the *law* – which favoured only those that had the power to enforce it; even *honour*, it appeared, was to most men no more than a fashionable coat, to be put on when they entered the drawing room, and taken off the instant they went out again.

In the end, I was able to glimpse hope only in one frail idea – that I clutched, and repeated like a catechism: *Go home. Attend to your own affairs. Never stir out of Somersetshire again.*

The dawn is at my window. My eyes wilt; but my mind craves the knowledge that this part of my history is over, and will not release me to my rest until I have pecked the last full stop on the page.

Which I may do pretty much at once; for the rest of my journey with Lubbock was almost without incident – save for the humdrum wilderness adventures of overturned boats, and wet feet, and empty bellies, of which I have already given you sufficient example. With the result that I at length reached Montreal, without having discovered anything further of any note, concerning either myself, or him, or the object of my quest.

The war had bred a clogged traffick between Canada and England; but – thanks to Major Litton's recommendation – after a delay of only three days, I was able to get a passage on the *Penelope*, with Captain Ferguson. And so one morning found myself gliding down the St. Lawrence River, bound once more for Bristol – watching the inky ribbons of forest unwind along either shore, and seeing, in their black impenetrability, the proof of what I already knew: that only a fool would come to this place, thinking it would yield him anything but pain and care.

And indeed, when I recalled the hopes I had brought with me to America, and then reflected on the manner of my leaving it again, I might have wept.

But I was past tears.

XXXVII

I had not intended to pick up my pen today. What prompted me to do so (as I am sure y^r honours very well know) was an unexpected incident this morning:

I had just risen from my breakfast – had taken up my dishes, and was approaching the hatch with them – when a sudden noise nearly made me drop them again: the fumbling scrape and clatter of a key in the lock.

The next moment – for the first time since I was brought here – the door opened.

Two bluff fellows stood without – their legs a-straddle, and hands held wide before them, like a pair of countrymen bracing themselves up to catch a bolting sheep. Beyond them, I could just make out a long, dark passage, with a scrap of light at the end of it.

"What do you want?" I said.

They said nothing; and for all their faces told me, they might have been wearing masks.

"Who are you?"

For answer, one of them stepped lightly forward, and snatched the tray from me; while the second thrust me against the jamb – pinioned me with his knee – slipped a hood over my head – and, before I had time to resist, spun me about, and tied my wrists together behind me. Then he half-turned me again, and hurried me from the room, prodding my back with one hand, and guiding me with the other – while his companion followed us, with a noisy tattoo of rattling china and slapping feet.

The combined effects of the cloth smothering my mouth and the furious heart-beating in my throat almost deprived me of breath; but I was just able to blurt out: "What – am I to hang, now?"

But still they did not reply; and, seeing that further questions would be useless, I resolved to follow their example, and hold my tongue – for if I could not master my fear, I might at least deprive them of the satisfaction of observing it.

(Is not mine as strange a case as ever man found himself in? 'Tis certain that in the character of my gaolers, y^r honours must have ordered my abduction; and yet in the character of my confidants, you remain the only friends I have here – or perhaps in the world; and if I deny myself the relief of opening my heart to you, I fear I shall go mad indeed.)

After perhaps a quarter of a minute, we emerged (as I deduced) into the open – for all at once, the sound of our steps became duller, and a breeze touched my fingers, and the darkness before my eyes turned from black to grey. We continued across a rough, hard surface, that I should guess to have been cobbles; and then upon a softer one; and at length, after a hundred paces or so, my guard tugged at the ropes binding me, like a carter at his reins, to signify I should stop. There was a knock – the click of a latch – and I was unceremoniously bustled into another building.

Blind and muzzled tho' I was, I was immediately conscious of the darkness, and the heat, and a pungent smell compounded of sulphur, and cloves, and liquorice, and some other aromatick gum or spice that I might have known if I had encountered it alone, but could not unmingle from its fellows.

I heard a few brief whispered words – tho' not clear enough, to make them out; then the grating of wood upon the floor – and the next moment was forcibly pushed down on to a chair, and then tied again, so that I was secured to the back of it.

This, I thought, *is not the prelude to a hanging – or, at least, not yet; but rather to torture.*

I felt exactly as a man must that imagined he was walking along the bottom of a deep valley – and finds it has suddenly given way, and tumbled him into some profounder abyss yet; for it had not occurred to me until that moment, that I need fear any ordeal worse than death.

Before I could stop myself, I cried out: "What am I supposed to have done?"

Again, there was no reply. I attempted to reduce my rioting thoughts to some semblance of order, in hope that – if I but reflected rationally for a moment – I might hit upon the answer myself. *Who might have read the earlier part of my history without being moved to anger – and yet, in what I submitted yesterday, suddenly discover a reason to punish me?*

I could think of three possible candidates for the office: the Indians, for my description of Benjamin's end; the Americans, for my observations upon colonists and property; and the ministry, for my account of the shameful conduct of British troops.

The Indians, I was certain, lacked the power to confine me in this fashion – even if they had wished to do so, which was extremely doubtful. The Americans might imagine they had a better reason for it; but I must be vain indeed to suppose they would put themselves to the trouble of punishing me, when there were so many worthier enemies to occupy them.

Was I then a prisoner of my own government? But here I was interrupted, by the sound of someone rapidly approaching, and then a slight pressure on the top of my head.

I grimaced, waiting for the first blow.

All at once, the hood was whisked away.

I found I was in a sombre room, lit only by a glazed opening in the roof, and furnished like a country apothecary's: the walls entirely covered with shelves full of books, and cabinets crammed with red and blue jars; and the table in the centre strewn with a whole company of knives and saws, phials and forceps and leech-glasses – tho' whether it had been assembled for the purpose of healing or hurting, I could not say.

A lean, swarthy man bent over me – who confounded all my speculations, for he had a markedly Spanish air, and I could not imagine there was a nation on earth that had less cause to quarrel with me than Spain.

"Why have you brought me here?" I said.

But he was no more communicative than his lackeys and, without favouring me with so much as a direct glance, placed a hand behind me and began methodically to probe my neck – his eyes fixed blankly on the wall, as if he had put them in abeyance, to devote himself entirely to what his fingers told him.

I thought: *He is measuring me for a noose; or for some infernal instrument of torment.*

I tried to quell my panick, by inhaling steadily, and compelling myself to study his face. It was coarse-grained – pitted with black pores, and shadowed with the ghost of a prolifick beard.

He moved in front of me, and looked coldly first at my cheek, and then at my brow. The memory of some dreadful device of the Middle Ages – a helmet with spikes upon the inside – impressed itself on my mind so powerfully that I almost fancied I saw it. With a mighty effort of will, I forced myself to remark that his breath smelled of garlick and cachou.

He kneeled before me – unbuttoned the leg of my breeches – rolled down my stocking – and peered at my shin.

And then I understood: he was examining my wounds.

The next moment he stood up – raising his hand, as a signal to someone behind me. Instantly, the hood descended on my head again; I was released from the chair with a few deft pluckings and tugs; then dragged to my feet, and marched quickly back to my room.

I have less idea than ever, of who y^r honours are, or what you are about – tho' I can only suppose that your motive on this occasion must have been to test my veracity, by comparing the scars upon my body with the injuries I describe in my narrative. In which case, I cannot acquit you of (at the very least) a certain careless cruelty – and that grieves as well as alarms me; for surely you must know by now that, at the venture of only a few kind words, you might have had as a gift what you chose to take by force, so sparing yourselves a quantity of trouble, and me a good deal of needless fear.

I shall rest now; and – if you leave me here until tomorrow – continue my story then.

XXXVIII

I own I hungered for an answer this morning. Your silence makes me tremble.

But I will not be cowed. For I repeat – whatever y^r honours may think: I am guilty of no crime.

So I shall buoy myself up as well as I can; and – in the hope I shall live long enough to finish it – today begin:

BOOK THREE

and last – unless (as now seems unthinkable) y^r honours should finally relent, and let me out of this place again, to resume my adventure.

We have endured one voyage together across the Atlantick; and I shall not tax you with another, saying only that we were eight weeks at sea – reaching Avonmouth on the last day of August 1776, as bilious and weak-kneed as a bucketful of puppies that have just narrowly escaped drowning. It was afternoon when we at length came into Bristol – to find it now as bloated by the troubles in the colonies as before it had been pinched by them: for the docks were choked with ships; the streets with soldiers and sailors; and the quays crowded with men and cannon – crates and barrels – pigs and cattle and sheep – all destined for the army in America. With the result that, by the time I at length set foot on English soil again, night was already falling.

This (strange tho' it may appear) was a contingency for which I was quite unprepared – for tho' I knew, rationally, that it was impossible to predict the hour of our arrival, yet I had sustained my frail spirits with the belief that it would be early in the morning. For a man prostrated on the ground will see as looming obstacles objects he might easily step over if he were standing; and in my weakened and exhausted state, the idea of having to relate my sorry tale to Uncle and Aunt Fiske – and even worse, the possibility of encountering Coleman – seemed so intolerable that I could only keep myself from the most abject despair by imagining that I should be able to slip ashore undetected, and on to the Wells stage coach, before anyone had recognized me. But there would be no coach now until tomorrow; and I doubted I still had money enough to hire a carriage – and besides, the thought of how my wife would receive me, if I roused her from her bed without first having given her notice of my return, now struck me as an even more fearful prospect than the rest. So, after bidding farewell to Captain Ferguson, I took up my little bag of possessions, and set off reluctantly for Queen Square.

It had occurred to me that I might have difficulty finding my way – for the events of the last twenty months had driven Bristol so completely from my head that I was unsure whether I should know it again. But as it turned out, the buildings looked familiar enough – tho' there seemed something tawdry and unreal about them, as if I were walking not through the city itself, but merely past some cheap piece of scenery, that had been painted to evoke it, and would be taken down again as soon as the play was over. This impression, far from diminishing, grew stronger with every step I took; so that when I finally knocked upon my uncle's door, I almost expected it to fall over – revealing nothing beyond, but a dusty unlit void.

But instead it half-opened; and Joseph's head poked out. His face was in shadow; but there was a kind of fidgety caution in his manner, that suggested surprise, and even apprehension; so – deducing that he had not expected a visitor at so late an hour, and could not conceive who it might be – I moved a few inches forwards, to let the light from the hall fall upon me. He instantly recoiled – his eyes wide – one hand clapped to his mouth – and the other thrust out before him, to bar my way.

"Joseph?" I said.

He shook his head frantically.

"Do you not know me? Mr. Fiske's nephew? Ned Gudgeon?"

He began to quake, and for a moment I thought he was going either to faint, or to run away; but with a great effort he mastered himself, and made a slow, orderly retreat – marching backwards, so as to keep me within view. But as soon as I tried to follow him, he stopped, and cried, "Wait!" – like a man pleading for his life; so I desisted, and watched as he picked up a candle, and hesitantly approached me again – as gingerly as if I were a mad dog, and he was ready to flee at the first snarl. I had not supposed that my appearance was so changed as to leave my identity in any doubt; but, knowing that any protest or sudden movement would only inflame his fear, I bowed my head, and submitted patiently to his scrutiny – confident that, at any moment, I should hear him cry out my name, and laughingly beg my pardon for showing me such an unmannerly welcome. So was amazed and dismayed, when he ended by falling back again, and shaking his head afresh – with the furious insistence of a waking child, trying to banish the last vapours of a nightmare.

"Good G–d!" I said. "Can you not make allowance for a few scars? This" – laying a finger on my cheek – "was caused by a burn. This" – moving it to my brow – "by an attempt to scalp me. I know it has healed a little awry, but–"

"But you are dead!" he blurted.

"Dead!"

"You were killed! The master had a letter – a year ago –"

"A letter?"

He nodded.

"From whom?" But before he had time to reply, my own tumbling thoughts threw up the answer, and I rushed on: "Ah! Mr. Coleman!"

I have had occasion before to speak of the strangeness of our minds; and mine now performed the peculiar trick of entirely splitting itself, so as to pursue two totally different courses at the same time. One half plodded along, like a dull clerk behind a brilliant lawyer, diligently searching for a logical explanation of what I had already grasped by intuition – which was not difficult; for I quickly saw it must be the likeliest thing in the world, that Hickling – supposing my wounds to be fatal, and eager to earn his reward – would have reported my death to Coleman as an accomplished fact. The other half, meanwhile, was fixed on Joseph's face; which had suddenly relaxed into an incredulous little smile, that told me I had at last come close to convincing him of the truth.

But when I took courage from my success, to move a little towards him, he immediately stiffened again, and frowning said: "But why would Mr. Coleman do that, if you are alive?"

My adventures had made me so reckless, and so heedless of distinction, that instead of ignoring the question, or telling him it was none of his concern, I at once replied: "He tried to have me murdered. And evidently thought he had succeeded."

"Murdered?" – the word just a movement of the lips, as if he feared by sounding it, he would give it lethal force.

I nodded. "But he failed, as you can see. And if you do not trust your eyes – here, take my hand."

And after a moment, he did so – crying, "Oh! – sir! – I congratulate you!"

Knowing that he finally believed me, and feeling the warmth and strength of his grasp and his unfeigned delight in discovering I was alive when he had imagined me dead, I began to weep – and ended by taking him to me, and sobbing on his neck. To which (when he had sufficiently recovered from his astonishment) he responded, by putting his hands on my shoulders, and hugging me to himself.

"What of my aunt and uncle?" I said, after we had stood thus for a minute or more. "May I see them?"

"Your aunt, Sir – I am sorry –"

"What?"

"She is –"

"Sick?"

"Dead, Sir."

You may think that, after all the other losses I had suffered, this would have seemed a small enough blow; but I found myself very deeply affected by it. On the voyage to England – despite trying to fortify my mind against useless speculation, which I knew could only weaken me further – I had been assailed by gloomy imaginings of what I might discover when I arrived; but for some reason or other the possibility of Aunt Fiske's death had not been among them. I should doubtless have taken warning, from seeing how age had crept upon her, the last time I was here; and yet she seemed such a vital part of my own nature – indeed, the very thread, that anchored me to my beginnings – I could not easily conceive that I might yet remain when she had gone.

"How?" I asked.

"You might say a broken heart, Sir. When she heard the news of your – of you – she retired to her bed, and never got up again."

So Coleman had taken aim at me, and killed her instead. The thought of it worked me to such a heat, I almost swooned – first from rage, and then from desperation: for I knew I could not prove he had attempted to cause my death, and that no court in the kingdom would find him guilty of hers.

"And my uncle?"

"He is sadly declined, Sir. You would hardly know him – and I doubt he would know you at all."

"Why?"

"Why, Sir – because he is become – become –"

"An idiot, you mean?"

He nodded – then began to shake his head instead. "He is well enough when he is not disturbed. But if something agitates him – something out of the usual course of things –"

"Well, we shall see."

"I beg you, Sir, to consider–"

But I had not come halfway across the world, to be denied admittance to my own uncle, who – however decayed his mind – must still, I was sure, recognize me, from the deep natural sympathy that existed between us. So – a little impatiently, perhaps – I snapped: "Where is he?"

"In the aerie. But –"

I could not but recall, as I limped towards the staircase, how – less than two years before – O'Donnell and I had bounded up those same steps, with Joseph snapping at our heels in a vain attempt to stop us. The poor fellow might have easily done now what he had failed to do then – for in my pitiful condition, it would have taken no more than a tug at my coat-tail to halt me; but tho' he was plainly uneasy, he followed me meekly enough – confining himself to muttering *that I must do as I pleased; but he was afraid I should only end by distressing both my uncle and myself.* And when we reached the top, he sufficiently remembered his office to knock upon the door, and open it with a flourish, and bow neatly, as he said: "Here is a gentleman come to see you, Sir."

I heard the ghost of Uncle Fiske's voice within, quavering, "A gentleman?"

"Tell him who!" I whispered.

Joseph hesitated; then said gravely, "Your nephew, Sir" – and at once stood aside, as if – having discharged his duty – he was now washing his hands of the business, and leaving me to accept the consequences of my own folly.

"My nephew?" whined the old man, with an edge of irritation in his tone.

"Yes, Sir," I began – intending to continue by presenting myself before him, and loudly saying my name, in hope the evidence of his eyes and ears together might jolt him into recognizing me. But the only light in the room came from a few bright twigs in the grate, that I suspected (for the evening was not cold) to have been made more to cheer my uncle than to warm him – with the result that I could not immediately make out where he was. So – knowing that he must be under the same difficulty in spying me – I lingered in the entrance, squinting into the gloom; and after two or three seconds thought I had him, sitting stock-still on the other side of the hearth.

"Uncle?"

His reply quite confounded me; for it came from another quarter altogether – and I at once saw that what I had taken for him was not a man at all, but the negro-head jug.

"What *nephew*?"

I looked again, and found the contour of his chair. Sickness must have shrivelled him, for he seemed to have been swallowed whole by the black maw between the wings, with nothing but a thin hand – trailing out like a pale tongue, and resting on the arm – to show he was there at all.

"Ned," I said.

"Ned!" He stirred, and leaned forward. And as he did so, the glow from the fire caught his face, sending forth a faint shadow, that mingled with the strange forms of the savage masks hanging on the wall – and was, indeed, as grotesque as any of them: for the mouth appeared to have collapsed in upon itself, thrusting his chin and beaky nose into the points of a crescent, so that he resembled Punchinello in a puppet-show. He gazed at me for a moment; and then went on: "Ned is dead, Sir. As that jackanapes might have told you, if he'd a pennyworth of brains in his woolly head."

"He did tell me, Sir. But it is not true. Matthew Coleman supposed I had been murdered – and with good reason, I'm sorry to say. But he was mistaken."

He did not answer at once, and I thought for an instant that the mention of Coleman's name had worked the same effect on him that it had on Joseph. But then he said: "Nay, Sir, save your breath – I saw Ned's bloody wig, and his ring, with my own eyes. I'm an old man; and you may have heard it said I'm mad – but I've not parted company with my wits quite yet, I promise you. So you'll have to try a little harder than that, if you want to find the way into my pocket."

"Not into your pocket, Sir – your heart."

"Ha! – very prettily said! And that proves it – for Ned could never have spoken so fit to his purpose. Will you not sit down, Sir, and drink something with me? I never liked a man the less merely for trying to cheat me; for 'tis in the nature of things, that we all strive to take advantage of another's weaknesses – and besides, I should have had no friends, else!" He made a phlegmy rasping sound, that began as a laugh and ended as a cough. While he was struggling to recover his breath, he delegated the business of communicating with me to his fingers – which fluttered wildly, waving me to a seat.

"Very well," I said; for tho' by accepting I might appear to be abandoning my claim, and conceding defeat, yet I knew that to refuse would be to throw away my only chance of continuing the conversation, and so changing his mind.

"Here, Sir," he said, when he could talk again – picking up a half-full rummer from the floor beside him, and holding it towards me with a shaking hand. "You take this, and I" – snickering knowingly, as if he supposed I should admire his roguishness – "I'll content myself with the bottle."

To hear this was something of a shock – for until that moment, he had said nothing that suggested he was so far degenerated as to forget the most ordinary rules of hospitality. But it was immediately eclipsed by a far greater one – as he sat back with a satisfied sigh, and continued: "In truth, Sir, Ned was very probably the greatest fool that ever lived. I never knew a fellow that was more easily deceived, or had less notion how the world really goes on. He might find you in bed with his wife – and if you but told him that you were sheltering there from the rain, he would not only believe you, but give you a suit of dry clothes, and insist you stay and eat dinner with him, too."

I had undergone some extraordinary adventures since I had last sat in the aerie – but none, surely, as singular as this: to be treated as a stranger by my own uncle, and diverted by him with a satire upon my own character? My feelings were so wounded, I scarce knew how to respond – and yet it was certain that the longer I allowed him to continue unchecked, the harder it must be to change his mind: for with every gibe, he entrenched himself deeper in a position from which it was difficult to withdraw – until, finally, the price of admitting his mistake, and attempting to make amends for it, would appear too great even to contemplate. So I replied: "Pray, Sir – you have said enough. Any more, and I fear you will regret it."

To my surprise, he gave a gargling sob; and his eyes suddenly sparkled in the fire-light. "Nay, Sir, nay – do not be cruel. You catch his voice pretty well, I'll grant you, when you've a mind to it – but that – but that –" He shook his head, and snivelled, before going on: "He was my nephew, after all – and I knew him from a boy – and my wife – my wife, Sir – she loved him like a son, for we had none of our own."

"I loved her, Sir. And you. You were –"

He twitched, as if a horse-fly had bitten him.

"I beg you – don't be so unkind." He fixed me with a wet, slabby stare, and then shook his head again. "You might have had more success with her, Sir – for she weren't so crafty as me. And if you had, I'd have thanked you for it, and winked at the pretence – for it would have kept her alive, I'm certain of it. You don't know what it is, Sir, to lose a wife, and be left alone in the world."

"I think I can guess," I replied. And then, before I had time to reflect, I found myself on my knees before him, saying: "'Tis no pretence, Uncle. I am Ned –"

"No!"

"I am – I swear it!"

His eyes grew large with panick – he gasped, and shrank back, crossing his arms before him, and screwing his face with pain, as if I were attacking him physically. Weary and angry tho' I was, I could not look upon him without being moved to pity.

"You shan't be alone any more," I said. "You shall come and live with me, if you wish it" (here attempting a smile) "as you always said you would, do you recall?"

He began to cry – like an infant that seems bent on refusing all comfort, and greets every soothing word with renewed wails, and every tentative caress with blows. He howled and puled; and, when I tried to embrace him, lashed me with kicks and punches – which, tho' they were too feeble to hurt me greatly, yet forced me to keep my distance. I pleaded with him to stop, and calm himself – but succeeded only in incensing him the more; so that in less than two minutes he was shaking and spluttering so violently, I feared he might fall into a fit, and die.

"Come, Sir," said a voice at my shoulder. I looked up, and saw Joseph holding his hand out towards me. Knowing I could accomplish nothing more by staying, I took it gratefully, and allowed him to help me to my feet and lead me from the room.

"I am sorry," I said, as we reached the stairs.

He gave no sign of having heard me, but fixed me with an impassive gaze, and said: "You may sleep in your old bed-chamber, Sir. I have told the other servants that you are a friend of the family. But it will be best if you leave early in the morning; for they will not accept my word against the master's – and you know what will become of me, if I lose my place here." And without waiting for my reply, he turned, and went back into the aerie, to try to mend the damage I had caused there.

I slept almost at once; but was roused again while it was still quite dark, by a troubling thought that would not wait till dawn to worry me.

It was this: that if Uncle Fiske believed me dead, 'twas a hundred to one my wife must, too – and tho' I did not doubt she had contrived to play the part of the grieving widow well enough, yet I could not but wonder if she might not privately prefer it to her previous state, and so be something less than delighted when the grave (as it were) suddenly opened, and restored to her a crippled husband, that she had not greatly liked even when he was whole. After pondering this difficulty for an hour or more, I at last hit upon a plan; and – as soon as the household began to stir – opened my door, and asked a passing servant to bring me pen and paper. I then sat down, and wrote a conciliatory letter, in which I apologized for my long silence – explained the reasons for it – described my sorry condition – and ended, by expressing as I warmly as I could the happiness I felt at the prospect of being reunited with my family. Which done, I summoned the same housemaid, and gave it to her, together with my last guinea – telling her *that if she would arrange for a messenger to deliver it without delay, and then discover what time the Wells stage coach left the Three Kings, she might keep sixpence from the change for her trouble.*

This unforeseen expenditure put me to the necessity of borrowing a guinea from Joseph, in order to pay for my fare – the humiliation of which, two years before, would undoubtedly have seemed painful enough to deter me from making it. But my recent adventures had so wonderfully eroded my pride that what had once been a great mountain, barring every way save the acknowledged path of a gentleman, had by degrees been worn down to no more than a smooth pebble, that I might easily accommodate to any shift, by the simple expedient of stepping over it. I promised my humble benefactor that he should have his money again in a week – and allayed my few misgivings by reflecting that it was laid out to good effect, if it served to prepare the hard soil of my wife's heart a little, and plant the seed of some softer feelings towards me.

But, having already unwittingly entangled poor Joseph in so many embarrassments, I did not wish to run the risk of adding to them, by lingering unnecessarily in the house, and so perhaps provoking my uncle's wrath against him a second time; so, after making my thanks and farewells, I hobbled down the hall as quietly as I could, and slipped out – even tho' the maid had told me that the coach would not be departing for more than another hour. I resolved, therefore, to try to extend my wizened muscles – which had almost wasted away again during my weeks of confinement on the ship – by walking three or four times around the square, before setting out for Thomas Street.

This exercise led me to a curious encounter, which I shall briefly relate, tho' I still do not know what it may signify – or indeed, whether it signifies anything at all. As I stepped into the street, I felt that faint but palpable force upon me, like the magnetick tug on a compass, that tells us we are being observed; and, turning towards its source, spied a small man on the opposite side of the gardens, wearing a neat blue coat and a trim wig. He was evidently watching me – or else the house – very closely; for when my gaze met his, he did not look away, as an idler would have done, but continued to stare, as if it was his business to do so, and he would not be deflected from it by the demands of common politeness. From his appearance, he might have been a bailiff, or a lawyer's clerk; but since I could not conceive that Uncle Fiske would have troubles of that sort, I quickly guessed he was probably a footman, that had taken a fancy to one of my uncle's maidservants and come to keep an assignation with her. And having thus (as I thought) settled the matter, I put it firmly from my head.

Only to find it no less firmly intruding again, when I turned into the farther walk and discovered he was still there – and still gaping at me, rather than (as should have been the case, if my hypotheses were correct) at the door. I now remarked, moreover, that he was older than I had at first supposed – at least of the middle age, and certainly too advanced in years to be wooing a girl; and that his clothes suggested more a decayed gentleman than a courting servant: for tho' well cut, they were pock-marked with little darns and patches. As I drew nearer, and could more clearly make out his face, I saw that it was drawn into a puzzled frown, as if he were rummaging his brain to know why I appeared familiar to him; and – in the same moment – it all at once struck me, that I had seen him before, too. I devoted my next circuit to trying to remember *where* – transposing his image, in my mind, from my uncle's drawing-room, to the theatre, to the mob that had pursued O'Donnell and me through Redcliffe; but in none of them did it seem to fit, exactly – and I at length concluded, that it must have been in some other place than Bristol. What of Somersetshire, then? I set him down in each of my neighbour's houses in turn – and as quickly plucked him out again; for he was a stranger in all of them. The *Sweet Jenny*? No – he did not belong there, either; and if he had been aboard the *Penelope*, I should have surely recalled him without difficulty – for we must have taken leave of each other only the day before.

This drove me, by degrees, to think I must have encountered him somewhere on my adventures – and so prompted me to begin scouring America, in hope of uncovering him there. But I had got no further than a fruitless search of Brunswick and Fiskefield, when my tour brought me back to him again; and – finding him in exactly the same posture as before – I was moved by a sudden reckless impulse to stop, and ask: "Forgive me, Sir, but have we met?"

He did not reply at once, but studied me with anxious brown eyes – like a dog, that does not know whether his master will strike or pet him. Then he shook his head, and replied slowly: "I do not believe so, Sir."

His voice did, unquestionably, have a slight American nasal twang; but it recalled no particular person or place to my memory. "We must both have been mistaken, then," I said.

He acknowledged that I had hit home, in supposing he had been under the identical apprehension himself, by reddening, and giving me a rueful, lop-sided grin. "That is not your house?" he said, after a moment, nodding towards my uncle's.

"No – it belongs to Mr. Fiske."

"That is as I thought," he said; and the next instant – as if to demonstrate that he had legitimate business there, and had only been waiting for this confirmation before embarking on it – took a few uncertain steps towards the door. But then his resolve seemed to desert him; and, without another word or glance, he suddenly turned, and shot off in the direction of Broad Quay.

All the way to Thomas Street, I wrestled with the riddle of who the fellow was, and where Fate had brought us together before; but could not find the answer.

And still do not have it today. But when I come to reflect upon the question, I cannot but feel it must concern yʳ honours, somehow – and your reasons for keeping me here.

XXXIX

However artfully I cast my bait, it seems yʳ honours will not rise to it. I confess I thought that my reflections on the man in Queen Square might have lured you to the surface for an instant – for I had been careful not to show my hook this time, by asking you about him directly; but rather concealed it beneath a tantalizing tit-bit of speculation, that I thought must tempt you into seizing it, and saying whether it was true or false. But instead you say nothing – not only on that subject, but on any other; as if you mean to punish me with silence, for having resorted to so pitiful and transparent a stratagem to try to catch a glimpse of you.

Or is the reality of the matter merely this: that you are become so indifferent to me, you can no longer even trouble yourselves to read what I write?

If that is so, I am lost indeed.

Not knowing what expenses I might yet be put to in getting to my house, and the state of affairs I should find in it when I arrived, I resolved to save myself a shilling, by taking an outside place on the coach. This, as it turned out, was a small enough hardship, for the weather was warm, and my perch afforded me a fine view of the landscape – which, after America, looked almost unimaginably crowded: the roads lined with cottages, and thronged with wag-goners, and miners, and farmers driving their beasts to market; the fields all yellow with the harvest; the hills sprinkled with sheep, and smudged with delicate shadows, that might have been dabbed on with charcoal; and the woods composed of so many gradations of green, as – after my weeks in Canada – quite astonished me: for if Nature there had seemed to possess but one pigment to form each colour, here she appeared to have at her disposal a dozen, at least. I could not look upon it, without succumbing to a hundred memories and associations, which made me long to tumble back into it, as a child into his mother's arms; and yet at the same time I felt strangely barred from it, like a prisoner peering at his birthplace through the grille of his cell. For it was not enough that I should recognize my home – I must know that my home recognized me, too; and Uncle Fiske had already given me reason to doubt, whether I should have that certainty, as easily as I had supposed.

It occurred to me, as I jostled along, that on receiving my letter, my wife might have sent a servant to meet me – or even have come her-self, if I had awoken a strong enough desire in her, either to welcome me, or (if I had failed in my intention), to d–n me for a troublesome fool. There was no-one I knew at the inn; but I resolved to wait for a while, in case she or her emissary had been delayed – occupying myself, in the meantime, by gaping at the cathedral; which seemed as impossibly large, in comparison with the buildings I had seen in America, as the country seemed impossibly small, in comparison with the wilderness. But nobody appeared; and at length (fearing that if I tarried any longer, I should only add to my offences, the crime of being late for dinner) I went into the stable-yard and engaged the services of a carter – who, less than an hour later, deposited me before my own house.

The sun was already low in the sky – touching the walls with gold and giving the windows at the western end that oysterish lustre that promises shady peace within, and the cool comfort of a favourite chair; the air was sweetly spiced with rose and privet; and from the paddock I could hear the huff and snort of horses, and the whisper of the thick grass as they stirred it with their hooves. All of which, you might have supposed, would have quite unmanned me: for had I not despaired of ever seeing this delightful scene again; and had it not become the object of all my remaining hopes? And indeed, I was aware of a great swell of emotion; but it was kept firmly plugged up within my breast by the same uneasy sense of exclusion that I had felt upon the coach – which had now grown to a feverish anxiety, very near to panick, that I knew would deny me every feeling of satisfaction and pleasure until it had been allayed.

I limped to the entrance; grasped the handle – and then reflected that if I merely went in, as unceremoniously as if I had only been away for a few hours, I might be judged wanting in proper feeling, and perhaps frighten one of the servants half to death. So I took a step back, and knocked on the door instead.

Almost at once (as if the fellow had been standing directly behind it, in readiness for my arrival) it was cracked open, to reveal a footman I had seen a hundred times before.

But never here.

"Stephen?" I said – my memory presenting me, in an instant, with his name. And then, when I had sufficiently recovered from my surprise: "Have you left Mr. Grimley's service, then?"

His eyes widened, but he neither replied, nor moved aside to admit me. Which was provoking enough, and should have earned him an immediate rebuke; but, not wishing to mar my homecoming with a show of ill-temper, I merely smiled, and said: "Well, will you let me in?"

Again, he gave no response.

"Do you not know me?" I said – conscious, as I did so, that this was the identical question I had asked Joseph, and already dreading the possibility that it would elicit the same answer. "I am the master here. Mr. Gudgeon."

Which at last goaded him into shaking his head, and saying: "No – the master here is Mr. Grimley."

I cannot now unpick all the strands of thought that suddenly seemed to tangle in my head. Was I dreaming? Was this some sort of a vile jest, conceived by my wife to punish me? Had I somehow, in all my adventures, forgotten where I lived, and had myself brought to my neighbour's house, rather than my own? Would Grimley himself appear the next instant – laughingly point out my mistake – and invite me to compose matters over a glass of wine?

I supported myself against the wall, and found the strength to say: "Where is Mr. Grimley? Let me see him."

"He and my mistress are gone from home today. But they did say that a man might come here, claiming to be Mr. Gudgeon –"

All at once I had an intimation of the truth – tho' I could not yet have expressed it in words; for I knew that Mr. Grimley's wife had died many years before, and that my letter had been addressed to my own. "Your mistress?" I said.

"Mr. Gudgeon's widow. He married her but a month ago. She instructed me to say that she is outraged at your presumption, in personating her late husband; and that if you will not leave, you are to be bound, and taken before the justice." Saying which, he shut the door.

I must have stood there for five minutes or more, struggling to assimilate this news to my poor brain. It seemed as uncatchable as a great ball of thread, that is too large to hold, and too smoothly twined to offer the tiniest protruding end, which might be pulled upon to unravel it. In the midst of my confusion, only one idea seemed to stand out plain: that this was a blow from which I could not recover; for how is a man to live, that is denied not only his property, but even his name, and everything that flows from it – the comfort of family, the support of friends, and the recognition of society? My solitary remaining hope seemed to lie with the magistrate – for if he upheld my claim, I should be able to resume my life; and if he rejected it (as it was a hundred to one he would; for if I had failed to convince my uncle, and Stephen, and my wife, what chance had I of faring better with a red-faced turkey-cock like Sr Will. Sutton, or one of his short-tempered brethren?), I should scarce be in a worse predicament than I was already. Several times – like a desperate gamester who resolves to risk all on a final throw of the dice – I raised my hand to knock again, and so set the wheels of the law in motion against me; but always at the last moment I dropped it again. What prompted me to do so, I am unable to say – for I was not aware of entertaining any other plan, or even the least idea that one might exist. When I reflect upon it, I can only think that my adventures in America had strengthened in me that brute instinct for preservation, that will always choose flight, rather than submit to captivity – and that now, in my extremity, rebelled against my rational mind; at length usurping it altogether, so that I suddenly found myself possessed by but one thought: I must, at all hazards, get away.

I quickly hobbled round the end of the house, and – pressing myself against the wall, to be as inconspicuous as possible – cautiously peered into the courtyard. It was empty. I hesitated for a moment; then, hearing no voices or approaching steps, hurried the hundred paces or so to the harness-room, and opened the door. Everything within was so exactly as I remembered it – the thin dusty light; the mingled smell of hemp and leather and grain, that seemed the very odour of a safe, well-regulated world – that for a moment I might have imagined Dan's summons to me, and all that had followed from it, to have been no more than a feverish nightmare, provoked by too much cheese at supper. But my aching leg and snatching breath testified that it was not so; and any inclination I might have felt towards fancifulness was displaced by a more urgent hunger: to know if what I had come for was still there.

I limped to the corner – kicked aside a drift of dirty straw – squatted down – and quickly brushed away the powdery surface of the floor. Beneath it was a small plank. I found the edge with my finger – lifted it – slipped my hand into the void – and after a few seconds' scrabbling felt the soft touch of shammy – and through it, the hard rim of a coin.

I almost laughed. This, at least, was a reason to thank my wife; for it was at her insistence I had placed the money here – she having one day heard from Sr Will., when a gang of ruffians were preying upon the neighbourhood, that he had secreted a hundred guineas in his garden, to ensure he should not be left penniless if they broke into his house and took everything they found there; whereupon she had immediately declared that she would not be satisfied until I had done the same. For some months I had resisted, saying *I hoped I was capable of protecting our property myself*; but she would not be swayed on so ticklish a point of fashion; and I at length conceded, to spare myself further chiding. It surprised me, as I now lifted the pouch out, that she had not removed it herself during my absence – but it then occurred to me that she might have judged it an exceedingly pleasant and convenient thing, to have a little fortune of her own, of which her new husband knew nothing.

I dropped it in my pocket; then stood up again – took down a bridle, saddle and hunting-crop from the wall – scooped a handful of oats from the corn bin – and squinted through the door. The coast was still clear; so I slipped out – crossed to the paddock – and unlatched the gate. Four horses stood grazing together, a little way off; but I could not spy Merry among them. This set me wondering (with something like jealousy, as well as disappointment) if perhaps Grimley had taken her – which would not have been astonishing, for she was as sweet and biddable a creature as I had ever known; but as I walked towards them, trying to settle in my own mind which I should have in her place, I suddenly saw her break from behind the others, and stand watching me with pricked ears. Whether this was merely chance, or whether she caught a scent of me that stirred some distant memory in her head, I cannot tell; but when I called her name, she at once started up and trotted towards me with a whinny of pleasure that brought the tears to my eyes – for this was the first unconstrained welcome I had received since my return to England.

I quickly drew on the bridle, and led her behind the shed, so that I might saddle her at leisure, without the danger of being observed. But so tractable was she, I was done sooner than I had expected; and within ten minutes, we were out of the field – past the stables – and entering the lime avenue that I had planted myself.

I did not wish to arouse suspicion by appearing in too much haste, but rode as hard as I dared – frequently glancing behind me, and clutching the crop to defend myself in case anybody tried to stop us.

But no-one did.

For the first two or three hours I had only one clear object: to get as far as I could before stopping; for the greater the distance I had gone, the larger the area my enemies would have to search if they tried to find me, and the less their chance of succeeding. This might have kept me travelling till dawn, but that my poor horse (who had evidently been so little used while I was in America that she had lost the habit of carrying a rider) began to hang her head, and a few moments later stumbled, so obliging me to get down, and – after having satisfied myself she was not injured – look about me for a place where we might pass the night. Whereupon I suddenly knew, from the familiar outline of the hills about me, that I was on the road to Hallmartin Park – where Dan had lived.

Which caused me some astonishment; for I had not consciously set out to come this way – naturally supposing that, since he must certainly be long since dead, it would be useless to appeal to him in my present crisis. But the more I reflected upon it, the more reasonable seemed the subterranean impulse that had carried me here. Even if the house were now empty, it was possible that one or two of the servants still remained in the village, and might recognize me, as Joseph had done. Moreover (the memory struck me with such force, as to set me quivering with excitement), had not Dan strongly hinted, during our last interview, that if his bastard could not be found, I should have the estate when he died? I had not seen his will, and was not enough of a lawyer to know what it might contain; but I could only suppose that it had not provided for my wife to inherit the Park in my place – for if it had, she and Grimley would undoubtedly have removed there. If I could secure Hallmartin for myself, I should, of course, eventually be obliged to resume the search for my nephew, and – if I was successful – give it up to him, as Dan had wished; but in the meantime, establishing my claim to my brother's property must help me to recover my own.

Recalling that there was an inn, at a crossroads about a mile ahead, I set off towards it, leading Merry at a brisk pace; and, before we reached it, had conceived a plan. It was very likely, if the situation was as I had supposed, that Grimley would guess my intentions, and follow me to Hallmartin; so over an indifferent supper of bread and ham, I told my fellow-guests (making sure the landlord heard me) that I was going to Bath. The next morning, after I had finished breakfast, and was buying some provision for my journey, I took care to mention the same destination to his wife; and when she had obliged me with a loaf, a lettuce and a knob of cheese, I made a great business of enquiring the right road, and taking it, until I knew I was out of sight of the place. I then turned down a rough track – that was already so stamped with hoofprints, I was certain mine would not be remarked among them – and into a wood, where I soon found a tranquil glade, with fresh sweet grass for Merry and water from a little brook for both of us. Here I resolved to spend the day; so allowing Grimley or his servants enough time to get to Dan's house – discover I had not been there – and leave again, before I finally ventured to Hallmartin myself.

My stay among the Indians had served me well in this respect, if in no other: it had taught me how to banish from my mind all large and troubling questions, whose issue I could not immediately affect, and attend instead to those small things near at hand that had the power to instruct or divert me in the present. By applying this practical lesson now, I gave myself the pleasantest few hours I had enjoyed in many months: listening to the tattle of the stream; watching the satin flash of dragonflies above its surface; or merely lying on my back, and seeing the oak leaves stirring in the breeze above me, like participants in some great lazy dance. We were disturbed only once, towards evening; when a gaunt-faced man burst through the trees, and stopped suddenly as soon as he saw me – his blue eyes wide with surprise, as if he was as startled to discover me here, as I was to be discovered. He was carrying a gun, which put me in a state of some alarm – until he abruptly turned, and plodded away again; revealing a pair of pheasants swinging from his belt, that told me I had nothing to fear from him: for he could not inform against me for trespass, without admitting he was himself guilty of the far worse crime of poaching.

It was already dusk when we at last set out again. I knew that by travelling at night, I was increasing the risk of being attacked by highwaymen – for which reason, I had stuffed all but a few guineas in my boot, by way of precaution; but I should also (I supposed) be reducing the greater danger of meeting Grimley and his men, which might cost me not only my money, but my life, if they took me before a magistrate and accused me of stealing my own horse. But as it turned out, we encountered no-one upon the road, save for a few weary harvesters returning from the fields; and entered the village, just as a fat white moon was beginning to rise above us.

I had intended to go first to the Three Pigeons, and secure myself a bed there; but as I approached the entrance, and glimpsed the bustle within, I suddenly reflected that if my enemies had pursued me here, it was almost certain they must have enquired after me at the inn, and perhaps offered a reward to any fellow that seized me, or gave them intelligence of my whereabouts. So I continued on my way; and in another ten minutes had reached the entrance to the Park.

The gates were closed, and seemed to have been reinforced, with boards behind and a phalanx of spikes arrayed along the top, that would have deterred a nimbler man than I from trying to climb it – all of which made me think that I had been right in guessing the house was shut up. But there was a light in the window of the lodge cottage; so I dismounted, and tapped upon it with my crop. This summoned a plump woman to the casement; who, after squinting out, and nodding to show she had seen me, disappeared again, and emerged a few moments later through the door.

"What is it?" she said – not irritably, but breathless with anxiety; as if she could not conceive why anybody should arrive at such an hour, save to bring news of some disaster.

"Nothing," I replied, "but that–"

"The doctor did not send you?"

"No."

"Oh!" she gasped, laying a hand on her breast and lowering her gaze.

I left her to her silent thanksgiving for a few seconds, and then continued: "I am here to see Colonel Gudgeon."

"Colonel Gudgeon?"

I nodded.

"Oh, alas, Sir – the Colonel died – 'tis more than a year, now."

I had known it must be so; and yet to hear it stated still stung me, and made my eyes smart with grief.

Seeing which, the woman shook her head sorrowfully, and said: "Was he an old friend?"

"You might say so."

"Oh!" cried the woman, half-sobbing and half-laughing. "There's a thing! I fear you are come to give me bad tidings – and end by giving them to you, instead. Did you serve with him in America?"

"I –" But I could not go on; for the gentleness of her voice, and the pitying tilt of her head, offered such a sweet prospect of sympathy as almost betrayed me into telling her the truth. In the effort of resisting it, I began to weep, so prompting her to rush to the gate, and thrust out her hand towards me – which, in my over-wrought state, I could not help taking.

"I am very sorry," she said. She was near enough now to see me plainly in the moonlight; and must have taken my scarred face and worn clothes as evidence that she had been right, in guessing I was an old soldier; for after a few moments she went on: "'Tis a hard thing to cast a man aside on half-pay, when he has been wounded in the service of his country, and can do nothing else to gain a living. Did you think the Colonel would assist you?"

313

There was no reason to undeceive her; so I nodded, and said: "Does anybody live there now?"

"Oh, yes, Sir – but you'll get no help from him, I fear!"

"Why? Who –?"

"Why – young Mr. Gudgeon. The Colonel's son."

A horse may sometimes become so habituated to the whip that at length it loses the power to stir him; and I fancy that the shocks of the past few days had worked a similar effect on my brain, which seemed too numb to respond to this information at all – so that for a moment I was not only speechless, but thoughtless, too. Then – as if someone else was saying it – I heard myself stammering: "But – but – is not Colonel Gudgeon's son dead?"

"Indeed, Sir – poor young Master Samuel Gudgeon died some four year since – or so I heard. The new master is Mr. Jeffrey Gudgeon, an American gentleman." She glanced behind her; then lowered her voice, and murmured: "A bastard, 'tis said – got with a Virginian lady, when the Colonel was little more than a boy himself. But perhaps you would know more of that than we do?"

"I – I –" I spluttered – but did not know how to go on; for I could not begin to conceive who this boy was, or how he came to be here; and at length was reduced merely to saying: "May I see him?"

She shook her head – so emphatically, you would have thought I had asked whether I might break down the door, and steal the plate.

"We are ordered to admit no-one, Sir, save the tradesmen – and then only when they are particularly required. But it will make no difference to your case, I am afraid; for he would not help you, even if you did see him." She hesitated, and looked into my face; and then – evidently concluding, from what she saw there, that I might be trusted with her opinion – muttered: "He is like no gentleman I ever knew."

Hearing which, suddenly seemed to knock my wits back into some semblance of order; for who could be less like any gentleman she had ever known than a boy that had been raised by the Indians? And had not the marquis found such a boy, and taken him to France, where he might have discovered his true identity, and come to England to claim his inheritance?

"Does he seem like a savage?" I asked.

"I never met a savage, Sir," she said doubtfully. "But he's a strange creature, sure enough. He never goes out – and barely opens his

314

mouth, but to eat and drink; and will not meet your eye, but always looks away. He has ordered changes to the hall, that make it appear more like a church than a house – tho' there's none to see them but himself, for he receives no visitors. And you might call him cruel, for he dismissed all the Colonel's servants when he arrived here."

"Indeed?" I said, thinking of poor Poist. "What became of them?"

She shook her head; and when she looked at me again, her eyes were large and bright: "But I know my husband and I profited by their misfortune. And I sometimes think God punished us for it, by striking down my mother."

Two years ago I would have ignored her – or else rebuked her for her superstition. But now I murmured: "I am sure He would not be so unkind. For they would have lost their places, whether you had taken yours or no."

My tongue shapes itself uneasily to such parsonish phrases, and I feared I had missed the mark with this one; but after a moment she grasped my hand tighter, and said: "Oh, thank you, Sir – that is a great comfort!"

I knew it would be vain to try to prevail on her to let me in – and even if it had not been, it was ten to one I would be apprehended before I reached the house, and either arrested, or thrown out again. So I asked if she would sell me a blanket, and a little food; to which she readily agreed – and then, wishing her better news of her mother, set out once more.

What I should do tomorrow I had not the least notion; but for tonight, Merry and I needed sleep. So I found my way to the old charcoal-burner's hut, that had been our fort, when Dan and I had played at soldiers; and tethered the horse, by the stream that had served as our moat, and was snugger than I had been since my last night in McLeod's house.

XL

Yʳ honours, it seems, are not content that I should relive the shocks of the past; but must give me new ones, too.

This morning the same two mute fellows again appeared at my door; covered my head, tied my arms, and then conducted me across the cobbles and into another building – all so exactly as before that I supposed they must be taking me to the same place. Until, that is, they plucked off the hood – and I discovered that I was in a room at least twice as large as the other, and as empty as that had been cluttered: for the white walls were quite bare, and the only furniture was two or three simple chairs. On one of which I was set down, before a great window – that should have afforded me my first plain view of my prison, but that (as y^r honours doubtless intended) the sun fell so directly upon my face, I could make out nothing but the outline of a roof, and a dark fuzz of trees beyond.

My previous encounter with the guards had taught me that it would be useless to ask them why they had brought me here; so I said nothing, and awaited the arrival of the doctor – or whoever else might have been appointed to attend to me – as calmly and patiently as I could. It was impossible not to feel a certain anxiety; but I held my head up, and looked steadily towards the door – comforting myself with the recollection that my wilder fears had proved groundless the last time, and would almost certainly do so again.

But the door never opened. Instead, I was all at once conscious of a faint diminution of the light; and, turning back towards the window, remarked a woman peering in upon me. My eyes were so dazzled, they could scarcely see more than a black shape, cut from the brilliance like a key-hole – but that was enough to make me clench my bound hands, and cry out involuntarily; for everything about her – her bearing; her stature; the angle of her brow as she leaned forward – conjured up the person I could most have wished to see again in all the world, and thought it least likely that I ever should.

The next moment, as if I had startled her, she stepped back – moving her head slightly to one side, and allowing me, for half a second, to glimpse her cheek. Which accorded perfectly with all the rest – being sweetly round and full, and hatched with silvery streaks, that must have been the traces of tears.

So that if I had not known better, I should have sworn I was looking at Mrs. Craig.

But perhaps I do not know better. For tho' I cannot conceive how she and I might come to be in this place together – it seeming equally improbable that she is either my captor, or a prisoner like myself; yet if there is one thing I can say with any confidence, after the weeks I have spent here, it is that I still have not the least clear notion where I am, or who y^r honours might be, or what your object is in holding me.

You must excuse me. My nerves are so wound up, and my brain so teeming with speculation, I cannot continue today – but will do so tomorrow, if you leave me in peace, and stir me up no more.

XLI

No word this morning. No interruption.

I thank y^r honours.

So now to my part of the bargain:

It sometimes happens that when our waking minds are at a loss what we should do, sleep will furnish us with the answer; and so it was, the night after my interview with the woman at the lodge – for having closed my eyes in a state of utter confusion, I opened them again with the certain knowledge that my next step must be to call on my brother's lawyer without delay.

Which presented something of a difficulty; for when he had inherited the estate, Dan – exasperated with doddering Mr. Wyatt of Bath, who had served the family for years, and doubtless fancying a fashionable London attorney would fit his station better – had placed his affairs instead in the hands of Mr. Batt, of Clifford's Inn. Whom I had never before met; and could only appeal to now by setting foot in the one place in the kingdom I detested above every other.

But there was no help for it; so (to spare y^r honours a long and tedious account of my journey, in which nothing pertinent to this narrative occurred) I returned directly to Bristol – repaid Joseph's guinea – gave him two more to take care of Merry, and to exchange my soiled linen for some clean articles of Uncle Fiske's – then hastened to Broad Street, and spent another on an inside place in the flying machine that left at nine o'clock. Arriving, the next morning, at the White Bear Inn in Piccadilly, stiff, tired and dirty, but having sustained no worse injuries than a bruised elbow and a bump upon the head.

My wife, in former days, had kept me permanently besieged with demands to go to London, and show ourselves in what she pleased to call *polite society* – weakening my defences with such a battery of *you do not care for me at all* and *I shall die of dullness else*, that I at length surrendered, and took her. But no sooner had we got there than she fell sick – a small enough wonder, when you consider the adulteration of the water, the choking vileness of the air, and the doubtful

317

origins of our dinner; with the result that the only *society* she saw, was that of a nurse and an apothecary. At the end of ten days, she was sufficiently recovered to go home again; after which (tho' she could not resist loosing a few shots after me as she retreated, saying *it was my niggardliness had made her ill, by forcing her to stay in a mean little inn*) I was less troubled by her importuning – on that head, at least.

That episode had been enough to persuade me that London was a diseased monster, that must either contain and mend itself or die; so conceive my astonishment when I now discovered that it was even grosser than it had been then – having, in the interim, drawn not only fields and gardens, but whole villages into its ulcerous maw, and filled every straining vein and organ with a yet more poisonous broth of luxury and excrement. The streets were a ferment of servants and beggars, ladies and whores, macaronis and hodcarriers, soldiers and tradesmen, chariots and waggons – all jogging this way and that at such a mad rate you would have thought bedlam must have split open at the seams and spewed its contents in every direction.

It had been my intention to conduct my interview with Mr. Batt, and – if he gave me no reason to remain – return again to Bristol the same night; for, besides heartily disliking London, I knew the expense of staying there would quickly exhaust my small stock of money. But I had got no further than Covent Garden when I saw the impossibility of this plan – being, by that point, so smeared with grime and filth that I must more have resembled a vagabond than a gentleman who might have business with a lawyer and deserve his confidence. I took a bed at a small inn, therefore – ordered some water and a towel, with which I washed myself, and cleaned my coat as well as I could – and then set out again; keeping to the lesser thoroughfares, in hope of avoiding further spatterings with mud, and looking all the while for a barber's shop, where I might complete my toilet. And pretty soon happened upon one, in a stinking little street called Maiden Lane.

It seemed a respectable enough establishment (while, as is often the way in London, keeping company with less creditable neighbours; for beneath it was a cider cellar, from which, even at that hour, I could hear drunken cries and roars); and tho' the proprietor was already occupied with a fidgety, actorish-looking fellow, he bobbed his head as I entered, and – in a pleasant Devon voice, that reminded

318

me of home – said *he would be glad to wait upon me in a few moments;* *and in the meantime, please to sit down.* Which, after the ceaseless battle of walking, I was happy to do.

There was an open newspaper lying on the chair, which I was obliged to remove; and, seeing nowhere else to put it, when I had taken the place myself, I left it upon my knee, and allowed my gaze to roam idly across the page. And, within a minute, was startled to glimpse, among the sea of unfamiliar names, one that I recognized: O'Donnell.

I had only glanced it in passing, and at once went back, to make sure I was not mistaken – reflecting as I did so that even if I were not, there must be a hundred other O'Donnells in London. But all doubts were immediately removed, as soon as I found it again, and saw:

TO-NIGHT was performed at Drury Lane for the first time a new *comedy, called THE RELUCTANT ADVENTURER, by Mr. Richard* *O'Donnell.*

Here I stopped, to enjoy the novel sensation (after so many of the other sort) of a happy surprise; for did not this tell me, not only that my former companion had returned safe from America, but that he had since enjoyed considerable success – and was, moreover, at that very instant, probably no more than a mile or two from where I sat? Which pleasant thought naturally provoked another: that tho' he could not attest to my identity without recounting how we met, and so exposing himself to the risk of prosecution – yet if I could find him, and persuade *him* of it, he might still be able to conceive some means to save me, as he had so often in the past.

Buoyed by this cheerful prospect, I returned to the review. And read (as well as I can recall):

The following are the principal characters:

Squire Dudgeon, a Somersetshire gentleman	Mr. WHITROW
Colonel Dudgeon, brother to the Squire	Mr. MATCHAM
Mr. Merchant, cousin to the Squire	Mr. PEARSON
Captain O'Dagger, a young Irish gentleman	Mr. O'DONNELL
Colonel Washhouse, an American gentleman	Mr. DAVIES
Miss Polltax, an American lady	Mrs. THOMSON
Mrs. Panacon, a tavern-keeper	Mrs. ALLIN
Calliope, a negro slave	Mrs. PERRY

Colonel Dudgeon, having lost his legitimate heir, wishes to leave his estate to his natural son by a colonial lady, and on his death-bed asks his brother to go to America to find the boy. The Squire reluctantly agrees, and sets out, accompanied by Captain O'Dagger, a young Irishman fleeing for his life after killing a man in a duel. O'Dagger soon surmises that they are engaged upon a wild-goose chase; but the Squire refuses to believe him, and insists on continuing his journey – so falling into a series of ever more comical adventures, from which the quick-witted O'Dagger is obliged to rescue him.

The performance was received throughout with very great applause; and with frequent bursts of that surprised mirth, that shows an audience has been struck not only by the humour, but also by the truth, of the author's observation.

Mr. O'Donnell's wit will, we hope, delight us for many years to come; but were he to lay down his pen tomorrow, we dare aver that The Reluctant Adventurer *alone would assure him a place in the firmament of genius. The character of the obstinate and irascible Squire Dudgeon, at once so risible, and yet so perfectly life-like, is destined to become firmly fixed in the publick affections.*

You might reasonably suppose that, after so many other unwelcome discoveries, I should have been sufficiently prepared for this one; but it took me so entirely unawares, as to throw me into a kind of stupor. And it was only by reading it slowly a second time, and then a third, that I finally persuaded myself my eyes had not deceived me. I was still so startled, even then, that I should indubitably have embarked upon it yet again, had I not at that instant become aware that the actorish man had risen, and was fixing me with a cold stare.

"Excuse me, Sir," he said, holding out his hand. "I believe that is my *Chronicle*."

"Indeed?" I replied, scarce thinking what I was saying. "Then I beg your pardon. I had supposed it was put here for anybody's use."

He gave me a cracked smile, without a hint either of merriment or warmth. "Perhaps, Sir, things are ordered differently where you come from," he said. "But in England, alas, we are still expected to pay for our diversions." And snatching the newspaper from my grasp, he pinned it under his arm – bowed frostily – and left.

I was conscious of a great welling of emotion as I sat down before the barber; but, by a prodigious effort of will, kept it from my thoughts while he was attending to me – even contriving to feign a polite interest, when he chattered proudly of his infant son, whose screams we heard from the basement. But once in the street again I could restrain it no longer; a hot surge of rage flooded my brain, making me gasp and tremble, and I knew it would be fruitless to call upon the lawyer until I had found some means of venting it – for one glimpse of me in such an agitated state would be enough to convince him I was mad.

For some minutes, I paced this way and that, pondering what to do – and at length, having conceived and rejected half a dozen plans, hit upon one that seemed practicable. Spying a coffee-house, therefore, I went in – called for pen and paper – and dashed off a note to my tra-ducer – of which (so distracted was I) I can recollect only the general sense: that if I ever had the misfortune to see him again, I should have satisfaction for the liberties he had taken with my character, and his publick betrayal of what – even after all that had passed – I still regarded as a sacred friendship. Having addressed it to Mr. O'Donnell, I hurried the quarter-mile to Drury Lane, and thrust it, together with a shilling, into the hand of a servant at the theatre.

Which, tho' it seems a small enough thing, had the hoped-for effect. The moment it was done, I began to be calmer, and in less than an hour felt sufficiently master of myself again to resume my journey to Clifford's Inn – where, upon asking at the gatehouse for Mr. Batt, I was directed to a staircase in the corner of the neighbouring court. A painted board at the entrance informed me I should find him on the second floor; so, having patted and pulled my poor clothes into the best semblance of neatness I could contrive, I climbed up, and knocked upon the door – at which an airy voice within at once called out: "Enter!"

The only lawyer's den I had ever set foot in before was Mr. Wyatt's – and his had been three-fourths filled with piles of forlorn-looking papers, that seemed to have given up all hope of anybody wanting them again, and merely lay in their own dust, like scurfy old dogs waiting to die. So I was surprised to discover myself in a tolerably light and pleasant ante-room, with well-tended shelves about the walls and a disciplined scent of ink and hot wax in the air, and a large desk in the centre – on which there were documents indeed, but all laid out in military ranks, that suggested they had been placed there with some thought to their purpose, and were ready, when called upon, to do their duty. Behind it was a dapper clerk wearing spectacles – which he slowly lifted from his nose and held an inch or two before his eyes, in my direction, as if he could not immediately tell what manner of creature I was, and needed to look more closely before determining how he should conduct himself towards me. But reconciling my scarred boots and ill-fitting coat and newly rolled curls proved beyond his knowledge of the world; and tho' he opened his mouth once or twice as if to speak, he could never bring himself to do it.

So at length, to spare us both further uneasiness, I said: "I wish to see Mr. Batt."

For some reason or other, this seemed to jog him into thinking that I was a singular kind of messenger; for he at once glanced down at my hands, evidently expecting to find a letter there. I was carrying nothing but my hat; but since (I suppose) a hat may very easily conceal something else, that was not enough to undeceive him – and with a supercilious jerk of the head he said: "If you have something for him, you may give it to me."

Seeing I had need of some more persuasive advocate than my own tongue, I drew a sovereign from my pocket, and held it towards him, saying: "I have something for you, if you will tell him I am here, and beg the favour of a few minutes of his time, to discuss my brother's estate."

He gaped at the money for a moment; then slid it from my hand, as deftly as a juggler, and said: "Pardon me, Sir, but your brother . . .?"

"Colonel Gudgeon."

He nodded – as if he had known it all along, and required no more than that I should prompt his memory; then knocked upon the door to the inner chamber – disappeared within – and emerged again after no more than a minute, with a discreet grin of satisfaction on his face. "Mr. Batt will be pleased to see you, Sir," he said. And ushered me into a room twice as grand as his own, with two great windows, and a marble fireplace that the King would not have been ashamed to warm himself by.

Batt turned out to be a fat, shiny fellow, with an immense brow, and cheeks stretched smooth like a well-plumped cushion. He wore a well-cut suit of sober black, that seemed almost as much a uniform of his office as a soldier's scarlet – and made me painfully conscious of my own uncommon appearance. But if he remarked the contrast, he gave no sign of it, but bowed politely; waved me to a chair; and then settled himself to listen with every evidence of complaisant attention – pressing his hands together before him, nodding encouragingly from time to time, and only removing his eyes from my face for one instant, when the clerk entered and placed a bundle of papers on the table. You might have taken this genial air for sympathy, but that it was belied by the unsmiling sharpness of his gaze – which put me on my guard, and quelled any urge I might have had to tell him more than was necessary to my object. So when I related my adventures, I carefully omitted all mention of the obstacles I had encountered since my return, reasoning that if I acknowledged any doubt as to my identity – even for the purpose of justifying myself against it – he could not but feel some himself.

But I quickly saw this was a mistake; for no sooner had I finished than Mr. Batt coughed respectfully, and said: "But I understood Colonel Gudgeon's brother to be dead, Sir."

I began to speak, but – holding up his hand to silence me – he lifted a sheet from the pile the clerk had set before him.

"Forgive me, Sir, but I have here a letter that distinctly states it. Um – um –" (searching the page with his finger). "Yes – yes – it is quite plain: 'While seeking his nephew in the wilderness, Mr. Edward Gudgeon was unfortunately set upon by savages, and murdered.'"

"Well – I was not murdered – as you can see."

"You were not, Sir – and I rejoice to observe it. The difficulty, tho', is this: I never had the honour of meeting Colonel Gudgeon's brother, and am therefore unable to say whether you are the gentleman or not."

"I tell you that I am."

"Indeed, you do, Sir" – with a puckering of the lips, and a judicious bob of the head – "and I have taken full cognizance of it. But, you see, it is something of a principle in my profession, when we are asked to consider an assertion of this nature, to enquire what grounds there may be for believing it to be true." He paused, and coughed again, before going on: "Have you any proof that you are Mr. Gudgeon? The testimony of his wife, for example?"

I was in a trap of my own making, from which there was no escape; for to open the door on so important a part of my story now would only cause him to wonder why I had left it closed before, and incline him to believe me even less. Seeing which, I cried out in desperation:

"Why should I lie?" But even as I did so, I could not help thinking that I had never heard so feeble and threadbare a response.

Batt flushed and smiled, like an indulgent uncle who has seen through some childish attempt to deceive him, but feels no ill-will towards its author: "Well, Sir, as to that, there are many possible answers. A man could reasonably imagine, for instance, that he might have a material interest in being able to prove his connection to so respectable a family, and such a considerable property."

I was naturally eager to discover what material interest he was speaking of, but could not do so without betraying my ignorance of Dan's will, and so weakening my position still further. So I tried to jolt him into revealing more, by asking: "Is that what Jeffrey Gudgeon imagined?"

He hesitated only a second before replying: "Well – I suppose there is no harm in letting you know, since it is a matter of publick record: Mr. Jeffrey Gudgeon had every reason to think he had a material interest, since Colonel Gudgeon had provided that he should inherit the estate."

"But how did he know it? I never found him. How can you be certain he is not an impostor?"

He sighed; and two little irritable spots of colour appeared on his cheeks. "I fear, Sir, I cannot discuss this matter with you any more, unless you are able to demonstrate you are who you say." He gave me a moment to reply; and when I could not, went on: "But to save you further trouble – and very possibly your neck, into the bargain – I shall go so far as to tell you this: first, that the young gentleman furnished ample evidence that he was Mr. Jeffrey – including a sworn affidavit by his mother, and a letter to her from Colonel Gudgeon, offering to make him his heir; and second, that even if your claim were true, and his false, you still would not have Hallmartin – for under the Colonel's previous will, it was to go not to his brother, but to another party."

"Who?"

"You will appreciate I cannot tell you that, Sir. I have already exceeded my duty; and it is for you to weigh what I have said, and determine for yourself how best to proceed." And without waiting for me to reply, he rose – bowed – and nodded towards the door.

This interview, as you may imagine, sent such a crowd of thoughts and questions flurrying through my head that it was not until I had descended the stairs, and almost reached the gatehouse again, that one finally broke from the others and captured my attention.

It was this: had Batt told me the truth about Dan's will?

If he had, then Dan had plainly lied to me – or, at the very least, encouraged in me expectations that he knew to be groundless. In which case, I must add my own brother – for whom I had risked everything, and lost all but my life – to the catalogue of those who had betrayed me. And if that were so, then the world was turned upside down indeed – depriving me of the only compass that still remained to me by which I might have hoped to find my way.

But *was* it so? Might not Batt simply have invented this particular, in order to dissuade me from pursuing my claim – which he evidently considered fraudulent and prompted solely by a desire for wealth?

I suddenly felt I could not know what to do next until I had the answer.

I returned to the staircase, and knocked a second time at the door of the ante-room. If the clerk was surprised to see me again, he did not show it; but listened respectfully as I explained what I wanted.

But when I had done, he shook his head, and muttered: "No, Sir, I cannot."

"Why? What harm would there be in it? 'Tis only to satisfy my curiosity."

He said nothing, but glanced towards the inner chamber.

"He need never know," I said. "And you" – taking another sovereign from my pocket, and laying it on the table – "will be this much the richer for it."

He stared at the coin like a dazzled rabbit; but at length jerked himself free of its spell, and shook his head again.

"There'll be two more of 'em when you're done," I said – drawing out my purse, and dangling it before him, to show this was no idle promise.

I could see the greed in his eyes; but some countering force (whether conscience, or merely fear, I could not say) continued to resist it, and for a moment his face became a battlefield – the brow clenched, and the mouth tugging first one way, and then the other.

And then, quite suddenly, peace was restored; his expression cleared, and he said: "Very well. But I cannot do it until Mr. Batt has gone. Go to the Temple Gardens, and I will come to you there, as soon as I am able."

I was on the point of saying that I did not know the Temple Gardens, and would sooner meet him at the Golden Keys, where I was putting up; but at that moment – as if hearing himself agree to it had brought home the gravity of the offence and weakened his resolve again – he let out a long, unsteady sigh. So I left, before he had time to change his mind.

I found our rendezvous easily enough, and – not knowing how long I should have to wait – installed myself in a solitary corner over-looking the Thames. It was my first opportunity for calm reflection since I had entered the barber's shop that morning; and I was appalled to find how far my circumstances seemed to have deterio-rated in those few short hours. Then, I had not supposed a man could lose more than his family, his property and his name; now, I saw that I had been robbed of something greater yet: the very marrow of my being, which seemed to have been sucked from my bones, and (to the very great amusement of the public) injected into the character of Squire Dudgeon instead. I felt as a man might in the age of supersti-tion, that believes he has sold his soul to the Devil – or rather (since I had not received anything in return), allowed the Devil to pilfer it, as a common pick-pocket filches a carelessly exposed handkerchief. For – and this was the worst of it – I was tormented with the growing conviction, that it was all my own fault. Had not Uncle Fiske – decayed as he was – been right in saying *I was the greatest fool that ever lived*? Had not all my misfortunes sprung from my own credulous nature, that had duped me into taking Dan at his word, without once troubling to look a little deeper and consider if it matched what was in his heart; and then led me to make the same mistake with every-body I had met?

The conclusion was inescapable. It pressed so hard upon me, I thought I should suffocate.

I involuntarily turned towards the river; but for all the relief it afforded me, I might have been contemplating the inside of my own head. The air was filled with a thick gauze of sea-coal smoke, through which I could see dark forests of masts and spars; and endless pro-cessions of ships, staining the water black with their tarry reflections; and lines of rickety wharves tottering off the banks on their slime-covered legs, like so many wretched souls trying to drown them-selves.

Drown themselves. Drown themselves.

326

Why should I not drown myself?

My mind had never before entertained such a notion; even now, I was surprised to find it there, and wondered that it did not vanish again as quickly as it had appeared. But, having once arrived – like some troublesome fellow that you would never think to ask into your house, but thrusts his way in uninvited, and will not be then got rid of – it seemed proof against every effort to expel it. For – save among those religious enthusiasts who believe a loving G–d would compound the misery of His most wretched creatures by condemning them to eternal damnation – there is but one great obstacle to self-destruction: the prospect of the undeserved pain it must cause those who are left behind. But how could that reasonably deter *me* – when all who might mourn my passing imagined me dead already, and would suffer not a jot more, if I made their supposition fact? Might it not, indeed, be not only the most expedient course, but also the most honourable, since by remaining I must quickly become a burden to my fellow-men – if only as a charge upon the parish?

How long my thoughts continued in this train I cannot say – but it must have been some considerable time; for the day had already begun to fade when I was suddenly roused from them by an indignant shriek close to my ear. I started up, and saw a black gull hovering not two feet from my shoulder, that seemed –

I hesitate to say what it seemed, for fear you will think me mad after all. But I am obliged to tell you the truth, even when I cannot account for it. And if you choose to explain it yourself as merely the fevered delusion of a brain temporarily disordered by despair, I shall not contradict you.

So: the bird seemed to be trying to attract my attention, and as soon as I had met its eye (a tiny bright pin-head in the dusk) it gave a little nod – rose up into the air – flapped past me – and settled beside a silver patch on the water, where a faint beam from the setting sun had broken through the haze and caught the mirrored white of a sail.

At the same moment, I was conscious of a corresponding scrap of light in my own mind; which for some reason (perhaps nothing more than an association with the luminosity of her skin) recalled Mrs. Craig to me – so vividly that all at once I heard her saying, as distinctly as if she again lay at my side: "We are near death a hundred times a day. But look – we are still alive. We are alive!"

327

I let out a moan; and screwed my eyes close, to contain the flood that filled them. I scarce knew if I was weeping for grief, or joy, or astonishment that – after having clung to my life against such monstrous odds – I was now contemplating doing Coleman's and Hickling's and Lord Jack's work for them, by simply throwing it away. But had no time to consider the question further; for at that instant, there came a sound of quick footsteps behind me, and a breathless voice calling: "Ah – there you are, Sir!"

I turned – blinked away my tears – and saw Mr. Batt's clerk, his face flushed with hurrying and the onset of a chill evening mist. In truth, I had clean forgotten about him, and for a second could not imagine why he was there; but he soon prompted my memory by drawing a packet from beneath his coat, and – after glancing this way and that, to make sure he was not observed – thrusting it towards me. I took it – gave him his two sovereigns – and then thanked him, and bade him a good night, before he had time to tell me anything of what it contained.

Which may seem strange, when I had proceeded such lengths to get it; but the truth is this: that tho' the recollection (I dare almost say, the *perception*) of Mrs. Craig had in some degree answered my suicidal feelings, yet it had not altogether banished them; and when the balance of life and death seemed so finely poised, I was reluctant to do anything that might strengthen death's cause, or bring the contest between them to a premature issue. Better, I thought, to let matters stand, and hope that life would work its effect, like a yeast left to leaven dough overnight.

So I slipped the packet into my pocket; returned to the Golden Keys; had a chop to assuage my hunger, and a mug of ale to soothe my nerves; and went to bed without giving it another thought.

And, for a wonder, slept.

XLII

Silence this morning. Not the least sign to show what you are thinking.

Which makes me anxious. I would sooner even be prodded or gaped at; for that at least gives me reason to hope you are curious about me still, and have not yet quite determined my fate.

Perhaps – knowing or guessing how near I am now to the end of my story – you have resolved to let me conclude, before dispatching me, or removing me to another place.

If so, then sense would tell me I should linger – resting today (it being Sunday); dawdling tomorrow; and spinning the remainder of my narrative so fine, it will take a week to unwind.

But sense may be mistaken. For what if I only succeed in wearing out your patience, and being snatched away after all, before I am done?

That is a risk I cannot afford to take. I should be like a mother, that endangers the life of her child, merely in order to add two or three days to her own. For if I can but finish my tale, I think it will be sturdy enough to live on in my place – finding its own way in the world (if it is permitted to do so); meeting its own adventures; and making its own friends, for ten or fifty or a hundred years after I am gone.

I know now: it is for that hope that I write.

I was woken by the lively drone of a hurdy-gurdy beneath my window, and the cries of a milk-seller a little further off; and for a moment, as they wove themselves about the smokey wraiths of my dreams, I could not remember where I was. But then the musick stopped, and there was a jeer of mocking applause, which reminded me of the theatre – and so, by a natural progression, brought O'Donnell and his comedy and Mr. Batt all tumbling back into my head.

You might suppose that this would have pitched me into the blackest despair – and, indeed, I should have supposed it myself, if I were the reader of this narrative, and not its author. But the yeast must have done its work; for tho' I was conscious of a bitter sense of injury and injustice, and an almost ungovernable rage, yet these emotions were mingled with another of a very different sort – which is not so easily described, but may perhaps be compared to the experience of a man that has been carrying a heavy burden for many miles and is suddenly robbed of it by thieves. He regrets the loss of it, sure enough – but at the same time cannot feel entirely ungrateful, that he no longer suffers its weight upon his shoulders. For had I not tried every possible way to retrieve what was mine – only to find each of them in turn blocked by an insuperable obstacle? What other course was open to me now than to accept defeat, and give up? And who was there to reproach me for it if I did? My wife? My brother? My uncle and aunt? My neighbour Grimley? Having – thanks to Mrs.

Craig, or the illusion of her – recovered my life, might I not dispose of it as I wished?

I quickly counted what remained of my little fortune, and discovered that it amounted to almost eighty pounds. That, carefully husbanded, should last more than a year in some bye corner of the kingdom – where it might even suffice to buy me a little hut, and a patch of ground, on which I could raise a few chickens and grow vegetables enough to feed myself. I already had a horse, whenever I chose to reclaim her; I might acquire a dog or two at small expense, to keep me company; and if I at last turned out too profligate a housekeeper to live contentedly in such a fashion, I could perhaps find employment as a groom. Two years ago I should have been unable even to conceive such an idea; now, I could view it with something akin to pleasure. It would be hard and solitary, certainly, but no more so than my present life; and I should be spared the wearying necessity of endless plotting and dissembling, and scuttling from one hole to the next like a frightened beast. And tho' I must feel a certain humiliation, yet I would not be the first gentleman to sink so low – nor the last, neither; and I could protect myself from the worst pangs of it by suppressing the true story of my life, and inventing another, more fitted to my new station; for while the shame of dishonour is carried in our hearts, that of indignity lies three-fourths in the eyes of others – and if they, not knowing how far I had fallen, saw no reason to despise me, why should I despise myself?

To glimpse, suddenly, such a prospect of freedom, where I should be master of my own fate, and my hopes for happiness would depend not on the caprice of lawyers but on the resources of my own nature, induced a kind of dizzying elation in me, much like the alchemical effect of a draft of champagne – and as short-lived; for as I finished dressing myself, I came upon the document Batt's clerk had given me the night before; and all at once the light at the window turned from gold to grey again.

I sat down – broke the seal – and read:

From the will of Colonel Daniel Gudgeon, October 4th, 1774

(written, therefore, a few weeks after I had last seen Dan, and agreed to look for the boy)

My estate at Hallmartin, with the messuage and all the appurtenances thereto, and all of my land; together with my books, plate and household furniture, and all the rest of the aforesaid sums of money, I do give, devise and bequeath to my natural son, Jeffrey Gudgeon.

From the will of Colonel Daniel Gudgeon, February 14th, 1772:

My estate at Hallmartin, with the messuage and all the appurtenances thereto, and all of my land; together with my books, plate and household furniture, and all the rest of the aforesaid sums of money, I do give, devise and bequeath to Matthew Coleman, only son of my dear deceased cousin Sara.

Matthew Coleman. Matthew Coleman.

I sank to the bed, cursing myself – yet again – for my own folly.

Did not this, at a stroke, explain all Coleman's conduct towards me – his rooted enmity, from the very beginning of our relation; his attempts to hinder me from looking for the boy; and his determination to have me murdered when I did?

It was undeniable. Only a blockhead could have missed it.

But then I rallied to my own defence – arguing that, in truth, it changed nothing: for it was no great news that I had been guilty of stupidity – a crime for which I had already paid many times over; and it was useless to punish myself further for what was past and beyond repair. Better just to tear the letter up – throw it on the fire – and cheerfully pursue the course I had resolved upon before opening it.

I came close – very close – to following my own counsel. But just as a splinter, or the head of a nail, may prevent us from squarely closing a door and turning the key, so my efforts to dismiss Coleman from my thoughts kept catching on two tiny snags:

ONE, that however much I wished to deny it, what I now knew about the will *did* alter the balance between us, if only very slightly – for tho' I could not prove what he had done to me, yet I could show what his motive for it was, and that might be enough to jolt him into trying to make terms with me;

TWO, that I still did not know who the supposed Jeffrey Gudgeon was, or how he had come by my brother's estate, but could not entirely put from my mind the possibility that he might indeed be an impostor, placed there by Coleman for his own purposes. Certainly,

the description of the boy given by the lodge-keeper's wife suggested he was not easy in his character, and shrank from scrutiny. Was it
not conceivable, even, that he (like Mrs. Craig's daughter at the
Mount) was not so much a recluse as a prisoner, forcibly shut away
from the world to keep him from blabbing some childish indiscre-
tion, that would betray the truth about himself?

I wrestled with myself for almost an hour, before conceding what I
had half-known all along: that I should never be easy beginning my
new life, until I was satisfied I had first tried every possible means to
recover my old one. I was almost certain that I should be no more
able to breach the enemy's defences through these cracks than I had
been through any of the others; but I was honour-bound to put it to
the trial.

Consoling myself that it would entail a delay of – at most – a day
or two, before I might revert to my plans with a clear conscience, I
bought a place on the night flying machine to Bristol and, after idling
the afternoon by London Bridge, went at the appointed hour to the
Bell Savage Inn in Ludgate Hill.

As I entered the coach, I heard something groaning in the breeze
above my head, and, looking up, saw the Indian beauty on the sign-
board waving me on my way.

The sun is almost at its height. I must make haste.

Arriving a little past noon the next day, I went at once to Queen
Square – gave my uncle's dirty linen to Joseph – received my own
back again, clean – and begged the favour of a little soap and hot
water, some wig-powder, and the use of a bed-chamber where I
might make my toilet. This being granted, I scraped and dusted and
preened myself, to reduce as far as possible the distance between my
former and present appearances – and was rewarded by seeing the
negro's eyes grow wide as I appeared, and hearing him say, "You
look very well, Sir."

"Thank you," I replied. "And now, I am bound for Mr. Coleman.
Can you tell me where he lives?"

His eyebrows flew up; but he kept the surprise from his voice as he
answered: "He is removed to Orchard Street, Sir. For Fiske and
Coleman is but Coleman now, in all but name; and he wished to be
close by the harbour."

Orchard Street, I knew, was but ten or fifteen minutes' walk away (depending on whether the drawbridge was up or down), and I set out briskly enough – but no sooner was I out of the square, than I began to be oppressed by a strange lassitude, that seemed to sap the power from my legs; and by the time I had reached the end of Marsh Street, my eyelids were sagging, and I caught myself glancing yearningly at every dark corner that I passed, and fancying I might crawl into it and sleep there like a dozy cat. This so far exceeded the usual symptoms of fatigue that, before my adventure, I should indubitably have supposed it heralded the onset of some sickness or other; but I knew myself better now, and quickly recognized it for what it was: a crippling dread of what I was about to do. For tho' we fondly imagine ourselves to be grown men, the fear of some future ordeal will often turn us into boys again, that will not go to school unless they are bribed with sweetmeats and soothed with the promise that it is but for a little while, and then they will be home again. So it was that I had reconciled myself to facing my would-be murderer, by inwardly saying, *It is not yet – first there is the stage-coach, where you may sleep and reflect; and then Queen Square, where you may compose yourself – do not be afraid – it is not yet.* But now those small consolations were behind me – nothing stood between me and (as it were) the tyrannical master, that I feared more and loved less than any man in the world; and I could not continue without the comfort of some token that my encounter with him would be brief, and there would be holidays again after. So I returned to my uncle's house; ordered Joseph to have Merry saddled and ready for me in an hour; and – thus armed against despair – embarked once more for Orchard Street.

Only to be told, when I got there, *that the master was gone to the warehouse at Broad Quay; but was expected home to dinner at three o'clock, and I might wait for him if I wished.*

Y^r honours may perhaps furnish my response to this news from the store of your own experience: for most men, I am sure, must feel much the same, when they discover that a crisis for which they have steeled themselves is suddenly deferred. The craven school-boy in me longed to hurry away, with no more than a vague promise to return at some point in the future; but I knew if I succumbed to his wheedling now, I should only have greater difficulty in overcoming it later, and I felt I could not bear the uncertainty of sitting in Coleman's house for an hour or so, with no exact notion of when he might appear, and so no opportunity to prepare myself mentally for the shock of seeing him again. So, after deliberating for no more than a few seconds, I turned about, and set off for the quays.

The port was even busier, if possible, than on my return from America, and I was obliged to stop at least a dozen times to let a flock of sheep pass, or by a sledge slowed to a slug's pace by the weight of barrels on its back, or a pair of silly urchins running with a plank to make a see-saw – with the result that it was long past two o'clock when I at length reached the warehouse; and, fearing that Coleman might have already left for home, or be preparing to do so, I did not even pause to peer in at the window, but burst directly into the office.

The light was dim, and the air marbled with tobacco-smoke; but it took me only a second to discover my cousin – for he wore a glaring yellow coat, that drew your eye to it like a beacon, and was sitting close to the door, at a table strewn with papers and bottles and glasses. Behind him stood a pair of elderly clerks, like witnesses at a wedding; and at his side was another gentleman, as brilliantly plumed as he was, in parrot-blue – who, as I entered, was saying: "I think I may promise you, Sir, that you shall not find the ministry ungrateful."

And I instantly knew him, too: Sr Will Sutton.

"It is enough, Sir, to know I have been of some small service to my country," replied Coleman – rising, and taking up his hat, in readiness for departure. At the same moment, Sr Will, with that member's faculty for sniffing the presence of a potential voter, apprehended my arrival, and turned towards me with a taking smile – that changed, almost at once, into a look of boggled astonishment.

"Your servant, Sr Will," I said, bowing.

"Good G–d!" he cried, gripping the arms of his chair, and starting back, so that it scraped upon the floor.

Which brought Coleman spinning round, to see the cause of the commotion.

His boyish face had thickened slightly since I had last seen him, and its peachy down had darkened into something like a beard; but he still had not learned mastery of his cheeks – which, as soon as his eyes met mine, turned a scorching scarlet.

"Cousin Matt," I said.

He blinked – he gulped – he glanced at Sr Will, with an apologetick little grin, that plainly said, *This fellow is mad, Sir; do not be deceived*; then gaped at me again, and blurted: "I have no cousin, Sir."

334

I caught Sr Will's staring eye. "You know me, Sir, do you not? Ned Gudgeon?"

Coleman did not give him time to reply; but rattled: "This is evidently the rascal that distressed my poor cousin's widow. I wonder at his audacity, in coming here."

"Well, but you must own," said Sr Will, "he is very like."

Coleman shrugged: "I cannot see it myself. But if others do, that only makes him the more dangerous."

His insufferable off-handedness set my temples throbbing, and brought the heat to my throat; but rather than stooping to answer it, I determined to prosecute my siege of Sr Will, instead – for I knew if I could but take him, I should have a base from which Coleman would find it difficult to dislodge me.

"Do you not remember, Sir? The last time we talked was just before the '74 election, at Mr. Grimley's house, on the eve of my setting out for America."

"That is true," replied Sutton slowly.

"It is not true," snapped Coleman.

"D–n me if it's not!" said Sr Will, growing slightly heated. "I swear, Sir, those were exactly the circumstances of my last meeting with Mr. Gudgeon!"

"I mean, Sir," murmured Coleman, hastily adopting a more conciliatory tone, "it is not true, because this man is not Mr. Gudgeon."

"Well, he's not Mr. Grimley," grumbled Sutton. "And there was nobody else there."

"Perhaps he heard of it from a servant. Or from Mr. Grimley himself," said Coleman. And then, when Sr Will tried to speak, rushed on, in a voice near to panick: "I grant you, he has learned his lines very well! But I give you my word, this is not my cousin Ned!"

"How can you be certain?"

"Cousin Ned is dead!"

"Did you see him killed? Or his body after?"

Coleman hesitated a moment, before saying very softly: "I have it on such authority as puts it beyond dispute."

"What authority?"

"That I should be glad to tell you, Sir. But not before this – this –" He cast me a sidelong glance, and completed his sentence with a twitch of the lip that expressed more contempt than any word could have done.

"The authority, Sir, of one Hickling," I said – addressing myself to Sʳ Will, but keeping my eye all the while on my cousin – "that Mr. Coleman commissioned to murder me; and that evidently claimed he had done so, in order to receive his reward."

Coleman's flush deepened; and a dark ooze of sweat appeared on the rim of his stock.

"Why?" demanded Sʳ Will – his voice suddenly as hard and jagged as a judge's.

"To keep me from finding my nephew – and so depriving him of my brother's estate."

"Well, that, Sir, you know to be false," snapped Coleman – seizing his opportunity like a nimble lawyer. "For as you will recall, far from trying to prevent young Mr. Gudgeon from coming into his inheritance, I helped him to it."

This point evidently told with Sʳ Will; for he did not reply to it, but merely looked at Coleman, with the puzzled gravity of a man who has just seen his weapon dashed from his hand. I felt the tide begin to ebb, sucking the sand from beneath my feet; and in a desperate attempt to turn it back again, cried out: "That is little enough wonder, when you intend to defraud him of it later."

"Do you hear that, Sir? First I am a murderer; and now a cheat."

"That is, indeed, a serious charge, Sir," said Sʳ Will. "What evidence have you for making it?"

This quite confounded me; for the truth was that I had none, save my own conjecture, and the testimony of the lodge-keeper's wife – neither of which (I was but too aware) constituted proof, or even grounds for a reasonable surmise. I tried to think how I might hint I had something more irrefutable, without being obliged to reveal what it was; but before I could do so, Coleman prosecuted his advantage:

"See! He cannot answer. Which is no great surprise, since – as he must know very well, if he is not a lunatick – both allegations are totally unfounded."

"Are they, you d–d rogue?" I roared. "I have seen the letter you wrote to Hickling! – saying, that the man that convinced you you should not see me again would not be the poorer for it!"

Coleman winced, as if I had touched him physically; and Sʳ Will returned again to me – in the manner of a spectator at a contest, following the fickle eddies of fortune from one combatant to the other, and then back again.

"Have you, indeed?" he said. "Is it still in your possession?"

I felt Coleman's anxious eyes upon me, and the intensity of his relief when I at last replied: "No."

"No!" crowed Coleman. "Because it does not exist!"

"Mr. McLeod had it," I said – hoping that my grasp of particulars might yet persuade Sʳ Will, and fluster my cousin into some fatal lapse or contradiction.

"Who is Mr. McLeod?" asked Sutton.

"I have never heard the name before in my life," said Coleman – trying to sneer me from the field, with a mocking smile that his trembling mouth could not hold for more than two seconds. "A phantasm, I suppose – a fiction, like the rest of his story."

"There is always the recourse of the law, if that is so," said Sʳ Will – in a manner that clearly conveyed he was very far from believing it was so.

"I mean to have it," answered Coleman hurriedly – precipitately stepping towards me, and then stopping. "If you will but assist me to lay hold of him."

But Sʳ Will – being far too artful a politician to engage himself unequivocally to one side, when the other might still prove victorious – merely settled his great rump more firmly in his chair, and grumbled irritably: "What! Have you no servants, then?"

"Jenkins! Taylor!" cried Coleman. Which brought the two old clerks tottering dutifully out of the shadows – and a smile to Sʳ Will's face: for they resembled nothing so much as a pair of dead leaves, blown from a dusty corner by the breeze. Coleman gaped at them – saw how ludicrous it was to imagine they could restrain me – and immediately snapped out: "Quick! Go and summon help!" And then, as they began to shuffle to the interior door to the warehouse, he whirled about – skipped past me – and stood barring the entrance.

I sprang towards him, meaning to wrench him out of the way and escape before his reinforcements arrived; for I knew that I had small hope of justice in a Bristol court – where even Sʳ Will. Sutton's testimony (if he were willing to give it) would count for little against the word of a prominent local merchant like Coleman, who might be depended upon to advance the magistrate's ambitions, and give him some pretty silks at Christmas for his wife and daughters, in exchange for my neck. But instead of moving forward to meet me, my cousin gasped and cringed, squeezing himself into the portal.

I looked into his eyes; and saw there – not fear, as I had expected, but something that incensed me more than all else together: disgust.

"If my appearance offends you, Sir," I said, tearing the wig from my head to expose the cicatrice on my brow, "whose fault is that?"

He did not reply, but merely shrunk back further, and thrust out his foot, to keep me at a distance.

My temper had been tugging at its mooring, like a boat in a storm. Now, all at once, the rope broke. I picked up a chair – gave him a mighty thwack upon the shin with it – and, as he doubled forward, raised my knee up into his belly. He *ooof*ed and retched, and crossed his hands before him to protect himself. I seized one of them, and forced the fingers into the ragged seam of my torn scalp.

"Here, Sir – this is your work! Can you feel it?"

He thrashed his head from side to side; and jerked his arm frantically – but I held it fast by the wrist.

"You are too nice, Sir. That is a weakness in a murderer. Better to do the business yourself – for then you may be sure it is not bungled."

His shoulders hunched; he made a frog-like croak – and puked a pint of souring wine over my breeches and boots.

I stepped back – I could not help it. Instantly he whipped up; braced himself against the door; and kicked me with all his force – sending me sprawling on to the table. I was conscious of slithering across a sea of papers, and hearing glass crash all about me; and then, before I could recover myself, of Coleman's hand at my throat, and his face no more than six inches above mine – his breath foul, and his lips purple with vomit.

I tried to throw him off by arching my back; but he pressed me down again – and as he did so, reached for something beyond the edge of my vision.

Even before I could see it, I knew what it was, from the rattling sound it made: an inkstand. The next instant, it appeared in his fist, poised above me like a club.

I stretched out, and dashed it against his temple as hard as I could.

I heard a thump – screams – and voices; then felt his weight lifted from me, and other hands grabbing my arms and legs, and dragging me to my feet – but who they belonged to, or what had happened to my assailant, I could not immediately tell; for I was totally blinded by a stinging shower of ink. When I had sufficiently blinked it away to recover a bleary kind of sight, I found myself being held by two meaty fellows stinking of beer, who, from their bright kerchiefs and knotted hair and chafed skin, I took to be seamen; while beyond them, Coleman sat in the chair I had but lately used to attack him – his coat liberally dappled with black and his hand clamped to the side of his head.

The instant he observed me squinting at him, he waved impatiently at my guards, in a manner that suggested he would not be answerable for his actions if they did not remove me at once; and then, as they were prodding and pulling me past him, looked up and said: "Sr Will is doing me the honour of dining with me today; and I will not break our engagement for this . . . animal. But you may say that I mean to bring charges as soon as I am able – for assault and slander, at the least." And then, turning towards Sr Will: "You will, I trust, Sir, be good enough to make a deposition corroborating those allegations, if nothing more."

But I did not hear Sr Will's reply; for at that moment I was pushed out of doors.

Even in so large and miscellaneous a crowd as was assembled upon the docks, my scarred and wigless head, and the ink-stains on my face and clothes, made me a conspicuous figure; and several times, when I felt a curious or sympathetick gaze upon me, I thought of crying out, *Help me, please! – I have been wrongfully arrested!* But I knew it was unlikely any man would do so, when he calculated the cost of challenging the two lusty young oxen guarding me; and that if I tried and failed, I should only make my situation worse, since the tiny chance I had of justice depended on my acting not as if I feared the law, but rather as if I believed it would vindicate me. Even that slight hope received a blow, when – after we had gone a hundred paces or so – there was a shout behind us; and we turned to see Coleman standing by the warehouse, gesticulating at us. One of the sailors at once returned to him, and a brief conversation ensued between them – that concluded with my cousin giving the fellow some money.

Naturally, I could not hear the words that accompanied it; but the sight of it filled me with a sudden dreadful apprehension: that he was paying them not to take me before the magistrates – where there must be some doubt, however small, about the issue – but rather to some remote place, where they could make certain of it by finishing what Hickling had begun and dispatching me themselves.

The more I pondered this explanation, the more probable it seemed; for what else might Coleman have come out to tell his men, that he could not have said to them in the office, before Sr Will? – and why, if you came to that, had he not merely ordered them to keep me prisoner at the warehouse, and summoned the constable there, if he had really intended to resort to the law? So that when the second guard swaggered back to us, with a great grin on his red face, and the clink of coins in his pocket, and we continued on our way, I began to look for some possibility of escape.

And, as chance would have it, one presented itself almost immediately. We had gone no more than another quarter of a mile when we met a party of five or six boozy tars rolling towards us – who hailed my pair of sheep-dogs as old friends, and demanded they go a-drinking with them at the Seven Stars. My fellows laughed, and said they could not, and playfully slapped away the grappling hands that descended on their arms and shoulders to draw them into the crowd – during which pantomime, they soon seemed to forget about me (except as the abstract cause of their unsociability) altogether. So that after half a minute or so, I was emboldened to edge from between them, and take a few cautious steps away – and then, when it was evident they had not remarked it, to set off as fast as I was able towards the town.

It was (it seemed) an impossibly long time later, that I at length heard a distant hue and cry from the harbour – and by then I was already entering Queen Square.

Impossibly. I see I wrote *impossibly.*

And now I come to reflect upon it, it does seem hard to believe, that two strapping sailors, charged with securing a cripple, could contrive to lose him on the quays of Bristol.

Which provokes a disturbing thought: Did Coleman really order them not to *kill* me, but to *let me go* – knowing, perhaps, that if my body were found, Sr Will, having seen our quarrel, would accuse him of murder?

If that were so, it would alter the whole ground of my reasoning. For every speculation I have entertained – about where I am, and how I came to be here – has been founded on this certainty: *that I escaped my cousin in Bristol.*

But what if I did not? What if they allowed me to imagine I was free – followed me discreetly – discovered where I was going – and then seized me, and imprisoned me in this cell, to prevent my troubling their master further?

In which case, y^r honours, I suppose, must be no other than – *Matthew Coleman.*

There is a shocking logick to this idea. I curse myself for not having thought of it sooner. Tho' I am still at a loss to know why, if it is true, you kept me sealed up alone, and encouraged me to expose your villainy, by writing my story?

The answer suggests itself even as I scribble the question: to torture me with uncertainty; and yourself with the knowledge of my hatred for you. Matthew Coleman's nature is deformed enough even for that.

I had submitted the day's account – gone to bed, and was nearly asleep – when I heard whispered voices without my window; which are still there as I write this. Thinking that perhaps y^r honours meant to punish me by whisking me away now, when I am upon the point of finishing, I determined to rouse myself, and continue by candle-light:

A servant (and more especially a black servant) must learn to suppress any wonderment he may feel at the foibles of his betters, if he is not to risk being whipped or dismissed for insolence; and it was for this reason, I suppose, that Joseph displayed no astonishment at the change in my appearance, or curiosity as to what had caused it. He helped me to clean myself – gave me an old scratch-wig of my uncle's – and accompanied me to my horse, with barely a word, beyond the most humdrum practicalities; and it was only when I was about to leave, and excused myself for giving him no more than a shilling by saying I feared I should soon be poorer than he was, that the footman's crust broke, and the man within cried out: "Why, Sir, what will you do?"

"First go to my brother's house, and see if there is any redress to be had there. And if (as I suspect) there is not, then live like a peasant, on the little I have."

"Oh, I wish you well, Sir!" he cried, his brown eyes big and bright. "And remember: as long as I am at your uncle's house, you will always have one friend in Bristol, at least!"

It was dark by the time I reached Hallmartin; but that suited my purpose, for I intended to break into the park over a fallen-down length of wall, that I recalled from my childhood. It was at the edge of a thick wood, so well concealed by bushes that a passer-by would not have guessed it was there – which, naturally, was why our father (and, I was pretty certain, Dan after him) had not put himself to the expense of mending it. And I very much doubted whether young "Jeffrey" would have even discovered it – or considered it much danger to his security, if he had.

It was only when I was approaching the village, and had begun to consider the particulars of my plan, that I was struck by a disturbing thought: *What would become of Merry, if* (as I had to concede was very probable) *I was captured, or some other mishap befell me while I was about my business?* The answer came to me suddenly as I passed the lodge cottage, and remarked a light burning in the window. I dismounted, and knocked upon the glass; and when the woman came out, enquired if there was any news of her mother. She said no, but appeared pleased that I should have remembered; so I summoned up courage to ask if I might leave my nag with her – saying *that if I was not returned within two days, she might keep her for herself.* To which she readily agreed; tho' as I left, I could not help glimpsing a man scowling at me from the casement – who doubtless wondered what my relations were with his wife, and what service she must have done me, to be rewarded for it with a horse.

The moon had shrunk since my last visit; but there was still light enough to make out the grassy track leading to the place. I looked about me, to make sure I was not observed; and then set off, dodging the tangle of overhanging branch.

I hear footsteps.
I pray you: not yet.
A key in the lock

XLIII

Yʳ honours must know this; and yet it is an element in my story, and I must include it.

Perhaps, if you *are* Matthew Coleman, you mean to torment me further by waiting until I am done, and then gathering all my book together (for it is a book now), and burning it before my eyes.

And still I must complete it. Including this:

Last night – I heard a key in the lock. The door opened.

And there, her face lit by a candle in her hand, was Mrs. Craig.

Behind her stood the two guards I have seen before here. Startled tho' I was, I had wit enough to remark that they were not the jolly sailors that had seized me in Bristol.

Mrs. Craig waved them away. They hesitated. She *shoo*ed them impatiently, crying, "Go! Go!"

After a moment, they left. Then she turned, and came towards me, saying: "My poor gentleman."

I was so aghast, I could do nothing but clutch the back of my chair, and stare.

"Come now," she said, smiling. "You cannot be so surprised as that. Did you not spy me the other day?" She paused; and when I did not reply, went on: "You did – I know it."

In truth, I was surprised enough; but even more was I ashamed – for a man that lives alone, with no prospect of seeing a friend from one day to the next, soon grows careless of appearances; and I was conscious that neither my person nor my quarters were in a fit state to receive a visitor – least of all Mrs. Craig. She must somehow have perceived this anxiety; for having glanced at the tangled sheet on my bed, and the soiled linen piled in a corner, and the papers strewn across the table, she looked tenderly at my unshaved face, and said: "'Tis no matter, Sir."

"I wish – I wish, Madam –" I stammered.

She chided me gently with a click of the tongue. "Nay, no more of it! If there are any excuses to be made, they are all on my part."

"Why? Are you –? Have you –?"

She shook her head. "Sir – I must begin by telling you – there are many questions I cannot answer – or at least, not yet. Where you are, or who is keeping you here, or–"

"Why? Because you do not know?"

"Because –" She hesitated, and then continued deliberately: "Because I am sworn to secrecy."

"Sworn to whom?"

"That I must not say."

"Is it a matter of honour?"

343

"It is, Sir. But also of expediency." She flicked her gaze back towards the open door, and then up at the window – suggesting that we might be observed, or overheard. "It was as much as I could do to persuade – to persuade" (with a little laugh) "their honours, to allow me this interview at all. It would go ill with both of us if I were to break the condition they imposed. Which is, that – except for giving you certain particulars of my own history – I must speak of nothing you have not already described or surmised in – in this."

She touched the page on which I had been writing – the page on which I write now.

"Have you read it, then?"

"I have, Sir. Every word of it." She sighed softly, and her eyes were rimmed with tears. "It near broke my heart. That is why I am here. Shall we sit?"

I bowed her to the chair, and perched myself upon the bed. She set her candle next to mine, and leaned towards me, so we might see each other clearly.

"I longed to come before, or at least to communicate with you; but they would permit nothing more than that I might occasionally send a flower with your breakfast or dinner, to bring you a little comfort."

"You are very kind."

She tossed my thanks aside with an impatient shake of the head. "No, Sir, I have not been kind to you. You were willing to die for me; and I repaid you by – by allowing you to believe something – that almost cost you your life. But I could not bear you to think that was what I intended. Your friend O'Donnell judged me more truly than you did, I am afraid; but on one point you were more right than he: I am not a murderess."

I crooked a finger in my mouth and bit down upon it with all my force. The pain made me wince, and almost cry out.

"What?" she said. "You wonder if this is a dream?"

"Yes."

"Do you often dream of me?"

I nodded.

"And I of you, Sir."

I do not know if her cheeks heated mine, or mine hers; but I could feel her warmth even across the table, and caught a whiff of rosewater, that I had last smelled in her bed-chamber at the Dexters'. Ten minutes before, nothing could have appeared more important than to be able to unravel some of the mysteries of my adventure, and perhaps even shake loose a forbidden clue or two, as to the identity of my captor, and my likely fate at his hands; but now a more urgent desire began to stretch and twitch within me, that made all such considerations seem dry and bloodless, and threatened to unseat them altogether from my mind. As a hungry man may salivate at the sight of a peach and the knowledge of what lies beneath its bloom, so suddenly my memory filled the darkness between us with the brilliance of her naked skin, and the laboured gaps in our conversation with the sounds of her pleasure. And I feared that if I missed the moment now, it might never come again – for who could say when she would leave, and whether she would return; or (worse still) if something that she had to tell me would so alter my opinion of her as to douse our ardour for ever?

"Madam," I began.

"Sir?"

I stretched forth my hand – and she moved to take it. But the sight of them together – hers pale, and sweetly rounded; mine shrunk and yellow and ivied with veins – produced an effect upon me that reason had been unable to work; for I could not but reflect that while she was scarcely changed since our last meeting, I had become a hideous cripple; and the thought of the disgust my deformities must provoke in her was enough to shrivel up my passion in an instant. So I forced myself back upon the path of sense; and, with a mighty effort at calm, said: "I am glad to hear you say so, Madam; for to think you had meant to kill me . . ." I shook my head. "But the rest of it? The plot to get money from England? The conspiracy with my cousin, to smuggle in goods and exchange them for Indian land?"

This sudden change of direction plainly took her by surprise; for she stared at me for a moment, before at length looking away again, and nodding.

"What of Miss Catchpole, then? Did she write for you, or –?"

She said nothing; but her face suddenly opened, like a window from which the shutter has been removed – and I saw the truth as plainly as if I had always known it.

"You are –?"

She nodded again.

"You are Miss –?"

"Yes."

"Why did you not tell me?"

"I feared to, Sir. I feared if you knew how I had deceived your brother – deceived you – you – you would –"

"What? Think ill of you?"

"Yes," she said – but too readily; so that I knew she had been searching for a way to confess something less creditable, and had grasped at my suggestion to spare herself the difficulty of doing so.

But so wonderfully quick was the sympathy between us, that she at once saw that I had seen it; and went on: "Well, in part it was that. But more – more that if you had been angry, and made a complaint against us to the courts, or to the company itself – then we would have been completely undone. And I could not have risked that, even to save you."

To which I could not help replying: "I should have risked it, to save you."

She said nothing, but accepted the rebuke by lowering her eyes, and gulping, like a patient swallowing some unpalatable preparation.

"And the boy?"

"I tried to warn you, Sir, not to look for him."

"He – he does not exist, then?"

"I cannot say."

I pointed to the door, and dropped my voice to a whisper: "They prohibit it?"

"No – no – I mean, I do not know. I bore your brother a boy, Sir, that is true . . ." Here she paused; and, plucking a handkerchief from her sleeve, began to twist it about her fingers. "And he was taken from me. I allowed him to be taken from me. But –"

"By savages?"

"What is a savage?" And then, before I could answer her, she smiled ruefully, and said: "Nay, I must not hide behind Bailey's Dictionary again. That was the cause of all the mischief before." She drew a deep breath, and blurted: "Not by savages, Sir. Not by what you mean by savages. Tho' the most devilish Indian could not have contrived a crueller torture." She suddenly winced, as if this last thought had only just struck her; and bit her lip – hoping, I think, that I would relieve her of saying more by changing the subject, or asking her a question she might refuse to answer.

But, having uncorked the bottle, I was not now going to stop it up

346

again; and at length she resumed: "Your brother, Sir, made a small provision for me and his – my child; but I soon discovered it would be quite insufficient to our needs. I could not stay in Wilmington – my father refused to permit it, for fear the scandal would harm his business; and the allowance I got from Dan was not a half of what I should have required to set up a respectable establishment of my own in the neighbourhood. When I complained of this to Mr. Grylls, he was very short with me, and said I could expect nothing more; but–"

I held up my hand to stop her; for not only could I not immediately recollect who Grylls was, or what was his part in the affair, but for some reason or other my mind seemed to associate his name not with America, but with Bristol – so adding to my confusion. Which Mrs. Craig evidently perceived – for she at once said: "The attorney, Sir – that Colonel Washington recommended to your brother?"

And instantly I recalled the fellow's frightened face, at the window of his house in Wilmington; and nodded.

She went on: "But a few days later he wrote to me, saying he believed he had an answer to my difficulty, and asking me to call upon him. I did not like to go out, for the infant was already showing; but I wrapped myself in a cloak, and slipped into his house as discreetly as I could. He was in an entirely different humour, this time – smiling, and attentive, and saying *he was certain he could help me, if I would but make up my mind to be reasonable.*"

"What did he propose?" I said – conscious of a certain apprehension in my own voice; for is not *make up your mind to be reasonable* a lawyer's way of saying *you must abandon your dearest hopes*?

"He said I must give up all thought of receiving a more liberal settlement from your brother; but that he was in the happy position of being able to offer me another way to provide for myself and my child. If I accepted it, he would at once arrange for me to be removed to a house in the country, where I might live as a lady until three months after the infant was born. I should then be obliged to surrender it, and take another in its place, to bring up as mine–"

"What!"

"Indeed, Sir" – acknowledging my surprise with pursed lips and raised eyebrows – "it was a strange request."

"What was the reason for it?"

"He would not tell me – beyond saying that, in doing so, I should

347

be rendering a great service to a very considerable family. Who would show their gratitude, not only by undertaking to raise my child as their own, with all the advantages of their station, but also by giving me a sufficient sum to buy a property for myself in the western part of the colony – where I should not be known, and where (according to Colonel Washington) good land might be had for less than in the east."

"And you agreed?"

"I could not bring myself either to agree or disagree – the thought of both was intolerable; and the most he was able extract from me was a promise to consider his proposal, and give him my answer in a day or two. But as I was leaving, something happened that decided the matter for me. In the street I met Mrs. Coleman, and one of her negro women that had helped me once when I had fainted–"

"Niobe!" I cried.

"Ay, thanks to you, Sir, I know now that was her name," she said – smiling weakly, and tapping a finger on my manuscript, before continuing: "Mrs. Coleman had always been kind to me; and when she saw me, she asked how I was going on, and what I meant to do, in the sweetest manner imaginable – and yet I could not but hear (or fancy I heard) a cloying condescension in it, that sprung from her consciousness of the difference between us. For was she not a respectable married Englishwoman, who would soon be going home; while I (in her eyes) must appear little better than a provincial whore, that was carrying her cousin's bastard, and might conveniently be forgotten as soon as she had reached Britain again?"

"I think perhaps you misjudge her," I said. "For we all remarked a great change in Sally when she came back from America the following year; and I now wonder if it was the thought of you that caused it."

Mrs. Craig flushed, and shrugged. "I should be sorry if that were so," she said. "But I never saw any sign that she cared so deeply for me. All I felt on this occasion was a kind of thin pity – which I found so irksome and humiliating, that I at once burst out: 'Thankfully, Madam, I shall not be dependent on Captain Gudgeon's charity; for I have just learned that I am to have an estate of my own.' She smiled, and asked me where it was; and when I told her, coloured prettily, and said: 'Well, I am delighted to hear it, Miss Catchpole. I congratulate you.' After which – after which –"

"You could not withdraw?"

"No, Sir. I was too proud."

"And you never learned what became of the boy?"

She shook her head.

"Why did you not tell Dan?"

"Mr. Grylls made me swear I would not. He told me it could not be considered lying, to say nothing – and that if the captain knew I had given his son away, he would assuredly cease to pay me." Which, I had to concede, was almost certainly true.

"But then, when your husband had squandered your fortune, and you thought of restoring it by getting money to invest in the Transylvania Company, you –"

"Yes, Mr. O'Donnell was right. I wrote to everybody I could think of. To your brother, telling him I wished to buy a property for his son. To Mrs. Coleman, saying that if she gave me a thousand pounds, I could multiply it by five in as many years – which I thought might sufficiently tempt her grasping husband as to make him loosen his purse-strings. But she was dead, and so was he; so naturally the letter fell into the hands of their son. And as for your brother – your brother –"

"He wanted his son in England, and sent me to fetch him – and you could not –"

She shook her head, and then bowed, pressing the handkerchief into her eyes.

"Nay," I said, "'tis not so hard to understand."

But, far from relieving her of her burden, my words appeared only to add to it; for her shoulders suddenly seemed to give way, and she began sobbing and wailing as unconstrainedly as a child. To witness such a frank show of emotion, in a woman who had remained mistress of herself even in the face of death, moved me beyond bearing; and in a moment I found myself kneeling before her distress – as she had kneeled before mine, on the road from Frigateville. She did not look up; but her fingers groped towards me – and, when they fumbled my neck, clasped it.

"I loved your brother very well, Sir," she said. "I should have made him a good wife, if he would have had me."

"I don't doubt it," I said. "But you deserved better."

She groaned; and clung tighter to me.

"If I had been in his place . . ." I began; but my throat was too swollen to say more.

"Nay, Sir," she whispered. "Your place is your own." And she moved her face next to mine, and dabbed at my tears with her lips – in so unmistakable a fashion as all at once re-awoke my awkwardness, and made me try to shrink back. But she held on to me all the more – pulling my head down, and kissing the scar on my brow.

"I – I pray you, Madam," I stammered. "I am – I know I am sadly altered."

"Not your heart, Sir. That is as true as ever. And as for this" – here she ran her tongue along the thick crease in the skin, as if she were savouring a delicacy. I struggled to free myself; but she clamped her hands to my temples, and laughing softly said: "Hush, Sir, you are like a wild goat. Did you think I should delight in you less because of your wounds? They are the badges that say what kind of man you are. The only shame attached to them is mine, for having caused them. And that, I hope, I can redeem a little –" Of which ambition she proceeded to give such a token, as must have convinced a leper.

"But what? – what of them?" I choked, looking towards the door.

"They cannot see," she said, "if we do this" – and, turning, blew out both the candles.

The next moment, we found each other again in the darkness; and the same bed that for so long has been the gloomy centre of my solitude, at last became my release from it.

Yᵣ honours will doubtless be wondering:

1. *Why had I not guessed sooner that Mrs. Craig and Miss Catchpole were the same person?*

and:

2. *Why did I not ask her, who was the "Jeffrey Gudgeon" that had supposedly inherited Hallmartin?*

To the first question, I can only reply that it never occurred to me Mrs. Craig would have deceived me on so material a point. And I presume to doubt whether it would have occurred to yᵣ honours, either, if you had first encountered her under the same circumstances – for even shrewd O'Donnell, you will recall, was blind to her true identity, even when he correctly surmised so much else about her.

As to the second matter – I had meant to do it, but must confess that more pressing concerns drove it clean out of my head.

But I think, in any case, I know the answer now.

*

Mrs. Craig (as y^r honours must know) gave me no clue as to who you are, or what your intentions towards me might be; and yet her visit has left me less fearful – for I find it hard to believe that you would have allowed her to see me today if you meant to hang me tomorrow. I cannot help taking it as a sign, indeed, that perhaps you have begun to relent a little, and may even one day let me go – so I shall proceed to my conclusion, if not with confidence, then at least with a particle of hope.

I shall be prompt, I swear it.

So: back to Hallmartin.

I discovered the tumbled-down wall with little difficulty, and quickly clambered through the breach – dislodging, as I did so, two or three stones from the dense web of vines covering it, and sending them to the ground with a clatter that must have been audible a quarter of a mile away. I waited, in case the noise had roused somebody; but the only response I heard was from a startled owl, that rose shrieking from the trees behind me; so after a minute, I continued. It was the first time I had entered the park this way since a summer night more than thirty years before, when Dan and Sally and I, having spent too long defending the charcoal-burner's hut against wicked King Louis, were obliged to scuttle for home, in hope of avoiding a thrashing; and yet the dark contour of the land and the shape of the little copses and the fleecy thickness of the grass beneath my feet seemed so immediately familiar that I could half-fancy I saw my playmates fleeing before me, as I panted behind on my shorter legs, calling out to them to wait. With the result that I knew without reflection what course I should take, to avoid pitfalls and marshy ground, and give myself the best hope of concealment – and suffered no worse surprise on my journey, than an unexpected encounter with a sheep.

Until, that is, I reached the top of the final rise, and caught my first clear glimpse of the house. For tho' the back was as I remembered it, the front had been been transformed – the walls topped with battlements – the door hidden by a crenellated porch – and the windows (as well as I could judge from the one of them that was lighted) stretched and sharpened into lofty gothick arches. So that I was at once put in mind of O'Donnell's words, as we approached the Mount: *Did you ever set eyes on a house that looked more like a castle?*

The sight of it cast such a strange spell upon me that for a moment I was unable to move; but then – perceiving that I should learn nothing of consequence by staring – I shook myself free, and resumed my stealthy progress towards it. And had reached the edge of the stable yard, when I suddenly heard voices within, and saw the glow of lanterns above the walls.

I crept to the entrance, and peered in.

Three or four men were standing about a coach. The horses were not yet harnessed to it; but it was plainly being prepared for a journey; for as I watched, a woman came out of the back-door, and handed the nearest fellow a bag, which he set behind, and began securing with a rope. Remarking which, one of his companions gave him a jocular stab in the ribs, and muttered something in his ear that provoked both of them to squeals of half-suppressed laughter, and soon had the whole company shaking and whimpering and wiping their eyes in merriment. I could not make out its cause; but there was a kind of forced excitement in their manner, that reminded me of nothing so much as a group of guilty schoolboys showing how little they cared for their master's displeasure at their prank.

This discovery was a blow; for not only did it keep me from slinking in through the back of the house, as I had planned, but it also suggested that "Jeffrey Gudgeon" (whoever he might really be) was intending to go away, and that I should very probably miss him, if I could not find my way to his presence at once.

I shrank back into the darkness, as discreetly as I could; but one of the men must have heard me, for he turned sharply, flinging up his lantern – and a second later pointed in my direction, and shouted something to his friends. But for a moment they seemed too astonished to know what action they should take; and by the time they had determined upon pursuit, I was already halfway to the rhododendron bush, that had served me so often during childish games of hide-and-seek, and did so again now. So I waited for them to dash past me, huffing and cursing; and then, when I could no longer hear them, crawled out, and hurried to the porch.

It was locked fast.

I limped to the edge of the terrace, and surveyed the front of the house. The moon had bleached the colour from the new stone walls, turning them white as bone – and giving the windows, by contrast, the senseless vacancy of empty eye-sockets. I looked from one to the next – from dining-room to parlour to hall – with growing despair. All of them were dark and shuttered – so cold and blank they seemed closed not only to me, but to life itself.

From some way off, I caught the sound of my pursuers returning.

It was then I remarked the light I had observed earlier. It came from the library, and appeared dimmer than before – so dim, indeed, that on first emerging from my hiding-place, I had somehow missed it altogether. But as I moved towards it now, I saw a pattern of two grey bars across it, that told me the sash was cracked open.

If y^r honours have followed my adventure from the beginning, you may recall that my first half-memory after I waked here was of standing before a window, and pressing my nose against the glass – and seeing something within that made my heart thud. But only today have I at last remembered what it was.

There was a candle burning at one end of the table, and a second, at the other, that had evidently been blown out by the breeze – leading me to suppose that the room was empty; for if anybody had been there, surely he would have lighted it again. Between them were a sheet of paper; a pen; an inkstand; a seal and a lump of sealing-wax –

And a porcelain figure of a shepherdess.

I knocked on the pane and waited. But heard nothing – save the whisper of garden plants, and the bawling of an infant in a far-off chamber.

I raised the sash, and climbed in.

As I did so, something about the document caught my attention. The writing on it was ornately scrolled, in the momentous manner of wills and deeds.

I read the first few lines:

> I, Jeffrey Gudgeon, do hereby give and assign my house at Hallmartin, with the messuage and all the appurtenances thereto, and all of my land; together with my books, plate and house-hold furniture, to –

Y^r honours are doubtless familiar with the effect of scattering crumbs upon the surface of a trout-pond. From the depths of the water, which a moment before had seemed empty, surges a jostling mob of fish – all drawn to one point, like iron filings to a loadstone.

So it was now. I heard the door open – a voice cry out; and then the darkness seemed to burst asunder, as I was set upon from every direction.

I fell. Something struck my head.

And then I remember nothing, save the swaying of a carriage or a boat, and a giddiness so fierce as to make all thought impossible – for my few brief moments of consciousness were entirely occupied with fighting it, and always ended with its screwing me back into oblivion. From which I only finally emerged, when I found myself in this room.

There. I am done. Do with me what you will.

XLIV

I could not pick up my pen yesterday, or the day before. And have no need to do so today; for my fate no longer hangs on what I write here.

But the fate of my story does. For what if (as I hope) others should some day come upon it, and eagerly drink their fill – only to find, at the last, that I have denied them the final few drops that would entirely sate their thirst, by neglecting to tell them what I know now, *viz.*, where I am, and who has kept me here, and why?

They – *you*, dear sir and madam – would reproach me with carelessness, or even cruelty. And worse – set down this narrative dissatisfied.

So:

On the morning after I completed what I imagined to be my concluding chapter, there were roses on my breakfast tray, and apricots, and a kind of bread I had never tasted before – hot, and as flaky as pastry, and wrapped in a white napkin. From which (so delicious was it) I was still picking the last fragments, when the door opened, and Mrs. Craig appeared. As soon as she saw me she stopped and curtsied slightly – extending her arms, and looking from one to the other, in a manner that made it plain she wished me to remark what she was wearing: a soft blue dress, and a hat bedecked with ribbons. The same that she had put on after our release from Lord Jack.

She looked at me questioningly, to see if I understood their significance. And must have perceived that I did; for the next instant she blushed and nodded with pleasure.

"I am come to take you to our host," she said.

"Who is he?"

She laughed. "That I must not say."

"Does he mean to hang me?"

"I cannot tell you that, either." She hesitated; and then – smiling, and pinching at her sleeve, murmured: "But do you think I should have worn this, to celebrate death?"

I looked away, not daring to say anything – for tho' it seemed almost inconceivable that she would be so unkind as to offer me such a token of encouragement, only to snatch it away again; yet after all that had happened, I could not entirely quell the fear that this might prove to be still another betrayal, and I should end by losing not merely my life, but the last scraps of my pride.

"Now, Sir," she said. "If you will permit it, I shall sit with you while you make yourself ready."

"Gladly. But there is little I can do, save –"

I was going to conclude, *change my shirt*; but at that moment she advanced into the room – and I spied behind her, not the guards I had expected, but two men I had never seen before. One was a footman, holding before him a peach-coloured coat, and clean breeches, and a pile of fresh linen, which he proceeded to place upon the table, before bowing and retreating without a word; the other a cheerful-looking barber, carrying a towel draped over his right arm – a rolled-up apron under his left – and a bowl of steaming water in his hands. He waved me back to my chair – bobbing his head, and repeating, *please, please* (the only English word he knew, it seemed), like a cheeping chick; then spilled the tools from his apron – slipped it on – and began to shave me.

"I have often wondered, Sir," said Mrs. Craig, settling herself upon the bed, and following the movement of the razor with a hawkish gaze, "whether that is an agreeable sensation for a gentleman, or merely leaves him feeling like a shorn sheep?"

"Did you never ask your husband?"

She laughed again. "He said it was no more my concern than the pain of giving birth was his, and I should have a care he didn't thrash me for wearying him with idle questions."

"Why, then," I said, "it is very agreeable indeed" – hearing in my own voice, as I did so, a lilting rise of delight, not only at the thing itself, but at the consciousness that I was enjoying a small intimacy with her that she had never shared with another man. "Much as a boot must experience, I suppose, when it is polished."

She laughed yet again – so freely and naturally, I was emboldened to say: "Poor Benjamin told me Mr. Craig beat you very often."

I had only been able to glimpse her at the edge of my vision; and now she suddenly started out of it altogether, as abruptly as if I had struck her. I tried to turn after her; but the barber said, "Please, please" – and firmly pressed my head back again.

"You must forgive me," I said; "I did not mean to pain you."

"No – no – We must be plain with one another, if we are – if we are to . . ." She did not finish the sentence; but it was hard to think of how she might have done, that would not have given me further grounds for hope.

So, taking her at her word, I resolved at once to address the question that had been exercising me: "Your daughter, Madam –" I began.

"Oh, she is not his, Sir!" she said quickly – suddenly appearing again, so that I could see the heat in her cheeks. "I had no children by him – save one, that died a babe. And he" – with a shrill giggle, that seemed to proceed more from awkwardness than mirth – "he was too drunk to get any more."

"Ah. But –"

"Sarah is the infant I exchanged for your brother's."

"Indeed. But what I mean is . . ." I paused; trying to think of a way to say it that would not sound like a reproach, and so agitate her more.

But before I could do so, she said gravely: "You guessed."

"I believe I did. She –"

"Yes."

There was a long silence; which she finally broke by asking: "Do you condemn me for it?"

I did not answer at once; for in truth, the notion was yet so new to me I still did not know what to make of it. But at length I stirred myself to say: "Was the idea already in your mind, when we first met?"

She shook her head: "It was Mr. Coleman suggested it, after I reached Frigateville, and told him of what had happened."

"Coleman!" I cried, with such a jolt that if the barber had not at that moment taken the razor from my face to rinse it, he would indubitably have cut me.

"He said, if you rattled a stick in their nest, you'd be certain to rouse up a crowd of hornets."

I could hear, from the way she repeated it, that she was smiling at the recollection; which only incensed me against Coleman the more, and made me snap out: "And what did he mean by that?"

"That you had already told half America you were looking for your nephew – which (he thought) would be enough to bring a hundred pretenders scuttling out of the wilderness, in hope of getting the estate. But if he and I concluded to let Sarah personate the boy, we might forestall any rival Jeffreys, and divide the spoils between ourselves. To which I readily agreed; for I had always thought it unjust, that a boy could inherit where a girl could not. And it seemed a fitting revenge upon a man who had abandoned me with his son – and then provided me with so little money to keep him, that I was obliged to give him up."

This I could not dispute; tho' I was still puzzled that Coleman should have so easily offered to share a property that, until recently, he had expected to inherit alone.

Which (by that mysterious mechanism that sometimes seems to make my mind transparent to her) she immediately perceived; saying: "Indeed, Sir, the same question perplexed me. At first I supposed he had done it out of friendship – for we were, after all, partners in business, and he had good reason to be grateful to me. But when I came to know him better, and saw how entirely out of character that would have been, I understood he must have had some other motive – tho' it was only a few months ago, that I found out what it was."

She paused, to see if I might have divined it myself. But being unable to discern her thoughts as distinctly as she could mine, I was obliged to shake my head – creating, as I did so, a great cloud of powder, that set us both gasping and sneezing; for having finished with my chin, the barber had begun occupying himself with my wig.

"I had your brother's letter," she said, when she had sufficiently recovered her breath. "And the miniature portrait he had commissioned of himself, which allowed me to prove 'Jeffrey's' identity beyond dispute. But he knew the truth about her; and when, after a year or two, she had secured herself unassailably against any competing claim, he might threaten to expose it – unless she agreed to transfer the property to him."

"And that is what he did?"

She nodded, and gave a strange lop-sided smile. "Sooner than he intended, I fancy. For while we were still at sea, she told me she was

357

with child. And within a month of our arrival it had become so obvious, she was obliged to live as a recluse, for fear of being discovered.

"Is the father – is the father –?"

At that moment, the fellow whisked the towel from my neck, and with a final *please* held up his mirror – in which I caught Mrs. Craig's reflected eye.

"O'Donnell?"

She did not reply, but slowly dropped her gaze – in a way that made me pretty certain I was right. But when – having nodded my thanks to the barber, and dismissed him with a wave – I turned to her again, and said, "Well?", she replied: "I should not have said that, Sir. I should not have told you so much. Come" – rising from the bed – "time to put on your finery."

I stood, and waited for her to leave; but instead she took the clean shirt from the table, and suspended it before her by the shoulders, like a nurse trying to coax a child into getting up. And then, when I continued to hesitate, smiled, and said: "Tch, Sir, 'tis a little late to be coy now."

Which made me laugh; for indeed – when I recalled the circumstances in which we had first seen each other naked, and all that had happened between us since – my shyness did seem absurd.

But I still turned away, to strip, and don my fresh drawers and stockings and breeches.

When at length I was done, she helped me into the coat – stood back to examine me, shaking her head in wonderment – then picked up the glass, and held it out, so I might see what had provoked her admiration.

I could scarce recognize myself. I had not imagined I should ever appear so again. Indeed, I doubt whether I had ever appeared entirely so *before* – for I was attired not merely as a gentleman, but as a gentleman of the *ton*. If I had found myself at that moment suddenly set down in the most fashionable assembly in London, I should not have been ashamed – tho' somewhat at a loss, I think, for topics of conversation.

"Be so good as to take my arm, Sir," she said. And for the first time since my arrival here, I walked from my room unhooded, unbound and unguarded – unless Mrs. Craig be counted a guard.

The passage was so ordinary – with walls of white, scabby plaster, regularly interrupted by closed doors – that I could not understand why I had been kept from seeing it before, since it told me no more about where I was than I had deduced already. But then we stepped into the courtyard, and the surprises began: for tho' the buildings around it were plainly stables and harness-rooms and offices, as I should have expected, yet they had a kind of luxurious torpor about them – the arches swag-bellied; the windows voluptuously curved, as if they had swallowed too much wine, and collapsed – that at once made me think we could not be in England.

"What country is this?" I said.

But Mrs. Craig only smiled, and shook her head.

We passed beneath a clock-tower, and into a broad gravelled way, hemmed on either side with tall yew hedges. It was one of those bright late-winter days, when you can feel the warmth of the approaching spring press upon you through a thin membrane of cold mist, and a few brave birds were already testing their voices in gallant little snatches of song. After perhaps a hundred paces, we emerged to find ourselves at the edge of a park – artfully laid out with mounds and hollows and little copses, and affording a distant prospect of a placid lake fringed by trees, with a white temple peeping out among them. There were five or six men and women sauntering along the shore – tho' they were too far off for me to see their faces, or even tell what manner of people they were. But they appeared to recognize us – or at least, Mrs. Craig; for as we came in view they waved their hats – to which she responded, by *halloo*ing, and flourishing her own.

"Who are they?" I said.

"You only know one of them, I think."

"Indeed? And –?"

"But I am sure you will be acquainted with the others bye and bye." And then, before I could pursue my questioning further, she squeezed my arm, and said: "Patience, Sir, patience."

She drew me to the right – and I suddenly beheld a huge square stone house, rising up not fifty paces before us. I say *square* – and, in truth, I suppose that is what it was; but there were so few straight lines upon its face as to give it a kind of buckled appearance, like something glimpsed through the haze of an intense heat. If the outbuildings seemed drunken, then the mansion was a bacchanalian riot – the windows bent, and framed with festoons of carved stone; the open door bulging like a giant key-hole; and the outline of the stairs leading up to it so sinuous, you would think the architect had used not a ruler to draw it, but a trailing vine.

I was obliged to stop for a few seconds, to allow my mind to absorb the evidence of my eyes. As I did so, Mrs. Craig took my finger into her mouth and nipped it – not hard, but enough to tell me, once again, that I was not dreaming.

We mounted the steps, and entered a hall crowded with colours and things – of which (so overwhelming was their combined effect, and so quickly were we moving among them) I can recall only a few particulars: a little bed of blue satin, with a silky cat asleep upon it; a naked goddess, lolling on the painted ceiling; the mechanical figure of a fiddler standing on a card-table – who nodded his head, and jerked his bow across the strings of his instrument as we passed. I was conscious that there were servants moving about us at a discreet distance – but none of them enquired our business, or showed the least surprise at seeing us there.

"Only a moment more," said Mrs. Craig – leading me into a large salon at the back of the house. Where I could see almost nothing; for it was a sea of light, that poured in at the great windows, and glanced off the pale walls, and scattered dazzling beams from a glass chandelier. To which I had scarcely begun to adjust myself, when she knocked upon a door at the end.

There was a muffled reply, that I could not make out.

She turned the handle. All at once, I heard an indignant shriek from within, and a thrashing of wings, and caught a glimpse of brilliant green feathers.

"Don't be alarmed," she said, smiling back at me as I hesitated on the threshold. "'Tis only Aurelius."

I followed her into a room as close and dark as the other had been airy and brilliant – with the result (which perhaps was intended) that I was even blinder than I had been before. All I could make out was a faint patch of shuttered daylight, and before it the black figure of a man in a wide hat. There followed a long silence, in which – from the angle of his head – he appeared to be examining me.

Mrs. Craig eventually broke it, by asking uneasily: "Shall I –?"

He nodded.

She slipped past him, and threw open the shutters.

Perhaps, if you have come with me this far, you have already divined the truth. If so, I can only wonder at your understanding –

360

for mine had left me totally unprepared for what I now saw: seated at a table strewn with clutter, his face shaded by his hat-brim, and three-fourths concealed by the upturned collar of his blue velvet coat, sat the stooping man. The Machiavel that had taken Niobe from us in Frigateville. The Marquis de Vieux Fumé.

"Pray, Sir – sit down," he said, half-rising and making a little bow, before sinking back into his own seat.

For a moment I was paralysed, as outrage, astonishment and curiosity contended for mastery of me. Then astonishment won, and I dropped into a chair, as inert as a sack full of oats.

"Martha," murmured the marquis, looking towards Mrs. Craig. She stared imploringly at him for a few seconds, like a child banished to bed – then suddenly nodded, and walked to the door, pressing my hand as she passed me. I naturally supposed he had dismissed her in this manner because there was something he particularly wished to say to me in private; but after she had gone he merely gazed at me, his chin on his hand, as if he was waiting for me to speak first.

Which finally I did: "Would you be so good as to tell me, why I am here?"

"Your cousin –"

"Coleman?"

"Yes. Mr. Coleman. He sent you to me. Together with Martha and her daughter."

"Why?"

"Evidently, to be rid of you, Sir. You were an obstacle to his plans. And Sarah had served her purpose as soon as she signed the deed, and thereafter could only be an embarrassment to him."

There was a maddening superciliousness in his words that seemed merely compounded by the unnatural ease with which he spoke them – as if he were determined to emphasize the distance between us by demonstrating that he was my master, even in the use of my own language. And when I remembered the unflattering references I had made to him in my narrative, I could not but feel he had some reason for it – which, as is ever the way, only roused me the more.

"So – you are in league with him, then?" I said – with a crack of ice in my voice.

He hesitated; and then his mouth (from the inch of it I could see, between the edges of his collar) twitched into a wintry smile: "You might think so, I suppose. It is not how I should have expressed it."

With some difficulty, I resisted the urge to grab him by the neck and shake him until he told me how he would have expressed it; and at length he went on: "I treated with Mr. Coleman before. I had some – some –"

"Dealings?"

"Dealings with him, yes, in America."

"Niobe and her boy."

"Yes. You know of that, naturally. Mr. McLeod told you." He waved the subject away with his hand, before I could snatch it up and oblige him to tell me about it himself. "And that encouraged him to believe that I should be equally interested in acquiring Sarah. And you also – tho' I suspect, from reading your history, that that idea only came to him at the – at the last moment."

My anger began to give way to unease. What manner of man acquires another human creature? Not a gaoler – not a master – not even the keeper of a madhouse. A slave-owner, perhaps – but I could not conceive that I had been brought here as a slave; for if he had wanted a lusty labourer, why should he choose a cripple for the office – and then shut him in a cell, where he could produce nothing but words, and dirty dishes, and soiled linen? Why choose Mrs. Craig, indeed; or even Niobe – who, tho' she was brought up to servitude, had been half worn out by it, long before the marquis had set eyes upon her?

"Interested in – acquiring us – for what purpose?" I said.

He did not reply at once, for at that moment the green parrot fluttered from its hiding-place and landed on his wrist – where he at once began to soothe it, by stroking its neck with his finger, and muttering *cuckoo, cuckoo* in its ear. So giving me time to conjecture an answer of my own, which unsettled me more than ever; for when I considered what I and his other *acquisitions* (or at least those I knew of) had in common, I could find only this: we were all people who had slipped beyond the protection of the law – with the result that he might do whatever he pleased with us, and we should have no recourse against it. I had heard of anatomists nailing live dogs to tables, and cutting them open, in the name of science; what if he were just such another – but used not beasts, but men and women, as his subjects?

I was not much reassured when at last he said: "I am – after a fashion – a collector."

"Indeed?" – my mouth so dry, the word almost stuck to it, and emerged as a desparing croak.

He nodded. "A collector of oddities."

"Am I an oddity?"

He smiled again; but gave no other sign of having heard me. "There is a great change coming, Sir. It is already upon us. The world is being parcelled out – divided up – turned into properties and nations. New boundaries are being made. And those who live outside them are being dispossessed." Perhaps he saw the bafflement on my face; for he paused, and his eyes drifted away, as if he were looking for an image that would make his meaning clear to me. And seemed to find one; for after a few seconds, he suddenly went on: "Like deer, that have nowhere to go, when the forest is cut down."

"But 'tis not so rare for a man to lose his land – nor a woman hers, neither."

"I am not speaking only of land, Sir. Nor only of physical boundaries."

"What other sort is there?"

He sighed. "Consider the woman that is raised a slave, and becomes free. The boy that is born an Englishman, and becomes a savage. The savage himself, whose home is destroyed, and must put on breeches and a wig, to be acceptable to his conquerors. The girl that is dressed as a boy, and goes into society as a man. They all have something to tell us, Sir, of what it is to be human, and whether we may yet hope to live together, in spite–"

He was suddenly interrupted by the parrot, which began shrieking *humaine! humaine!* like an angry tutor correcting his pupil's French; and it was a few seconds before he had sufficiently calmed it again, to go on.

"And I have been favoured with the means to offer some of them a refuge, and see what we may learn from them."

"And what did you expect to learn from me?"

"Ah" – with a grumbling in the throat, that might have been a costive laugh – "as to that, Sir, something quite different from what you actually taught me."

"You are too cryptick," I said – annoyed at his manner; which seemed more designed to amuse himself than to inform me. "Can you not speak plainly?"

"Well, Sir, Mr. Coleman told me you were a dangerous madman, who had deceived himself into thinking he was the late Ned Gudgeon."

"And did you believe him?"

He shrugged. "I own I wished to. To find a man who truly imagined himself to be another – that would have been wonderful indeed. And it was not so hard to persuade myself. Why should Mr. Coleman have lied to me?" I made to speak, but he shook his head, to show he knew my answer already; and went on: "Besides which, his letter was accompanied by a . . . a . . . declaration from Sr Will. Sutton – attesting that he had met you, and you were very plausible. And also" – with a tiny smirk – "very violent."

I resisted the urge to justify myself – reasoning that if he had not been convinced by my narrative, there was nothing I could add now that would change his mind.

"So I resolved to shut you up, where you could do no harm, and see what I might discover by allowing you to write freely – giving you only such occasional direction as was needed to elaborate important points."

"But why did you not at least tell me where I was?"

He sighed – in that galling manner that I recalled from Frigateville, that expressed wonder at my not perceiving it myself, and exasperation that he must explain it to me. "What is a man to do, that fears an attack but knows not which way his enemy will come?"

There seemed something familiar about the phrase; but I could not immediately recall where I had heard it before – so, to avoid appearing a still greater fool, I held my tongue.

"Those are your words, Sir," he said. "You wrote them on the fourth or fifth day you were here. And" – glancing down at a sheet of paper on the table – "this is how you answered yourself: 'He must fortify his position on every side.

"'Tomorrow, therefore, I shall begin a full narrative of my adventures.'"

"I see–" I began.

But he evidently doubted whether I understood him even now; and – waving me to be quiet – continued: "That is what I wished for. A full narrative – from which I might be able to judge the truth about you. And my only hope of getting it was to leave you in ignorance. For as long as you were uncertain of your captor's identity, you could not know whether it would serve you best to flatter the Americans, or the British, or somebody else entirely – so offering you no other recourse, but to be honest."

It was impossible not to acknowledge the justice of this; so instead of reproaching him, I merely asked: "And were you able to?"

"Judge the truth? I believe so." He hesitated a moment, before going on: "Mr. Coleman told me you did not know who you were; and in that I agree with him."

"Do you, indeed?"

"I mean–"

"D–n your French impudence! What of my injuries? What of Mrs. Craig's testimony? What of the evidence of your own eyes, if you come to that? Do you not know me as the poor wounded fellow you found at Tsiyahi, and carried to McLeod's–"

I might have continued in the same vein for another five minutes; but at that instant the parrot (perhaps imagining Tsiyahi to be the hiss of a cat) suddenly shot into the air again with a loud cry – startling me into silence, and allowing the marquis to say softly: "Why – as to that, Sir – a burned face may deform a man beyond recognition." And he turned down his collar – to show me a cheek even more scarred and livid than my own.

I cannot easily describe the effect this revelation worked on me. It was as if, for the first time, I saw the marquis, not as a kind of inscrutable machine, designed for some jesuitical purpose I could never entirely fathom, but as a man like myself, constructed of nerves and feelings and corruptible flesh. And, at the same moment, that our damaged countenances made some more particular connection between us, like a subterranean tunnel linking two houses – tho' I could not distinctly perceive what it was, and was still trying to bring it into clearer view when he went on:

"I mean, Sir, it is true you did not know who you were when you first came here. But not in the way Mr. Coleman claimed."

"How, then?"

"You had been changed by your journey. And in narrating it, you discovered just how much – and that consciousness changed you again."

This thought was so foreign and unexpected, I could do nothing but gape like an idiot. He picked up a little bell from the table and shook it, before continuing: "Our experiences, I think, have been strangely similar, Sir. We each began life in the centre of things, and

365

were then gradually propelled beyond the margins."

I recovered my wits sufficiently to say: "You accept that I am Ned Gudgeon, then?"

He did not answer at once; and when at length he did, I was astonished to see tears in his eyes.

"I accept it, Sir, as I accept that I am Michel Pierre Georges St. Valéry de Neufchatel, Marquis de Vieux Fumé. That is indeed my name. But I am not the same man that first bore it. He is gone – as surely as the old Ned Gudgeon. Ah" – glancing up, as a footman appeared, and then quickly plucking off his hat and bowing towards me – "you will, I hope, take a glass with me, Sir?"

I could not yet find it in myself to say thank you; but I contrived to nod, and the fellow was sent away again, with an earful of jargon – of which I was able to make out only the solitary word: *vin*.

"Like your brother," said the marquis, "I am a veteran of the late war in America. I was educated as a mathematician – wrote a treatise on algebra – and was presumptuous enough to believe I understood the nature of the world. But what I saw in Canada" – shaking his head – "that was something entirely beyond my comprehension – something there is no equation to express."

All at once, my memory seemed to break open, and spill out its darkest monsters: fleeing women, and burning children, and Nancy McLeod's butchered entrails, and blind Benjamin's bleeding eyes; and the dreadful chorus of their screams – so intolerably loud, I would have thrust my fingers in my ears but that I feared I should only trap it within my head rather than keeping it out. And then, I found myself weeping, too; and felt the marquis's hand upon my shoulder, and heard him murmuring, "I know, Sir, I know" – which is how the servant discovered us, when he returned with two goblets and a bottle of wine.

After the fellow had gone, we pledged each other; and then my host smiled, and remarked: "There is this to be said for standing beyond the margins: we see things that others do not. Your story, I find, is full of curious observations and reflections – which I hazard would not have struck you had you stayed at home in Somersetshire, and never set out to find your nephew."

"That is true, I cannot deny it. And G–d knows, in spite of everything, I have enjoyed the writing of it."

"I am glad to hear it." He cast his gaze back and forth across my face, as if trying to see whether I was in earnest; and then, in a tone so changed it seemed almost diffident, went on: "Perhaps, Sir, you might yet turn your misfortunes to some account – as I have attempted to do, with mine."

"Indeed? How?"

"You have some facility with the pen. And there are other stories to be told – other stories that must be told – if we are ever to succeed in the great work to which I have devoted my life, of understanding ourselves a little better. But – that is for you to determine." He shrugged – as if it had been but an idle thought, and it was of no consequence to him whether I heeded it or not; but, from the gravity of his manner, I could not avoid the impression that his true feelings were very different, and that his real motive in hurrying on was to prevent my rejecting the idea, before I had had time to consider it. "Your future is now your own affair. I have written to Mr. Coleman, saying you are as sane a man as I have ever met – and saner than the great majority; and you are free to go, if you wish."

Free to go. *Where?* Back to England, to resume my struggle against Coleman and my wife and my neighbour Grimley? And what then? What difference would it make, that I now had the word of a French nobleman to support me?

Almost none.

"What of Mrs. Craig?" I said. "Is she free to go, too?"

He nodded: "But she prefers to stay here with her daughter – whose singular upbringing has made her a quite remarkable case. They cannot return to your country; nor yet to their own – for the Mount was quite destroyed, and it would be folly to try to rebuild it while the war continues. Martha makes herself very useful, in helping to organize the community – as you may imagine."

I nodded; and was about to speak, when (perhaps trying again to forestall a definite answer) he rose abruptly, and said: "Come – there is something I wish to show you."

He led me through the light-filled salon and teeming hall – down the serpentine steps – and across the park. When I had seen him in Frigateville, his limp had appeared no more than a gallick affectation; now, it became another emblem of our fellowship, and we hobbled along together like a pair of old soldiers. Coming, at length, to a little plantation of firs – with a thin eddy of smoke drifting up from the centre of it.

At first, I could not conceive how anybody might have got in, to make a fire there; but, taking my arm, the marquis guided me to the other side, where I saw a narrow breach in the trees. He stopped beside it, and called out, "Friend, friend," very loudly and solemnly – before parting the branches, and slowly entering.

We had gone no more than twenty paces when we came to a small thatched shelter, with a few miserable logs smouldering in front of it. There was a stench of human filth – but no sign of the human that might have caused it. Until, that is, we stooped down, and peered within the hut. For there, cowering in the corner, sat a wretched, trembling, white-eyed youth, clad in a few rags and animal-skins, and clutching his knees to his chest, as if they were some bastion, that might protect him against harm.

"Here, Sir," said the marquis. "This is the European boy brought up by Indians. Like you, he has lost his entire family. And is still in such a state of shock he cannot even speak."

I edged nearer, so I might see the lad more closely – at which he cringed and whimpered so much I immediately stopped again, for fear of frightening him more. And stood there gazing upon him, till I was blinded by my own tears.

For until that moment – like a ship that is carried forward by its own impetus, even after the sails have been lowered – I think I had half-believed, against all the odds, that he might yet turn out to be the object of my quest. But now, as I beheld him quaking before me, and reflected upon the sufferings we had both had to endure to bring us together at last, I knew with absolute certainty that this pitiful creature was not my nephew. And I wept with grief – at the folly of our conduct, and the vanity of our desires, and the coldness of our hearts; but also with a kind of wonderment, at the impenetrable strangeness of fate. For if my deluded search for Dan's bastard had cost me my wife, and my property, and my acquaintance, and very nearly my life, had it not in some manner balanced the ledger by entering the like items upon the other side: Mrs. Craig for my wife, and the occupation of writing for my estate, and the prospect of a new life for the old? And (to conclude the reckoning), his honour for the rest; for I flatter myself that I was not wholly mistaken in conceiving of him as a friend as well as a captor – and now he has ceased to appear in the latter character, hope I may know him better in the former.

With which devout wish, tho' I trust I shall some day open another account, yet under this one – begun in the confinement of his honour's prison, and concluded beneath an oak tree in the liberty of his park – I now set the final line, and close it for ever.

XLV

Epilogue
It is six months since I put the last words to my narrative – during which time it has lain in a chest, where I had intended it should remain, until I was dead; for like a child that will not look upon a coffin, for fear he will die, I superstitiously imagined that even to glimpse it might be enough to conjure up the nightmares it related, and so destroy the sunshiny world into which (I believed) I had finally waked. I should, perhaps, have reflected that a happiness vulnerable to such feeble magick must be too fragile to endure – and so indeed it has proved; for I now find myself obliged to take my story out again, and add a postscript that even a week ago I could not have conceived of, and that it pains me to write now.

But write it I must, dear sir and madam; for you and I set out upon a journey together, and having unwittingly left you at a false conclusion, I cannot rest until I have brought you to the true one.

On the evening following my interview with the marquis, I took a walk with Mrs. Craig – which ended with our sitting together in the little temple. And there – as the great red sun dissolved in the water below us, and the moon usurped its place in the sky above – we made certain promises to each other. I cannot repeat them here, for to do so would be to expose to the publick gaze treasures that must remain locked within our hearts, if they are not to become dull and tarnished; but perhaps (and I hope it is so) you may be able to supply the sense of them, by looking within your own. But I think it is betraying no great secret to tell you our conclusion: that tho' death must inevitably one day part us, yet life (in so far as it lay within our power to command it) should never do so again. Of which our best hope at present, was to remain together at the marquis's, if he would consent to it, and repay his hospitality by making ourselves as serviceable to him as we could.

The next day, he readily agreed to this proposal; and – saying he would show me where I might live – conducted me past the woods screening the lake, to a part of the park I had not seen before. It was laid out as a kind of loose-woven village, with little buildings of every sort – stone huts; a brick cottage; a conical tent covered in skins; barns and animal-sheds – all arranged in a great irregular circle about a larger structure in the middle, that put me in mind of a small market-hall, and was evidently a meeting-place: for it was full of people, one of whom appeared to be talking to the rest from a central dais. I could tell the speaker was a woman, but not who she was, or what she was saying – until we were almost upon her, and I caught the words *gelé* and *plante*, and thought there seemed something familiar in the flat, un-French way she spoke them.

I glanced towards towards the platform – and, to my astonishment, saw Niobe.

I raised my hand; observing which, she stopped – looked towards me – and started. Then she mastered herself again, and bowed her head, with something like a little smile – before turning away, and continuing her address.

If the marquis remarked this brief exchange, he gave no sign of it, but merely took my arm and, smiling, murmured: "That, Sir, is our parliament."

He led me at length to a small knoll, a little apart, that was bare on top but fringed with trees, like a monk's pate. And here he told me I might build my house.

Which, in the due course of things, during the next few weeks, I did – or, rather, *we* did; for I was blessed with many helpers: among them a dark-eyed woman from the Indies, that had come to France as a sea-captain's whore, and been turned out of doors when he died; a boy (it was said) that had been suckled by a she-bear, and would accept no reward for his labours but honey; and a broad-backed African, who had somehow lost his tongue but possessed a great stock of frowns and smiles, by which he was able perfectly to communicate. Niobe remained aloof; but her son (whose name, to my shame, I had never troubled to learn before, but now discovered to be Jonathan) proved wonderfully deft at fixing lintels, and setting casements square in the wall. And Mrs. Craig's daughter Sarah – tho' still awkward and reserved in conversation, and unable to resolve the question, from one day to the next, whether she should appear in the world as a man or a woman – showed the worth of her strange education by wielding a hammer more easily, and driving in nails more truly, than any carpenter I ever knew. With the result that I soon had a snug cabin, and was able to turn my attention to another undertaking, that I had been projecting since my first day at liberty, *viz.*, to see if I might win the confidence of the poor boy raised as an Indian, and so by degrees bring him out of his fearful solitary darkness into the warmth and brightness of our common life.

The marquis approving this idea, one day after breakfast I took myself to the little copse; and after calling, "Friend! Friend!" at the entrance, cautiously approached the wretched hut. When I was near enough to be seen, but not (I hoped) so near as to appear an immediate threat, I sat with my back against an oak trunk – took out a book – and began to read. The poor fellow at once dropped the lump of bread he had been chewing (which somebody had set on a dish before him, as you would for a half-wild dog) and retreated into his corner – from where he gaped at me unwaveringly during the whole twenty minutes I was there.

I stayed thirty minutes the following morning – forty the next – and an hour each day thereafter; and by the end of a week he had grown sufficiently accustomed to my presence to take his eyes from me occasionally, and even to attend to such essentials of his toilet, as rearranging his blanket, or picking the lice from his hair. This encouraged me to make a first tentative attempt at conversation – which (having discovered from the marquis that the boy had been taken from a Cherokee town that had suffered the same fate as McLeod's) I resolved to do by plundering my small store of Cherokee words.

"Ela," I said, pointing to the ground.

He did not respond.

I shaded my eyes, and looked towards the sun: "Nunda igehi."

Again, nothing.

I knocked my head against the tree behind me, so hard he must have heard the crack of it: "Ata'ya."

He did not smile or laugh, as I had hoped; but for the first time, the dominant emotion in his eyes seemed not terror, but surprise.

For the next two months I returned every morning, and most afternoons – helping him to recover the English he had heard in the earliest years of his life, and teaching him more, and coaxing from him his name, Da'yi, and fragments of his story, that I then (partly for the pleasure of it, and partly in deference to the marquis's wishes) began to write down each evening, while it was still fresh in my mind. At the same time, I told him something of where he was, and who his fellows were, and repeatedly promised him that, if he chose, he might come and meet them in perfect safety – of which I would give surety, by swearing not to leave his side for a second. For a long while, I despaired of his ever accepting; but one sweet warm morning towards the end of April, I arrived to find him standing before his shelter, and hugging his blanket about his shivering frame, and saying, "I am ready, now; I am ready."

I had arranged for the whole community to welcome him – not as a body, for that would have intimidated him, but in little groups of two or three. He seemed very much pleased, not only by the evident warmth of this reception, but also by the appearance of the village, which I fancy must have reminded him somewhat of his Indian home; and within another month, had removed entirely from the copse to a small hut about a hundred yards from mine. At first, he still spent most of every day with me; but he soon had so many other friends that it was all I could do to persuade him to sit with me half an hour after dinner, so that I might learn more particulars of his history, to be included in my record.

And what, meanwhile – you may wonder – of Mrs. Craig? She was occupied with her own duties: organizing work in the fields and orchards, and preparing the surplus fruit and cheese and honey for market in the neighbouring town – at which she was so accomplished that, under her care, the community soon came to provide for most of its own material needs, and to depend on the marquis for little but his protection. But she and I usually contrived to meet for an hour or two each day, and pass the night in each other's company, either at her house or mine; and continued in this fashion until the middle of May, when we were wed, in a ceremony like no other I have seen – with the marquis calling upon the Supreme Being to bless our union, and the whole community afterwards gathering to shower us with blossom, and sing us to a great feast in the village hall.

That evening, my new wife removed to my cabin, leaving her daughter mistress (or master) of her own; and we entered together upon a life of such contentment as neither of us had ever known, or would have conceived possible. Of which the sweetest moment came but last Wednesday, when I was seated at work before the house, and heard Martha behind me; and the next instant, felt her arms about my neck, and her cheek pressing mine, and heard her whisper: "I have something to tell you, Sir, I hope will make you happy."

"What! Are you –?"

"Yes, I believe so." She came past me; sat upon my knee; kissed me – and then, laughing, asked: "What shall we call it?"

"If it is a girl, Martha. If a boy, Michael, after the marquis."

She shook her head, brushing my face with her hair. "I say, Edward for a boy. Or else Benjamin."

"Let us have three boys, then, and remain friends," I said. And then, kissing her again: "That is the best news I ever heard."

I could not have guessed what news of a different sort we were about to receive.

Not long after my arrival in the village, I had been surprised one morning to see our host before the parliament, with half a dozen elegantly dressed men and women – one of whom was examining the tongueless African through an eyeglass, and another offering the bear-boy morsels of honeycomb on a stick. On enquiring who they were, I was told *that the marquis often brought visitors to observe the inmates, and learn something of their history*; which at first very much affronted me, since it seemed to reduce us to little better than those poor bedlamites, whose wild ravings are a favourite spectacle of fashionable society. But when I questioned him upon the subject, the marquis replied *that it was the best means he possessed, to open the eyes of the world to the great variety of human experience*; and on discovering that my fellows rather welcomed the attention than anything else, and that I was never likely to be an object of it myself, I soon grew quite reconciled to the idea. So that when – going home last Thursday – I caught the sound of distant applause, and turned to see a group of strangers standing about the dark-eyed woman, and beating a tattoo with their hands to accompany her as she performed a dance, I thought no more about it, and continued on my way.

And was therefore not a little astonished, when, twenty minutes later, there came a knock on the door; and, opening it, I found the same party gathered before my house. At its head was a tall lady, who stared at me for a moment, and then gave a too-eager smile, as if she were conscious of having made a mistake.

"Nous cherchons les esclaves échappés," she said.

"Malheureusement, vous vous êtes trompés," I said, pointing out Niobe's cabin. "Ils habitent là."

"Merci, monsieur."

She bowed, and left, and I turned to go in again; but as I did so, I felt a hand upon my shoulder, and heard a whispered: "One moment, Sir."

I knew that voice. I spun about – and found myself gaping at O'Donnell.

"Good G–d!" I cried.

"Hush, Sir!" He cast an anxious glance at his retreating companions; and then, without another word, pushed me into the house, and leaned against the door to shut it.

"Why are you here?" I gasped.

"I am come to rescue you."

"*Rescue* me!"

He nodded. "There are horses waiting at the gate. How soon can you be ready?"

"I – You are misinformed, Sir. I am not a prisoner."

This intelligence evidently puzzled him; for he frowned, and stammered: "But – but I –"

"I *was* confined, it is true," I said, to relieve his confusion. "But I remain here by choice."

He said nothing, but gazed about the room – with a disdainful twitch of the eye-brow, that at length goaded me into saying: "What? You are surprised to find I should be content with so little?"

"No, Sir. Only that you should be content without your freedom."

"But d–n it, Sir – I have told you – I am free!"

He stepped back, plainly startled at my vehemence – and indeed, I was startled by it myself. It seems obvious, now, that his words must have pricked a hidden nerve; but all I was conscious of at the time was a kind of panick – provoked by the sensation that my former life had come to reclaim me, and that I must exert all my power to throw it off, before its hold on me became secure. But I could not see the pain and shock on O'Donnell's face without feeling I had employed too much force against him; so I smiled, and in a gentler tone said: "Come, Sir – I do not mean to seem ungrateful, but –" And then, suddenly conscious of all that we had to tell each other, and the impossibility of telling it while we continued to conduct ourselves in the manner of a pair of prize-fighters: "Let us sit down, and talk like friends."

If I had hoped this would mollify him, I was disappointed; for (by the strange see-saw principle that so often operates in our affairs) my apology seemed only to confirm his own belief that I was at fault – so that in the same measure that my temper cooled, his grew hotter. I watched the familiar little spots of colour appear on his cheeks, and his hand move to his sword – and feared he was about to issue a challenge, that I should be obliged to refuse for want of a weapon. But then he must have reflected that the record of our transactions showed such a fine balance of profit and loss on both sides as to give neither of us an exclusive right to anger; and, with a little grimace, he pulled out a chair, and folded himself on to it.

"How did you find me?" I said.

"Ah – that is something of a history."

"I should like to hear it."

He leaned forward, so as to see out of the window; and, having satisfied himself (I suppose) that there was no immediate danger, began.

"Well, Sir, to spare you all the ins and outs of it: I went to your brother's house, to enquire after you, and found your cousin Coleman living there. I asked where you were; to which he shortly replied that you had died in America – as I very well knew. I answered that I knew no such thing; for I had received a letter from you, not six months since, that showed you had returned to England; and that if you were dead now, it must be his doing. At which he flew into a rage – saying *that he'd hear no sermons from a murderer – that I should have a care what I said, or he would have me committed to a justice – &c. &c.* I responded by calling him out – reminding him that I had told him once before, if he repeated the charge that I was a murderer, I should have satisfaction for it."

"And did he fight?" I said – my voice buoyed up by a sudden surge of excitement, and the fervent wish, that he would answer yes.

O'Donnell shook his head. "He at once summoned his men, and ordered them to put me out of the house; but not, I observed, to take me before the magistrate – from which I could but conclude, he supposed he had as much to fear from the law as I did."

I recalled my own experience in Bristol; and nodded.

"I was still standing in the road, brushing the dirt from my clothes and considering what I should do next, when a woman suddenly appeared from the lodge cottage, evidently in some distress, and–"

"Ah!" I cried. "The lodge-keeper's wife."

"Yes," he said. "She was anxious to know if I was a friend of the other gentleman, that had left Merry? I enquired who Merry was, and she told me, a horse; so, recalling that you had mentioned a favourite nag of that name, I asked her to describe the man she meant. And she did." He paused, and gave a little smirk.

"Why," I said, "what did she say?"

But he only shook his head, and murmured: "Enough to tell me it was you. But when I asked what had become of you, she grew very agitated, and looked nervously behind her to see we were not observed, and at last said" (here catching her tone so perfectly, that if I had closed my eyes I might have supposed her in the room with me) "you had been taken away, she knew not where, but her husband did, because it was he together with four other fellows had kidnapped you. And G–d had punished them for it; for three days after–"

"I know!" I interrupted. "Her mother died!"

He gave me a wondering glance; and said: "Very good, Sir. Whatever else your adventure may have cost you, your wits have not suffered by it. Yes – her mother had died; and when her husband returned from bringing you here, he began drinking even more than before; and she could not help thinking it was a curse, for what they had done to you, and for keeping your horse. So I told her, I was certain G–d would forgive her, if she returned Merry to me, and found out where you had been carried, and sent word of it to me at the Three Pigeons (where I should be putting up that night), so that I might come and free you."

I could not help remembering my own assurances to the poor woman; and wondering what peculiarity it was in her nature that had made both O'Donnell and me affect such a confident knowledge of the Almighty's intentions towards her. But all I said was: "And did she?"

"I fancy she cannot write; for she came to the inn in person – tho' she ran a great risk in doing so, and was in constant terror that her husband might follow her there, and demand to know what she was doing. And I fear he did; for shortly after she left, I heard raised voices from the yard – one of which, I am certain, was hers."

This was disturbing news, and I said: "I should be truly sorry, if she has suffered more on my account."

"I too, Sir. But that is for another day. Now we must look to ourselves. If he succeeded in beating the truth out of her, as seems very likely, 'tis almost certain Coleman must know it by now, and have sent some of his fellows after me."

"Why should he do that?"

"Why, Sir" – clicking his tongue in exasperation at my obtuseness – "because he is afraid of what you will do to him when you are at liberty again."

"He has nothing to fear from me."

"Nothing?"

I shook my head.

"Well" – after a puzzled pause – "he cannot know that. And–"

"Then I shall write, and tell him so," I said, reaching for pen and paper.

"But–"

"I pray you, Sir" – holding up my hand to stop him – "I shall not be long doing it. And then you may carry it, and perhaps it will serve to protect you, if you encounter him upon the way."

"Like Washington's letter," he murmured – and I again had the giddy sense of my former existence lapping about my ankles, and threatening to draw me back into itself.

But I ignored it as well as I could, and quickly scribbled six lines, renouncing any claims I might have against Coleman, and declaring my firm determination never to trouble him more. And having done it, and given it to O'Donnell, felt calm again, and sufficiently clear-headed to order my thoughts and ask what should have been my first question: "But why were you looking for me at all?"

"As to that, Sir – I had truly supposed you dead, when I wrote my play; for that was the rumour Coleman had put about, and I had no reason to doubt it then. So when I got your note at the theatre, I was naturally mortified; and as soon as my engagement there came to an end, I resolved to seek you out, in hope of making amends."

What is a man to do, that is repaid a debt when he no longer wants it? "No amends are necessary," I said. "I was a great fool, and an ungrateful friend; and if you were able to profit from my folly and ingratitude by putting 'em in a play, I am heartily glad of it."

"You are very generous, Sir. But I know it made you angry – and with good reason."

"It did, Sir, it did –" I began; but went no further, for how could I explain that I was angry no more – or rather, that the anger I had felt then was locked away in an unvisited attic, together with the cause of it, and all the other lumber of my discarded self? It must be a hard notion for him to grasp, and I feared trying to convince him of it – for if I failed, he would conclude my ordeal had made me mad; and if I succeeded, that I had cast him off, along with everything else, and become quite indifferent to him. But at length he spared me the trouble; for looking about him at my modest home, as if searching again for some clue as to why I should be reluctant to leave it, he spied dear Martha's cap hanging on the door, and said: "You are married, Sir?"

"Yes," I said – suddenly seeing, that here was a motive he might be expected to understand. "Do you recall Mrs. Craig?"

His eyes grew owlish: "What – do you mean –?"

I nodded.

"How?"

I began to tell him, and soon discovered how eagerly he would swallow, as a tale of love, what he might have choked on as philosophy. He had never shown me so much attention before – fixing his eyes upon my face, and nodding encouragement when I paused, and smiling with gratification when he perceived how nearly he had guessed the truth concerning the conspiracy. The only particular I omitted was of Sarah Craig's child; for if he had not known of it before, it was not my office to inform him of it now.

When I was done, he remained silent a long time, as if in contemplation; and then rose, and said: "Well, Sir, I congratulate you."

I stood up myself, and held out my hand.

He took it stiffly; and said: "And my compliments to your wife."

"She would thank you for 'em herself, if she was here. And please to give mine to yours, if . . .?"

"I have not that happiness" (with a small, weary smile). "Miss P., that said she would wait for me for ever, could not wait six months, it turned out, and wed a Gloucestershire glass-maker while we were still in Carolina."

"I am sorry to hear it."

"Nay, Sir –" He shook his head abruptly, snatched up my letter to Coleman, and began towards the door – his shoulders sharp and narrow, like a boy's; his pace light and hasty, as if I had caused him pain, and he was impatient to be gone from me. At sight of which, the neglected attick seemed to burst open – pouring out upon me such a deluge of confused emotions as all at once threatened to sweep away my resolve: guilt, and rage, and (so near the edge of consciousness I could not have put it into words, or even acknowledged its existence) a shadowy sense of being somehow diminished. I could only keep myself from running after him by gripping the back of my chair, and willing him to be quick; so was dismayed when – with his fingers on the latch – he turned again, and said: "I neglected to mention, Sir, that I have some intelligence concerning your family, which you might find–"

"Nay – nay –" I said, waving him away.

"No" – after a second's pause – "no, you are right." He grew dim and watery through my tears – and then I heard the door click, and saw him no more.

At first I dared not move, and clung to my chair like a drowning sailor to a spar – until I was certain that he must be out of hearing, and I could no longer betray myself by recalling him. When I suddenly became aware that I was weak with fatigue, and that a violent head-ache had begun to clang my skull; so, after drinking some water and chewing a piece of bread, I crept to my bed – and in a few moments was asleep.

What I woke to was so like a dream, I might have imagined I had not waked at all – were it not for the evidence that still lies before me now.

It was dark. I heard a cry of pain from the next room – that almost at once dwindled to a muffled moan, as somebody clamped a hand over the mouth that made it.

Then a man's voice I could not identify.

Then Martha's, saying: "He is not here."

A loud smack, followed by another cry – which was stifled again, as quickly as the first. But not before I had guessed it came from a woman.

I had no gun or sword, and could not immediately think of anything else I might press into service as a weapon; but as I stumbled to my feet, my hand brushed against the brass candlestick beside the bed. I snatched it up, and flung open the door.

The shards of a cracked mirror may sometimes shift, so as to give the illusion of reflecting several disconnected scenes, rather than a single coherent one; and there was a similar fragmented air to what I observed now, by the dim light of two candles. To the left, an ear-ringed rogue was clutching Niobe's hair with one hand, and a piece of wood with the other – which he had evidently been using as a club, for her face was bleeding, and she was staring at it white-eyed, in anticipation of the next blow; in the middle stood Martha, wincing at Niobe's moans, but still marvellously composed; and to the right, crouched in a corner, a man whose face was lost in shadow – until he glanced up at me: Coleman.

He made a little sob, and raised a pistol towards me – but he was trembling so much that the legs of his stool rattled upon the floor; so that I knew, even if he fired, it was three to one he would miss.

So, forcing myself to be steady, I said: "Did you not meet Mr. O'Donnell on your way?"

He shook his head – which I took to signify no, but might have meant only that he was incapable of keeping it still.

"That is a pity; for if you had, he would have given you a letter I entrusted to him, saying that you have nothing to fear from me now. Provided, that is" – glancing quickly at Martha and Niobe – "you will leave me in peace here, with my wife and friends."

"I supposed I had nothing to fear from you before," he said – and suddenly drew a little pipe from his pocket, and blew hard upon it, making a shrill shriek that was evidently intended to whistle up the other members of his party, who were doubtless searching for me elsewhere.

At which – without stopping to reflect – I hurled the candlestick at him.

He ducked. It struck the wall, and rebounded – smashing the window behind him. Martha and I both dashed forward, intending to wrest the gun from him, if we could; but Niobe's tormentor sprung between us – hurling Martha against the front-door, and striking me such a savage blow on the mouth that I was sent sprawling on to the table, where I lay, too hurt and shocked to get up again.

Whether because I was slightly concussed, or simply because of the strange position from which I witnessed it, I cannot say; but everything after that seemed to occur more slowly – as if the course of time itself had become half-frozen and reduced to a sluggish trickle. I saw Niobe try to escape during the hiatus – only to be knocked aside in her turn, as the front door burst open, and another brace of ruffians armed with muskets tumbled in, in answer to Coleman's summons; I heard her cry out, and then begin to scream "M'aidez! M'aidez!" – until the ear-ringed rascal leapt upon her again, and gagged her with her own kerchief; I saw my cousin rise, and try to quell the din of cursing men and clattering furniture by shouting, "Quiet! Quiet, d–n you! Do you want to bring the whole pack of 'em after us?" Which had its effect; for in less than half a minute the room was reduced to a semblance of calm – with nothing to be heard, save Niobe's whimpering and the ragged gasps of my poor Martha as she struggled to recover her breath.

I saw the other two curs approach me, one from each side, and felt them grab my arms and press me down. I saw Coleman follow them, and stand above me, his gun quivering in his hand. I saw one of the scoundrels nod towards it, and glance up at Coleman with raised eyebrows; and Coleman shake his head – and then nod, as the fellow handed him a knife, and smirking muttered, "Less noise with this, Sir."

I saw my cousin attempt to point the knife at my throat – his hand so tremulous it quivered like a compass needle that cannot find north; and heard him stammer, "You – you were –" I think he meant to taunt me, by saying, "You were right: I should have done this myself"; but he was not sufficient master of himself, and after a moment turned pearly pale, and thrust his sleeve against his lips, as if he feared he would puke. Then – muttering, "Wait!" – he staggered to the broken casement, and began gulping air.

I saw his face lit by some faint glow without, that seemed too warm and buttery to be the moon. The next moment I thought, *He is puking.* And then, with a kind of distant amazement, *He must have been drinking blood.*

And then I heard the shot, and saw him fall.

All at once, his men ran roaring to the door, frantically catching up their weapons; and roared the more when it sprang open – to reveal the tongueless African, laying about him with a great yoke; and Sarah Craig in her animal skins; and Da'yi in his; and half a dozen other creatures, that must have appeared to them like the figments of a drunken delirium. All of whom fell upon them – dashing their guns from their hands, and dragging them howling into the night.

But what caused me the most astonishment, was the figure that would doubtless have occasioned them the least. He walked in after they had gone – his wig slightly askew and his pistol still smoking, so that I knew it was he had killed my cousin.

"Mr. O'Donnell!" I blurted. And at once fainted away.

*

Dear sir, dear madam – we are nearly done. Indeed, we approach the very pith or kernel of the story.

It was a blackbird waked me again. I was lying in my bed, my back and limbs and face still stiff from the buffeting they had received; but I contrived to turn my head enough to see that I was alone – tho' the pillow beside me still bore the imprint of Martha's head, and there seemed a faint disturbance in the air, as if somebody else had been in the room only an instant before. A fierce light from the window stabbed my eyes – from which I concluded, with some astonishment, that I must have slept the night.

I caught the sound of the front door closing; but no more than half a minute later, heard it opening again – and then, after a brief pause, tip-toeing footsteps, and O'Donnell's voice calling: "Are you fit to be seen, Sir?"

I tried to answer; but my swollen mouth would not do as it was bid, and all that came out was a frothy moan.

"I shall take that for a yes," he said; and entered.

I struggled to sit up; but again my body betrayed me.

"Pray, Sir, be easy. I am come only to satisfy myself your wounds are not mortal, and to bid you farewell."

I attempted to protest, and plead with him to stay longer, and – tho' the words were as mangled as before – must somehow have conveyed their meaning; for he shook his head, and replied:

"I am engaged at Drury Lane for the next season, and fear I shall be late, even as it is." He hesitated a moment; and then went on: "I waited, I own, for your wife to go out before presuming to call on you; for I wished to speak with you alone. First" – here he took a crumpled packet from his coat; but instead of handing it to me, as I had expected, merely tapped it against his knee, and continued: "First to explain how I came to be here last night, three hours after you supposed me to have left. The truth is, I had gone not a hundred paces from your house when the idea came to me that I might conveniently serve both your interests and mine, by visiting Miss Craig and soliciting her hospitality for the night – so giving myself a welcome respite after my journey, and ensuring that I was close by, in case . . . in case you should require my assistance."

I tried to say, *I thank G–d for it*; and *I thank you, Sir, with all my heart*; but, hearing the tortured gallimaufry I made of it, he waved me to silence.

But my eyes must have told him what my tongue could not; for he went on: "I beg you, Sir, spare yourself – there is no need for that. I only mention the matter at all so that I may do myself the justice of observing: that before I entered her house I had not the least notion that she had a child, or that I was his father – for whatever else you may consider me guilty of, I would not have you think me a black-guard. But now I have seen the boy – well, he is a brisk little fellow, and I have promised to do what I can for him."

He plucked a watch from his pocket; and – glancing hastily at it, as if to emphasize how pressed he was and so deter me from attempting to speak again – hurried on: "Second: tho' it is beyond my power to undo the unwitting injury my comedy caused you, I have left a bank-bill for £200 on your table, which I beg you to accept – not, naturally, as payment for the slight you have received, for that is a debt of hon-our, which money can not acquit ; but rather as your proper share of the receipts that our adventures together have earned thus far – and that one day, perhaps, if the piece continues a success, may make us both rich."

I knew it would be churlish to refuse, even if I could have done so graciously; so I merely nodded, and forced my giant lips to mouth: *You are very kind.*

"Third: I brought Merry for you, Sir; and since you will not be going with me, have taken the liberty of tethering her before the house. And fourth" – here he paused, and raised the packet in his hand, as if to signify that he had come to the solemnest part of his purpose, and this was it: "when I embarked on my search for you, I went first to Bristol, to see your Uncle Fiske – whose condition I need not tell you, and who mumbled only that you were dead. But Joseph testified that he had seen you, and also said another gentleman had recently called, enquiring after you, and saying *he had something important to communicate to you.* I decided to apply to this person, in hope he could tell me something of you; and was startled, on asking his name, to hear that it was Grylls. But when Joseph told me I should find him on College Green, I presumed 'twas another Mr. Grylls – for the one you and I saw must surely still be in America."

I suddenly recalled the small fellow in the blue coat that I had encountered in Queen Square – and matched him with the attorney we had seen peering anxiously from the window of his house in Wilmington.

O'Donnell went on: "But I was mistaken – 'twas the same man – and a miserable little weaselly figure he cut, too. He had been hounded by the rebels – deprived of his property – and forced to flee to England, where he was treated little better. He had hoped the government would reward his loyalty with some place or office; but in this (like so many others) he was disappointed – and in desperation he sought to provide for himself by offering such secrets as he possessed to any who might buy 'em."

"What secrets?" I spluttered.

"That I do not know, Sir, but you may discover for yourself soon enough, if you will. It was impossible not to pity the wretched fellow, for all that he had forfeited any claim to honour or respect; and rather than immediately beating him (as no doubt he deserved), I told him – kindly enough – that he must write everything he knew about your family, and give it to me to deliver to you; that if he did so honestly and without demur, I should pay him five guineas for his trouble; but that if he dissembled or offered the least obstruction, I should kill him. He was too cowed to make even the feeblest protest; and at once set to work. And" – at last laying the packet on the bed – "this is his testimony. I leave it to you to choose, whether to read it, or – if you fear it may only bring you further unhappiness – to burn it unopened."

And then – before I had time even to attempt a reply – he leaned forward – hugged me – and murmured in my ear: "There, Sir. I have done what I came for. Now – not a word. We have said all that is needful, once before. And will have occasion to say it again one day – of that, I am certain." And then sprang up again; and, with the slightest of bows, was gone.

G–d knows how long I lay there after he had gone, looking at the packet, as powerless as a rabbit trapped by a snake. *If you fear it may only bring you further unhappiness.* Was it that that paralysed me? I cannot say, for my mind was too agitated to reflect clearly; but I was obscurely conscious that some great issue hung on what I did next. At length I reached out, and took it up – but even then weighed it upon the palm of my hand, as if that might help me guess the gravity of its contents, and so determine whether to open it or not.

Then I steeled myself, and – before I had time to change my mind – broke the seal.

The letter within began and ended with pitiful sycophancy; and some of what lay between I already knew from Washington and Martha. But the rest: that I should never have guessed, if I had lived a thousand years.

A few days after I had been obliged to tell Miss Catchpole she could expect no more, and must make shift with what she had, I received a secret visit from Mrs. Coleman. She appeared in the greatest distress, and it was some time before she was able to honour me with the reason for it; but what I at length understood was this: that on the evening Colonel Gudgeon learned Miss Catchpole was with child, he had confided his dilemma to Mrs. Coleman. She had sat with him half the night, trying to comfort him – at length becoming so weary and over-wrought that, scarce knowing what she did any longer, she took him to her bed. With the result that she now found she was pregnant herself – with an infant that had been conceived two months after her husband's departure to the Indies, and therefore could not be his. She was at her wit's end; and implored me to help her, if I could.

You will readily imagine how eager I was to be of service, when the reputations of so distinguished an officer, and so respectable a lady, were at stake; but at first I was at a loss what to propose. And then, all of a sudden, I saw how easily the matter might be composed, if only Colonel Gudgeon's two infants could somehow be swapped. I therefore arranged for Miss Catchpole and Mrs. Coleman to be removed to two different houses, some distance from the estate (it was easy enough to find a doctor who would swear it was necessary, for their health), where they remained for the duration of their confinements, and for a little while after; and then contrived the desired exchange, between Miss Catchpole's boy and Mrs. Coleman's girl. This permitted Mrs. Coleman to return home with a child three months older than her own – which, since it must have been conceived while her husband was yet with her, could conveniently pass as his. Miss Catchpole, I have to say, was not easily reconciled to this arrangement, but I finally persuaded her that Colonel Gudgeon would under no circumstances marry her; and seeing that no more advantageous settlement was possible, she at length consented to it. Without, I should add, ever learning who the other mother was, or where the additional money came from.

From which you will see, that Colonel Gudgeon's bastard was, in reality, no other than Matthew Coleman.

I must have read this last sentence at least a dozen times. To begin with, it conveyed no meaning to me at all; but gradually – like the feeling returning nerve by nerve to a numbed hand – an apprehension of it seemed to creep through my brain, setting off first one thought, and then another, and then a third. Of which the most urgent was: what should I tell Martha?

The strongest impulse in me at first was to say nothing. For after all the disappointments she had known, the losses she had suffered, and the horrors she had witnessed, it would surely be needlessly cruel to torture her with another? Even the sturdiest shoot can bear only so much trampling before it dies; and to inflict what might prove the mortal blow, when I could as easily withhold it, seemed more than I could bring myself to do.

But what if I did not? Would that not be to treat her as an infant, rather than as a woman – and so perpetuate the fatal delusion (as I now began to see it) of our life in this place? For I could not but recall what she had once told me herself: *You cannot cast off the history that made you, and begin afresh* – the truth of which had been brutally demonstrated not twelve hours ago, by the sudden reappearance of Coleman. And yet (it seemed) we had lived here as if it were not so, like two children playing at man and wife – which is well enough for boys and girls, but not for men and women: for, as any parson will tell you, once they had tasted of the fruit, Adam and Eve could not return to the Garden, but were doomed to roam the world instead.

I was still debating the question when I heard her return; and – to delay the critical moment – hastily thrust the packet beneath the pillow.

She was smiling as she entered the room, and carried a bunch of late roses. She kissed me; then stood back, so the graceful curve of her head was caught in the light from the window, and said: "I have been to Sarah, my love, and brought you some flowers." And then – remarking my expression, and my difficulty in speaking: "What's the matter?"

I did not know how to reply; for to say "Nothing" would set me irrevocably upon one course; while to say anything else (however tentatively at this juncture) must bind me to the other. She stared at me for a moment; and then – perceiving that I would not tell her the cause – looked about to see if she might discover it for herself. And the next second fixed her gaze upon the pillow, and rushed towards it – from which I can only conclude that my hand must have been as irresolute as my brain, and failed to cover up the paper totally.

I tried to stay her; but she threw off my grasp – dropped her bouquet – snatched up the sheets – and retreated with them to the corner of the room, like a fox with a pilfered hen.

She read in silence – save once or twice for a little gasp, accompanied by a frown, or a quick shake of the head, which in another woman would have signified no more than slight exasperation, but in her, I knew, was the evidence of profound distress. And yet, strangely, I did not find myself wishing I had kept the news from her. For I recognized, suddenly, that if ours was to be a true marriage, it was not my office to protect her from a knowledge that was properly hers, however painful it might be; but only – if I could – to help her bear it. And, in the same instant knew (for it was, indeed, the same point, merely viewed from another angle) that I could no longer stay in the marquis's community. I had angrily resisted O'Donnell's charge, that I had lost my freedom; but now I was obliged to concede that he was right. A man that chooses to remain in gaol is no less a prisoner on that account than one that is kept there by force – indeed, he may be said to be more so; for a captive body will escape as soon as the shackles are removed, and the door unlocked, but a captive mind may be depended upon to restrain itself. After the ordeal of my adventures and my incarceration, it had been undeniably pleasant to find myself living as a boy again, seemingly secure, and with all my wants provided; but the security had proved illusory – and (I now saw) a boy cannot be a husband and a father and a man. I fervently hoped that Martha would go with me; but if she would not, I must go alone – for I should be doing her no service, and betraying the very vows we had made each other, if I were to remain, and try to play a part I knew to be false.

When she was done, she did not cry out, or weep, or fall to the floor; but pressed herself against the wall, and let the papers flutter from her hand. I waited for her to speak; but she only shivered, and crossed her arms – seeing which, I rose with some difficulty from the bed, and went to her.

"My dear," I began hesitantly, touching her shoulder.

She winced, as if my fingers had been a hot iron; and suddenly burst out: "I cannot stay here. We must leave this place."

"I think so too," I said; and embraced her.

*

387

This morning, beneath a sky untroubled by a single cloud, and in a place as close to natural perfection as I have ever seen, we buried my brother's bastard boy. The air was sweet with the smell of hay and apples and the first fires of autumn, and we were serenaded by the ruffling of the trees above us and a chorus of distant sheep and goats.

When the ceremony was over, and we had each flung a handful of flowers on to the coffin, I went to stand with Sarah and the marquis and our other friends, leaving Martha to kneel alone by the open grave for a few minutes: for her grief was not only the deepest, but mingled with such currents of regret and self-reproach as I could scarcely guess at, or hope to relieve.

At last she rose; and the mute African stepped forward, and began to fill the hole with clods of earth.

No-one spoke on our way back to the village; Martha and Sarah, no doubt, because their thoughts were beyond the reach of their tongues; and the marquis because he was too well-bred to express his own. Which, I fancy, were somewhat melancholy; for, tho' he had made no attempt to dissuade us from our resolve, yet ever since we had told him of it he had only been able to rouse himself to short bursts of conversation – after which he would always sigh, and lapse into the distracted air of a parent about to send his children into the world.

For which reason, as we approached my house, I said: "Come, Sir, it is just as well. Whatever else we are, Martha and I are not human oddities. There are others more deserving of your kindness."

Tho' his mouth was half-hidden by his collar, I think I saw it twitch. At last he said: "Where will you go?"

"Why, as to that," I replied, with a shrug, "perhaps we will stay in France. Or return to England again. Or America. Wherever the day takes us."

"And how will you live?"

"We have Mr. O'Donnell's money –" I began.

"And our wits," said Martha suddenly, pressing my hand. "They have served us well enough until now."

He stared at us for a few moments; and then – as if to spare us all the pain of farewell – nodded sharply, and turned, and began to limp hurriedly away, before we had time to thank him, or bid him adieu. But then, after he had gone a hundred paces or so, abruptly stopped, and lifted his stick like a giant pen, and made a writing motion with it. To which I raised my own hand in reply, and nodded.

And indeed, dear sir and madam – tho' I can say nothing else with any certainty of our future – *that* I promise.

Finis

Acknowledgements

Thanks to Philip Trower, for providing me with eighteenth-century wills; to Gordon Bennett; to Nick Le Poidevin, for his immense knowledge of property law, and his willingness to put it at the service of fiction; to Susan North and her colleagues at the Victoria and Albert Museum, for guidance on Ned Gudgeon's wardrobe; to Anne Armitage, at the library of the American Museum in Bath, for help in finding contemporary sources; to Yvonne Gibbs; to David Clements, for his expert advice on eighteenth-century ships; to Heather Joynson, for information about horses and harness; and to Louise Greenberg, Jony and Georgia Mazower, Sally Darius, Derek Robinson, Tony Hipgrave, Michel Rist, Colin Samson and Henry Sclater for their friendship and support. On the other side of the Atlantic, I'm indebted to the staff at the Cumberland Gap Visitor Center in Kentucky, the Oconaluftee Indian Village in Cherokee, North Carolina, and the Fort Loudon Visitor Center/Museum in Tennessee; as well as to Margot Emerick, for her hospitality, and to Ralph Emerick, for recklessly entrusting me with his van for my research trip to the 'back country'.

I'm immensely grateful to Dominic Power, Nicholas Alfrey and Emma Farrer for reading early portions of the manuscript, and for their encouraging responses.

Special thanks, as always, to my wonderful agent, Derek Johns, his assistant, Anjali Pratap, and all their colleagues at A. P. Watt; and to everyone at Faber who gave me such tremendous backing: Stephen Page, Sarah Wherry, Angus Cargill, Walter Donohue, Anna Pallai, Kate Ward, Will Atkinson, and the incomparable Jon Riley – the kind of brilliant, perceptive and supportive editor most writers dream of, and very few ever have the good fortune to work with.

Many other writers, both famous and almost forgotten, gave me information and inspiration. I can't list them all, but would like to single out Janet Schaw and Nicholas Cresswell for their vivid accounts of what it was like to be a British visitor to the American colonies on the brink of the revolution; and the rather better-known Marquis de Chastellux for a very different European view written a few years later.

Finally, I must acknowledge the huge contribution of my family: my nephew Richard and niece Catherine for their interest and encouragement; my mother, for the heroic campaign of research she undertook on my behalf (so saving me, as always, many months of work) and for her intelligent and constructive comments on the text; Tom, for the inspiration of his own work, and his perceptive reading of mine; and Kit, for putting up with me during a critical time in his own life.

And Paula, for everything.